Praise for Deb Kastner and her novels

"Multilayered [story line] while having
a strong emotional edge..."
—*RT Book Reviews* on *The Heart Of A Man*

"[A] delightful romance..."
—*RT Book Reviews* on *A Wedding In Wyoming*

"Deb Kastner creates two very likeable characters
with her seemingly effortless writing style
in *Black Hills Bride*."
—*RT Book Reviews*

"Kastner treats readers to a breathless romance..."
—*RT Book Reviews* on *A Holiday Prayer*

"[A] sweet second-chance story..."
—*RT Book Reviews* on *The Doctor's Secret Son*

DEB KASTNER

The Heart of a Man

and

A Wedding in Wyoming

HHARLEQUIN® LOVE INSPIRED® CLASSICS

Recycling programs
for this product may
not exist in your area.

ISBN-13: 978-0-373-60648-1

THE HEART OF A MAN AND A WEDDING IN WYOMING

Copyright © 2014 by Harlequin Books S.A.

The publisher acknowledges the copyright holder
of the individual works as follows:

THE HEART OF A MAN
Copyright © 2006 by Debra Kastner

A WEDDING IN WYOMING
Copyright © 2009 by Debra Kastner

This edition published by arrangement with Harlequin Books S.A.

For questions and comments about the quality of this book,
please contact us at CustomerService@Harlequin.com.

® and TM are trademarks of the publisher. Trademarks indicated with ® are registered in the United States Patent and Trademark Office, the Canadian Intellectual Property Office and in other countries.

HARLEQUIN®
www.Harlequin.com

Printed in U.S.A.

CONTENTS

Books by Deb Kastner

Love Inspired

A Holiday Prayer
Daddy's Home
Black Hills Bride
The Forgiving Heart
A Daddy at Heart
A Perfect Match
The Christmas Groom
Hart's Harbor
Undercover Blessings
The Heart of a Man
A Wedding in Wyoming

His Texas Bride
The Marine's Baby
A Colorado Match
*Phoebe's Groom
*The Doctor's Secret Son
*The Nanny's Twin Blessings
*Meeting Mr. Right
†The Soldier's Sweetheart
†Her Valentine Sheriff
†Redeeming the Rancher

*Email Order Brides
†Serendipity Sweethearts

DEB KASTNER

lives and writes in colorful Colorado with the Front Range of the Rocky Mountains for inspiration. She loves writing for Love Inspired Books, where she can write about her two favorite things—faith and love. Her characters range from upbeat and humorous to (her favorite) dark and broody heroes. Her plots fall anywhere in between, from a playful romp to the deeply emotional. Deb's books have been twice nominated for the RT Reviewers' Choice Award for Best Book of the Year for Love Inspired. Deb and her husband share their home with their two youngest daughters. Deb is thrilled about the newest member of the family—her first granddaughter, Isabella. What fun to be a granny! Deb loves to hear from her readers. You can contact her by email at DEBWRTR@aol.com, or on her MySpace or Facebook pages.

THE HEART OF A MAN

Then Moses said to the Lord, "O my Lord, I am not eloquent, neither before nor since You have spoken to Your servant; but I am slow of speech and slow of tongue." So the Lord said to him, "Who has made man's mouth? Or who makes the mute, the deaf, the seeing, or the blind? Have not I, the Lord? Now therefore, go, and I will be with your mouth and teach you what you shall say."
—*Exodus* 4:10–12

To my sweet middle girl, Kimmie, who is the absolute last word on fashion in our house. This incredibly talented girl can make anything with a piece of fabric and some thread. My own personal image consultant, she continues to remind me fashion can be comfortable, just as I continue to break that rule by wearing sweats when I write. Much thanks and gratitude to my oldest daughter, Annie, who transcribed much of this book for me onto the computer, as I am one of those dinosaurs who still prefer to create in longhand.

Chapter One

"How do you do that?"

The question came from her best friend since childhood, Camille O'Shay. They had grown up together in a tiny rural Texas town, attended the same college and now were sharing living quarters in the heart of downtown Denver.

"Do what, Millie?" she asked absently, her eyes carefully scrutinizing the gentleman under her authority, her eyes taking in every seam and pleat as she tucked and pinned.

"Completely change people's appearances, Izzy, like someone's fairy godmother or something," Camille said with a laugh. "I'm completely astounded by your ability to wave your wand and work wonders."

Isobel Buckley shrugged. "It's my job to dress and press these gorgeous gals and pretty boys and get them looking their best for the boardroom. The final product depends on me. It's hard work, not waving wands, that yields a final product I can be satisfied with."

She wasn't telling her friend any new information—Camille was well familiar that Isobel was a personal shopper and image consultant for a select, high-end clientele. And Camille likewise knew Isobel was every bit the perfectionist she sounded.

"You know, when you think about it, it doesn't really take much to make high-quality fashion look good on those pinup model hunks you work with," Camille observed wryly. "Although, of course, dear heart, you do it better than most."

"What's that supposed to mean?" Isobel was busy straightening a silk tie on one of those so-called pinup model hunks who wanted to look his best for a national conference, and was only half paying attention to her friend's happy chatter.

"Turn around for me," she told the man, who willingly complied.

"Oh, nothing," Camille replied, not sounding the least bit convinced as Isobel turned her attention back to her friend for a moment. "I was just wondering if you could do the same kind of work with an *average* man, someone who hasn't ever read a men's fashion magazine."

"What are you talking about?" Isobel said, throwing a quick glance in Camille's direction. "You're babbling nonsense."

"Am I?" she shot back, her grin reminding Isobel of a cat crouched to pounce on a helpless mouse. "What do you think about adding a run-of-the-mill variety guy to your clientele? The kind of guy *I* usually date, as opposed to the kind of guy you *could* date if you weren't so caught up in your career?"

Isobel rolled her eyes. "I'm going to pretend you didn't say that."

"So are you up for it?" Camille actually sounded excited, as if she were taking the idea for real.

"I beg your pardon?"

"Making a normal slob of a guy into *Mr. Right.* Blue-collar material, ya know? It would be fun."

Camille was definitely warming up to the idea, while Isobel was beginning to cringe. Her friend was sounding all too serious about this fanatical, half-baked scheme.

"Here's what we'll do. I'll pick the guy, and you'll have six weeks to make him into a real man. The man of every girl's dreams."

"You're kidding, right?" Isobel took a deep breath and held it. She could only hope.

Camille shrugged, a noncommittal gesture. "Maybe. Maybe not. But don't be surprised if I come knocking on your door with a fellow who desperately needs your help for a makeover."

Isobel pinched her lips, deciding to ignore her friend's obviously off-the-top-of-her-head twaddle. It would come to nothing in the long run.

She hoped.

Not more than two days later, her dear childhood confidante made good on her threat. Bursting into Isobel's office, Camille announced in a loud, triumphant voice, "I've found him!"

"I'm sorry," Isobel said, distracted by the pile of paperwork she was muddling through, piece by agonizingly slow piece. "You found whom?"

"The guy, of course. The one you're going to wave your magic wand over." She looked disappointed for a moment. "Our average guy, remember?"

Isobel smoothed her thick, long brown hair with her palm and sighed, desperately wishing she *didn't* remember. "I would ask if you were joking, but I know you better than that. What possessed you to go through with this crazy scheme? This isn't even remotely close to real life, Camille."

"I wasn't even looking! I'm telling you the truth. No one could have been more shocked or amazed than I. All I was doing was talking with a regular patron at my hotel—a *rich,* quite handsome, very well-connected patron, I might add."

"All the people who spend time at your hotel are rich," Isobel reminded her friend blithely. "And well-connected. Handsome, though. Since when is that a requirement for hotel patronage?" she teased.

"Oh, Isobel. You have no idea. This guy is out of this world!" She stopped suddenly and clapped a hand over her heart, sighing loudly and dramatically, even as a dark blush stole up her cheeks. "Addison Fairfax.

"But that's not the point." She faltered for a moment, and Isobel found a bit of humor in the fact that her dear friend was actually flustered over this *Addison Fairfax.* It took a lot for Camille to show interest in a particular man, preferring in general the whole of mankind.

"Go ahead, Camille," Isobel encouraged with a smile and a sly wink that let her friend know she was on to her. "Handsome and…?"

Camille placed a hand on her reddened cheek and continued. "We were making our usual small talk, you know, and I was telling him about my brilliant idea for you to make over some regular guy—not anything like Addison, of course. He dresses divinely."

She followed her high-speed discourse with another long, drawn-out sigh.

Isobel chuckled.

"Well, the next thing you know, he's telling me all about his problems. You are the answer to his prayers, Isobel, I kid you not. Neither of us could believe it!"

"I might as well hear it," Isobel said with a groan. "Go on."

"Okay, I'll tell you," she agreed, casually stringing it on with a laugh. "But Izzy, you have to promise to listen all the way through before you jump to any conclusions."

Isobel smiled. She was certain she'd be *jumping to conclusions* long before her friend was finished telling what was sure to be a wildly fantastical story—but she *could* promise to keep her thoughts to herself, at least until she'd sorted the whole wild, bizarre idea out in her mind.

"So, it's like this," Camille began with a flourish of her hand.

"Once upon a time," Isobel teased.

Camille threw her a mock glare. "If you're going to keep interrupting every time I speak, I'm never going to get through this."

Isobel chuckled. "Sorry. It won't happen again." She made the motion of zipping her lips closed with her thumb and index finger.

"So there's this man I was telling you about, Addison Fairfax, who often uses our hotel for his meetings and conventions," Camille said, her voice growing with excitement at every word. "He's the CEO of Security, Inc. You know it?"

"I've heard of it," Isobel replied. Of course she knew

the name. It was only one of the most prestigious financial firms in Denver, probably on the continent.

Everyone had *heard* of Security, Inc.

"You can only imagine how successful Addison is, not to mention how wonderfully handsome he looks. He's always polished, precise and dressed meticulously."

"So, what's the problem?" Isobel asked, wondering how she could help such a high-and-mighty being, and why on earth he would think to pay her for it. Sounded to her as if he had it made.

Unless, like many of her clientele, he was simply too busy to worry about fashion. But then, where would be the challenge in that? He was the type of man Isobel worked with on a regular basis in her business, not something out of her league.

"Oh, it's not Addison," Camille said, holding her hands up, palms out. "You can trust me on this. That man is perfect just the way he is."

Isobel laughed. "It sounds as if you have a genuine, fully loaded crush on the man."

"A *crush?*" Her friend sounded mortified. "I would never stoop so low. I haven't had a crush on a man since ninth grade." She sniffed, her nose in the air like a cat who'd been offended.

"Tenth grade. Mr. Monahue, our history teacher," Isobel reminded her with a smile.

Camille chuckled. "Oh, he was cute, wasn't he? If I recall, I wasn't the only one who thought he floated over the ground."

Isobel shook her head, smiling at the memory. *Every* tenth-grade girl in Mr. Monahue's class had had a crush on the charming teacher.

She shook her head again, her mind returning to the

present dilemma. "Okay, so Addison Fairfax is *interesting*," she said, rephrasing for her friend's sake and to keep the conversation on line. "But I still don't understand what that has to do with me."

"It's his younger brother, Dustin. Now, Dustin is a mess—a regular slob, in Addison's words. And Addison actually wants to *pay* you to whip him into shape. Six short weeks of work and an enormous salary tacked on as a bonus. Think of it, Isobel! You don't even have to stop your own work to help him."

"Why would I want to do this, again?" Isobel asked, crossing her arms and tipping her executive-style black leather chair as far back as it would go, wishing for a short moment it would crash backward, sending her down through the twenty-two floors below and away from her glassy-eyed friend and the half-cocked ideas spouting from her lips.

"Remember our conversation from the other day?" Camille reminded her, dangling the thought out before her like a carrot to a rabbit.

"I remember *you* saying a bunch of stuff. I don't remember *me* saying anything at all. Most particularly that I wanted to participate in such nonsense."

"Oh, but you do, Isobel, whether you want to admit it now or not. Think of the tremendous challenge involved. I know you love the idea, deep down. Admit it!"

Isobel crossed her arms and shook her head. Vehemently.

"Don't you see? Dustin Fairfax would be a test of your true strength as an image consultant." Camille raised her hands to emphasize the mental marquee board. "I mean, they make gorgeous hunks into ugly bums all the time in the movies. Don't you think you could do the opposite for one poor man who needs what only your special brand of fashion sense can bring to him? He'll be a new man!"

Isobel admitted—in her heart, anyway—that she was intrigued, despite every bone of sense in her body screaming to the contrary. Something about the whole setup just didn't seem right, though she wasn't sure what was bothering her.

It sounded innocent enough on the outside, but something...

"How old is this man?" she asked after a slight but pregnant pause.

"Dustin?" Camille asked, her eyes gleaming with the victory she sensed was coming.

Isobel was quite aware Camille knew her better than anyone. They'd spent their whole lives together, been best friends forever. Camille would know that once Isobel capitulated in the least, she had her bagged and roasted for sure.

Camille certainly looked like a tiger hunter in full triumph, stripes sighted down her scope.

"Well, I know Addison is thirty-three," her friend supplied thoughtfully. "And since Dustin is his younger brother, I would guess he'd be about thirty, give or take a year."

"And what, exactly, is wrong with him?" she asked, feeling as if she ought to be taking notes. "I have to know the truth, here, if you want me to help."

"Oh, nothing's wrong with him, really," Camille exclaimed with a high laugh. "Addison said he's just— flighty. That's the word he used."

Isobel raised one eyebrow. Here, she suspected, was where the roof caved in.

"At least by Addison's standards, Dustin doesn't dress very well. He's not sophisticated. That shouldn't be a huge challenge for you."

"He's not a homeless man or something like that?" Isobel was still cautious. Too much about this story still didn't mesh. Something was off just a little, though she couldn't put her finger on just what it was.

She gave Camille a hard, serious stare. "Dustin is aware this is going to happen to him? He has agreed to work with me?"

"He happens to own a small flower store on the 16th Street Mall. Retail, you know? He's successful, in his own way, I guess, though he's a long way from the clientele you're used to working with."

Camille paused, running her tongue along her bottom lip. "And as for your other question, he hasn't exactly been told. Yet."

Isobel opened her mouth to argue but Camille held her hands up to cut her off.

"As soon as you agree, Addison will make sure Dustin knows to expect you. It's all been arranged, but Addison didn't want to speak to his brother about it until I'd finalized things with you."

"What if Dustin says no?"

"He won't," Camille said with a firm nod. "He might want to, but he won't. You see, there's money riding on this venture. Apparently quite a lot of money."

"He will get a lot of money if he learns to dress well?" Isobel asked, stymied. "But deep down he really wouldn't want to do this. Is that what you're really telling me?"

"It's complicated," Camille explained with a patient sigh. "Addison was left to execute his father's will, and

Izzy, the poor man is beside himself, with the situation being what it is. I feel so sorry for him. What a predicament!"

"Go on," Isobel urged, not at all certain she wanted to hear more.

"Apparently their father was afraid Dustin would squander his inheritance away instead of doing something useful with it. Addison is terribly worried about his brother. I guess he's kind of stubborn, and he's definitely his own man. Marches to the beat of his own drummer, so to speak."

She paused, clasping her hand over her heart in the melodramatic way that was uniquely Camille's. "Can you imagine the tremendously heavy burden their father left on poor Addison?"

"How so?"

"Addison was named Dustin's trustee in the will, even though Dustin is a full-grown man. You can imagine how *Dustin* felt. And Addison certainly didn't ask for the formidable task of bringing Dustin into line. According to the terms of the will, Dustin has certain obligations to meet—delineated by his father—in order for Addison to release the funds to his brother."

"He has to learn to dress well?" Isobel asked again, befuddled. "In order to get his hands on his rightful inheritance?"

None of this made the least bit of sense, and Isobel was beginning to feel very much as if she'd stepped into another dimension.

What kind of a man was Dustin, that his father would put such insane demands on him?

One thing she knew for certain—*she* would balk at such radical and unusual demands being placed upon her. If Dustin were *half* the independent spirit Camille had described him to be...

Camille laughed. "No, of course not, silly. He has to make a splash in society or something outrageous like that, and of course clothes make the man, right?"

"It's a good start," Isobel said with a laugh and a shrug. *I'd be looking for a little more than that in a man.*

Camille giggled. "After I told Addison about you, he thought you'd be the perfect person to bring Dustin around. You, of all people, can guide him in making a true contribution to society. Those are the exact terms of the will. Can you believe it?"

"I see," Isobel said under her breath, though she wasn't sure she did. The idea was intriguing, of course; definitely intriguing. The thought of transforming a scalawag of a man into a prince would be a challenge, but it also sounded kind of fun.

"Okay," she said after only a brief pause to consider the short- and long-term ramifications of her decision. She didn't want to examine her own motives too closely. "I'll do it."

She didn't ask how much money she would make. She was taking on this *project* for the challenge, and she trusted Camille that the time she spent would be worth her weight in gold. Literally.

And she was surprised by how excited she was at the prospect of making over the erstwhile Dustin. It had been a long time since she'd done something truly stimulating, and her heart was pounding with anticipation.

"I knew this was something you'd want to do," Camille squealed, throwing her arms around Isobel's neck and dancing her around in dizzying circles. "Oh, how wonderful for you!"

"Wonderful for *me?*" she asked, laughing at her friend's excited antics. "I thought Dustin was the one to benefit from this deal."

"Oh, he will," her friend agreed immediately. "He most definitely will. But won't it be such fun for you, as well? Admit it. You love the idea. *Pygmalion* at its best."

"I suppose the idea has merit," she agreed. "I do have one condition, however, and I refuse to take on this *project* unless it is met unconditionally."

"What's that?"

"This Dustin guy—he has to go into this experiment with his eyes wide open. If he doesn't agree to the makeover, if he is not comfortable with the idea of working with me or if he expresses doubts or disinterest, I do not want to move forward with this." Isobel listed items on her fingers. "The project must all be conducted on the up-and-up, with everything laid out up front for Dustin and for me. No surprises and no reluctant subjects. Do you understand what I'm getting at here?"

"I'll speak to Addison immediately," Camille assured her, obviously trying to rein in her high, excited tone and appear more businesslike and reserved. It didn't fool Isobel for a moment.

Her friend continued, gulping in air to remain calm. "He said he would be the one to speak to Dustin about it and firm up the final details. After that I'll be able to let you know when and where you two can meet and get the ball rolling toward Dustin's new look. He's got to agree. He just has to." She winked. "Especially when he meets *you.*"

"What's that supposed to mean?" Isobel squawked, feigning offense and pressing her lips together to keep her smile hidden.

"Why, you're so pretty you'll knock his socks off. And then, my dear friend, you can replace them with preppie argyles."

"Oh, I just love it when I get to play fairy godmother," Isobel teased, waving an invisible magic wand through the air. "But this sounds just a little too weird to be real."

Camille laughed and whirled about on her toes like a ballerina. So much for her businesslike demeanor, Isobel thought, smothering her grin. She didn't know where her friend got all her energy, but she wished just a little of it would rub off on her.

"There's a first time for everything, Izzy," Camille said, clapping her hands in anticipation. "And you, my dearest friend in all the world, are going to be the best thing that ever happened to Dustin Fairfax. He won't even know what hit him."

Chapter Two

Dustin lifted the drumsticks into the air, adjusting his grip on the wood so he could play the drum set that curved around the stool on which he sat. He closed his eyes and with a flick of one drumstick, adjusted his backward black-and-purple Colorado Rockies cap to keep his curly black hair out of his face.

His music of choice, at the moment, anyway, was a trumpet-licking jazz CD he'd picked up over the weekend. Eclectic was the only way to describe his taste—in music, or in anything else he had a strong opinion about.

The drum set was new—or at least, new to him. A friend who had been a drummer in a high-school band was getting rid of it to make room for a baby crib.

Dustin had grabbed the opportunity and bought the set for a song. He'd never played a percussion instrument in his life, but he figured now was as good a time as any to learn.

It wasn't the first instrument he would have taught himself to play in his life.

How hard could it be?

He made a couple of tentative taps on the snare drum

with his sticks, and then pounded the bass a few times with the foot pedal.

Smiling with satisfaction, he began pounding in earnest, perfect rhythm with the beat of the jazz CD. He didn't care at the moment whether or not he sounded good. He was only trying to have a good time. Technique would come later, with many strenuous hours of practice, he knew.

He sent a timely prayer to God that the insulation in his house would be sufficient to keep his neighbors from knocking his door down with their complaints about the horrible din.

Suddenly, out of nowhere, someone clamped his hand tightly on Dustin's shoulder.

Dustin made an instinctive move, standing in a flash, turning and knocking the man's hand away in one swift motion of his elbow and then crouching to pounce on the unknown intruder.

"Hey, take it easy," Addison said with a deep, dry laugh Dustin immediately recognized. "I didn't mean to startle you. I tried knocking, but you couldn't hear me over all that racket. Sounded like the roof was caving in or something."

Dustin chuckled.

Addison shook his head and laughed in tune with his brother. "The door was open, so I just let myself in. I hope you don't mind."

Dustin wiped his arm against his forehead, as his hands were still tightly gripping the drumsticks. "Naw. Guess I was pretty distracted, messing with this thing." He popped a quick beat on the snare drum for emphasis, then clasped both sticks together and jammed them in the back pocket of his jeans.

He crossed his arms over his chest and stared at his suit-clad big brother. "What are you doing here, Addy boy?" he asked in genuine surprise.

Addison rarely visited Dustin's small house, which was located in Wheatridge, one of the many sprawling suburbs of Denver. In fact, he'd never been there without a direct invitation first.

He had shown little interest in Dustin's hobbies, or anything else for that matter. They had never been close, even as children. Addison was the jock, and Dustin the artist. It had always been that way.

Addison wasn't fond of anything artistic, from drama to Monet. Football, baseball, soccer—these had made up Addison's teenage world.

And Addison had always been the brains in the family, in Dustin's estimation. As the CEO for a major financial corporation, and an important person in the Denver social scene, Addison didn't have time to dabble with anything beyond the walls of his chic, downtown penthouse condo and lush corner office. His only interest in the arts as a successful adult was as his business required, and nothing more.

"I've come about Dad's will, Dustin—specifically, the terms of the trust fund," Addison said tersely and abruptly in the crisp business tone he always used. Dustin sometimes thought Addison hid behind that tone in order to keep his emotions on a back burner. The two brothers certainly weren't as close as Dustin would have liked, though he put the blame for that more on his father than on Addison.

Dustin clasped his hands behind his back. His father's will was not something he really wished to discuss, though he knew it was inevitable. It had to be done, and sooner rather than later. Addison was right on that one point, anyway.

Their mother had died when Dustin was fourteen and Addison was sixteen. He remembered her as a sweet, delicate woman who always smiled and always had an eye and an open hand for the poor and needy. She had kept the house full of laughter and singing, and always had a prayer or a song of praise on her lips.

His father, on the other hand, was as cold as stone, a strict disciplinarian who practiced what he preached— that God helped those who helped themselves.

Never mind that *that* particular "verse" wasn't really in the Bible.

Addison Fairfax, Sr., had worked long hours establishing the firm Addison Jr. now led and held a majority interest in.

Dustin knew his father had wanted him in the company, as well. Addison Sr. had been bitterly disappointed when, as a young man following his own strong, surging creative impulses, Dustin took a different career path.

To Dustin, being boxed up in an office all day would be like caging a wild beast; and the thought of spending all day crunching numbers—especially anything to do with money—made him shiver.

It was enough just to balance his checkbook every month. That was not the kind of life for him, caged behind a desk with nothing but figures on paper for company.

He wanted to help people, but in another, more creative fashion. One on one, where he could reach out and touch his customers, smile and encourage them to smile back at him.

He pinched his lips together to keep his smile hidden

from his brother's observant gaze. It was an understatement to say that math had never been one of Dustin's better subjects.

And so now it came down to his father's last wishes, laid out plainly, literally in black and white. Dustin had been at the formal reading of the will. He knew what it contained, especially in regard to what he was expected to accomplish in order to win the coveted trust fund, which Dustin desperately wanted, but for reasons he would disclose to no one.

At least not yet.

And that was no doubt why Addison was visiting him today. It was up to his big brother, as trustee of the fund in Dustin's name, to see that Dustin cleaned up, became a pillar of society and made a *real* contribution to the world in some way not explicitly drawn out in the will, but legal nonetheless.

Dustin knew Addison wasn't thrilled with the job. He had enough responsibility with his own work without burdening himself with his younger brother's supposed faults. But there was one thing Dustin knew about his older brother—he would follow his father's dictates to the letter without question.

Even if Addison didn't necessarily agree with the terms. Besides, it was legal, drawn up and finalized by their father, who'd known exactly what he was doing.

"You want the money, don't you?" Addison asked crisply, his golden-blond eyebrows creasing low in concern over his blue eyes, all traits of his father.

Dustin had his mother's curly black hair and green eyes. It was a startling contrast between the two brothers, and just one more way they were different from one another.

Dustin took a deep, steadying breath. "Yes, I do," he said solemnly. "You know I do."

That was as much information as he was willing to offer, which no doubt perplexed his older brother.

"Hey, Addy boy," he said, cheerfully changing the subject, "you want a soda or something?"

"I've asked you repeatedly not to call me that," his brother responded through gritted teeth, shaking his head in warning.

"Why do you think I do it?" Dustin responded with a laugh.

"You little punk," Addison said affectionately. He grabbed Dustin around the neck and scrubbed his knuckles across Dustin's scalp, just the sort of rough-housing they'd done as kids. "Don't forget I'm bigger than you. I can still knock your block off anytime I want."

"I'd like to see you try," Dustin challenged, grabbing his brother by the waist in what amounted to a wrestler's hold.

Addison sighed and abruptly released his hold on Dustin. "As much as I'd like to monkey around with you, bro, I just don't have time today. I'm behind on my schedule already just by being here. Can we just get this painful business settled as quickly as possible so I can return to work?"

This business. Was that all it was to Addison? Another piece of business to settle and then move on? It was only Dustin's life they were talking about.

And so much more. If only Addison knew. But Dustin wasn't ready to trust his brother with more information than he'd already given.

Dustin felt like no more than a thorn in Addison's

side at times, a trial to be borne through and just as quickly forgotten.

Addison was staring at him. "I'm sorry to say this, little brother, but you need a makeover," he said soberly, though his eyes were gleaming with amusement at the prospect.

Dustin grinned and crossed his arms over his chest in an instinctively protective gesture. "Oh, like a facial and a mud bath, right? You want me to get a manicure and a massage?"

Addison cleared his throat and looked out the nearest window, gazing for some time before speaking. "This is a very serious matter. You joke about everything," he said softly.

Dustin shrugged. "Of course. In my book, it's better to go through life with a smile than to be grouchy all the time."

"Grouchy? Is that how you see me?" He sounded genuinely surprised.

Dustin shook his head. "I was speaking in relative terms."

"Yes, well, I'm not sure I believe you, but let us get back to the subject at hand. As it happens, per the will, I've hired a girl—"

"No way." Dustin cut him off with his voice, and concurrently made a severe chopping gesture with the flat of his hand. "My personal life is mine. I won't be set up, even by you."

"I'm not talking about your personal life, Dustin," Addison said, sounding as if he were straining to be patient, and yet with the hint of laughter to his voice. "I'm talking about your image. Who you know, where you go and especially how you dress. A change you and I both know would make our father happy."

Dustin looked down at his old tennis shoes, faded blue jeans and worn gray T-shirt. "What's wrong with the way I dress?"

"That's exactly the point, my man. This woman I hired, Isobel Buckley, knows what's in fashion and helps people change their image. She does it for a living, and I'm sure she could advise you better than I. Honestly, baby brother, you don't have a clue. Admit it. You're a world-class chump."

Dustin felt pressure building up in his chest. Addison was forcing his hand, and they both knew it.

And they both knew he would cave, eventually, before it was all said and done.

He *had* to cave. For the sake of the money. There was no other way.

For a moment, he considered tackling his older brother and wrestling him to the ground, as they had often done as youngsters. It would serve his big brother right to give him the good pounding he had threatened and that he was now certain Addison deserved.

With deep restraint he denied the urge, knowing it would do nothing more than prove Addison's point. Bad clothes and bad manners.

A chump.

"Frankly—" Addison continued in his best, solid business voice "—and you know I'm right in saying this, Father was concerned about the way you would spend your inheritance."

Addison paused, leaning one hand against a nearby table and pulling his brown tweed jacket back to put his hand in his slacks pocket.

To Dustin, it was like seeing his father all over again.

"You have no vision, Dustin. You own a small flower shop, you bang like an Aborigine on this drum of yours in the name of *fun,* and that's all you have to show for yourself. For your time. For your life."

"Is that you or Dad talking?" Dustin goaded through clenched teeth.

It wasn't a fair question, and Dustin immediately regretted his hasty query. It was clearly his father's intention to make Dustin into a different man. Addison was merely the messenger.

The urge to pounce on his burly brother and mess up his fancy suit was growing by the moment, but he knew better than to shoot the messenger, no matter how tempting it might be. It wouldn't solve anything in the long run, and he needed access to that trust fund.

"It's *my* life," he complained, sounding as surly as a little boy. "What's wrong with my flower store?"

"Nothing is wrong with your little shop. But have you ever thought about opening up a chain of stores? What about making a real name for yourself in the Denver social scene? Why not cater to a higher-level clientele, boost your own income?

"You spend as much time gallivanting around town, and who knows what else, as you do putting your strength and effort into your business." Addison took an extended breath. "What you need is to go to the right parties and rub elbows with the right people. Build up relationships that mean something. Really make something important of yourself."

Addison rubbed his palms together like sandpaper on wood. "I'll help you. I have the connections, Dustin.

But you can't meet the right kind of people in jeans and a T-shirt."

Dustin shook his head and grunted in disdain. "Relationships that mean something? Mean what, exactly? More money? More prestige? A nicer car? I'm never going to be like you, Addison. That's not what I want out of life."

"Perhaps not," Addison agreed with a curt nod. "You and I have traveled different roads. Nevertheless, I do think Ms. Buckley can help you with this trust-fund issue, and I insist you meet with her."

Dustin balked inside, but he didn't let it show. He didn't like being ordered around, especially by members of his family. "How long?"

"Six weeks. That shouldn't be too much of a strain, even for you." Addison began to pace, a sure sign he was losing his patience. Dustin knew his brother didn't like this any better than he did.

And why should he? Dustin knew Addison wasn't a bully at heart, childhood pranks notwithstanding. He was as pinched by their father's will as anyone.

Better to wrap things up and let Addison get on his way. Back to work in his posh office, where he was more in his element.

"At the end of the six weeks, then, I get my inheritance money?"

Addison met his gaze straight on, staring as if trying to read his soul. Dustin let him look, knowing his own expression was unreadable. It was something he'd practiced.

"You know I'm taking a calculated risk here." Addison cleared his throat and continued pacing back and forth in front of Dustin, his arms clasped behind his back. "And I expect a full return on my investment."

"Meaning?"

"I want you to cooperate with Ms. Buckley fully. If she gives me a bad report, I will put your trust fund on hold and you won't be able to touch it."

Dustin opened his mouth to protest against these rules, but Addison held one hand up, palm out. He clearly didn't want to be interrupted.

"If, however, you make a genuine effort toward your reform, the money is yours, with no limitations from me or anyone. I know that's what you want. You just have to make an effort."

He gave Dustin a genuine smile, but Dustin just winced at his brother's stilted effort.

"This will work, Dustin, if you just give it half a chance."

Dustin clenched his jaw tightly, still hardly believing his brother had set up such a scheme. Addison wasn't married—he was as careful in dating as Dustin himself was. And for good reason.

Every woman in the world wanted to change a man; it was in their very nature to meddle that way. Every man alive knew that, and ran from it with his whole being until he inevitably got caught in some woman's snare.

It was the extraordinary, seesawlike balance between men and women that Dustin didn't even try to comprehend, and generally attempted to steer away from.

That was at least partly the reason Dustin remained single at age thirty. His experience with relationships with the opposite sex had, frankly, made him more than a little world-wise when it came to women.

He liked being on his own, being his own man and answerable to no one but himself and God.

And for some strange woman to get paid for meddling in his private affairs, pushing her ideals on him—what kind of woman would take such a job?

This Isobel Buckley must be on a real power trip. He could only guess at what kinds of torture she would concoct for him.

Still, it was only six weeks.

What could happen in six weeks?

Chapter Three

Isobel was more than a little anxious about meeting the man she'd heard so much about. With all she'd been told, she had absolutely no idea what to expect when she actually met the real person.

Dustin Fairfax.

She had thoughtfully recommended a public venue for their first meeting, knowing both of them would feel a bit more comfortable with other people around, especially at this first encounter.

She admitted being nervous herself, at least inwardly, which was silly, really. She did this for a living, after all.

But this was different. The nuances weren't lost on her, and she was certain they weren't lost on *him,* either. Dustin wasn't coming to her for her expertise and help—or at least it was not his idea to do so—and she wasn't even certain he was coming willingly.

Camille and Addison had made the arrangements, and here she sat, in a quiet deli on 16th Street, waiting for Dustin to show up.

If he actually materialized.

She still wasn't convinced he was a willing guinea

pig in this experiment, and that fact was something she meant to establish before this day was over. She wouldn't blame him if he found somewhere else to be and didn't make their meeting at all.

He was already twelve minutes late to their appointment, not that she was counting. She tried to distract herself by watching the people around her, the usual eclectic hodgepodge of faces and accents that made Denver so interesting. Coffee shops were the best for finding interesting people to view.

But no matter how hard she tried, her gaze kept straying back to the front door, her adrenaline rushing every time the bell indicated a new customer was entering or exiting.

She had purposefully taken a seat at a corner table where she could easily see the entrance. She wanted to have a moment to watch Dustin before they were formally introduced.

She wiped her palms against her conservative navy blue, calf-length-split rayon skirt, ostensibly to straighten it—for at least the tenth time. She straightened her back and adjusted her posture, an incidental habit she was hardly aware of but often performed.

Suddenly a man burst through the door like a Tasmanian devil, lifting his hat and scrubbing his hands through his thick black hair. He looked around, his eyes sweeping across the tables with a glazed, harried look.

He was obviously searching for someone, and he definitely fit the profile she'd been given for Mr. Fairfax—six feet tall, medium build, black hair, green eyes.

Isobel froze, not giving any indication she saw him at all. She lowered her eyes to the table and pinched her lips.

She was afraid this was how it would be.

Her first impression wasn't good.

Dustin's black hair, what she could see of it from under a backward-faced, navy newsboy cap, was long—nearly shoulder length—and thick and curly. She wondered if anyone had ever told him his hairstyle had gone out in the eighties.

Way out.

The thought made her laugh, and she politely covered her mouth with her hand.

His big green eyes were friendly, though, and he was smiling. Those were immediate pluses, in her book. Not many people faced life with a grin these days. It was a rare blessing to see.

Polishing up the outside of a man would be a piece of cake for her, but how could she ever hope to turn some weirdo into a socialite?

Apparently, that was one worry she could cross off her list. Kindness showed in every line of his face. Somehow, after seeing him in person, she felt in her heart she could work with him.

His clothes were another matter.

He was attired in faded, holey blue jeans and a navy blue T-shirt that had seen better days. She couldn't even decipher the writing on the front. And his old tennis shoes—once white, as far as she could guess, but now a scuffed gray—were abominable.

She bit her bottom lip thoughtfully. Part of her screamed to duck under the table, however ungracefully, and hide from the man. Back out of the plan. Get away from it all.

But then she remembered her purpose here, and with this thought came resolution. This was a job like any other job, however different in form it—*he*—presented itself.

It was time to buck up and do what she was hired to do.

Of course, Dustin was an unconventional scalawag who was continually late to his appointments. Hadn't she discussed this very thing with Addison and Camille? Why else would Addison feel compelled to hire an image consultant to clean him up and generally organize his life for him?

And how hard could it be, really?

Her mind was already envisioning a sharp pair of scissors in her hand, lopping off great handfuls of his thick black hair. Her smile widened.

"Mr. Fairfax," she called, waving her hand. "Over here."

The man turned at her voice and smiled as he approached. "Please, call me Dustin," he said, his voice deep and resonant. "All my friends do. And you must be *Iz-a-belle*," he said, pronouncing her name with a crisp Italian accent. His emphasis was strongly on the last syllable. "Belle. It has a nice ring to it." He laughed at his own joke, but Isobel just shook her head.

She stared at him for a moment, trying to get her bearings. No one had ever, in the whole course of her life, called her Belle before.

Everyone, even her mother, called her Isobel. Camille called her Izzy sometimes, but they had known each other forever.

"Isobel Buckley," she corrected subtly, hoping he'd take the hint.

"Dustin Fairfax," he said, turning his chair around

and straddling it. "But of course, you already know my name."

"Yes," she agreed mildly, linking her fingers on the tabletop to keep from fidgeting. It was important that Dustin have confidence in her dignity and refinement if he was going to take any advice from her. It wasn't his problem she was feeling as if she were walking on shaky ground at the moment.

"Don't feel awkward on my account," he said with a wink.

Despite herself, her heart fluttered. The man was certainly a charmer, if a badly dressed one. And how had he known she was feeling off-kilter? Had he seen it in her expression? She determined then and there to take better control of herself and the situation.

She cleared her throat and looped a lock of her deep brown hair around her index finger, twirling it in lazy circles. "Let's start at the beginning," she suggested.

"Sounds reasonable," he agreed. That he was genuinely amicable was clearly apparent to Isobel and worked immediately in his favor. He appeared unusually relaxed and free of the usual stark brassiness most men his age wore about themselves like a cloak.

Dustin was simply himself, and he offered that openness willingly to her; and, she suspected, to all those he encountered in the—what was it?

Oh, yes. *Flower shop.*

If she was successful in her endeavor, she very well could be about to change all that. It was one of the things his brother had mentioned—in the negative category of Dustin's life.

One small shop was all he owned. He didn't even

have a second one located across town at one of the many available malls and outlets.

She felt a shiver she couldn't identify as anticipation or warning.

"You were late," she said without preamble. She had to start somewhere.

"I had the worst time finding a place to park," he explained with a shrug and an easy grin. "You know how Denver parking can be."

"You drove your *car?*" Isobel asked, surprise seeping into her voice.

"Doesn't everybody?"

She knew he was teasing her, but she couldn't resist answering him. "I assumed—well—that you could walk here from your shop. Or take the mall bus, although I admit that doesn't appeal to me, either."

His grin widened. "I did walk. My shop is only a few blocks down from here. But what would have been the fun in telling you that?" He chuckled. "I drove my car to work, though, since I live in the suburbs. I'm telling you this in case you want to tool around in it later." He gave her a wide, cheesy grin.

Dustin was clearly on the far side of sense. What had she gotten herself into?

"As I'm sure you'll quickly learn," he clarified, "I'm not everybody. Run-of-the-mill does not apply to me. I often walk, but I have a nifty little sports car and I like to drive it."

"Oh," she said lamely.

"And you came in…?"

The question dangled before her, taunting her silently for an answer.

She blushed. "A Town Car."

"Yeah? Huh. Well, what do you know? That doesn't surprise me in the least. You look the type. You wouldn't catch me dead in a Town Car, though."

"Why is that?" she asked, intrigued despite wondering if his attitude might be condescending to her. It didn't show in his tone or facial expression. His smile was genuine and kind. He had a strong, masculine smile that made her heart beat faster in response.

He was pulling her under his spell and she knew it, but she was helpless to stop herself. Maybe that was exactly what he wanted, and she was playing right into his hand, but she'd never been as cynical as she oftentimes thought she should be.

She immediately decided to take Dustin at face value unless he proved her wrong. It was only fair, and he seemed nice enough.

She cupped her chin in one palm and leaned forward to better hear his answer.

"Well, I can't afford it, for one thing," he said. "At least, not until I get my inheritance." He laughed at his own joke. "And for another, I think fancy cars give off kind of a hoity-toity attitude to the general public, don't you?"

Isobel nearly choked. Town Cars were a regular, accepted part of her existence as an image consultant, and something she'd taken for granted. She had been raised in a small Texas town and had not grown up with such luxuries, yet she admitted now she'd never given a single thought to how a person on the streets of Denver, perhaps someone less fortunate than herself, would consider the mode of transportation she chose.

"But you said you drive a sports car," she countered

tightly as it occurred to her. It was an accusation, and she knew it sounded like one.

"That's true. I do," he said, smiling. He didn't look the least bit offended, but he offered no further explanation.

"And that's okay with you."

His grin widened. Then he lifted his dark eyebrows and shrugged.

"Are you hungry?" Dustin asked, meeting her gaze squarely. She had the feeling he knew exactly what she was thinking and was playing rescuer to her own guilty conscience.

It was an unnerving feeling. She shook her mind from the thought and said, "No, thank you. I try not to eat much after noon."

He glanced at his watch, as if he weren't already aware it was well after the noon hour. "You're kidding. That can't be good for your health."

Isobel chuckled. Ten minutes into their first conversation and *he* was already trying to change *her.* What an amusing paradox.

"A drink, at least?" he coaxed in a warm, rich voice. "You aren't going to sit across from me with nothing while I stuff my face, are you? I missed lunch and I'm starving."

"All right," she said, giving in gracefully to this one small concession. "I guess I might enjoy a good cup of hot tea. Herbal. And make sure it has no caffeine or sugar."

He stood and saluted. "Yes, ma'am. I'll bring you just what you ordered."

"Thank you, Dustin," she said with a sigh as she watched him approach the counter. She wasn't sure if he'd heard her or not, for he didn't turn or acknowledge the comment.

"Dearest Lord, what have I gotten myself into?" she prayed under her breath as she stared at Dustin's broad back. "I'm feeling a little overwhelmed here. This is a new one for me. A little help? Please."

Actually, she could use a *lot* of help. She felt she was way out of her league where Dustin Fairfax was concerned.

He quickly returned to the table with a loaded tray, placing it on the table before turning his chair around properly and seating himself.

"One cool-mint hot tea for you, and two large, completely indigestible pastrami sandwiches with extra jalapenos and onions, extra-large French fries and a large cola for me."

With a cheeky smile he leaned on his elbows and began unwrapping his first sandwich.

"Are you *trying* to give yourself a heart attack?" she quipped.

He burst into laughter and had to cover his mouth to keep from spitting food. Putting his index finger in the air in a gesture for her to hold on for a moment, he chewed and swallowed his large bite of sandwich, then chased it down with a big drink of cola.

"This stuff doesn't bother me," he assured her. "I'm as healthy as a horse."

She eyed his meal in disbelief, then twisted her lips and met his sparkling gaze. "Right. Tell me those same words again in ten years."

"I had my cholesterol checked when I turned thirty. Honest."

She shrugged. "Eat whatever you want. They're your arteries."

With a grin, he picked up his jumbo-sized sandwich and took another big bite, right out of the middle of the bread.

Etiquette was evidently going to have to be added to Isobel's list of things to go over with Dustin in their six weeks together.

She was amazed at how fast the sandwiches and fries disappeared, especially since Dustin was doing most of the talking during the meal.

He cheerfully talked about his childhood—about growing up in the Fairfax household, how he had felt having a controlling father and a competitive older brother like Addison around.

He glossed over the death of his mother, though Isobel thought it must have made a huge alteration in the life of a considerate, impressionable young man, both then and now. Certainly such a tragic event would have had a great deal of influence on the man Dustin had become.

Addison was Dustin's only sibling, and according to Dustin's many laughter-filled stories, they had done their share of fighting and wrestling when they were young. Addison had always been bigger, but Dustin was slick, smooth and, he told Isobel with a smile that could spark up a lighthouse, he could run faster. So the disputes had remained fairly even, and Dustin spoke of his brother with affection.

He asked Isobel about her family, but she said as little as possible, other than that she was an only child and grew up in a small town in Texas.

Since Dustin's parents had been together forty-five

years until his mother's death, Isobel felt awkward discussing her own parents' divorce when she was an infant, and the many ways that had affected her.

Besides, everyone's parents got divorced these days. Why should she have been any different?

She didn't remember her father, and though she'd made peace with that, it rose up to haunt her now. She felt overly emotional trying to discuss her childhood, though Dustin had been open about his.

Not that she'd had a bad life—her mother had become a Christian soon after her father had left, and Isobel had been raised healthy, happy and loved, with plenty of hard work to bind them together in strength and lots of support from their home church.

Still, she didn't like talking about it, especially to a man she hardly knew. She didn't even want to think about it.

When she said as much, Dustin seemed to take it in stride, though he tried time and again to engage her in talking about herself; if not her childhood, at least what she was doing now.

"I have a small condo in the city that I share with my best friend, Camille. Have you met her?" she asked inquisitively.

He shook his head vigorously. "No, but I've heard she's a great girl."

"Camille would have a fit if she heard you calling her *girl,*" Isobel replied. "We're both twenty-eight, you know."

"Oh," he said, frowning as he strung out the syllable. "*Old* ladies, then."

She couldn't help it. She kicked him under the table, and thought she made good contact with his shin.

He didn't even acknowledge that he'd been kicked at all, except perhaps in the tiniest widening of his all-male grin.

"I have the rest of the afternoon off," he said with his usual casual bluntness. "If you want to take advantage of me, that is."

Isobel choked on her tea. She knew her face was flaming, and it didn't help that Dustin only chuckled mildly when he realized what he'd said, or rather, how it had sounded.

He shook his head and cuffed the side of his head to indicate he hadn't been thinking. "What I was really trying to say was—"

"I know what you were trying to say," she said, surprised she could speak. "And I'm going to surprise you by taking you up on that invitation, however awkwardly it may have been worded," she teased, enjoying the way his attractive smile widened when their eyes met.

She fought a grin as she considered her plan. Oh, she would take advantage of Dustin, all right—or rather, of his easygoing nature.

Isobel was certain she could make him a changed man in a single afternoon. She thought even Addison would be impressed, not to mention pleased, with such a feat.

Maybe Dustin would get his inheritance after all, if she had anything to do with it.

And she did.

Chapter Four

"Do you want to take a ride in my sports car?" Dustin offered, jingling the keys in his pocket as he held the deli door open for her and gestured her through ahead of him.

She glanced up at the dim sunlight. At least it didn't look as if it was going to rain, or worse, snow. Colorado winters were unpredictable. "Tempting as the offer sounds, a ride won't be necessary. We can walk where we're going."

As soon as they stepped out onto the sidewalk, he automatically repositioned himself so he was walking closer to the curb. The sign of a true gentleman, Isobel thought. Maybe this wouldn't be so hard after all.

Dustin kept his hands in his pockets and whistled as he walked, glancing at her from time to time and genuinely smiling, although a bit as if he had a secret he wasn't yet ready to share with her. He seemed in no hurry, but rather content just to walk slowly and casually, as if they were old friends.

And he was certainly taking this well, having to

make sudden changes in his life dictated by another person he had only just met and had no reason yet to trust.

If she were in his position, she knew she would be balking and pulling at the reins at such outrageous and uncomfortable demands.

Then again, maybe he didn't really know what he was getting himself into.

Yet.

She stopped and gestured at a shop door. "We're here."

Dustin glanced up at the sign and froze.

"No way," he said, his voice low and guttural. "No possible way."

"Now, Dustin, be reasonable," she pleaded, reaching up to place a hand on his shoulder, hoping he would take the hint and look at her.

He did.

And when their eyes met, Isobel felt exactly what he was feeling—the shock, the panic, the desire to run.

Truth told, she felt like running, herself, and pulling him along. But that wasn't what she was here to do, and Dustin had to start somewhere. Here was as good a spot as any.

She would not back down, no matter how his bright green puppy-dog eyes implored her to do so.

"It's not as bad as all that," she assured him, not certain how committed she sounded.

He shook his head. "Says you."

"Trust me?" she urged.

His gaze asked, *Why should I?* His jaw was clenched, but he stepped forward and opened the door for her. "After you."

She grinned in triumph, her heart pumping at the

battle of wills she had just fought and won. This was a big victory for her—her first—and would no doubt be one of her best. It would pave the way for other small successes and triumphs.

The end result, of course, would be a final product of which she could be proud—and more importantly, of which *Dustin* could be proud.

"Ricardo, please meet my friend, Dustin," Isobel said as her regular hairdresser rushed forward and kissed both her hands.

Ricardo was unique and not a little odd with his spiked purple hair and dozens of gold necklaces that encompassed his broad, hairy chest, not to mention his bombastic personality and shrill voice.

His personality and flashy looks took some getting used to, but when it came to hair, Ricardo was the best in the industry.

Dustin, his eyebrows raised and his expression one of pure panic, was halfway out the door before Isobel caught him by the elbow.

"No way," he whispered in her ear. "Look at that guy's hair. I'm not letting him anywhere near me with a pair of scissors. He obviously has no clue what he's doing."

She laughed. "Hairdressers don't do their own hair," she said, nudging him back into the room. "Haven't you ever heard the elementary-school logic problem about the small town with only two barbers?"

He looked at her as if she'd gone mad. She smothered a smile.

"Obviously not." She burst into laughter at the horrified, stubborn look on his face. He was adorable when he was being mulish.

With a flourish of her arms, she continued with her story. "So, then. There were only two barbers in this small town. One of the barbers had a neat trim, and the other's hair was chopped at odd edges. Now think about it, Dustin. Which of these two barbers would you rather go to?"

Delighted, she was aware of how his eyes immediately began to sparkle with understanding and his amused gaze turned on her.

He chuckled and shook his head. "I've never heard that one before, and I'll admit you have a valid point. But then again, I have no reason to trust Ricardo, despite your clever stories." He winked at her. "I haven't seen the other barber, so to speak," he reminded her, his voice grave but his eyes alight with humor.

"Oh, yes, you have," she countered, grinning back at him. She ran her fingers through the thick lengths of her long, chocolate-brown hair, circling the ends with her fingers. "You're looking at her."

"*That* man does your hair?" he said in an incredulous whisper. "Surely not."

"Oh, but he does. Ricardo is a genius. He not only cuts my hair, but he has a clientele list that would blow your mind. The best haircuts in Denver are provided by this man, I assure you."

Dustin yanked off his newsboy cap and scratched the top of his head, still looking as if he might bolt. "I can't believe I'm doing this," he muttered.

Isobel wordlessly took his arm and led him farther into the hair studio. Ricardo, who had no doubt heard most of their conversation, elegantly gestured to a barber chair and indicated Dustin should sit. Isobel was surprised the hairstylist's expression didn't betray a thing.

He drew a smock around Dustin and directed his gaze to Isobel. "What would you like done with the young man, my dear?"

"His hair," Isobel joked.

"Really?" Ricardo made a gesture of surprise, his hands over his mouth. "And here I was all ready to give him a pedicure."

Dustin's eyes widened and his jaw dropped at what he no doubt considered a threat. Pinching his mouth closed with a frustrated twist to his lips, he quickly tucked his feet under the smock, making Ricardo howl with unabashed laughter.

"Cut it short," said Isobel decisively, and Dustin cringed, shirking his shoulders and glaring first at her and then at Ricardo.

She paused a minute to let him stew before continuing her direction to Ricardo, not allowing herself the satisfied smile she was feeling inside.

"Not too short, though. A business cut. Something to keep his curls in order. And he's still young—keep the front long enough to comb back."

"I'm going to look like a toddler," Dustin grumbled good-naturedly.

"Not with Ricardo's help, you won't," she assured him, moving forward to place a hand on his shoulder. "He is perfection itself."

She turned halfway away from him and muttered, "Not like you *could* look like a toddler."

"What was that?" Dustin asked immediately, sounding suspicious.

She turned back to him and grinned. "Oh, nothing. I was just thinking aloud."

Dustin's gaze met hers in the large mirror in front of them. He still didn't look convinced.

"Trust me," she pleaded. "I really do know what I'm doing."

He gave her a clipped nod.

Knowing no amount of verbal persuasion would help, she stepped back then and let the master hairdresser go to his work.

The first thing Ricardo did, after giving Dustin a thorough shampoo and returning him to his chair, was to turn Dustin away from the mirror, which Isobel immediately understood and thought was an excellent idea. The worst thing that could happen would be for Dustin to run out before his haircut was finished.

Half a haircut would definitely not be an improvement on no haircut at all. She curled her fingers around in front of her mouth to hide her amusement, but Dustin caught her motion and glared at her anyway.

Dustin closed his eyes as Ricardo trimmed the back of his hair flush with his neckline. The more the hairdresser snipped, the curlier Dustin's hair became, but they were soft, natural curls instead of the long, frizzier style he'd worn before.

Finally, Ricardo dropped a bottle of hair gel into Dustin's lap without a word.

"What am I supposed to do with this?" Dustin growled, picking up the bottle and eyeing it suspiciously. "I'm a wash-and-wear kind of guy."

"Allow me to demonstrate," Ricardo said, not taking no for an answer. "You put a nickel-sized amount of the product on your palm and then work it through the tips of your hair with your fingers. Work the hair up and out. There is no need to work it into your scalp."

The hairdresser took the bottle from Dustin and held out his palm. He squirted a dollop of orange gel in the exact shape and size of a nickel, dropped the bottle back in Dustin's lap, then rubbed his hands together and began stroking his fingers expertly through Dustin's hair.

Dustin was still staring at his lap, hardly watching what Ricardo was doing. "I've never in my life…" he said, sounding stunned, or at least stubbornly uncomfortable.

"There's a first time for everything, right, Dustin?" Isobel asked quietly, totally amazed at his transformation. "Take a look at yourself."

Holding her breath for his response, Isobel turned Dustin's chair back toward the mirror.

Dustin stared at his reflection, hardly recognizing the man staring back at him. Who was this slick-haired man?

Perhaps he *had* worn his hair in the same style for a few years longer than he should have. Isobel may have had a point.

Of course, that was her job, wasn't it? To find the best places to make changes in order to make him a better man?

He still wasn't completely sold on the idea, but this was one point in her favor.

That said, he wasn't at all convinced about putting sticky orange gel in his hair every morning. But he had to admit the guy staring back at him in the mirror had his own charm.

Between the haircut and the gel Ricardo had meticulously applied, the hairdresser had done an outstanding job taming the wild curls Dustin had battled all his life. Ricardo had parted his hair just off to the right side of center and combed every strand of hair neatly back into place. Only a few stray curls escaped.

As Isobel had instructed, the hair on his forehead was combed back in the current style. He had to admit it looked good, though he wasn't at all sure he could duplicate the process when he was alone in his own home.

But in the end, the score was: Isobel one, and Dustin zero.

He stared in the mirror one more second, memorizing every detail.

He looked, well, contemporary.

And though there was no way he would admit it to anyone—especially Isobel, who would no doubt report such findings straight to Addison—Dustin found he rather liked his new look.

Especially with a hat.

"Double or nothing," he mumbled under his breath with a quick shake of his head.

"What was that?" she queried back, looking wary and more than a little suspicious.

He adjusted his newsboy cap backward on top of his new haircut, winked at Isobel and walked out the door without a word.

Chapter Five

Dustin didn't wait for Isobel to call him. Part of him—probably the sensible part—wanted to hide from her and tenaciously avoid her for as much of the prescribed six weeks as possible, but something about Isobel intrigued him. Completely apart from the stupid agreement he'd made with Addison, perhaps even in spite of it, he wanted to get to know her better.

Besides, in the long run it *was* the only way to get to his trust fund. He wouldn't examine his motives any deeper than that.

Isobel was certainly a beautiful woman, with her deep brown hair filled with red highlights and her warm brown eyes. She was tall and lithe. Maybe she could stand to gain a pound or two, in his opinion, but she still had the hint of womanly curves that would turn any man's head.

What caught him most, though, were her gorgeous bee-stung lips and knockout smile, especially when it was directed at him.

Perhaps it was this thought that made him hold his breath as he dialed her number.

"Dustin," she said when he greeted her. She sounded surprised, but did he hear a bit of excitement in her voice, as well, or was it his imagination and a healthy dose of wishful thinking? "I certainly didn't expect to hear from you so s-soon," she stammered.

"Well, I figured you owe me one." He waited for her response, a grin pulling at his lips.

Dead silence.

He listened to the telephone line crackling and the praise music in the background, obviously coming from Isobel's stereo.

"Look at it this way. I put up with your torture yesterday, so today you're on my terms. And that's why I'm calling." He chuckled.

"That's not how this scheme is supposed to work," she protested immediately in a high, strained voice that only made Dustin's smile widen. "We're not supposed to be having a social relationship. I'm working on you, remember?"

"How are you going to help me become an honest, hard-working citizen if you don't know anything about me?" he countered. "Granted, you chopped off my hair without even knowing my middle name, but I don't think you can turn me into the best I can become without knowing a little bit more about the *real* me."

"What *is* your middle name?" she asked, sounding distinctly uncomfortable.

"So, you want to know now, do you? *After* you whack my hair off?" he teased. "How fair is that?"

"Dustin," she pleaded.

"James."

"Dustin James Fairfax. That's very nice. Now I will

know that crucial bit of information for future whacking and/or cutting."

"Is that a threat?"

"Oh, no," she said with a laugh. "Consider it a promise."

"That doesn't sound good," he said. "Even more reason for us to get together today, though, if you ask me. Which you didn't," he pointed out wryly.

She sighed extravagantly. Pointedly.

"What did you have in mind?" She sounded as if he were about to ask her to walk the plank.

The horrible pirate captain. That was him, all right. Fit him like an old pair of sneakers. He held in the callous chuckle that would befit his pirate status, but he was tempted.

Instead, he told her why he'd really called. "I thought you could join me at my flower shop. To see what I do all day, you know? The regular nine-to-five thing my brother doesn't really think I have going on."

She breathed an audible sigh of relief, and this time it sounded genuine. "That actually sounds reasonable."

"And you sound surprised."

She laughed. "Perhaps I shouldn't be. I have an active imagination. You'll learn that about me as we work together. I'm more tempted to believe the moon is made of green cheese than that astronauts have landed."

"I thought so—something like me holding you at sword point as you walk the plank?"

"Mmm. Something like that," she murmured thoughtfully.

"Aaargh," he said playfully in his best gravelly pirate's voice.

Dustin gave her directions to his shop on the 16th

Street Mall, and they planned to meet at ten o'clock, a half hour away.

In the meantime, Dustin set out to fix his hair, which he had been ignoring until this point, since no one had been going to see him. At least no one who would care.

His old style had been easy—shower, comb it and leave it alone. But this hairstyling business—this was new to him.

And yet he had to make the effort. For the acquisition of his trust fund. He would do well to remember his true purpose in this six-week make-a-new-man-out-of-him process—getting his money.

Why then, as he combed through his hair, did he think his primping and preening might have just a little to do with Isobel, the woman?

He used the gel, but that only made his hair worse.

Every single hair on his head was sticking up, and from Dustin's viewpoint, each and every strand was going in a different direction from all the others.

He looked like a startled porcupine.

Dustin was befuddled. Ricardo had made it look so easy.

With a frustrated growl, he picked up the gel bottle and squirted another large dollop of gel into his palm, then slathered it through his hair.

Now his hair was not only prickly, but stiff as a needle. He took his bristle brush, the one he'd used for years, and slicked his hair back.

Oh, boy.

He gave his reflection a sinister look with shaded eyes and a whacky half smile.

This was better, if he were going for the crazy-man look.

He sighed aloud and began to part his hair on the

side. Curls immediately began popping up, but he thought he looked better than he had before, if only marginally.

Less than a half hour later, Dustin he was in the back room of his shop, designing a floral arrangement for an upcoming wedding, when Isobel showed up, making her way slowly through his shop and appearing to take in everything. She stopped several times to admire one bouquet or another, even leaning forward to inhale the fragrance of the sweet-smelling blooms.

When she reached his work table in the back of the shop, she stood silently, watching him as he selected various flowers and placed them in an eye-catching manner within the arrangement.

"You're very talented," she said softly, stepping forward.

"Thanks," he responded, grinning at her. "It's a great way to express my creativity. Arranging flowers is something I particularly enjoy."

"I would hope so, considering you own this place," she teased. "If you hated flowers, I would have a real problem trying to reform you, now wouldn't I?"

"I meant it's one of many things that bring joy to my life," he corrected with a laugh.

"Oh," she said softly. Then, obviously trying to change the subject, she gestured at the vase he was working on. "That looks complicated."

"It's not just putting flowers together," he explained, handing her five yellow carnations and gesturing to the arrangement. "It's so much more. If you let it be, flower arranging can be a real work of art, like painting or sculpting."

Isobel clutched the flower stems, wondering what he

meant for her to do with them. She'd come here today, as he had put it, to see him in his natural environment, so to speak, and to assess what needed to be done in the remaining six weeks.

She'd certainly not come to arrange flowers, and she had not the least idea what she was doing. Her artistic tendencies, such as they were, leaned toward fashion, not flora.

She eyed Dustin, who merely gestured toward the arrangement and grinned. "It's for a wedding," he informed her, adjusting a bloom here and there as he spoke. "The bridesmaids will be in yellow."

"Hence the yellow carnations," she said, winking back at him. "But please don't expect me to place these flowers in the arrangement. I'm sure I'll do it wrong, and then you'll just have to start it all over again."

"How will you know unless you try?" he asked quietly, but with emphasis. "Give it a go, Belle. It will tell me a lot about you."

He gestured at the unfinished bouquet. "The worst that can happen is that I'll have to help you, and I really don't mind doing that. It's a risk I'm willing to take," he said with a chuckle.

She flashed him a surprised look at the nickname, but didn't comment on it.

Dustin was trying to figure *her* out. Why would he do that? Everything felt all backward, and Isobel's stomach was filled with psychopathic butterflies.

She was supposed to be analyzing *him*.

It suddenly occurred to her that perhaps an attempt at working a flower bouquet would do just that. Give her a chance to see him interact with her as she destroyed his beautiful floral arrangement with her incompetence.

Would he become angry, or was he more of a patient man? Isobel would bet on the latter, but there was no time like the present to see for sure.

She stepped forward and tentatively began placing carnations carefully within the arrangement, gently and one at a time.

Dustin whistled low and clapped his hands slowly and in rhythm, each touch of his palms echoing in the large, colorful room and reverberating through Isobel's heart. "I knew it."

She looked up from her work, surprised, and met his gaze. "Knew what?" she asked, her mind half-distracted with her work.

"That you're a natural artist."

"You're kidding," she said honestly, feeling some-how elevated by his heartfelt praise. "I've never done this before. The closest I've come to flower arranging has been jamming a bouquet of flowers I bought at the grocery store into a vase."

Dustin laughed and then winked at her as the bell rang over the door, indicating customers were entering the store.

Isobel stood quietly by as Dustin assisted several of his obviously well-appreciated clientele, some of whom looked to be affluent, and many of whom had just walked in off the street amidst their 16th Street shopping.

This was what Isobel had been waiting for. It was an excellent opportunity to observe Dustin in his natural surroundings, when he was dealing with his everyday life and not her chaotic uprooting of his life, and she took advantage of the moment.

Oddly enough, she found herself enjoying her perusal of the man in his natural environment.

The first thing she noticed about Dustin was that his smile never left his face. Nothing seemed to ruffle him—not an irate customer being, in Isobel's opinion, absolutely ridiculous in her demands and refusing to calm down despite his best efforts. Not even this forced intrusion of Isobel into his life disrupted his careful attitude as she attempted to turn a frog into a prince.

Part of her problem, she thought—glad she was watching him from a distance and he would not be able to see her expression—was that Dustin was one very cute frog.

Even in faded blue jeans and a plain black T-shirt, Dustin was a man that women would naturally notice— *and* find attractive.

He wasn't handsome, at least not in the classic sense of the word, but something about him drew Isobel to him, and she knew she couldn't possibly be the only woman who felt that way.

Dustin was irresistible in the way of a tough, self-reliant stray tomcat. Not necessarily in the mood for a cuddle, but ready to jump in and stir things up.

And though he was big and independent, his green eyes emanated warmth and kindness, and that attracted Isobel more than any of his physical features could.

And then there was his hair.

She thought he looked infinitely more approachable with this new cut. He had obviously tried to emulate Ricardo in recreating the style, but he'd used too much gel and his hair looked stiff and stubbornly unmovable.

Even so, a few curls slipped out, the most noticeable of which was the curl across his forehead. She had the *most* indescribable urge to brush that lock of hair back where it belonged.

Suddenly, she realized the store was empty and she was still staring at Dustin.

Only, now he was staring back, and his green-eyed gaze was full of amusement.

He approached her slowly. "What do you think?" he asked, standing so close to her she could smell the cinnamon gum he was chewing.

She didn't want Dustin guessing what she was really thinking, so she glazed him with her most cheerful smile and said, "Oh, I don't know."

He lifted an eyebrow, silently challenging her off-the-cuff explanation.

She paused, searching for the right words. "Charming. Absolutely charming."

That she was talking about *him* and not the shop would be left unsaid. She could hardly be expected to think straight when his gleaming eyes so cheerfully held her gaze. She barely remembered to breathe.

He smiled. "Why, thank you, ma'am," he said with a put-on western drawl as he tipped an imaginary cowboy hat to her. "Glad you like it. I'm rather fond of the place myself."

Isobel chuckled. Addison had indicated that Dustin didn't put enough time and effort into his work, but Isobel saw he was wrong.

Dustin cared a great deal.

"The shop looks very successful," she said thoughtfully, hoping her astonishment didn't register on her face or in her voice.

From everything she'd been told about Dustin, she admitted—at least to herself—that she had pegged him for a flighty man who couldn't settle down or make a commitment to anything.

So it was no surprise that she expected his flower shop to be somewhere between thoroughly disorganized and completely run-down.

She wouldn't make that mistake again.

From now on, the only opinions she would form would be from her own factual observations, and not what she had been told secondhand. As it was, she had a lot of backpedaling to do in order to get to a place she could really start with Dustin.

"I'm here seven days a week," he qualified, as if in answer to her unspoken question, "though I don't always work regular hours. In that sense Addison is right, I guess."

She could stand it no longer. His close proximity was getting to her. He was leaning into her space, so close she could smell his gum.

Taking a deep breath, she clenched her hands together at her sides and pinched her fingernails into her palms, but to no avail. Try as she might, she could not stand it a moment longer.

With one trembling hand, she braced herself against his shoulder. Reaching on tiptoe, she ran her fingers back through his sticky-soft hair and put that stubborn lock of hair back into its rightful position.

"There," she said, stepping back and placing her fists on her hips, happily surveying her handiwork. "Much better."

"I can't promise it will stay that way." As soon as he laughed, the willful curl dropped right back down on his forehead.

"I don't believe it!" she exclaimed. "I just don't believe it."

"Told ya so."

He shrugged, grinning at her stunned expression, and then slowly made his way around the store, straightening items and locking up, whistling a song Isobel recognized but couldn't identify as he worked.

Her heart was in her throat, beating an irregular tattoo as she watched him clear the cash register and prepare his daily deposit. Isobel wondered if this would be the end of Dustin's *planned day* together.

Oddly, though it was past her normal working hours, and though Isobel had gathered more than the amount of information Dustin had meant for her to have, she found herself hoping it wasn't.

Of course, she had a lot of work to do with Dustin's transformation. But really, she admitted privately, she just liked spending time in Dustin's company, and she didn't want the day to end for personal reasons.

He cleared his throat, his back to her as he covered up a display of roses with soft, silky netting. "I, uh—that is—I hope you don't have anywhere you need to be just yet."

Isobel let out the breath she hadn't known she'd been holding. "No, I don't have anything special planned tonight. Why?"

He shrugged and looked away from her, though she caught his secretive smile first. "I thought maybe you could go out with me."

There was a brief, brightly flashing moment when her heart caught in her throat at the words *go out with me* before reality set in.

With a start, she reminded herself of the true relationship between the two of them. She was only here because Dustin's brother had ordered it to be so.

Dustin probably hadn't given any thought to what he was saying. He had simply misphrased his question.

She tried to speak but found her mouth too dry to form words. Clearing her throat, she tried again. She could not—would not allow herself to—make a big deal of nothing. "Where?"

Dustin turned and leaned his back against a wall, one foot flush against the surface.

Isobel's gaze was immediately drawn to his face. His smile was the genuine article. His eyes glowed in the half-light of the security lamps.

Again she considered how attractive he was to her, though not in the conventional way.

Cute.

That's what Dustin Fairfax was. It wasn't a new or currently fashionable term, she was sure, but it *was* Dustin. She'd picked up the word from her youth, when boys would walk by and her girlfriends would exclaim, "Oh, he's so cute!"

And that's what Dustin was, not that Isobel was going to share her newfound insight with him. She had no doubt he'd be appalled by her conclusion.

Men wanted to be thought of as handsome and dashing and strong and mysterious.

Definitely not *cute.*

"I just want to take you for a walk," Dustin answered vaguely, startling Isobel from her reverie.

For a moment she couldn't figure out what he was saying, and then she abruptly remembered she had asked him where he planned to take her this evening.

"It's a nice night for a stroll in downtown Denver. Would you like that?"

She nodded, wondering if he could have presented a scenario which she would have refused. She couldn't think of anything at the moment.

He reached around the cash register and picked up a bouquet of red roses he had prepared, and then escorted her out the back door, locking it securely and turning on the security alarm.

She wondered about the flowers. Did he mean to give them as a gift to her?

She was pleased by the thought.

But if he did plan to give her roses, why had he not done so at the shop?

Maybe he had a special hand-delivery to make, and planned to drop the bouquet off during their stroll.

He was being mysterious again, with that half grin hovering on his face. What was he up to this time?

She wasn't sure she wanted to know.

And yet she did.

"How did you come to be in Denver?" he asked as they walked along the crowded sidewalk. "I know you said you grew up in a small town in Texas. What made you move to a big city?"

"Fashion," she said thoughtfully, but said no more than that.

He chuckled. "Care to elaborate? I'm picturing you following this trail of translucent pink-scarf material until you reached your destination."

"Hmm?" she asked, glancing at him. "Oh, right. Texas." She cringed inside, but quickly determined to give him the short, happy version of her childhood, and leave it at that.

"As I mentioned before, my best friend, Camille, and I grew up in a rural Texas town. I remember summers riding horses from sunup until sunset."

"You learned fashion from riding horses?" he teased lightly.

"No. My mother didn't— Well, my father wasn't around, and so Mom had to work extra hours to keep us afloat. I had a lot of time alone, so I taught myself to sew on my own when I was eight."

"What, uh—" He hesitated. "What happened to your father, if you don't mind my asking?"

She did. But his voice was lined with such sympathy and compassion she knew what he was thinking.

That her father had died.

She should just leave him believing what he liked. She hadn't told any lies.

Exactly.

And if it were anyone else she'd known for less than a week, in any other circumstances but these, she *would* have left well enough alone.

Instead, she found herself blurting out the truth. The whole truth, for once.

"My father left my mother for another woman when I was three years old. They're divorced."

Dustin's tone didn't change. Neither did his expression. "I'm sorry to hear that. Are you close to your father?"

Isobel bit back the retort that sprung to her lips. "I never saw him or heard from him again. Even the government couldn't find him to get him to pay child support."

"I'm sorry," he said simply, and then wrapped her in a warm, tender hug.

Isobel took refuge for a moment in the sheer masculine strength of his embrace. Slowly the bitterness eating at her heart began to crumble.

Dustin was so strong, like a fortress against her painful thoughts. She felt safe in his arms.

But she wouldn't cry. Not for her father. She'd decided that long ago.

He wasn't worth it.

At length she straightened her shoulders and broke the embrace. Dustin immediately stepped back, his face awash with pity and compassion.

Isobel did not want to be pitied, not even by Dustin.

Especially not by Dustin.

But his next words put her back at ease. "So, you said you taught yourself to sew. You must really have a gift for it—from God. I'd love it if you would tell me more about it."

It took her a moment to compose herself.

"Mom had a sewing machine she'd kept packed up away in the attic. One day Camille and I decided to be explorers. High adventurers, you know?"

Dustin chuckled.

"So, we visited the attic and found the sewing machine. I was instantly in love. I instinctively knew how to use it. I can't explain it to you, except perhaps that it was trial and error. And I did instinctively know a lot of things, as if it were already placed in my mind for me to use."

Dustin grinned. "God," he said firmly.

"God," she agreed. "Anyway, the work kept me busy. And happy. I always had a knack for knowing what was in fashion. As you said more than once, I believe it is, for me, a gift from God. And I thank Him for it every day of my life."

"Amen," Dustin said softly and fervently under his breath, though not so low that Isobel was unable to hear it.

Suddenly he stopped and tugged on her elbow to get her to stop, as well. "We're here. This will be perfect for what I have in mind."

What he had in mind? What in the world was that supposed to mean?

Isobel looked around her, puzzled. People buzzed in and out of shops and up and down the sidewalks, reminding Isobel of a swarm of bees. None of the shops looked like somewhere Dustin would deliver flowers, but she shrugged. What did she know about the business?

Everyone everywhere had a sweetheart, it seemed. Why not someone in one of these quirky shops?

"All right, so now what?" she queried, flashing him a confused smile. At least he'd gotten her thinking about something other than her father's cruel betrayal.

He grinned back, his eyes gleaming with mystery. "Now," he said, "we go down there."

Isobel's eyes widened as Dustin indicated a long, dark alley she hadn't noticed was there until he pointed to it. It was dark and dank, definitely the sort of place she usually avoided at all costs.

"C'mon, Belle. Bring back some of that adventuresome spirit into your life and let's see the world." Again, he gestured down the alley.

She hung back. The alleyway was so long she couldn't see its end, and the bright light from the streetlamps didn't reach into its darkness.

She was frightened.

She knew she was being ridiculous. She'd taken care of herself all her life. And if that wasn't enough, she had a big, strong man with her. In a real pinch, she trusted Dustin enough to know he would protect her.

But an irrational sense of fear flushed through her nonetheless. Her heart leapt into her throat and lodged there, beating double time.

"No, thank you," she said, her throat tight. "I think I'd rather not accompany you at the moment. I'll just wait out here for you."

Dustin scowled. "Oh, no, you won't, Belle," he said in a low, crackly voice that wouldn't be denied.

And with that, he put his arm around her and gently but firmly, and without giving her the opportunity to protest, led her step by step deeper into the darkness of the bleak, damp alley.

Chapter Six

Dustin gently urged Isobel to follow him around the corner. He kept his grip tight to reassure her and to remind her he was there by her side.

Though she remained silent and walked with her chin high, he sensed he was taking her well out of her comfort zone; although, to be fair, dark alleys were out of *most* people's comfort zones.

Suddenly she clasped a hand on his sleeve, her grip tight. "What are you doing?" she whispered quickly in a low, stiff voice.

"*We* are visiting an old friend," he said with a low chuckle. "Or at least, she'll be a friend once you've met her. Trust me?"

She shrugged and marginally loosened her grip on his sleeve. He knew he had her on that one—it was the same question she'd posed to him just before she'd had all his hair lopped off.

She gave a clipped nod.

Dustin spotted old Rosalinda huddling against an aged brick building, using the side of a large steel trash bin to ward off the nip in the air. The alley was damp, and without the benefit of cleansing sunshine, snow still lingered here and there.

The one wool blanket she apparently owned was wrapped tightly about her shoulders. It was ragged and full of holes. Dustin made a mental note to bring her a new blanket the next time he saw her. Or maybe a sleeping bag.

"Rosalinda," he called, loudly enough for his voice to echo in the alleyway. His intention when he'd yelled was to keep from startling her with his approach, but the old woman jumped to her feet with amazing dexterity for her age and immediately reached for her shopping cart, which Dustin knew contained all her worldly possessions.

For what they were worth.

Not much. Not by anyone's standards. It made his heart ache just to watch her.

He glanced down at Isobel, unsure of her reaction to a situation that was heart-wrenching at best, and wondering not for the first time if he'd made a grave miscalculation in showing her this hidden facet of his life.

He was surprised to see that her eyes were alight with the emotions he imagined were raging through her as she took in every aspect of the situation.

Fear still glittered in their deep brown depths, but there was another, more prevalent emotion shining through above the fear.

Compassion.

Dustin grinned, his heart pounding as he looked at the beautiful woman at his side. He knew he'd been right about Isobel.

She was as attractive on the inside as she was on the outside.

"It's Dustin." He waved his hand at the old woman and she lifted a hand in response. "I've brought a friend with me."

Isobel raised her hand and waved, offering a quivering smile as she did. She squeezed his hand and stepped close into his shadow. It wasn't, he sensed, that she was afraid of Rosalinda, but rather that she had never been put in this position before.

Perhaps she needed his guidance.

He chuckled and stepped forward. "How are you doing, Rosalinda, sweetheart?" he asked heartily. "You look absolutely stunning."

As he spoke, he plucked a single rose from his bouquet and grinned widely as he presented it to the old woman with a bow and a flourish. "A rose for my Rosalinda."

Isobel hoped her mouth wasn't gaping open. After the initial shock of seeing the poor, tragic state of Rosalinda's circumstances, she had recovered enough to realize Dustin was obviously trying to help in his own adorable, quirky way.

But when he gave her a rose, Isobel's head had gone into a whirl. The gift of a simple flower seemed so completely incongruent with the situation, and yet was such a tender gesture, made so simply and honestly, that it brought tears to her eyes.

And she was not the only one affected by Dustin's gift. Rosalinda's face crinkled into a thousand wrinkles as she flashed her nearly toothless grin.

She reached over and patted Dustin on the back with one gnarled hand. "What would I do without you, Dustin? You always make me smile."

After a moment, Rosalinda turned her attention to

Isobel, smiling her gap-toothed smile. "Your young man here never fails to brighten my day."

The first thing to register was that this wasn't Dustin's first visit to the old woman, but rather one of many.

And then the old woman's words hit her with their full impact.

Isobel opened her mouth to speak, to clear Rosalinda of the grievous misunderstanding that Dustin was *her* young man.

It was odd enough for her to be looked upon as a youngster in the old woman's eyes—she hadn't been called *young* for years—without Rosalinda somehow assuming she had a thing for Dustin.

But just as she was about to clear the air on the inaccuracy, Dustin squeezed her hand and gave an infinitesimal shake of his head.

The message was clear.

Leave it be.

Isobel ruffled as if she were a cat with its hair being brushed the wrong way, but she quickly realized Dustin was probably right.

The old woman almost certainly wouldn't remember the connection between her and Dustin, anyway, though she certainly remembered Dustin from his previous visits to her.

"Here, darling Rosalinda. This'll do you for a spell." Dustin discreetly handed the old woman a folded piece of blue paper.

Rosalinda wrapped one knobby hand around his fist and brought it to her cheek, unabashed at the tears flowing from her eyes.

"Thank you, Dustin," she said with quiet dignity.

"Now, Rosalinda, I've told you before and I'll tell you again, all the thanks belongs to God." He grinned charismatically. "I'll spare you the sermon if you promise to eat. Jesus is the reason, and all that."

"Isn't that a Christmas saying?" Isobel broke in, brushing her hair away from her face with the tips of her fingers. "Jesus is the reason for the season or something like that, right?"

"As far as I'm concerned, it's good all year round," said a laughing Rosalinda. "At least the part he quoted is."

"I second that motion," Dustin added.

"I suppose you're right," Isobel agreed thoughtfully.

Dustin patted Rosalinda on the back and smiled down at her. "Keep the faith."

Isobel could see the faith shining from both her companions, gleaming in their eyes as, one at a time, their gazes met hers.

Every sweet morsel of the scene amazed her—Dustin for having the courage to share his faith in this way and Rosalinda for the courage to recognize her real treasure was in heaven.

Impulsively, she leaned down and patted the woman's hand, an act that was new and foreign to her.

She wasn't the touchy type.

"Thank you," Rosalinda said in her old, crackly voice. She turned her radiant smile upon Isobel.

"But I didn't do anything," Isobel protested, her voice a high, tight squeak. Her heart was pounding a mile a minute.

"Rosalinda, we'll be seeing you again soon," Dustin said, his tone friendly and respectful. "God bless and keep you."

"And you," Rosalinda replied shakily.

Dustin took Isobel's hand and tucked it into the crook of his arm, then turned them both around toward the light of the street.

"You told Rosalinda you didn't do anything for her," he whispered close to her ear. "You're dead wrong about that, you know."

Dustin glanced down at the woman next to him as they stepped into the muted brightness of the streetlamps, stopping her with the touch of his hand as the streamlined mall bus drove past.

Cars weren't allowed on 16th Street, only pedestrian shoppers and the free mall buses, which ran both ways along the street for the convenience of the patrons who didn't wish to walk from end to end of the mall.

Right now, Isobel looked as if she might have run right into that bus if Dustin hadn't stopped her when he did. Her expression gave a brand-new meaning to *dazed and confused.*

He laughed.

She started as if suddenly awakened.

"What's so funny?" she asked warily, pulling away from him. "Are you laughing at me?"

Dustin's expression instantly sobered. She wouldn't look at him, so he used his finger to turn her chin so his gaze could meet hers. "I would never do that."

"No? What, then?" She didn't sound as if she believed him, and she was pulling away from him again, looking anywhere but at his face.

"You're just so sweet," he admitted after a long pause, and trying to choose his words with care. "What can I say?"

"Sweet?"

To Dustin's surprise, she looked genuinely offended, cocking her hands on her hips and glaring back at him as if he'd just called her a bad name.

What had he said?

At least she was looking at him again, he supposed, approaching the issue with his usual humor.

"Sweet?" she repeated, her voice an octave higher than usual. "Dustin James Fairfax, I may be many things, but *sweet* is definitely not one of them."

Dustin shoved his hands in his pockets and pulled his shoulders in tight. When she used his middle name like that she sounded like his mother.

"Sorry," he said, not quite contrite but refusing to admit it. He wondered how he was going to manage six weeks with this woman.

And they called *him* flighty.

"Well?" She stood frozen in the same intimidating position, staring him down.

If she was trying to make him feel smaller, it wasn't working. She wasn't going to intimidate him, no matter what she did.

He wouldn't let her. A lifetime of intimidation had made him strong against those kinds of tactics.

She was still staring at him.

"*Well* what?" he snapped, getting tired of all her wily female games. He'd given her a compliment, after all. What was the big deal?

She remained silent, continuing to stare at him as if he'd grown an extra nose.

"Are you waiting for me to take it back?" he asked, his voice gruff. "Because if you are, you'll be waiting for eternity."

And even then he wasn't sure he was going to be

ready to concede, he thought mulishly, crossing his arms over his chest.

She sighed loudly and rolled her eyes. "What I *want* is an explanation."

"Oh, that," he said as if he'd moved long past the scene she'd just witnessed, though now that he was really looking at her he could see her head was still spinning from the encounter.

"Yes," she said blithely, imitating his tone, which he now realized sounded faintly temperamental. "*That.* I take it you do *that* often?"

He shrugged noncommittally. He hadn't really given his actions much thought, other than that they helped another human being. Wasn't that what everyone did? "I get out when I can."

"Well, I think that's spectacular." Her expression told him more than her words could have done. She looked at him as if he were truly someone special.

He turned to her and grasped her gently by the elbows. Her eyes were shining in the soft twilight and his heart was beating double time. No one had ever looked at him that way before. "Do you really think so?"

"Dustin, that was incredible. Remarkable. *You* were remarkable."

"No, Isobel, I'm not. I'm just a man. I do what I can," he repeated again. He felt like squirming under her intense scrutiny and had the feeling she was looking at him like some kind of superhero or something.

"Why did you give her that piece of paper?" she asked quietly. "I don't mean to pry, so feel free not to answer if you don't feel comfortable in doing so. I thought it might be for food or something. Dinner."

"A French dinner," he corrected with a laugh, shaking his head at her expression.

"Even more intriguing."

"Well, I'd have bought her a bag of groceries, but what would she do with it?" His hands slid up her arms to her shoulders. "She doesn't have a microwave or a refrigerator."

Isobel's expression was so melancholy he wanted to hug her, but he didn't know her well enough to fold her in his arms. His words would have to do, though that didn't seem like nearly enough.

The harsh reality was that he couldn't save Rosalinda, he could only be her friend.

"I can't just give her money, Isobel. She'll buy a bottle of liquor with it. That's a fact."

Isobel shivered despite the fact the evening was warm for winter in Colorado. The old woman had been so sweet, so fragile. And yet the reality was she was a homeless alcoholic.

"She's made her own choices," Dustin said firmly, taking Isobel by the shoulders and gently brushing his palms down her upper arms. He felt her shiver, and knew it wasn't the brisk night air.

"We can help, but we can't change her ways unless she wants to change. Right now, Rosalinda isn't ready for that kind of commitment. All we can do is give her what she's willing to take, and maybe in some subtle way keep tabs on her to make sure she's okay.

"A friend of mine owns a restaurant and has a heart for the homeless. It's a fancy, high-class French joint. I'll have to take you there sometime for dinner. The food is delicious. I think you'd like it."

Isobel brushed over what almost sounded like an invitation. A date. But, of course, that was ridiculous. She was working for him—or rather, his brother.

A date with Dustin was out of the question. So why did it sound so appealing?

"And he seats the homeless people right in the middle of the dining area? Wouldn't they feel uncomfortable in such a setting?" she asked in disbelief. "Not to mention the guests."

"Not he. She. Linda."

Isobel didn't outwardly react to the news that Dustin's friend was a woman, but she couldn't deny the internal tug of disappointment—or was that jealousy?—she experienced upon hearing the information.

He paused, his fingers playing with the curl on his forehead. "And she already had in mind what you were saying. In fact, she built a special room for the comfort of the homeless."

He was impressed that Isobel had thought of Rosalinda's comfort first, rather than the rich patrons who usually frequented the restaurant.

As if suddenly realizing his grip on Isobel had tightened, Dustin suddenly dropped his arms and stepped back, clasping his hands behind his back and clearing his throat. With a light smile, he began walking down the street, nodding his head for her to follow.

He didn't look back to see if she was behind him or not, but assumed she would keep pace with him, as she had all evening.

He was wrong.

Isobel narrowed her gaze on his back, her hands on her hips. "You haven't told Addison about this little hobby of yours, have you?"

He froze midstep, his back and shoulders turning rigid.

"That's what I thought," she said, taking his posture as an answer.

"Don't even think about it," he said, his tone low and tense. "I didn't bring you with me today to show off to you, Belle. I don't want Addison knowing a thing about what just happened."

Isobel smiled softly at Dustin's pet name for her. She had no idea where he'd dreamed it up, but for some reason she liked it—though, if the moniker were to come from someone's lips other than Dustin's, she was sure she'd be mortified.

Stepping forward to catch up with him, she laid a reassuring hand on his arm. He had to know she respected his motives. How could she not? He had the gallantry of a medieval knight.

But if his brother knew of his compassion for the homeless, wouldn't that be a big plus in his favor of getting the trust fund? Dustin might not have to endure these six weeks with her if he only came clean with what he did in his spare time.

It just didn't make sense to her.

"Dustin, I would never do anything without your permission, but I really think Addison's opinion of your *contribution to society* would change if he could see you with Rosalinda—and all those other homeless people I suspect have been touched by your good heart. Don't you think it would be worth a try?"

"That would ruin everything," he snapped tersely. "Stay out of it."

Isobel knew the stress Dustin's older brother was putting on him was starting to wear thin. She could see the strain in his expression. And yet for a long moment, he didn't speak.

She stayed quiet, patiently waiting for the explanation she sensed was forthcoming. She'd not known him long, but she knew him enough already to know he had his own reasons for doing things; he wasn't exactly conventional in his methods.

Eventually, Dustin sighed and she sensed the tension slowly easing from his body. He clenched his fists for a moment, and then gradually released them.

Finally, he turned to look at her, his gaze warm and tender, his arms stretched toward her, almost pleading as he approached her.

"Sorry, Isobel, I don't mean to take it out on you. I shouldn't have been so irritable." He shrugged his shoulders. "This whole money thing is a bit much sometimes, but I shouldn't take it out on you. Sometimes I just want to punch something, you know? Like a brick wall?"

"I can't even begin to imagine," she said earnestly, placing a hand over her heart as a gesture of sincerity.

"I mean, I know you're right in one sense," he said thoughtfully. "That if I told Addison about Rosalinda, he might be more inclined to release the funds to me."

He took a deep, steadying breath and shook his head. "I would have all this money to use to build a homeless shelter or something."

He paused a moment, jamming both hands into his already untidy hair. "There's just something that feels *wrong* about telling Addison."

Isobel nodded. "'But when you do a charitable deed, do not let your left hand know what your right hand is doing, that your charitable deed may be in secret; and your Father who sees in secret will Himself reward you openly.'"

"Matthew 6:3-4," Dustin choked out. "So you're a Christian, then. I thought you might be."

She nodded. "I taught my fifth- and sixth-grade Sunday school class that verse last year." She smiled at the memory.

"A Sunday school teacher, huh?" He winked at her. "You sure don't look like any Sunday school teacher I know. I probably would have gone to church more often as a kid if I'd had a teacher as pretty as you."

She blushed a bright, becoming pink, though Dustin had only been voicing an opinion he'd had since the moment he'd first seen her in the deli.

"Well," he said, deciding to have mercy on poor Isobel, who was hemming and hawing and squirming, "at least you get what I'm trying to do here."

He watched as she slowly calmed down, and he was perplexed. She obviously wasn't used to compliments, yet she was a beautiful woman, inside and out.

It gave him pause to wonder what her past had been like.

At length, she smiled at him. "And here I am, standing here staring at you like a constant reminder of your trouble. Like a porcupine rubbing against you."

"A porcupine?" he repeated, in a high, stilted voice, sounding stunned.

He turned and looked her over with an amused grin, his eyes twinkling with merriment. "I don't *think* so. Not in a million years."

"But it bothers you to have me here," she hinted without the least bit of subtlety. She wasn't about to mince words now.

"No," he answered definitively. "You, my dear Isobel, are the best thing that has happened to me in a long time. Maybe ever," he added in a quiet undertone.

He looked away from her, suddenly studying the still busy activity of the street.

Isobel felt a choking sensation at his words, and became even more emotional when his gaze suddenly turned back to her and she stared into the sincere brightness of his eyes.

Eyes that pleaded with her to understand, to walk with him in this one thing.

And how could she do less?

He was so real, so in the moment, that it almost frightened her, more now than at any other time since she'd been with him.

"But you won't tell," he said softly, again looking away from her, stuffing his hands in the pockets of his jeans in a gesture she now recognized as a subtle form of anxiety in the most carefree man she'd ever known.

It was just another incongruity in Dustin Fairfax, another puzzle Isobel meant to solve before her six weeks were over.

She heard the catch in his voice and knew his words were a question, though he'd artfully phrased it as a statement.

"No," she assured him, her voice suddenly unable to go above a whisper. "I won't tell."

Chapter Seven

Dustin arrived at the Regency Oak Towers in the Denver Technical Center shortly after 5:00 p.m. Dressed in his usual jeans, T-shirt and a bomber jacket, he felt a little uncomfortable entering the flashy hotel lobby.

He cringed at the very thought of the time, because five *sharp* was when Isobel was expecting him, and he knew exactly what that fact meant for him.

He was gonna get chewed.

It was her job, after all. Miss Perfectionist, with her intimidating habit of constantly looking at her watch, a habit he doubted she even noticed.

With Isobel, Dustin knew, even a minute late was *late,* and he was at least ten minutes behind—maybe more, with the way his life tended to run.

He didn't know the exact time because he forgot to wear a watch.

Okay, so he didn't *own* a watch. But what was a little semantics between friends?

Isobel would consider it showing his true colors, and it would no doubt make the *image consultant* part of her wish to give him the tongue-lashing he so richly deserved by his actions.

Dustin found it amusing to think of Isobel this way, on a high horse and full of righteous indignation…as long as it wasn't aimed right at him.

He chuckled under his breath. Whether or not she followed through on her career-focused instincts remained to be seen.

Would she take him to task on a few measly lost minutes?

The Tech Center, the major business hub in Denver, was surrounded by huge international firms and was the centerpiece for out-of-town business. Thus, a number of high-end hotels with excellent service and gigantic conference rooms to service their affluent and prestigious clientele were at virtually every corner of the complex, each vying for the upscale business.

Wishing not for the first time he'd picked up one of those five-dollar, big-faced watches at a discount store as he had considered doing for Isobel's sake, he pushed through the highly polished revolving glass doors and made his way into the hotel.

He really did hate watches—they made him too aware of time. They made him tense and stressed when he didn't want to be—and especially when he needed to be at his best.

Like now. And he was *late*.

At least he could have brought Isobel a bouquet of flowers to ease the way into her good graces. He owned a flower shop, after all. He hadn't even considered the obvious.

How dumb was that?

He was still pondering his error when he was hailed

by a bouncy, lively Camille, who looked like—by her hair and the way she flittered around—she'd had a few too many double-shot espressos. Dustin had never met her in person but Isobel had described her with remarkably accurate detail, right down to the Irish red hair.

She was waiting for him behind the concierge desk. Her palm drummed out a nervous rhythm on the desk and she sang softly with the beat she had created, all the time waving to him with her other hand.

"Dustin," she called sharply as he wandered aimlessly through the lobby. She continued her energetic arm movements, waving over her head so there was no way he could possibly have missed her.

He removed his ball cap and scratched the top of his head. His gaze remained on Camille as he smiled a bemused hello.

"Dustin Fairfax. You're just the way I pictured you." Her voice was a rich, vibrant alto, bouncy and full of life. Quite a contrast to Isobel's soft, high voice, Dustin mused.

He nodded.

"She filled me in on every detail of what has happened to you so far. For what it's worth, your hair looks great. I heard all about it—Ricardo is really something, isn't he? He does my hair—but I'm not afraid to tell you I was scared out of my wits when Isobel first recommended him. As long as the guy does his job well, though, don't you know what I mean?"

Dustin didn't have an opinion on the issue—he only wondered if he would be allowed to get a word in edgewise if he did. Camille was like a machine gun; her words shooting out so quickly he couldn't make heads or tails of any of them.

This was something Isobel hadn't mentioned when she'd told him all about her best friend. She'd obviously told Camille more about him than she'd told him about her closest friend and roommate.

Camille continued to prattle on, waving her hands enthusiastically as she spoke. "Isobel wasn't fibbing when she called you the next major hunk to take Denver by storm."

The woman didn't seem the least bit embarrassed or shy about her statements. It wasn't that she appeared a ditz, not aware of what she was saying, and blathering on and on about everything. Rather, her soliloquy appeared to be a clear-cut judgment of how she saw things in the world. No blushing or pandering with Camille, just an honest assessment, straight up.

He kind of liked it, and immediately saw how Camille complemented Isobel. It gave him insight into why they had become fast friends.

He already liked this happy, carefree woman who was Isobel's best friend from childhood, and thought he understood why Isobel shared such a close-knit bond with such a happy, outgoing person.

"Did Isobel really say that about me?" he queried, his grin widening.

Camille barked out a laugh. "Ha! You know Izzy better than that by now—or at least I hope you do!" she said, waving her hands in denial.

"She'd never say anything like that—not in so many words, anyway. But Izzy is the best image consultant in the industry, if I do say so myself—and I do. You can bet by the time she's through with you, you'll be just exactly what I said you will be—the next major hunk to hit the Denver area."

Dustin replaced his cap. "I don't know about that," he replied, honestly but not warily. "Isobel's been good for me, that's for sure."

Camille eyed him with intelligent, amused, interested green eyes. "Do you think?" She laughed heartily at her rhetorical question.

He answered it anyway, nodding vigorously. "Yeah. I sure do."

"I'm Camille, by the way. Isobel's best friend. She told you about me?"

Dustin laughed. "She told you about me, didn't she?" he queried.

"Well, yes. She tells me everything, of course. You're just—"

Dustin cut her off. "A hopelessly backward male who needs some refinement?" he offered.

Camille laughed with delight. "I like you. I really like you."

"I like you, too," Dustin said honestly.

His mind brushed quickly over the details he knew about Isobel's friend.

Camille had joined Isobel in pursuing their higher education in Denver from some kind of Texas backwoods childhood, choosing a career in the hospitality arts, whereas Isobel had pursued the fashion industry. With Camille's bubbly, open personality it was no wonder she was a successful businesswoman, having risen to assistant concierge of one of the most prestigious hotels in the metro area.

"I think you'd better get up there," Camille said. "Isobel is anxiously waiting for your arrival."

"*Anxious* being the key word," Dustin said, groaning. He lifted an eyebrow. "Up where, exactly?"

"Fifth floor. It's the second conference room to the left."

"Got it. Thanks for the help. And it was nice meeting you, Camille." He fingered the rim of his cap and tipped his head.

"Oh, no," Camille protested with a friendly wink. "The pleasure is all mine. I hope we see each other again soon."

"I'm sure we will," he responded politely, his mind already half on what was to come.

Actually, he wasn't exactly sure what *was* to come. But he had more pressing matters at the moment.

He wasn't too fond of the glass elevator that skimmed its way up and down the exterior of the hotel, but the view of brightly lit downtown Denver in the dusky twilight was almost worth the way his stomach turned upside down as he rose floor by floor.

Almost. He didn't especially like heights—particularly in see-through elevators.

He was most heartily relieved to reach the fifth floor, and he quickly stepped out onto the firmness of the hotel floor, letting out a deep breath as his feet touched the solid, unmoving floor.

Staring at the beckoning door to the conference room, he ran his tongue across his dry lips and sighed deeply, then removed his ball cap and stuffed it into the back pocket of his jeans.

The things he was willing to do for a trust fund.

Dustin thought the convention room he entered must be the hotel's largest, for it had effectively been transformed into a fashion runway.

Isobel had said the hotel would be the location of a prestigious spring fashion show, but he had never expected an actual *runway*. Not in the middle of a conference room more suited for, well, *conferences*.

There was a small, gold-curtained stage near the back, obviously constructed just for the event. The chairs for the guests had been assembled in straight rows around the runway and were draped in shimmering strips of gold.

The only thing missing from the sparkling picture was Isobel.

Dustin shoved his hands into his bomber jacket pockets and just stared at the spectacle for a moment, taking it all in and feeling a tight, cold fist in the bottom of his gut.

This was where Isobel belonged, amongst all this glitz and glamour. For a moment, he thought he might have caught a glimpse of her heart.

But shimmering and gold was all that Dustin was not. If she was thinking to change him into this, she would have to think again.

"What's wrong?" Isobel asked, having come up from behind him and noticing his low brow and the stubborn set of his chin. "You look like your dog just ate your ice-cream cone."

He jumped back like a kid caught with both hands in the cookie jar.

"What's wrong?" she asked again, patiently looking up at him.

Dustin's features evened out, settling into his usual cheerful countenance. "Nothing's wrong. You just startled me."

"I don't believe you," she said frankly as she met his guilty-eyed gaze, and felt a little hurt at his reticence to confide. "But I'm not going to push you into telling me what you were really thinking."

He gave a dry laugh. "I thought that was your job—pushing me around."

She felt heat rush to her cheeks and knew Dustin would be able to see the result of his teasing on her reddened face, if teasing was indeed what he had meant by his remark. He had sounded quite serious, and his expression gave nothing away. She didn't know whether to laugh or cry.

Deciding to ignore his unsettling comment, she changed the topic. "Well, I'm glad you're here," she said in as light a tone as she was able. "We have a lot to do this evening, and we need to get started right away if we're going to accomplish anything."

"Do?" Dustin stiffened. "I was hoping you were going to say you just wanted to give me a tour of this place. You know, show me the ropes of what you do around here."

She lifted an eyebrow.

"I'm interested in what you do for a living," he insisted, giving her his best cheeky grin. "This is all new to me."

"Trust me," Isobel purred. "I'm going to *show you the ropes*."

Dustin narrowed his gaze on her, his green eyes gleaming with amusement. "I've heard that tune before," he reminded her in a dry, suspicious tone.

Isobel laughed gaily, curving her arm through his. "Come on. I promise this won't hurt nearly as much as your haircut did. It's nothing permanent or irreversible. Who knows—you might even like it."

He snorted. "Famous last words. I notice you didn't

say it wasn't going to hurt, only *not as much*. What am I supposed to take from that?"

She frantically pulled in the smile that threatened to crease her face from ear to ear. Dustin needn't know how funny and boyish his expression looked as she purposefully goaded him.

She leaned into his arm, running a delicate hand across his biceps. "Never tell me a big, strong man like you will let something as harmless as a new set of clothes scare him."

"Clothes?" he choked out, pulling down on the rim of his ball cap. "That definitely has the same ring to it as *haircut*."

Isobel laughed again and continued to pull him forward toward the stage. "C'mon, big boy, and let me introduce you to a couple of my good friends, Jon and Robert. I'm sure you'll like them."

Dustin threw her another suspicious look. "Who are Jon and Robert?"

"They work in the industry. You should feel honored. These guys are giving us their time for free as a favor to me."

"Oh, joy," he said, with just a touch of sarcasm lining his voice.

Isobel sniffed, letting him know she was offended by his candid remark. "They happen to be top-of-the-line experts—the very talented and creative assistants of Wanda Warner."

He shook his head, his gaze letting her know the name didn't ring a bell. "And she would be...?"

"Oh, *please* don't tell me you've never heard of the most popular western clothing designer on two continents. I'll be mortally offended if you do."

He shrugged. "Sorry. No."

He didn't sound sorry.

He sounded amused.

She wanted to shake him. What planet was the man living on that he had never heard of Wanda? She was always appearing on the news and specialty television shows, and her face regularly turned up in local and national newspapers.

She even had her own television shopping network that was shown worldwide.

It was almost as if Dustin purposefully kept himself distanced from the world—a virtual hermit if not a literal one. Did he not even read the daily paper?

"Well, you're about to be introduced," she said firmly, earning a groan from Dustin. "And, please, Dustin, try to be nice to them," she added, remembering their encounter with Ricardo the hairdresser. "It will go easier on you in the end."

It was a veiled threat, and he groaned again, rubbing his forehead with his palm.

She set her face in a businesslike expression, unwilling to let Dustin take the enjoyment out of what was most certainly—at least for her—going to be a fun and extraordinary evening.

Grabbing him by the hand, she tugged him toward the stage, up three steps onto the platform and eventually through the sparkling gold curtain to the back, where her colleagues were waiting.

She was totally aware Dustin was literally dragging his feet, scuffing along like a boy on his way to the dentist's office, but for the moment she chose to ignore his antics and stall tactics. "Jon, Robert, come meet your designated project for this evening."

She felt him pull back again, slamming on the mental brakes, so to speak; but she didn't feel entirely guilty at provoking him.

Jon and Robert were obviously twins, aged somewhere in their mid-twenties. They had polished good looks, but were not the least conservative in their dress. Their clothes were colorful and loud, if carefully coordinated, and definitely western, right down to polished snakeskin cowboy boots.

Isobel knew Dustin wasn't used to working with highfliers like these.

Still, he could be just a little more of a willing participant, in her opinion. He had, after all, agreed to this arrangement between the two of them in the first place. He was the one who would benefit from it in the long run, if he would just give her half a chance, instead of fighting with her every step of the way.

It wasn't exactly as if she were going to be drawing blood.

Dustin surprised her by releasing her hand and offering a firm handshake to each of the two young men in turn.

"Glad to meet you fellows," he said with none of the reticence or patronization she expected. "I hear you've got plans in store for me."

The two men looked at each other and then back at Dustin, breaking into friendly grins.

She wasn't sure if it was a blessing or a curse that Dustin appeared to have decided to trust her and had capitulated in his attitude.

Finally, he was submitting to her plans with the good grace he usually showed. The night-and-day difference astonished Isobel.

"What's going on here tonight? A fashion show?" Dustin asked, smiling down at her in that quirky way of his that at once conveyed his unspoken apology for his earlier behavior and sent Isobel's heart leaping into her throat, beating a quick, sharp, patent rhythm that she was beginning to recognize as uniquely pursuant to Dustin's warm smile.

It was Dustin's signature on her heart.

He could really be charming when he wanted to be, and right now, he was laying it on full force.

"The fashion show isn't until later this week," Jon said, leaning casually against the nearest wall and crossing his feet at the ankles. "You oughtta ask Isobel to get you a ticket. Five-star event, but our Isobel has that kind of clout, you know."

Dustin cocked an eyebrow and looked down at her, his expression unreadable. "No, I didn't know that about Belle. Not that it surprises me," he continued softly, chuckling under his breath.

Isobel shrugged, feeling uncomfortable with the attention the three men were paying her. To the last man they were staring at her with pride, the younger guys with a touch of envy, and it made her uncomfortable.

"I'm sure you'd really enjoy it, Dustin," Jon said, kindly taking the focus off of her, and not a moment too soon. She'd been on the verge of turning and running. She grinned at him, silently thanking him for rescuing her.

Dustin stiffened, his face screwed into a ball of lines. Isobel realized he was holding back a laugh.

"I'm sure I would," he said in a blithe tone Isobel hoped Jon and Robert wouldn't recognize. "Our Isobel is full to bursting with ideas on how to spruce me up, make me another man."

She knew exactly what he was implying with every word he spoke, so she not so gently laid her heel down on his toes in silent warning, leaning back until she was certain he felt it.

He'd *better* feel it. The cad!

Next time she would stomp.

"What we're doing tonight is kind of like a fashion show," Robert offered, brushing a hand through his curly mop of hay-colored hair.

Isobel gave a small, startled shake of her head to warn the young man off, but the damage had already been done.

"And by that you mean?" Dustin asked warily, looking around at the three of them.

"You'll see," Isobel said, just the littlest bit too brightly.

To her assistants, she merely said, "Guys, why don't we get started?"

Chapter Eight

"Jon and Robert, as I briefed you earlier, and as you can now obviously see for yourself, my client needs a fashion makeover in a mean way."

She cringed inside. She had almost said *friend,* and deep down she knew it was true. Dustin was very much becoming a friend.

But she had to keep her professional boundaries, not get her priorities mixed up. She had a job to do. He was her client—and that was only for what was left of the six weeks they would spend together.

"I'm *mean?*" Dustin queried, raising both his eyebrows. Isobel had opened herself up for it, and he just couldn't resist teasing her about it.

"I hope that's not meant to be literal, Belle." He grinned at Isobel and winked.

She held a straight face, but he could see the sides of her lips twitching. "Wait and see, Fairfax."

She clapped her hands twice. "Jon and Robert, let's get started."

Started, Dustin soon discovered, was trying on an inordinate number of outfits—slacks, dress shirts, jeans, casual shirts—even shoes! More clothes than he'd ever seen—or *wanted* to see—in his whole life. Where did they get all these things?

But the three fashion moguls in his company were undaunted, and continued to send him back and forth from the dressing room with new sets of outfits. They commented amongst themselves at each new combination of garments, but didn't let him hear a word until Isobel was ready to proclaim her final opinion.

And the tuxedos, sports coats, and hats.

So many different kinds of hats! There was an entire rack of them!

He was given baseball caps—which he didn't mind too much; felt fedoras, which, in his opinion, made him look like a gangster out of the 1920s; and even one top hat which, he had to admit, looked pretty classy.

Even on him.

There were so many clothes, and he quickly found he would have the unfortunate experience of putting on and taking off every single item.

It wasn't exactly his first choice for a night out. Not even in the ballpark.

And his feet were beginning to hurt from some *very* uncomfortable oxfords squeezing his toes together.

"Oh, now *that* is a nice look," Isobel commented on one particular outfit, making her opinion known as she had on every other. "It's casual, yet it lends the distinction of class."

Dustin stared in the three-way mirror, shaking his head in astonishment. For once, he couldn't formulate the words to tell her how he felt.

Maybe it was because his brain had turned into a speeding highway, one thought after the next threatening to collide with one another. He couldn't find room in his mind to make audible speech.

The tight indigo-blue designer jeans they'd given him were all right, he supposed, though in truth he much preferred his jeans loose and well-worn.

But a pink shirt?

It was a nice, snap-down dress shirt, made of extra-soft material Dustin couldn't identify. It fit his broad shoulders perfectly and tapered to his waist, where he tucked it into his pants.

In other circumstances—or more precisely, other colors—Dustin would have been impressed by the shirt, maybe even have worn it, despite the western look to it he wasn't real keen on.

But pink?

No way.

Not on this man.

"It's gorgeous," Isobel proclaimed, clapping her hands together in sheer delight.

"It's awful," Dustin replied instantly, cutting her off before she could rant and rave some more.

"And I'm taking it off. Now."

He made good on his threat and began unsnapping the shirt, not even bothering to go back into his dressing room to do so.

"But Dustin!" she protested, slapping her palms over her cheeks as he peeled off the shirt right in front of her.

"I draw the line at *pink,* Isobel," he said, trying to keep his voice sober, though he knew a gleam of amusement must have shown from his eyes. He wasn't really angry as much as annoyed.

How could she think he would be the kind of man

who would wear pink? He wasn't *that* comfortable with his masculinity.

Deep down, he wondered how much she really knew about him, when she couldn't even pick out appropriate colors for him to wear, colors that matched his lifestyle and personality.

It seemed to be the sort of thing an image consultant ought to know instinctively, and especially after spending some time together with him.

"But it looks good on you," she protested again in a gravelly tone, moving her hands to her hips. "Spectacular, even."

"You have got to be kidding." He wasn't going to argue about this.

"You are so closed-minded," she retorted, angrily stepping forward to face him.

"Mebbe," he growled low in his throat. "But I," he informed her through gritted teeth, "will never, ever wear anything *pink.*"

He paused for effect.

"Not a pink shirt, not pink pants, not pink shoes and not a pink hat," he said, feeling as if he were quoting something from Dr. Seuss. "I won't even wear pink pajamas, thank you very much. So can we please move on to another subject? Like *blue?*"

Isobel let out a loud huff of breath as Jon and Robert, whom Dustin had mentally tagged *Riff* and *Raff,* chuckled under their breath.

"Some people's children," Isobel muttered irritably as she turned to find something new on the wardrobe rack. She pushed the clothes hangers around loud enough to make sure every one of the men in her presence knew she *meant* to stir up a ruckus.

"What was that?" Dustin queried, chuckling and raising an eyebrow.

"Nothing," she snapped, keeping her back to him and continuing to riffle through the clothes.

"You mean nothing I'd want to know about," he corrected casually.

She whirled around and glared at him, her eyes spitting fire. "Whatever."

Dustin knew then that he'd really offended her, and he took the offensive to make it right with her again, submitting to the ministrations of Riff and Raff and cracking jokes that made the men, at least, loosen up and laugh a little bit.

But it took another long, excruciating hour before Isobel finally settled on an outfit that both pleased her and that Dustin didn't whine about.

"You are so lucky," she informed him, her tone still a little sharp and exasperated. "Do you know how many men can get away with pleated slacks with cuffs, and actually look good in them?"

He rolled his eyes but then grinned in her direction, trying to ease the tension between the two of them but still not ready to give in to her demands. "No, Belle. Tell me."

Either she didn't hear the irony in his voice or she was ignoring it. Or maybe her answer would have been the same either way.

"Close to none," she said crisply, brushing her palms together as if brushing off any rebuttals he might have made.

"Honestly," she continued before he could speak, "so many men wear pleats and shouldn't. You need broad shoulders to balance the look, and of course a trim, tight torso."

Dustin grinned and patted his stomach. "Three hundred sit-ups each and every morning, first thing. Guess it's done the trick."

"Evidently," she said wryly, looking anywhere but at him.

He chuckled.

"Besides you, Dustin, I can only think of one man who really does those pants justice, and he's a television hunk."

Both of Dustin's eyebrows hit his hairline at her words and his mouth dropped open.

"Hunk?" he teased.

She brushed his comment off and kept her eyes carefully averted. Isobel didn't want to be thinking about his nice physique right now, unless it was related to the clothes she wanted him to wear.

"Whatever."

Truth be told, the real hunk was standing before her, and despite their differences in opinion over fashion styles and what he should wear, she knew she was succumbing to his innate charm.

He was one of those men who didn't have the slightest idea what they had going for them—which was just as well. He'd be a dangerous, and no doubt arrogant, man if he knew the effect he had on women.

On her.

She mentally shook herself out of her emotional relapse. She still had work to do, and she wouldn't let her latent feelings for Dustin keep her from getting the job done.

Without a single word to him, she held out her hand to him.

He took it without comment and allowed himself to be pulled through the golden stage curtain and on to the runway.

"This is very important, Dustin, so please try to follow my instructions to the letter." Her voice was low and crisp.

"Yes, ma'am," he replied with a playful salute. "Whatever you say."

"Spotlights, Jon," she called loudly. Immediately a hot, bright spotlight put Dustin and Isobel at the center of the action.

"Spotlights?" Dustin queried warily, dropping her hand. Something was up, and he wanted to know what it was. "What's with the spotlights?"

"You'll understand in a minute, hon," Isobel said with a short laugh.

"Why do I think I'm not going to like this?" he asked wryly, lifting his left eyebrow. His muscles tensed as if in preparation for the worst.

"Oh, it won't hurt. I promise."

Dustin just shook his head.

"It's that simple, really. All I want you to do is put on some attitude. Be your usual confident self, only with a little punch."

"And?" he asked. It sounded as if he might be gritting his teeth, and Isobel well knew she was gritting hers.

He wasn't going to like this.

"And," Isobel continued, half holding her breath, "I want you to walk down to the end of the runway, turn around as if there were big crowds of fashion-conscious magazine editors out there in those chairs watching you, and then walk back to the curtain."

She paused. This was an important moment. If she couldn't get him to comply in this one area, to show off the confidence she believed he possessed, then it would be all uphill from here.

How else would she ever begin to get him up to snuff for the really important moments, when people would be present?

Watching him. Judging him.

"Nothing could be simpler, Dustin. It might be fun, even." Her voice cracked, and she wondered if he noticed the slight lapse.

"Not a chance," Dustin informed her in a deep, slow, firm monotone voice that indicated he would brook no argument.

"I'm not asking you to do anything illegal," Isobel retorted, mild anger showing in her tone despite her best efforts. She'd known this wasn't going to be easy, but she'd hoped for the best, despite it all.

He grunted.

"What could be easier that walking the runway? No one is here to see you but me."

"Don't forget Riff and Raff," he pointed out, crossing his arms and sounding just a bit like a pouting child, at least to Isobel. "And as for the runway, I can tell you right now I would look like an idiot strutting around like that, showing off some dumb clothes."

He looked at her then, his gaze pleading in a way his words could never do. He looked as if he were in pain, and it struck right at her heart.

After a moment, he groaned. "Don't ask me to do this, Isobel. It isn't me."

She wanted to let him off the hook. Her heart was screaming to give the poor man a break.

But this was for his own good, she reminded herself. He needed to do this, needed to see what it felt like under the spotlight.

"Please?" She was begging now, and they both knew it. "For me?"

He shook his head, but at the same time stepped forward and onto the runway, glowering down at her from his new height. "Very well," he said, his voice tight. "For you."

With a frown, he started down the runway. It wasn't long before Isobel detected his intentions weren't entirely honest. Fire and ice fought inside her as she watched him make a mockery of her life, and his chances of getting the trust-fund money.

It began subtly, with a turn of his hips and an occasional hand flipping in the air in an unusually cocked manner. Then he started strutting and jerking all the way down the aisle.

The only sound was the click and thump of the boots he was wearing with the outfit Isobel had devised. It didn't take a neurosurgeon to figure out he was doing a man's imitation of a female runway model.

Poorly.

For Isobel, it was the last straw.

She threw down the clipboard she was holding and let it clatter to the floor.

The noise stopped Dustin in his tracks, though he didn't turn and look at her.

"That's it," she said, unable to keep the anger and frustration she was feeling from her voice. Rage surged through her in hot waves.

And the worst part was she didn't care. "You want to change, Dustin Fairfax, do it yourself. At this moment, I couldn't care less about you, your brother's crazy ideas or the money in your stupid trust fund."

She drew in a large, loud breath and glared at his back. "I quit."

It was the first sensible thing she had said all day— maybe for weeks, she thought to herself. It was as if a weight was lifted from her shoulders, now that the stress of the situation was gone.

And the sooner she got away from Dustin Fairfax, the better.

She turned and hiked toward the door, not daring to look back to see what Dustin was doing.

"Isobel," he roared, and she froze solid in the spot despite her best efforts to keep moving.

Every bone in her body screamed for her to run, but there seemed to be a short between her brain and her limbs. She couldn't move a muscle.

"Turn around." His hard voice was a command, and she knew she should be offended, but she didn't move.

She couldn't.

"Isobel, please."

The tender, genuine ache in his voice as he spoke moved her heart as no cold command could have.

She didn't stride off in indignation.

She turned.

If his genuine honesty had compelled her to stop and turn around, it was the hopeful pleading in his wide green eyes that made her stay.

"Belle, look at me," he said, his voice low and hyp-notic. "Just stand there a moment more and watch me. Please."

How could she not?

She was mesmerized by him. His every move was slow and calculated, and graceful in the way of a large wildcat in its mountain home.

Slowly, sweat dripping unheeded from his forehead, step by excruciating step, he walked down the runway, putting every effort into transforming himself into the poised and well-postured man Belle wanted him to be.

He exceeded every aspect of a true runway model. His male ego would settle for nothing less. His boots made no sound this time as he glided along; all she could hear was his labored breathing.

No swaying hips or obnoxious comments in a falsetto voice followed these movements, and she was overwhelmed by the pull of his will alone.

He was sleek, smooth and oh, so masculine, in a way none of the male models of her acquaintance could even remotely simulate. His face was a study in strong lines and smooth planes as the lights teased his shadowed expression and his concentrated steps.

After what seemed an excruciatingly long time, Dustin reached the end of the runway and paused. Electricity crackled in the air.

Isobel held her breath in unconscious anticipation, thinking he might do something boyish and silly and totally Dustin to ruin the moment—something like taking a running leap off the constructed platform and screaming like a banshee all the way down.

And yet...

He broke for only one moment in order to flash her a cheeky grin that made her heart skip a beat. Then he was absolute model material again, as he carefully removed his sports coat and, with a beautifully executed turn that reminded her more of a dancer than a model, turned back toward the stage, flipping the jacket with casual ease onto his shoulder.

With another smooth turn he stepped confidently to the end of the runway and pulled at the silk tie, then unbuttoned the top button of the rose-pink shirt he vowed he'd never wear in public.

Pink or no pink, the man oozed masculinity.

When he was finished with his spotless routine, he gave a subtle, after-work casualness to his overall appearance, like he'd finished his workday and was just beginning to relax and kick back.

Isobel had never seen anything like the performance Dustin Fairfax was giving her right now.

Everything from his confident male swagger to the stray lock of hair that fell over his forehead was as professional as it was endearing. She swallowed hard, forcing herself to keep breathing, to keep watching this magnificent sight. She was certain she'd never see anything quite like this again.

Dustin pivoted once more and walked back up the runway until he disappeared behind the sparkling gold curtain.

Isobel didn't move, not at all sure what to expect next. She thought perhaps she ought to follow him backstage, but her legs felt like jelly and she wasn't sure she could walk even if she wanted to.

A few moments later, Dustin slid back through the curtain, and Isobel released the breath she hadn't even realized she'd been holding.

The coat was gone, his pink sleeves were rolled up over his elbows, he'd unhitched the second button on his shirt and his baseball cap was back—or more accurately, *backward*—on his head.

He cocked his chin and raised his hands in question, turning around once for her inspection, laughing at his own performance.

Isobel just stared at him, thinking he looked every bit as handsome the way he was now as he did dressed up out of his measure.

Maybe more.

"Well?" he asked when she didn't speak. "Am I forgiven?"

Chapter Nine

Isobel supposed she was giving a bit of a peace offering when she showed up at Dustin's door Saturday morning, with a dozen or so new outfits for him in the trunk of her car.

This time she'd included a few casual outfits she hoped he might actually wear, for she now knew Dustin's personality well enough to know he would never really convert to wearing business suits and ties.

That just wasn't Dustin.

That being said, there would be times when he could not avoid wearing a suit, and at the moment, both of them knew this six weeks was in that category. The grand finale was a posh dinner hosted by his brother. Dustin would *have* to dress up for that.

Feeling oddly nervous, she took a deep, cleansing breath and glanced at her watch.

9:00 a.m.

Isobel was a morning person by nature, and it hadn't occurred to her until this moment, when she was literally standing here on his doorstep, that Dustin might not be.

She wished she'd thought of it earlier.

If Dustin was a night owl and liked to sleep in late, he was not going to appreciate her gesture of goodwill when the sun was still low in the east and bright in the sky.

She hesitated a moment before raising her hand to knock. For a moment, she thought of turning around, leaving and returning later in the day.

But, after all, she was already here, she reasoned, so she might as well go ahead and knock. If he was rumpled and grumpy and growled at her to come back later, she would.

She knocked several times, pounding harder with each effort. She called Dustin's name, thinking he might be deeply involved in some project and, in typical Dustin fashion, had become entirely unaware of the world around him as he worked at whatever it was he was doing.

His ability to lose himself completely in whatever he was doing, working at everything he did with his whole heart, was actually a quality she much admired in him, as she herself was always ultra-aware of her surroundings and what was going on about her, often to the point of distraction.

At this particular moment, however, his tendency to get lost in things was annoying her. She had handpicked the outfits she had with her to give him as a present, and she was going to be very disappointed if he wasn't home or wouldn't answer his door.

She realized in hindsight she probably should have called first as a common courtesy, but she had wanted to make her appearance at his door a complete surprise—hopefully a good one.

Well! She had done that, all right. He was so surprised he wasn't even home.

Crestfallen, she shifted her attention to her surroundings. There were two cars in his driveway. The first was a practical compact car, appropriate for a single man to get around with, she supposed, though in truth a little boring for her perception of Dustin.

The second was a beat-up piece of junk Isobel barely recognized but supposed she would classify as some sort of old-time sports car.

His *sports car!*

Could it be?

She laughed aloud as she looked the car over. She would doubt if the thing even ran, were it not that he'd said he'd had it with him when they first met—offered her a ride, in fact.

Maybe she should have taken him up on it.

She stifled another laugh, but couldn't help the grin that continued to line her face.

So much for first impressions.

With Dustin, nothing was ever what it seemed on the surface. Everything about him was a mystery, and what he offered openly was completely incomprehensible to the normal female mind.

At least hers. But then, she thought wryly, not too many people she knew would classify her as *normal*.

Her curiosity piqued, she stepped around the side of the house and found a Kawasaki motorcycle, every piece of chrome polished to a bright shine, parked against the redbrick wall.

Isobel chuckled. Dustin definitely wasn't a Harley man, but it didn't entirely surprise her to find he tooled around on a motorcycle.

He marched to the beat of his own drummer, that was for certain.

She examined the motorcycle, as she had never actually been this close to one before. It looked a little dangerous, with all those pipes and rods. Her heart beat a little faster.

Suddenly and quite abruptly, she became aware of music.

She froze in place, her ear tuned to discovering the location of the pleasant sound, which she had quickly identified as some form of classical music being played on a piano.

But where was the delightful music coming from?

She couldn't quite place it, and suddenly had an incorrigible need to know. Maybe it was that incomprehensible connection she felt with Dustin. She hadn't known him that long, yet for some reason she thought it might be him, despite the fact that he had never mentioned music, much less played the piano in front of her before.

Was she right? Was it Dustin?

She walked slowly around to the back of Dustin's house, letting herself in through the unlocked picket gate and feeling a little like an intruder prowling about where she didn't belong.

She wasn't sure what Dustin would think of her letting herself into his backyard that way, but once struck, she could not help but continue until her curiosity was met as to where the sound originated.

The music led her on.

She turned the corner of the brick house. Dustin's backyard was overgrown with weeds from end to end, hadn't been mowed in ages and, most surprising of all, hadn't been landscaped.

Not a single flower bloomed. No color budded from the ground.

And him owning a flower shop.

Dustin was a paradox. An enigma.

And she was more determined than ever to figure him out.

After she had found out where the music was coming from. The longer she listened, the more intrigued she became.

There were sliding glass double doors at the back of Dustin's modest home, and one was open a crack, though the long white drapes were still pulled against the blazing sunlight.

She crept forward, every moment half expecting Dustin to jump out from behind a bush or shrub, shouting "Gotcha" at the top of his lungs and frightening her half out of her wits.

It would be just like Dustin to do that.

But then, who would be playing the piano?

Every nerve on end, she pulled the glass door open mere inches more, only because, she told herself, she now had no doubt whatsoever that the music was coming from within Dustin's house.

Someone was in there playing, and she had to know for certain who it was.

And it was not, she assured herself, any sort of jealousy that led her on, like the unwanted thought that some beautiful woman was in Dustin's house playing on his piano and to his delight.

It was the music and nothing more.

In moments she had confirmed her theory. The piano

melody was definitely coming from his house, and she closed her eyes for a moment to savor the warm, familiar classical refrain.

Whoever was playing, he—or she—was good. No, not good.

Gifted.

Hardly knowing she did so, she slid the door half-open so she could slip inside the house. She followed the sound of the music like a tiny mouse at the mercy of the Pied Piper.

Not thinking. Feeling.

She crossed through an empty room that looked as if it served a variety of purposes. There was a computer, a wide workbench with a variety of wood products on it and a table spread with flower cuttings.

Not, she thought with a small smile, flowers fresh from his own garden.

The room had a wood floor that looked as if it had seen better days. It needed a mop and a good dose of wax, not to mention some elbow grease.

As soon as she hesitantly stepped through the open double doors onto the white shag carpet that covered the next room, she finally located the source of the wonderful music.

Dustin sat straight-backed at a highly polished baby grand, his eyes closed as his fingers flowed effortlessly over the keys.

This room was full of light from the many windows and, unlike the room she'd come from, was fully furnished with what looked like expensive, high-end wood furniture and a posh set of black leather sofas and chairs that looked fabulous against the plush white carpet.

Nicely framed black-and-white art posters lined

every wall, placed with a remarkable sense of balance that finished off the room with class and distinction.

Isobel couldn't help the smile that tugged at the corners of her lips. Apparently he hadn't completely lost a sense of his upbringing.

Suddenly she realized the music had ceased and she froze in place, almost afraid to turn her head in Dustin's direction.

After all, she was, technically, an intruder. Whether that was a good thing or not was still to be decided.

As much as she would have liked to avoid it, her gaze turned almost of its own consent toward the piano, holding her breath at what she might find there.

Dustin's eyes were open, one eyebrow arched. His arms were crossed over his chest, and his inquiring gaze was upon her.

And that was all.

He didn't even look particularly surprised she had suddenly appeared in his house without being invited. He looked as if he might be wondering *why* she was there, and was only mildly and amusedly curious at discovering the answer to that.

Isobel's face flamed as she realized she *had* no explanation, no rational excuse at all.

She cleared her throat and looked at the floor, stalling for time, though she knew he wouldn't wait forever. She would have to think of some excuse at some point.

Preferably sooner than later.

"Well?" he encouraged, unabashed laughter lining his voice.

"I followed the sound of the music," she blurted at last, then felt her face flame at the weakness of her poor explanation.

He laughed aloud then. "You followed the music. From your condo in downtown Denver?"

She scowled at him, though in truth she was put out with herself. What kind of fool walked into someone's house uninvited, especially a man she'd only known a short time?

"From your front porch," she answered in a clipped tone. "I dropped by as a surprise to, uh—to give you a present," she stammered.

Dustin's grin disappeared as soon as he heard the word *present*.

A *present*?

Up until this time their acquaintance had been casual, even businesslike, although admittedly he considered her a friend at this point.

He intended to get to know her over these six weeks. He hoped to stay friends with her after his brother's crazy experiment was over.

But still…

What had he missed?

Some sort of three-week anniversary or such?

It wasn't his birthday.

His male mind scoured the details of their acquaintance for a clue to his oversight and he felt sweat beading on his forehead.

The crux of the matter was that *he* didn't have a present to give to *her*.

He didn't know why it mattered.

She was the one who'd wandered into his house without an invitation, and somehow she'd already turned it around so he was the one pulling at his collar and fidgeting on his piano stool.

Women.

No wonder he was single at thirty.

He'd never understand the female mind, not if he lived to be a hundred.

"Don't look so shocked, Dustin. It's not personal," she said with a chuckle. "It's a professional gift, and your brother paid for it. So you can take a deep breath and relax, cowboy."

Dustin scrunched his face and cringed dramatically. And it wasn't all for show. For one thing, he didn't want anything to do with his brother's handouts, even in the form of beautiful Isobel Buckley.

"Oh, now, stop that fidgeting and take it like a man. I know you can handle it."

She paused long enough to make him fidget again. "Anyway, I picked everything out myself."

"Everything?" he asked warily.

"Every last piece."

He gazed at her warily. "Piece of what? Dutch apple pie, I hope."

She chuckled. "You wish. You men and your stomachs. I'm sorry to disappoint you, but I'm speaking of clothes, as I think you already know."

He cringed again. "I was hoping you wouldn't say that. And yet, somehow I knew deep down in my heart, despite my growling stomach, that was what you were going to say. I wonder why?"

She propped her hands on her hips, and he knew she wasn't buying his propaganda. "If I didn't know better I'd think you were afraid of new clothes."

He chuckled, placing a fist on his hip, mimicking her moves and her voice. "If I didn't know you better, I'd think you were obsessed by them."

She tossed him a catty grin. "What an astute observation. How long did it take you to come up with that one?"

They stared at each other. A silent moment passed between them.

"So?" Dustin asked, amused, though maybe still a little uncomfortable. He was not in a big hurry to get to the *clothes* part, but resigned himself to the inevitable.

"So?" Isobel repeated, obviously pulling back from her thoughts and looking a little dazed.

"So are you going to get those new clothes out of your car so I can see them, or what?"

"I...uh..." Isobel stammered. "I wasn't thinking about the clothes," she admitted, her words muddled together as they tumbled from her mouth.

Dustin threw both hands up to his unshaven cheeks and drew in a sharp, dramatic breath. "You've astonished me."

She narrowed her eyes on him.

"It's a compliment." He nodded his head vigorously when she raised her eyebrow.

"Hmm...I wonder."

"Well," he prompted with a grin, "if you weren't thinking about what an incredibly changed man I'll be in your new clothes, just what exactly were you thinking about?"

She cleared her throat and looked out the window. "Your music," she mumbled under her breath.

"My what?"

"The piano. I followed the sound into your house. Although in my defense I did try knocking on the front door first."

Her face was a delightful shade of pink, growing red, and Dustin's grin widened.

"And of course I didn't hear you. I pound around so voraciously on these old ivories it makes the dogs howl clear down the street."

She lifted an eyebrow.

"And just wait until I start wailing along with the music," he added, laughing with her. "I'll have the whole neighborhood up in arms in a matter of minutes."

"I'm sure that isn't true," she replied instantly. "From what I heard of your piano playing, you're pretty good." She paused. "Actually, that's an understatement. If you sing half as well as you play, you'll have no trouble impressing me."

"Is that what I'm doing?" he queried lightly, his gaze brushing over her.

She swallowed hard and straightened her hair with her palm. "You tell me."

Not in a million years, he thought as his heart raced as fast as his thoughts. He wasn't about to admit to anything but his name, rank and serial number. And that was if he could speak at all.

He ran his fingers across the ivories, so swiftly that they didn't make a sound. It was one of the nicest feelings in the world, his fingers on the keyboard.

"I do love playing," he admitted softly.

"Play something now, then. For me?" Her voice was soft and so compelling he didn't even think about toying with her.

With a clipped nod and pinched lips holding back any expression of emotion that might betray him, he brought both hands to the keyboard, brushed his fingers lightly across the ivories and began playing a familiar hymn. It was slow and emotional, and Dustin closed his eyes to capture every nuance.

Isobel also closed her eyes, savoring the beauty of one of her most beloved hymns. How had he known "The Old Rugged Cross" was one of her particular favorites?

Suddenly, Dustin switched gears and started playing an upbeat praise song Isobel recognized from one of the CDs in her car. He was hitting so many notes one after the other Isobel was certain his fingers must be flying over the keys.

Her eyes popped open in surprise and Dustin smiled at her without missing a beat.

"Sing with me," he said, and looked out toward the sunshine-jammed window before breaking into an upbeat tune with his deep baritone.

"Oh, no, I don't think—"

"Isobel." Dustin cut her off with a warning look. "Remember, I know how to be every bit as stubborn as you do."

"Yes, but I—"

"Is-o-bel." He drew out her name, pleading this time instead of ordering.

She couldn't resist the soulful look he gave her with his big green eyes. For some reason this appeared to be very important to him, and she immediately capitulated to his endearing puppy-dog look.

"Okay, but don't say I didn't warn you," she said with a laugh.

"I will take full responsibility for your actions," he assured her, joining her laughter as their gazes met and held.

"Now, let's see," he said, flipping through a stack of books on the top of the piano. "What do you think we should sing?"

"'Mary Had a Little Lamb'?" Isobel suggested, placing a hand over her mouth to suppress the laughter surging from her.

"Come now, Belle," he said fondly. "Surely you can do better than that!"

"You choose, then," Isobel said, suddenly tense. She was not at all comfortable with her own voice, though she hesitated to mention her fears to Dustin. "Just make it something easy."

Once again massaging the keys with his fingers before he started playing, Dustin broke into a simple praise melody Isobel was completely familiar with, one with a straightforward melody and without much range.

It figured.

He couldn't choose a song she'd never heard before, so she could honestly beg off. It had to be the most likely song in the world she *might* be able to sing.

Oh, well. It was his problem. He'd asked for it, and had more or less told her to sing.

He might just come to rue it.

She joined in, tentatively at first and then, as Dustin smiled his encouragement, slowly and steadily with more gusto.

She couldn't have been more surprised if he had pinched her.

It was *fun* singing with Dustin.

Her voice might not be anything to write home about, but his certainly was, and for some odd reason she almost felt as if they sounded good together, as if their voices somehow blended.

But of course that was ridiculous. Water and oil didn't mix, no matter how hard a person might shake them.

She was relieved when the song ended.

Dustin sat straight-backed on his piano stool, staring at her, his hands folded in his lap.

When she finally had the nerve to look at him, he merely raised an eyebrow.

"What?" she finally asked when he continued to sit stone-faced and unspeaking.

"Well?" he prompted in return, looking and sounding as if he expected something from her.

"Well, what?" she asked, exasperated. She couldn't stand to play games, especially right now when she was feeling self-conscious. She was embarrassed enough as it was, without him rubbing it in.

"What was the big shock I was supposed to experience when you sang?" he asked her bluntly, looking her right in the eyes.

"What do you mean?"

He shrugged, as if the answer were obvious. "From the way you talked, I expected—well, I don't know—something awful."

"Wasn't it?" Shock rippled through her body at his intimation.

"No. Not at all." His voice was warm and reassuring.

"But I thought…my voice…I mean I really can't…" she stammered, but he cut her off with a shake of his head.

"What?" he asked, his voice gentle and firm. "You can't *what?*"

She didn't answer. She couldn't. She just stared at him, knowing he would force the issue anyway, but unable to say the word.

"Sing?" he suggested in a whisper, his gaze full of compassion.

She let out a relieved breath she hadn't realized she'd been holding. "Exactly."

Somehow, it was easier when he put it into words for her.

"Isobel, you have a nice voice. Trust me."

He sounded so genuine Isobel's heart did a flip-flop into her throat.

"I don't sing off-key?" she asked, her voice squeaking with surprise.

"Who told you that?" He sounded more surprised than she felt.

She blushed, trying to think where she'd first received that impression and what had led her to feel that way. "Why, no one, I guess. I used to sing all the time when I was a toddler and in preschool," she remembered with a sudden fondness. "I always liked music, especially Sunday school songs."

Her mind drifted to less happy times. "I remember," she said, choking on the words, "that my mother used to yell at me when I would sing."

"Aw, Belle," Dustin said, empathy dripping from every syllable. "Everyone's parents holler at their kids when they get too loud."

"Yes," Isobel replied quietly. "I know. I probably am making a big deal out of nothing." Her heart ached, screaming to the contrary.

In a moment he was by her side, grasping her hands gently in his, stroking her fingertips in a calm, rhythmic manner. "Of course, it's not nothing," he said in a gravelly tone.

He paused a moment and continued fervently, "Talk to me."

He led her to the couch and seated them both, never letting go of her hands.

"I remember a specific time," Isobel said slowly, looking over his shoulder so she wouldn't have to meet his eyes.

He nodded. "Go on."

"I was about five, I think. My mother was on the phone. I was singing with the television—one of those old children's programs. I didn't know who Mom was talking to, or that it was important. But suddenly she slammed the phone down and turned on me. Her face was as white as paper, and I remember noticing how bad she was shaking."

Dustin continued stroking her fingers with light reassurance.

"She yelled and yelled, until her face was bright red. She said my voice was annoying, and she wished for once I would just shut up. She kept yelling the words 'shut up' over and over again."

"She was in a really bad way," Dustin said. "Did you ever find out what was going on?"

Isobel shook her head. "I never did find out what that phone call was about. I always thought it must have been my father, but I don't know. I do know I never sang again."

"So you assumed that you must sing off-key?" he asked seriously.

She could feel her face growing warmer by the moment. "I don't know. I thought perhaps I was tone deaf. I always stand quietly in church and let others do the singing, though I praise God in my heart."

"You should sing," he admonished promptly, wagging a finger at her.

She shrugged, asking with her gaze for him to tell her what he was thinking.

"In the first place, Belle, today you hit every single note right on key, with a beautiful tone of voice I'm sure many people would love to hear."

"Oh," she said mildly.

"And second of all, you broke through today, Isobel. You sang with me. Don't go backward from here.

"Third," he said, his voice turning a little gruff, "that's not the point of music in the first place."

"I'm not following you," she said, honestly confused by his words.

"What is music really for, Isobel?" he queried seriously. He stood and returned to his piano stool, leaning his elbows on his knees and staring right into her eyes.

When she was silent, he answered his own question. "To worship God."

"Of course," she whispered reverently. It was something she'd always known, yet Dustin was showing it to her in a new way.

"And do you think God cares if a person sings a bit off-key? If he sings from the heart, I expect that song comes off as beautiful to God's ears as the entire heavenly host put together."

Isobel just stared at him.

His smile wavered and he pinched his lips together. "And I'm preaching, aren't I?"

She shook her head. "No. Not at all. I've never heard it put that way. You're absolutely right. And it's a lovely thought."

She looked away from his bright gaze, seeking refuge in one of the posters lining his walls.

"What?" he asked.

She laughed at herself for her own folly. "I'm somewhat hesitant to admit this, but I wasn't thinking of God's ears so much as yours."

Dustin broke into laughter.

She was cute, that one. Cute, truly intelligent and completely fun to be around. He loved the way she spoke her mind no matter what, even if it got her into trouble or was potentially embarrassing.

He could respect a woman like that.

But that was more than he wanted her to know. He felt vulnerable enough around her as it was.

In fact, he couldn't ever remember a time in his life when a woman had touched his soul as she had in three short weeks. She was truly unique, and he silently thanked God for the opportunity to get to know her better.

What had started as an unmitigated disaster of a plan concocted by his brother was now time Dustin found himself looking forward to, more and more as the days went by.

He only had three weeks left.

Chapter Ten

Isobel was still staring at him, a peculiar look on her face, when Dustin started from his reverie and realized he'd been woolgathering.

"Why did you stop singing completely? After a while, didn't you wonder?"

"Well I never…I mean, other people were so…and I…" She paused from her stammering and took a deep breath. "You can't really know if you're good or not," she finished lamely. "After a while, it just seemed easier that way. Besides, my voice sounds different to my ears than it does everyone else's."

He decided to interrupt her soliloquy and spare her further agony.

"Isobel, sweetheart, let me put you out of your misery. You have a sweet, pleasant alto and you hit every note right on key."

"No squeaking?"

"Nothing remotely reminiscent of any kind of animal," he assured her, shaking his head and chuckling at his own joke.

"Oh," she said, still sounding surprised and a little stunned. "Thank you."

"And remember, I'm a musician, so I know what I'm talking about."

"You are that," she agreed readily. "Who was your teacher? Where in the world did you learn to play the piano like that?"

It was an obvious attempt to change the subject, but Dustin let it go.

He coughed and brushed his fingers across the ivories, trying unsuccessfully to hide a bittersweet smile. "I didn't."

"You didn't what?"

"Have lessons," he admitted painfully. "Although in my defense, I did practice several hours every day when I was a kid."

"No one taught you," she repeated, sounding stunned.

He could tell she didn't believe him.

"My parents didn't believe in the extracurricular—except maybe for competitive sports, and that was my brother's department, not mine. Anything in the arts was definitely out of the question."

"But your dad was a multimillionaire!" she exclaimed. "Surely he could afford something as simple as piano lessons."

Dustin ground his teeth against the first reaction that stabbed through his chest and threatened to exit his mouth. He would not say aloud how much it hurt him, no matter how soulfully her eyes looked at him and begged for him to share.

It took him a good moment to regain his composure, and the fact that Isobel was scowling—presumably on his behalf at his mistreatment by his parents—made the task of pulling himself together even more arduous.

It would be easier if he didn't know she cared. But for some reason, she did. It showed in her glistening brown eyes and in her hurt expression.

"My father was a strict businessman," Dustin explained hoarsely. "He worked his way up from a poor family to a multimillionaire by sheer effort and will-power. Frankly, he didn't see the point of studying fine arts, so we didn't."

"But there was a piano in your home," she said, stating the obvious.

"Oh, yes," he said, drowning out her last word. He had lived in a house, but despite his mother's best efforts, he realized now it had never really been *home* to him.

He squeezed his eyes shut and cleared his throat again. This was more difficult than he would ever have imagined. "It was the most expensive grand piano they could find. It was purely for aesthetic purposes, to make the room nice. It didn't mean anything significant to anyone. No one ever played it."

"Except you."

"Except me." He felt hollow inside as he made the admission, yet he felt compelled to go on, to tell her the whole story before he lost his nerve.

"My father was almost always away from home, building his business, so I rarely saw him. Every time my mother left the house to shop or meet with her friends, I practiced on the piano."

Isobel's eyes were bright with unshed tears, as she moved to stand behind Dustin, and he swallowed hard.

"That must have been hard for you," she whispered, placing her small, soft hand on his arm.

He nodded. "It was. I didn't have any music books or anything to work with at first. I had to wing it completely on my own."

"You succeeded admirably."

He nodded to acknowledge her compliment, and then continued with his story, his voice coarse with emotion. "When my mother died, music was my only solace. I bought music books and put what I learned on my own to use, learning notes and staffs and keys and stuff."

"All on your own?" she asked softly. "Without any help from anyone?"

"Not a soul even knew I played the piano until long after I'd reached adulthood."

"I can't believe your father," Isobel said angrily, squeezing his arm in protest. "I'm surprised you aren't permanently emotionally scarred by what that man did—or rather, didn't do."

"Who says I'm not?" he joked, forcing a chuckle through his dry throat.

"Dustin," she retorted, moving to sit on the soft leather sofa opposite the piano. Leaning forward, she ran her fingers casually over the coffee table, as if examining its planes and ridges.

"Play me a song," she urged him. "Something sweet and classical."

"Whatever the lady wants," he said with a wink, glad to have something positive to do, something to take the sad expression from Isobel's face.

He ran his fingers across the keys as was his unconscious habit, and then was instantly lost in the beautiful music of Bach. It happened all at once, as it had in childhood, his forgetting all his problems and cares as music swept him away.

He closed his eyes, savoring every note and measure, wanting the music to be especially pleasing to Isobel's ear.

He wanted her to hear what he heard, feel what he felt with music.

As he finished the piece, he took a deep, cleansing breath and turned to see how Isobel liked it, hoping the music had brought some manner of peace to her, as it had done with him.

To his surprise, she didn't appear to have been listening at all.

But when she turned to him, her eyes were glowing. "Bach was wonderful, and despite what it may look like, I really was listening to you."

"Glad to hear it. It sure didn't look to me like you were listening," he groused under his breath, trying not to look like a pouting child.

"All I can say is that you continue to impress and astound me. Your piano, your singing, your work at the flower shop—you are truly gifted by God in so many ways."

"Hobbies," he corrected. "Believe me, I'm no kind of genius or anything."

"You know, I don't think I even *have* a hobby. I spend all my time working. At night I get takeout and then fall into bed completely exhausted."

Dustin laughed, genuinely this time. "That's not good for you, you know."

"I know, I know. It's a bad habit of mine that I just can't seem to break."

Isobel was suddenly aware that she had intruded on

his privacy. She had quite literally walked in on him
when she hadn't even been invited into his house. And
then she had continued to push and prod him around
his house as if she owned it.

"I'm sorry," she blurted, feeling her face flush with
heat. "I came here to give you clothes, not to take up
your whole day with my prattling. Let me go get them
for you."

She rushed out of the room and out of the house,
gulping fresh air as she exited the door, and feeling
just a little bit faint.

What was it about Dustin that made her long to linger? She would have to watch herself around him. She
seemed to lose brain cells when he was near.

She pulled out a folding clothing rack and set it up
with one hand, a trick she'd learned in college. She then
carefully placed each outfit on it in what she would consider a reasonable order.

She smiled as she surveyed the colorful variety of
materials and fabrics. Dustin would definitely be overwhelmed by the quantity and magnitude of her gift.
She'd have to try to go easy on him so he didn't have a
heart attack on her.

Carefully, she wheeled the rack up the driveway and
bounced it up the single cement step to the porch, using
both hands to stabilize the shaky rack.

Dustin came to help her, propping open the screen
door for her, opening the main door wide, then holding the screen with one foot so he could assist her as
they yanked and pulled till they had the rack in the
carpeted foyer.

It was frustrating but not impossible to trek toward
the den on the thick plush carpet, with both of them

working at it. The wheels squeaked and groaned, complaining all the way.

Isobel sighed in relief when she reached the den. "That was quite a challenge," she said. "I have a tuxedo for you for the Elway benefit," she teased. "It's black, with a black-and-white-striped ascot. You'll look great in it."

When he didn't reply, Isobel thought he was being stubborn. She turned, expecting to see Dustin by her side, frowning and throwing a boyish, if adorable, fit.

"Thanks for coming today," Dustin said gruffly, not looking at her.

"I was glad to. I—I'm glad you weren't angry with me for intruding."

"Never," he said, opening his arms to her.

Isobel stepped into his embrace without a word. With her head resting against his chest where she could hear the rapid beat of his heart, there seemed to be nothing left to say.

Chapter Eleven

Dustin was in his flower shop completing an arrangement for a wedding, but his heart wasn't really in it. Try as he might, he just couldn't keep his mind on his work.

He had discovered a soft side to Isobel, a woman he'd first thought was made of steel and who might not possess a heart at all.

Shows how much he knew.

She was a woman who followed classical music to its source without considering the consequences.

This Isobel followed her heart before her head. She was willing to take a chance even when she thought she'd fail, like singing when she thought she couldn't carry a tune.

He laughed at that now. How sweet she was, tentatively singing the praise song despite her fear, not realizing that not only was she right on key, but that she had a sweet, pleasing voice.

Why hadn't anyone ever told her what a lovely singing voice she had? Of course, if she never sang, that would pretty much explain it.

Well, he decided, jamming flowers into the arrangement with both fists, *he* was going to tell her. And he'd tell her over and over again until she believed him.

Until she believed in herself.

Suddenly, he knew what he had to do, and it couldn't wait, not one more second. He stopped arranging the bouquet and told the two employees hard at work he was leaving.

He couldn't remember being this excited about anything in a long, long time.

Maybe ever.

Making one quick stop at a local music store, he hurried home, anxious to begin this new project he'd concocted on a whim but knew in his heart might be one of the best ideas he'd ever had.

Once home, he shed his coat and went straight to the piano. With gentle reverence, he opened his new package and carefully placed the lined, blank staff sheets before him.

For a moment he felt overwhelmed, about to dive in far over his head with nothing but one quick gulp of air. The lines and blank spaces were intimidating, challenging him to fill in the notes.

Could he really do this?

He'd never composed music before, only played it. He hadn't the remotest notion of whether he could create a piece of his own, compose his own melody and write his own words.

Yet he had to try.

For her.

Besides, to his surprise, music was already beginning to form in his head. He realized it was already there, fully formed in his mind. All *he* had to do was get it down on paper.

Soon he was completely involved in the project, a pencil behind his ear and that stubborn lock of hair falling down on his forehead.

It was more complicated than he thought it would be, but he was certainly improving as he went along.

He was writing music!

He realized now it would take quite some time to finish the piece, far longer than he'd originally thought. But he was determined to complete it before the six weeks were up, so he could give a gift back to Belle for all she'd done for him.

Dustin didn't raise his head for several hours. He was so fascinated by the process of putting the music in his head onto paper that he threw himself wholeheartedly into the work.

When he looked at the clock, it was ten after seven at night. At first he thought he might go back and work some more, but there was something else niggling at his brain, something he was supposed to remember.

What was it?

He was growling under his breath about how he needed to start writing things down so he could remember his appointments, when it hit him.

He was supposed to be at the John Elway Foundation benefit. It was a high-class event and Dustin knew Isobel had had to pull strings and call in some favors to get invited.

And, he realized with a sharp spike in his adrenaline, he was supposed to be there at seven o'clock sharp.

He was late.

Really late, since he still had to put on the tuxedo Isobel had left him. And then it was at least a thirty-minute drive downtown, and that was if the traffic was good.

He looked in the mirror, critically surveying his appearance. His hair was a bit mussed, but that could be easily remedied with a comb and some gel. His black T-shirt was brand-new, and his jeans were still discernibly black, through a bit faded in spots.

He shuffled though the clothes rack Isobel had brought him and immediately came upon a nice black-and-gray sports coat. He chuckled and pulled it down from the rack even as his plan formed.

Isobel would have to be pleased by his ingenuity in the heat of tardiness.

Besides, he didn't like tuxedos anyway.

Isobel stood in the corner of the large, highly decorated conference room and watched the entrance door like a hawk. Occasionally she would tap her foot in an impatient rhythm.

Where in the world was Dustin?

He'd *promised* to be her escort tonight, and though she was generally quite comfortable mingling with the crowds on her own in such situations, for some reason tonight she felt as if a part of her was missing.

It was an unsettling notion, and Isobel didn't really like it. Certainly she wouldn't mention her awkward feelings to anyone, especially Dustin.

If he showed up.

She would not look at her watch again, knowing it would only be one or two minutes since the last time she'd looked.

Instead, she looked again at the door, thinking he might be planning to make a grand entrance just to surprise her and throw her off guard, as Dustin was so very fond of doing.

For a moment she dwelled on that unlikely fantasy, most especially the first glance of Dustin in a tuxedo. She had no doubt he would be breathtakingly gorgeous. Tuxedos always made men look dashing and elegant, but she suspected Dustin would look especially charming.

But he wasn't there.

At least she thought he wasn't until she made a casual sweep of the room and her gaze stopped on Dustin. He was at the opposite end of the crowd, already in an animated conversation with the mayor of Denver.

No wonder she hadn't recognized him. She'd been looking for a man in black.

What was he wearing?

Though he was obviously unaware of it, Dustin looked as if he'd crawled out from under a rock, and Isobel wanted nothing more at that moment than to crawl right underneath the very rock Dustin had come out of—after she'd had a chance to wring his neck.

Steam rose from the tips of her toes to the tops of her ears.

He had *promised!*

On time, and dressed in a tuxedo.

Zero for two, by her count.

How could he do this to her?

As if sensing her stare, Dustin turned around and looked straight at her. His smile brightened noticeably as he saluted her with his hand. He then turned to the mayor, said something that made the mayor chuckle and made a beeline for Isobel.

"Hey, Belle, I've been talking to the mayor. Did you know he goes to—"

"You're late," she said flatly, cutting him off. She was

in no mood for his cheerful chatter. She had so many things she wanted to say to him that her words were all mixed up in her head. "You—you—"

"Wascally Wabbit?" he suggested, chuckling at his own jest.

"How can you joke at a time like this?" she demanded in a huff of hot air.

He made a sweeping gesture that encompassed the whole room. "Is this a party, or what?" he asked in a bright voice, obviously ignoring the female warning signs she was inwardly wrestling with and which she was sure showed in her posture and on her face, not to mention in her voice.

"Yes, Dustin. It's a party. An *upscale* party," she emphasized.

He merely shrugged.

"Look how everyone is dressed—in tuxedos and cocktail dresses. This was supposed to be a test drive of the new you, remember? All I see is the same old Dustin Fairfax."

He looked down at his own clothing and frowned. "Well, yes," he admitted with a groan. "I had noticed I'm a bit underdressed, but then, I usually am."

"And your excuse is?"

He looked at her blankly for a moment. "My excuse," he repeated halfheartedly. "Am I supposed to have an explanation?"

He looked a bit rattled by the simple request, which surprised Isobel for a moment. She'd expected him to be blurting wild excuses a mile a minute.

But he wasn't.

Isobel took that moment to push him.

"I'm sure it's fascinating, how you were on your way

to the benefit and some homeless person needed to borrow your tuxedo for a night out on the town."

"Hey," he protested. "Lay off, already. I have a good reason."

"I'm sure you do," she said wryly. "I'm just surprised you haven't divulged it yet. You always seem to surprise me."

"I…it's just that I was…" His eyes lit up even as he struggled for words.

He stopped suddenly, set his jaw and met her eyes squarely. "I was busy with a project at the house, and I lost track of time. It's as simple as that."

"And the clothes?" she prompted.

"I thought you would want me to be here as soon as possible, so I improvised and rushed to get here as quickly as I could. I've been to these events before, Belle. I knew the choice I was making."

His excuse sounded lame to both of them, but Isobel found her heart softening to him. Why did he always have that effect on her?

"Did I mention I'm more comfortable than any other man here?"

She glared at him.

"Please, Isobel," he begged softly. He touched her arm and implored her with his soft green eyes.

Suddenly he was serious, his tone grave. "*Please* don't ask me to explain more than I have. I can't." He frowned. "I won't. Can you find it in your heart to forgive me?"

She couldn't help it. Her heart capitulated.

She reached up and touched the hard line of his chin, running her finger along the rough-whiskered edge. "You missed a spot."

"Did I?" he asked, chuckling. "Guess that's what happens when you try to shave and tie your sneakers at the same time."

Her eyes dropped to his well-worn sneakers, her gaze once again full of surprise.

Dustin inwardly cringed. As soon as he had said the words, he realized he had just brought the subject back to his clothes, which was the last thing he wanted to talk about and certainly the very last thing he wanted Isobel to be thinking about.

Holding his breath and expecting a firm reprimand, he was saved by the announcement of dinner being served.

He breathed a sigh of relief as people immediately began milling around them, looking for their place cards among the many tables and making far too much noise for anyone to have a real conversation.

"Where are we?" he asked, moving closer to her. After a moment, he placed an arm around her shoulders to keep them from being separated by the hungry crowd.

She reached into her bag and drew out a carefully folded piece of paper. "Table eight," she said, glancing across the room. "Although I admit I'm not sure where that is. I should have checked earlier."

He slid his hand down across her waist and then slid his hand into hers, linking her fingers with his. Isobel suddenly forgot what she was doing as the pad of his thumb stroked over hers.

She shook her head in confusion.

"Don't worry. I know where it is," he said, winking down at her and squeezing her hand. "I saw it when I came in. Just stick with me."

Dustin was glad he had taken the time to look, so this time, anyway, he could come off as the hero.

Gallantly offering his arm, he escorted her to the table and held a chair for her. She was glowing with pleasure, and he suddenly realized that she was completely in her element here—the fine dining, fancy clothes and fancy talk.

He, on the other hand, felt completely overwhelmed. Too many people, too much noise and definitely too much silverware.

It wasn't that he'd never seen such a layout, but he hadn't used one since he was a kid under the instruction of his nanny and the cook before a big dinner at their home. And even then he'd been relegated to the kids table with only one fork and no knife at all.

"I—er—" He paused and cleared his throat. Leaning in close to her ear, he whispered, "Why doesn't everyone just use one fork and scrap the rest of the silver? Less for the dishwashing folks, you know?"

She chuckled and tapped his nose playfully with her finger. "You can be really adorable sometimes, do you know that?"

Her words created a funny, fluttering feeling in his gut. He cocked an eyebrow and flashed her a cheeky smile. "I hope so."

Using her index finger under his chin to pull him closer to her, she whispered, "The small, sharp fork is for appetizers. Next to that is the one for salad. Then you have your main-dish fork."

He turned his head just slightly, putting them eye-to-eye and nearly touching foreheads. "Whose idea was it to make it so complicated?" he asked in a stage whisper that he knew didn't mask his alarm. "My father's, probably."

"Let's keep it simple," she said with a small nod that closed the gap between their foreheads until they were touching. Her brown eyes beamed with fondness and amusement. "There's a trick to it. Start on the outside and work in."

"Perfect," he said, his voice softening even as his gaze warmed on the beautiful woman beside him. "And I mean you, not the silverware. Although now that you mention it, I do recall Nanny saying something to that effect."

Without conscious thought, he leaned in slowly, crossing the small gap between his lips and hers.

His heart racing in his chest, he gave her plenty of time to figure out what he was doing, to be the one who, in the end, made the choice.

Though her arm stiffened under his hand, she didn't move a muscle to pull away from him. Only her eyes, her breathlessly warm brown eyes that felt as if they were staring right into his soul, widened slightly.

He didn't need more confirmation than that. He took her gaze as a yes and closed his eyes as he brushed his lips over the bee-stung softness of hers.

At the touch of his lips on hers, Isobel slammed back in her chair so intensely she thought she might tip herself over. She quickly tucked her elbows into her side to keep from flapping around in what she supposed would be a most inelegant manner.

If she fell, she fell; but she wouldn't make a scene doing so.

Dustin, too, pulled back, but his movement was only to straighten his spine and turn his gaze straight forward, away from her. He looked every bit as stunned as she felt, as if he hadn't initiated the contact.

"Sorry," he said gruffly. "I forgot you work for my brother."

Isobel felt the impact of his words like a dart in her heart. She hadn't meant to have it look as if she were turning *away* from his kiss—it was the sweetest moment she had ever known.

In that moment, she had finally come to the realization that Dustin wasn't just some sort of challenging makeover project.

And she was attracted to that man, as a woman was drawn to a man. He was no longer a challenging project.

He was a man.

But that wasn't the reason she had jerked away. It was a sudden sense of guilt that had caused the fatal movement.

He was her client—at least in a sense. And although there were no set doctor/patient types of rules in the fashion industry, she was struck by her own sense of responsibility to the work she'd been hired to do, and to those she was accountable to.

It was a silly thing, really. She considered herself rational and down-to-earth, and here she was being flighty and nonsensical.

She attempted to smile at him, but he would have none of it. He was pretending she wasn't even there. She had never seen Dustin look so grim, not even when faced with a table full of silverware.

He was punching into his salad—with the correct fork—as if he had to spear and kill the lettuce in order to eat it.

And he wouldn't look at her, or even in her direction. Not for one second.

He was polite and cheerful with the other guests at the table, keeping the conversation moving right along, but Isobel could tell something was wrong and she knew she was the cause of it.

Oh, why had she pulled away from him? He was taking it all wrong.

Try as she might, she could not engage Dustin's attention. Throughout the meal, she attempted to add to the conversation, especially when Dustin was voicing his own opinions.

But he wouldn't speak to her, wouldn't even look at her.

Not a glance.

It appeared the only way she was *really* contributing to the evening was in making the most easygoing, laid-back man she had ever known become stiff and tense.

Frustrated, she got up and began milling around the room, unsuccessfully attempting to put Dustin and his ill humor out of her mind.

As if that were possible.

What was she supposed to do?

Apologize?

Ask for another kiss so she could do it right and not offend him this time?

In the end, she decided it would have to be his move. She'd just have to wait and see.

Chapter Twelve

Isobel waited.

She waited. And waited. And waited.

For a whole week she waited.

By the following Saturday, she had decided Dustin wasn't planning to contact her at all.

Ever.

Why she should be surprised by that was beyond her, she decided. After all, she was the one hired to make over Dustin, and not the other way around. She should be contacting him.

Not to mention the fact she was certain she had offended him when she'd pulled away from his kiss at the charity banquet.

No wonder he wasn't calling her. Who wanted to be rejected?

She should have followed up the next day, she realized, mentally kicking herself for her tactical error. She'd been acting as if she were in an emotional relationship with Dustin, and not as his image consultant, which was the truth of the matter.

He owed her nothing.

She owed him a job well done.

What had she been thinking?

She could have—*should have*—called him Sunday afternoon and professionally reviewed what he *should* have worn to the banquet. She should have been calm, cool, collected and proficient.

The truth was that he had pulled it off. And in all honesty, it hadn't bothered her as much as it should have, especially given her profession.

Maybe it was just that the look was completely, uniquely Dustin.

Of course, critiquing his clothing would no doubt have led to an argument, but at the very least they would have been talking. And they'd always worked out their differences before.

Now, too much time had passed for her to call and nag him about his clothing selections. In fact, try as she might, she couldn't think of one single viable reason to call him now at all.

Short of the money—and she refused to be that shallow ever again.

She had dropped the ball.

She was still mulling over her dilemma when the phone rang, intruding on her thoughts like rapid gunfire. She jumped and put a hand to her chest to still her banging heart.

"Isobel?"

"Dustin!" she exclaimed. She hoped she didn't sound as relieved as she felt, but knew he could probably hear the excitement in her voice. "It's good to hear from you."

"Yeah," he said with a chuckle. She could imagine him shaking his head in mirth. "I kind of thought you would call me on Sunday and chew me out for my jeans and T-shirt combination."

She laughed, relieved at his usual warmth and candor. "Your jeans, your T-shirt and a few other choice items." His tennis shoes came to mind.

"Why didn't you?" he asked, sounding suddenly serious, his voice low and gruff. "Call me, I mean. Surely my tennis shoes alone are worth a few good words, if nothing else. I was really surprised when you didn't contact me at all. Not even a phone call."

"I…" Isobel started, and then stopped again. She was about to say she had been afraid to make contact with him after the way she had acted, which was the truth of the matter.

But she couldn't tell the truth. She felt vulnerable enough simply thinking the thoughts. To dare to speak them aloud was unimaginable.

"I was busy," she said, amazed at how calm and sure her voice sounded to her own ears. She didn't sound shaky at all.

She wasn't accustomed to lying, and as she said the words the remorse she felt in her heart made itself into a prayer for God's ears. Later, she would have to apologize to Dustin.

"Busy?" Dustin repeated, laughing loudly. It sounded forced to Isobel's ears. Guilt gushed over her like an ice-cold waterfall.

"Too busy for me? But I'm supposed to be first on your schedule," he complained, his lips tight. "I'm sure my brother made that clear to you, and I'm pretty sure he's paying you a load of cash to see that I'm first on your *busy* agenda."

"Why, yes," she said, not able to hide her surprise at

his vehemence. He sounded almost as if he were chastising her, like a parent with a child, and her hackles rose. "You *are* my highest priority, of course. I had a matter which I could not put off. It was—unavoidable."

"I see," Dustin's voice softened though he still sounded strongly suspicious.

She knew he didn't believe her, yet his next words were, "I'm not going to press you, Isobel."

Her throat tightened until she felt she was choking. She couldn't have spoken if she'd been given a million dollars to do so.

How did he understand her so well when she didn't even understand herself?

"Well then, Belle," Dustin said, his pure baritone caressing each syllable. "Can you come out with me *today?*"

"Yes, but, wh-where are we going?" she stammered, suddenly unable to keep her nervousness in check any longer.

Dustin could hear the hesitance in her voice. "Did you already have other plans made? Because we can always postpone if you'd rather. It does have a direct correlation with fashion, however."

He really wanted to spend the day with her, but couldn't help himself in giving her an out if she didn't want to go.

"Then how could I possibly refuse?" she immediately reassured him, though Dustin thought her tone was rather forced and affected.

Dustin restrained a laugh. "Perfect. I'll pick you up in a half hour. That is, if you tell me how to get to your house."

"It's a condo," she corrected halfheartedly. "I'll give

you directions. But where are we going? I don't recall you saying."

"I didn't say," he replied cheerfully. "It's a surprise."

"Surprise?" she repeated, her interest clearly piqued, judging by the high, squeaky tone to her voice.

He laughed with his whole heart. What woman didn't like surprises?

A little more than a half hour later, Dustin arrived at Isobel's house. The moment he rang the doorbell, she opened her front door. He wondered if she'd been waiting for him. She was dressed in a pretty pink number and even had a sweater tucked around her shoulders.

"Shall we go?" he asked, cordially offering his arm. She tucked her hand though the crook and smiled.

"Lead on, good gentleman."

He was happy to do so, and she was a willing participant, at least until she spied his means of transportation.

She stopped and stood as stiff as a brick wall, staring with her mouth pinched tightly shut and her eyes wide. Her hands were clenched into fists at her side.

He just grinned, having known this particular idea was going to take some selling on his part. "I take it you've never ridden on a motorcycle before."

She continued staring for a moment. "You could safely say that."

He struggled not to continue laughing, knowing Isobel would not appreciate his good humor. "Then this will be an adventure."

"Or a nightmare," she countered.

He surveyed her outfit again, a short skirt and a blouse made of some soft, silky pink material. And high heels.

"Go back in and change," he ordered lightly. "Jeans

and a T-shirt. I won't take no for an answer, so you may as well just go."

"You're kidding, right?" Her expression clearly let him know she hoped he was jesting with her, and would pull a comfortable Town Car out of his pocket.

"Didn't I say this was a fashion expedition?" he prodded cheerfully, flashing her a cheeky grin.

She planted her hands on her hips and glared at him. "A T-shirt?"

"And tennis shoes," he continued as if she hadn't spoken at all. "You just can't ride a motorcycle in heels, Isobel, no matter how much you'd like to."

"But I—"

"Go!" He cut her off in a brisk, no-nonsense tone, chuckling as she dashed back up the walk.

Isobel appeared five minutes later in navy blue designer jeans, a red T-shirt that read Shopping Is my Therapy and a worn pair of white tennis shoes.

"Wow," Dustin said, whistling softly and running his hand along his jaw.

"Wow, what?" she said, flashing her gaze at him. "Are you making fun of me?"

His amused gaze met hers. "Well, to tell you the truth, Belle, I really didn't think you *owned* a pair of tennis shoes. And those even look well-used." He pointed to her feet. "I am impressed."

"Knock it off with the sarcasm, Dustin," she said, pushing his shoulder playfully. "I wear tennis shoes all the time."

He lifted his eyebrows in disbelief.

"I do," she said, pulling herself to her full height of five foot seven. "Inside my house. When I work *out*."

He laughed heartily. "Today you're going to be wearing them out."

She hesitated. "I have a nice pair of black boots that—"

"Have a two-inch heel on them," Dustin finished for her.

She made a face at him.

"So I'm right."

"Don't gloat," she said, shaking her head but smothering a laugh.

"Who's gloating?" he asked with a criminal grin. "I just like getting my way."

"I've noticed that."

This time he was the one to make the face. He then moved to his bike and removed the leather jacket and helmet he had stored at the rear of the seat and fastened down with bungee cords.

Isobel put the jacket on without comment, but when he held up the helmet, she threw her hands up and shrieked in earnest.

"Oh, must we?" she asked, shaking away from the helmet and putting both hands out in unconscious defense. "I have a lovely pair of sunglasses I can wear. That's the law, isn't it?"

Dustin rolled his eyes. "Isobel. Don't be stubborn. I don't give two hoots about the law. Your health might have crossed my mind, though."

"But my hair—"

"Will be all tangled and frizzy by the end of the ride with your sunglasses," Dustin cut in. "Unless, of course, you wear this."

He dangled the helmet in front of her by one finger.

"Helmet head," she muttered, but she took the offending headpiece and awkwardly placed it on her head nonetheless.

Grinning, Dustin adjusted the straps under her chin and made sure it was a secure fit.

"You'll live," he teased.

"That," she said with a pouting twist of the lips, "remains to be seen."

Isobel had never in her life even remotely considered riding on a motorcycle. The only risks she took were calculated.

She left the death-defying feats like motorbikes to men like Dustin.

So she was surprised at the pleasant surge of adrenaline that shot through her as she clutched her arms around Dustin's waist and he put the cycle in gear, quickly accelerating so the wind rushed around them and the cycle purred into life.

"Woo-hoo!" she shouted as they zipped through suburban back roads and Dustin showed off the capacity of his motorcycle.

"Fun, huh?" he yelled back at her.

"Can this thing go any faster?"

Dustin roared with laughter and cranked his bike up.

He never would have thought Isobel would actually *like* riding a motorcycle. He'd only brought it out to prove a point, and maybe because he was still a little angry at her shallow behavior at the benefit.

But all of that seemed inconsequential now.

It was a beautiful, sunshiny winter morning, so typical of Colorado weather and yet always an enjoyable surprise. He had a powerful vehicle beneath him, the wind whipping around him and a beautiful woman clutched to his back.

What more could a man ask for?

Impulsively, he popped a wheelie and buzzed down the street on one wheel. Isobel held him more tightly but seemed to make the move with grace.

She made some sort of sound he couldn't quite discern. He thought she might be laughing.

At the end of the street he pulled his bike to the side of the road and pulled his helmet off, scratching his fingers through his thick, ruffled black hair.

"How was that?" he asked, out of breath but with a smile on his face.

Isobel flipped her faceplate up. Her complexion was rosy and her brown eyes were sparkling with delight as she smiled back at him.

"Incredible," she answered, sounding out of breath. "I feel so…"

She hesitated at length, so he completed her sentence for her.

Several times.

"Free?" he suggested. "Alive? Impressed? All shook up?"

She laughed and waved her hand at him. "All of the above."

"You need some spontaneity in your life, Belle," he said sincerely. "Too much of your life is planned exactly by the book."

"Dustin," she said, pulling in a loud breath and placing her hand flat over her rapidly beating heart, "you are definitely all the spontaneity I can handle in one day."

He grinned widely.

"But no more pop-a-wheelies, okay? I thought I was going to slide right off the end of the motorbike. It's a good thing I had you to hold on to."

Now why did he not feel chagrined?

Instead, he threw back his head and laughed heartily. "Quite a jazz, isn't it?"

She nodded, the motion amplified by her oversized helmet. "It is that, yes." She paused, then poked him in the chest with her finger. "Don't do it again."

He laughed and grabbed her hand, giving it a gentle squeeze. "I promise. But we have to use the freeway to get where we're going today. Are you going to be okay with that?"

"Oh, sure," she agreed with a smile of anticipation that made her look childlike and vulnerable, and made Dustin's protective instinct surge to the surface. "Just no more—"

"Yeah, right," he agreed, knocking her helmet lightly with his fist. "I promise. No more pop-a-wheelies. At least for today."

Then he turned back in the seat and revved the motor, smiling to himself when she scooted in close to his back and clutched tightly to his waist.

Chapter Thirteen

Twenty minutes later he pulled up at their first stop of the day, a deep brown, stone-hewn church with stained glass windows and its front double doors painted a bright cherry red, though the paint was peeling to show the wood beneath.

Isobel craned her neck up to see a pointed steeple complete with a belfry.

"A church?" she asked as she pulled her helmet off and brushed her hair back around her face. She didn't bother to state the obvious, that they weren't exactly in the best part of town.

Dustin swallowed hard. It was hard to concentrate on her words when the sunshine played off the highlights in her hair in such a beautiful way. "Where were you expecting to go?"

She placed her helmet on the cycle and fumbled with the bungee cords meant to tie it down. "I don't know. The only thing I can say for sure about you is that I can't say anything for sure about you."

"Hmm. And here I thought women were attracted to

men of mystery," he said, swishing an imaginary cape across his shoulders.

Her face turned a delicate shade of pink and it took her a moment to answer. When she did, it was in a tight, squeaky voice. "I—uh—*they* do."

He opened his mouth to tease her some more, but she cut him off.

"In theory." She stared into his eyes. "But you know, in real life it can be—frustrating. Sometimes I feel like I don't know you at all."

"And sometimes I feel I know you better than anyone else on earth," he countered, crossing his arms over his chest.

They stared at each other for a long moment, each either unable or unwilling to break the tense moment by speaking.

Finally, Isobel broke eye contact and looked back up toward the steeple, gesturing at the big bell. "This is a really pretty church."

It was lame, but it was a start.

"Yeah," he agreed, his voice deep. "Too bad it's off the main way where no one can see it. Hardly anyone knows it's here."

He paused and ran his fingers though his hair. "It's almost a hundred years old. But believe it or not, the bell still rings."

"How cool," she said. "But you still haven't told me why we are here."

"Tell you?" he asked with a wink. "How about I show you?"

He took her hand and pulled her toward the red doors. "I can't wait for you to see this."

With great aplomb, he opened one of the doors and gestured her in.

"I'm breathless with anticipation," she teased as she walked by him.

He yanked gently on the back of her silky dark hair as he followed up behind her.

"Belle," he whispered in her ear, causing a shiver to run all the way up her spine.

To Isobel's surprise, the small sanctuary was buzzing and alive with a veritable hive of teenagers. Though the room looked as if it would hold no more than one hundred and twenty parishioners, there were at least forty youths hanging about.

From Isobel's perspective, they ranged from junior high to nearing high-school graduation. It was a beautiful sight, seeing all these kids together inside a church, with nearly every conceivable shade of skin represented—not to mention *hair*—and everyone smiling and mixing about.

But what was this about?

She turned to Dustin, questioning him about what she was seeing without saying a word.

"Watch and learn," he said with a clipped nod and a mysterious grin.

Nodding back at him, she slid into the last pew at the back of the sanctuary and leaned in to see what would happen.

As Dustin moved into the middle of activity, he experienced a moment of pure nerves that nearly made him freeze to the spot.

What would Isobel think about what was about to happen?

Would she understand the passion of his heart?

A moment later, he forgot to be nervous as the youths began gathering around him. He knew and loved each and every one of these kids.

"It's the music man," one of the older boys crowed loudly.

"Hey, Dugan," Dustin responded. The boy approached and they popped fists, then hands, and then wrapped their arms around each others' shoulders and gobbled like turkeys.

It was an old and traditional male sort of rite of passage, and Dustin didn't think anything of his usual decorum until he heard Isobel roaring with laughter in the background.

He turned to her and gave an elaborate mock bow before calling for the kids to get organized.

It took a few minutes and a lot of noise to get forty teenagers moving in the right direction, but eventually the kids were seated by section, and were relatively quiet and ready for his direction.

Moving to the piano, he said, "Let's start with some warm-ups, and then we'll go ahead and tackle the anthem for next Sunday."

As he ran scales for the teenagers to follow, he surreptitiously glanced back at Isobel to see how she was taking what was happening.

She was sitting straight-backed in the pew, her hands clasped in her lap and her face unreadable. Her gaze was glued to the teens, so he couldn't see her eyes to discern whether or not this meant something to her.

Well, maybe this would surprise her.

He ran his fingers over the ivories, as was his habit

before playing, then cranked into a modern, upbeat version of "Amazing Grace."

The piece featured one girl soloist and one guy, who then came together in a touching duet in the middle of the last verse. The young voices had a purity to them he knew he would never find in adult voices, and he coveted every moment, feeling blessed to be their director.

He loved both the music and the words, and closed his eyes as the song ended, his heart reaching out to God in worship.

Praise God.

When he opened his eyes, his first act was to peer back at Isobel.

She had her eyes closed, too. He hoped that was a good thing.

The hour's practice flew by as Dustin led the choir in a variety of sacred tunes, some modern and some classic.

He was proud of his kids, proud to bursting. They had come far in the short time he had been teaching them, and not just vocally, either.

Spiritually, they had grown closer to each other and to God. Gone were the gang-type references and fist-fighting Dustin had dealt with in the beginning.

And as bad as the boys had been, the girls had been even worse, with their petty rivalries often blowing up into catfighting that easily put the boys' fistfights to shame.

Boys fought fair. Dustin knew what to expect from the male gender.

But girls?

Man, when their fur was flying, it was no holds

barred. Girls used *all* their resources—scratching, pulling hair, biting, poking at eyes, using knees and elbows... Well, he was glad he'd worked past that stage with them for the most part.

Once again he glanced back at Isobel. She continued to sit straight-backed and unmoving, and her face gave nothing away.

Disappointment washed through Dustin.

He had trusted her, opened his heart to her and shown her a part of his life he'd kept secret from the world until now.

He thought she'd understand.

And she couldn't care less.

He set his jaw, gathered himself together and called for prayer time.

The kids gathered around, taking hands and speaking softly amongst themselves.

When he called for prayer requests, several of them jumped right in with their problems. One young lady's grandmother was in a hospital dying from cancer. A young man named Jay asked for prayer for his older brother, who he thought might be using drugs.

Suddenly he heard a soft, sweet voice behind him, as Isobel took his hand and joined the circle. A tingle spread down Dustin's back.

"This isn't anywhere near as serious as some of the things I've heard from you," she said, making eye contact around the circle. "But I'd appreciate prayers for my mother. She's thinking of moving to Denver from a small town in Texas where she's lived all her life. It's a big move, and frightening."

She shrugged. "I guess she wants to be near her grandchildren. That is, if I ever get married. And if I ever have children."

The teens' reaction was half laughter, half hooting calls to Dustin to help out his girlfriend's mother and marry Isobel. They were especially interested in the *kids* part.

In response to their interest, Dustin couldn't help but give Isobel a smacking kiss on the cheek, which caused her to turn bright red, though she was laughing.

She flashed him a look that told him he had most definitely committed a major felony and ought to be ashamed of himself.

He absolutely wasn't feeling any sort of remorse, especially since he was enjoying the amusement of the teenagers immensely.

The kiss had been nice, too, though he'd never admit that to Isobel.

After the noise had died down to a bearable level, Dustin called for prayer.

The teens prayed openly and spontaneously for the needs that had been mentioned and some that hadn't. Isobel was squeezing his hand tightly, and he found himself rubbing the pad of his thumb against hers.

He wasn't sure why she was shaking with emotion until he peeked though one half-closed eye and saw there were tears on her face.

He wondered if *he* had somehow inadvertently made her cry, and then realized with a metaphorical thump in the head that he was thinking like a guy.

Isobel's tears were clearly tears of joy.

He closed his eyes, smiled and gripped her hand back tightly. Funny how the moment was suddenly causing a scratch in his own throat.

Probably just the start of a cold.

But whatever he told himself to explain away his own emotions, he couldn't deny the way his heart raced to life when he heard Isobel pray.

"Father, thank You for this blessed and talented group of youth, and for giving me the opportunity to enjoy their lovely voices today. These young people offer their voices as the purest form of worship, and their faith puts my own to shame. Shower them with Your love and blessing, Father, and I pray You'll address all their individual needs, both those spoken and those left unsaid."

The church was so quiet after Isobel's prayer that even the tiniest sound echoed. Dustin thought those around him must have been able to hear the frantic thump of his heart.

After a few more minutes, Dustin ended the prayer. "Thank You for hearing our needs, Father. All this we pray in Jesus' name. Amen."

The kids immediately broke into a buzz of activity, grabbing coats and purses and personal CD players. Many spoke to Isobel as they left, and her smile was genuine as she made compliment after compliment to each of the young people.

As the last of the youths left, the church once again became quiet. Dustin closed the red wooden doors and turned back, leaning against the old, solid wood. Isobel stood just where he'd left her, at the front of the sanctuary.

She had her arms clasped about herself as if she were feeling a chill, and her gaze arched up to the large cross at the front of the church.

"Thank you," she said quietly as he approached, her voice scratchy with emotion. "I know you risked a lot in bringing me here. Again, you've shown me a side of you that I *know* your brother doesn't know about, in allowing me to participate in what transpired today."

Participate. Not watch.

Dustin grinned. "They are a pretty awesome crew, aren't they?" he asked promptly. "I'm really proud of them."

"As you should be," she agreed in a heartbeat. "They are almost every bit as awesome as their wonderful director."

Before he could see it coming, she reached on tiptoe and kissed his cheek.

"Scratchy as usual," she complained in a teasing voice.

He ran a hand across his jaw, his mind still swimming. "Mmm. Yeah, uh, sorry."

"Don't be," she said, waving off the comment. "I find I'm getting used to the unshaved look. Who would have known?"

He laughed and ran a hand across her silky hair. "Should we call that progress?"

"Oh, no," she said, shaking her head. "I'm not the one on trial here. Besides, if anything, I'm moving backward."

He groaned. "Don't remind me."

"While we're on the subject…" Isobel began, and then stopped with a pregnant pause.

"Oh, what now?"

"This isn't about clothing," she assured him. "For now, anyway."

He blew out a breath and grinned at her. "That's a relief."

"However," she continued, automatically switching to her business voice as she faced him, "I do have a few questions."

"Shoot," he said, looking as if he meant it in the literal sense of the word.

"Am I correct in interpreting that you do this on a permanent basis?"

Dustin nodded. "This, and three different choirs at other churches in the area. Each group sings once a month."

"You have *four* youth choirs?" she clarified with a cough.

"My home church completely approves of my ministry," he said, sounding just a bit defensive. "I went through the vestry to get my marching orders."

"And I know you haven't told Addison about this," she repeated, a statement rather than a question.

"No," he said emphatically, his eyes widening as he realized where she was going with this. "And I'm not going to tell him now."

Two minutes ago she seemed to understand. Now she was pushing him again.

He bristled.

She touched his sleeve. "Why not?" she queried softly. "Surely if Addison knew of your work here, he would gladly release the trust fund to you. He would surely see this as I do. Dustin, this is not like your work with the homeless people. This is a legitimate ministry. You should at least consider the idea."

"No," Dustin snapped, his jaw tight.

He made eye contact with her and held the gaze, his green eyes flaming. "This ministry isn't about a trust fund. It's about me, the kids and God, and I plan to keep it that way."

He clenched his fists at his side. "Promise me, Isobel. Say you won't give me away."

Isobel couldn't move for a moment, couldn't breathe as she looked upon this strong, handsome, godly man who had so much to offer the world.

Finally, she broke the silence. "I promise, Dustin. Your secret is safe with me."

Isobel saw his shoulders and jaw relax at her words, and she relaxed a little bit herself.

"I knew you would understand," he said in a low, husky voice.

"And yet," Isobel said with sudden insight, narrowing her eyes warily on him, "this *is* about the trust fund, isn't it?"

He cleared his throat and pulled at his collar, even though he was only wearing a T-shirt. He shifted uncomfortably. "How do you mean?"

"I mean," she said firmly, taking his other hand and turning him toward her so she could look him right in the eye, "that you do not want the trust-fund money for yourself at all. Do you?"

He looked away from her gaze and shrugged noncommittally.

"Come clean, Dustin Fairfax," she ordered, using her hand to turn his chin back to her. "Admit the money is for the kids."

"So what if it is?" he growled, turning and walking away from her.

Isobel ground her teeth. Why was it so difficult to get any real information from him? He was like a mule when it came to his feelings. Sometimes she felt as if she were talking to a brick wall.

Stubborn man.

"For college," he said suddenly, turning back to her with a half smile on his face.

Isobel didn't say a word, waiting in anticipation for Dustin to continue.

His gaze showed the love and compassion he felt for the teenagers, as he clearly considered the words to explain what was in his heart.

"Some of the youth feel a call to ministry. Others just want an education in a Christian environment. But private colleges are ridiculously expensive—way out of the reach of the most well-to-do student to whom I teach piano lessons. These kids are from this neighborhood. They would never get there on their own."

"I'm beginning to see where you're going with this," Isobel said, her excitement growing as love expanded in her chest.

"Scholarships," he finished. "I want to provide a way to help the kids get a much-needed lift in an otherwise menacing world."

"I still say you should tell your brother," she urged. "Surely if he knew—"

"No!" The subject was clearly and adamantly closed by the sheer tone of Dustin's voice. He stood taller, hovering over her. "You promised."

"I did. And I will keep that promise, Dustin," she vowed.

Suddenly he grinned at her, the light, buoyant smile

that was classic Dustin. His smile alone was a tremendous relief.

"I haven't shown you everything yet," he said mysteriously.

When she smiled, he winked.

"Close your eyes," he said, taking her hand in both of his.

"Lead on," she said, closing her eyes as he'd requested, relaxed and entirely trusting him to keep her safe.

Slowly, gently, he led her around several twists and turns until she had no idea in what part of the church she was. It smelled musty, like old wood.

"'Kay, open," he said, sounding as excited as a little boy on Christmas morning. "See what you've been missing, Belle."

He emphasized his special nickname for her, chuckling with happiness.

They were in the belfry, the long thick ropes that led up to the big bell dangling directly in front of both of them.

"Are you ready?" he asked, leaning in toward her and stretching his arms until his hands met and clenched the ropes.

Isobel also clasped her hands around the ropes, but she could hardly concentrate on anything but being in the cradle of Dustin's arms. His musky western aftershave wafted around her and made her feel dizzy. His strong arms were tight around her; his warm breath tickled her neck when she turned.

She couldn't breathe and she couldn't move.

And suddenly she realized she didn't want to do either. She had no desire to move out of the comfort of his arms.

Ever.

"Ready?" he whispered close to her ear, and suddenly bells were ringing in Isobel's heart.

Chapter Fourteen

Isobel would never understand why people made such a fuss about Valentine's Day. Why make a special day to celebrate love? It only caused the majority of people to feel bad about themselves, and realize how alone they were in this world.

Not Isobel, of course.

She didn't buy into the commercials.

Well, okay, she usually splurged on a box of chocolates for herself. But chocolate was chocolate—a female ritual, right? So what if it happened to come in a heart-shaped box?

Only, this year Valentine's Day wasn't about a box of chocolate.

She had a date. Even though it technically wasn't a *real* date, she couldn't stop her mind from thinking about it.

Or rather, *him.*

The last six weeks had been a genuine eye-opener for her. She was sure she'd learned more from Dustin, her supposed student, than he could ever have learned from her in twice the time.

He had shown her the world, taught her to really look at people and not just their clothing. He had made her care.

Care about the homeless. Isobel had been to see Rosalinda twice on her own since that first day, and the old woman was beginning to trust her.

Care about low-income youth. The choir had stunned her and opened her eyes to issues she'd never before considered.

Care about *him*.

Oh, but she was in trouble.

Because even though her own feelings were beginning to manifest in her heart and crystallize in her mind, she was terrified even to consider if Dustin might feel the same way about her.

There was no use pretending any different.

Talk about heartbreak.

From the beginning, Dustin had been the epitome of a gentleman in every way. She'd never met a man like him. He even opened doors for her.

But that was Dustin.

A true gentleman.

Yet there was nothing personal about that. He would, she was sure, be just as polite to any woman of his acquaintance.

Her thoughts drifted back to the kiss they'd shared, but she didn't dare put stock in it. She'd been wrong before, associating physical affection with emotional strings.

Worse, at least in the long run, was that he hadn't made many changes in their six weeks together.

In fact, she wasn't positive he had taken to change at all, she thought, her mind sweeping over the events that had taken place at the John Elway Foundation benefit—and before and since, for that matter.

The Elway benefit had been sort of a midterm test for him, and he had blown it big-time. They had talked about it afterward—or rather, she had lectured. But what difference did it really make?

This was one of the major reasons she was standing on Dustin's doorstep at noon, when Addison's fundraising function wasn't until eight at night.

Or at least that's what she told herself as an excuse for the truth.

The fact that she knew this was their last day together, and she wanted to spend as much time as possible with Dustin, might have something to do with it.

But she wasn't about to admit it.

Her throat tightened. She was a professional, and Dustin was a business transaction.

She would not let herself cry.

At least not until she was back in the safety of her own condo.

Dustin opened the door on the first knock, surprising her. It was almost as if he'd been waiting for her arrival, which was impossible since she'd indicated she would show up closer to five o'clock.

"Hey, there, Belle," he greeted heartily and affectionately.

Isobel smiled at him, but her heart dropped like a stone tossed in the ocean. She was going to miss him so much the pain was indescribable.

For a moment she considered, as she stepped into the foyer and shed her jacket into Dustin's ready hands, that perhaps this didn't have to be the last time she saw Dustin.

She'd had a job to do, and she'd done it. She would make certain Addison was impressed with her work no matter how much she had to torture Dustin into a tux.

She would corner Addison and remind him what a gifted brother he really had. Steer the trust-fund issue by emphasizing Dustin's stellar personality and gentle heart.

Surely Addison would hear—and had to know, deep down, anyway—the truth about his brother.

Dustin *would* get his trust-fund money. That objective had become all-important to her, now that she knew what the man was really like.

"You don't look surprised," she accused, putting her hands on her hips and staring up at him. "At my being early, I mean."

"I'm not," he stated, mimicking her movements. "As a matter of fact, I guessed you would make an appearance right about now. Actually, I wouldn't have been that surprised had you shown up at dawn."

Isobel was mortified and shot back, "Is that why you were standing at the door?"

He laughed. "What, you mean peeking though the peephole in anticipation of your arrival? I don't think so."

He closed the door and leaned his back on it.

"I'll go, then," she said, very aware of the way he casually blocked the door.

"Oh, no you don't. You're here, so now you have to wait and see the real reason I was so close to the door when you knocked."

"Oh, really," she said wryly, crossing her arms in defense of who knew what. "And what is this big mystery I should be aware of?"

Dustin's gaze swept across the floor and into the different rooms visible from the foyer. He appeared to be looking for something.

"What are you looking for?" Isobel asked at last.

"It's a she, not a what," he said vaguely, still looking around.

Isobel felt like she'd been shot in the heart, and not by Cupid's arrow, either.

Thick, green slimy jealousy oozed through her bloodstream as every nerve in her body quivered with this new information.

She?

He was chasing some woman around his house.

And he expected her to stand here and watch!

Who in the world was she, and more to the point, *where* was she?

Isobel had the sinking feeling Dustin was going to tell her something she really didn't want to know. She wanted to clap her hands over her ears like a child and wail, "La, la, la—I can't hear you!" at the top of her lungs.

Only her dignity saved her, and then just barely. She straightened her spine, tipped her chin and prepared for the worst.

For meeting the woman Dustin had apparently given his heart to, if the sweet, gentle sound of his voice when he talked about her was anything to go by.

"She's around here somewhere," he assured her, stepping away from the door and drawing her into the house with his hand at the small of her back.

Isobel allowed herself to be led, even when she felt like turning and running away.

"I can't wait for you to meet her," he continued, apparently, if the tender tone of his words was anything to go by, completely unaware of her stiff gait.

He led her to the living room and seated her on the couch. She couldn't help but feel a little jealous.

"She's pretty temperamental," he warned congenially, flashing Isobel a bright smile. "Hang on a minute and I'll see if I can find her."

Isobel sat straight-backed on the edge of the sofa, her hands brought up and clasped—not clenched—in her lap.

Composure, she coached herself.

She would maintain her dignity and refinement no matter who Dustin brought through that door. No matter how beautiful or poised that *woman* was.

She could be poised, too.

Please, God, let her maintain her poise.

And then Dustin appeared in the doorway and she screamed as if the house had caught fire.

Dustin nearly lost his footing, not to mention his surprise, as he scrambled to cover at least one ear against her racket.

She'd never been so surprised in her life, and she couldn't contain the joy flowing through her.

So much for dignity and refinement.

The fluffy little white kitten Dustin was holding in his arms stole her heart with its first tiny mew and one look into its luminescent blue eyes.

"I know you own your condo, Belle, but I didn't have time to check into your covenants before I got her. She was sort of an impulse purchase, but I couldn't seem to help myself."

He reached forward, offering the tiny, adorable fur

ball out to her, and she instantly clasped it to her. "One of these *homeless* things, was it?" she teased.

He laughed.

"Is a kitty okay where you live?" His expression was an adorable mixture of excitement and anxiety.

He was almost as cute as the cat.

"Dustin," Isobel said, her throat tight.

She was half in shock as the kitten purred and pushed at her with its tiny paws, trying to find the most suitable position for a nap.

She'd never in her life taken to an animal as she did that little kitten. Her heart was swirling around in her chest—and not just because of the cat. Dustin's worried look was enough to make any sane woman forget to breathe.

She didn't say anything, enjoying the kitten and the small, innocent thrill of torturing Dustin a moment or two longer.

At length, he groaned. "I did the wrong thing again. I'm sorry."

"Dustin," she murmured, fairly at a loss for words but suddenly needing to comfort him.

"I was at the Humane Society yesterday," he explained in a gravelly voice. "I saw this little kitty and it reminded me so much of you, Belle. She's fancy, but she's also a real cutie."

Stroking the soft fur of the now comfortable cat, Isobel laughed and said, "Don't tell me. Let me guess. You volunteer at the shelter in your *spare* time."

She was pleased to see a little color darken his face. He shrugged and chuckled. "You caught me."

"Is there anything you don't do?" she teased, smiling and winking at him.

"Shoulder massages," he quipped merrily. "But I could work on that. In fact, I really think I should."

So saying, he moved behind the sofa and began working the knots out of Isobel's shoulders. His strong hands were soft and tender, a real paradox, but one she didn't wish to ponder at the moment.

She hadn't realized how tense she'd been until Dustin's gentle touch unwound her tight, tired muscles and she started to relax.

"The weight of the world shouldn't be on these delicate shoulders of yours," he said huskily, his warm voice close to her ear.

She sighed. "I know what you mean. It feels like it sometimes, though. I think I take life too seriously most of the time."

She'd never admitted that to anyone, but Dustin's kind ministrations were having a funny effect on her brain—and her tongue.

She found herself telling Dustin things she'd never told another living soul, not even Camille. She quietly admitted what it was really like living with a bitter mother and no father at all.

She told him how she always wondered if she was the reason her father had left, and not for another woman, as her mother had said. Isobel always wondered if her mother resented her, though of course she'd never shown it in any way.

But she would always wonder why her father had never come back.

She told him how badly she wanted to get away from Texas—to do more, *be* more, than most of the people in the small high-school class she'd graduated with, the majority of whom were still working on the family farm.

Just like the movies, right? Farm girl makes good in the big city.

Except it wasn't good—or at least not as good as she'd thought it would be. The same hollowness in her heart followed her everywhere.

Dustin just focused on her, asking quiet questions once in a while and letting her know with verbal assents that he was listening.

All the while he kneaded her shoulders and neck, thinking he might at least be able to help with some of the physical tension, even if he was not able to reach the emotional pain she carried.

A deep, gut-wrenching pain chewed at him all the while.

He didn't just want to commiserate.

He wanted to fix her problems.

Suddenly Isobel glanced at the digital clock on the end table next to the sofa and clapped her hand over her mouth. Her face flamed with embarrassment as she realized just what she'd done.

"I've been talking nonstop for over thirty minutes, Dustin," she exclaimed. "Why didn't you tell me to shut up?"

He chuckled. "Because I like listening to you," he replied gently, slowly brushing his hand down the length of her sleek brown hair. "And I think you needed to talk about some of that stuff. It's not healthy to keep things like that inside."

She shifted away from him, standing with the kitten still curled in her arms. She stroked the purring fur ball slowly, petting all the way down her back and smoothing any ruffles in her soft coat.

"What shall I name her?" she asked quietly, for some reason suddenly shy to look at Dustin after all she had revealed. She kept her eyes on the cat.

She felt, rather than saw, him smile as he came around the couch and up behind her, gently placing his hands around her waist. This time, his touch didn't make her immediately stiffen, though the longer they stood there, the harder it became.

"You're going to keep her, then?" he asked softly, close to her ear.

She fought the urge to tense at his nearness, wondering why he affected her so.

Her heart knew the answer without question, but she pushed the epiphany aside just as quickly as it arose in her mind.

"Snowball?" he suggested, reaching around to stroke underneath the kitten's small chin. "She's as white as new snow."

"She is," she agreed, holding the fluff ball in the air so she could see its bright, curious blue eyes. "But somehow I think she has another name, if only I can figure out what it is."

"Take your time," he said, giving her waist a squeeze. "There's no hurry to name her. You can keep her for a week or so and get to know her own little special personality."

And as soon as he had said the words, Isobel knew her cat's name.

"Epiphany."

Dustin turned her around, took the cat in one arm

and brought his other hand up to her cheek, stroking it gently as he petted the cat.

"That's a good name. I like it. Unusual, but I agree it fits her."

She gazed up at him and nodded.

"You're shaking," he said.

"Am I?" Her breath increased as she tried to still whatever physical symptoms were giving away the uneasiness of her heart. "It's a little cold in here, I think. Maybe that's it."

He lifted an eyebrow.

"Well, maybe I'm nervous about tonight. I mean, it's a really big night for both of us. A lot is riding on our presentation, right?"

"Right," he parroted, sounding not the least bit convinced. But then, under his breath, he continued, "I hate tests."

He brushed the pad of his thumb across her cheekbone, his gaze warm and tender. Isobel never wanted the moment to end.

Her *moment* would end all too soon as it was. Tonight was it, and then *it* was over. She wanted to savor every second with him.

She looked up at him—more charming than she'd ever imagined possible with that kitten cradled in his arm.

Dustin stared back, transfixed. He brushed his hand gently through Isobel's hair, using the tips of his fingers to feel the softness.

"Your hair is so beautiful," he said huskily. "It picks up all the highlights of the sun."

Emotion washed fiercely through her and she knew she was shaking.

But as his hand returned to her face, she realized he was shaking, too.

She plucked the kitten from his grasp, knowing subconsciously they were both using the poor cat as a pawn, and moved to the safety of the opposite side of the room from Dustin.

She couldn't be next to him right now. She couldn't control the emotion—the *love*—flowing through her.

When had this happened?

She was going to do or say something really stupid and ruin the event for him—more than the evening, but the opportunity to win his trust fund.

Panic surged through her in nauseating waves. What was she to do?

Dustin stood across the room from her, his arms relaxed at his sides, his gaze on her.

He looked calm.

Handsome.

Perfect, in his faded jeans and plain black T-shirt.

She wouldn't change a thing.

What on earth was happening to her?

"Can I keep Epiphany here at your house until after the banquet?" she asked, surprised that her voice worked at all.

He looked down at the kitten, and then grinned up at her. "Absolutely."

She couldn't help thinking that tonight, when she picked up Epiphany, Dustin probably wouldn't be around much longer.

And she wondered if he was thinking the same thing. His gaze was suddenly pensive, his lips tight as their gazes met.

She wondered if they could part as friends. She hoped as much with all her heart.

Yet she had been hired to do one specific job, and that task would come to total fruition this evening at the banquet.

Dustin was ready.

They had been practicing every spare second, had discussed scenarios to make him appear more of what Addison was looking for.

He was going to wow more than his brother with his newly refined looks and manners. He would confidently present himself to his brother and receive the trust fund that was his due.

Dustin would be everything his brother hoped for, and more. She knew in her heart he wasn't going to blow it this time.

And then...

And then he would be nothing but a memory, out of her life forever.

Chapter Fifteen

Dustin fidgeted for the umpteenth time in as many minutes. He hated having a shirt buttoned clear up to his neck. He felt like he was choking, but resisted the urge to pull at his collar, an effort that was sure to be superfluous.

His red cummerbund was tight around his waist and made his back itch.

His whole outfit was bothering him. But right now, his mind was mostly on Isobel.

His heart pounded in anticipation of seeing Isobel—in a gown, jeans or otherwise. As far as he was concerned, she looked great in jeans and a T-shirt.

She looked great in every kind of clothing. How could a man ask for more than that?

In his book, clothes didn't make the woman.

Her *heart* did.

He'd never met a woman like Isobel, and he wasn't foolish enough to think he ever would again. She was one of a kind.

A keeper.

Somehow, he had to find a way to keep her in his life.

A quick rap on the door pulled him abruptly from his thoughts.

Scooping Epiphany into his arms—and wondering briefly why Isobel had named the fur ball Epiphany in the first place—he opened the door.

The vision standing on the other side of the door was beyond words.

His breath swooshed out of his lungs in a rush. He dropped his arms slack to his sides, his mouth gaping—he hoped not too wide. The kitten made a mew of protest and gingerly hopped to the carpet.

He barely noticed her scurry away, tail held high in exasperation.

Dustin's gaze was riveted on Isobel, whose flowing red cocktail dress was gently blowing in the breeze, making the ruffles at the edges of the dress, just over her knees, stir and rustle like leaves in autumn. The red material made the brown in her eyes look like rich, dark chocolate, and she was gleaming with happiness.

He couldn't take his eyes off her.

"Dustin?" she asked, her light, twinkling voice sounding hesitant.

"Mmm," he answered, not exactly a question. It was more that he couldn't form coherent words at the moment.

She shifted uncomfortably, losing her smile to a shaky, pinched mouth. She stayed on the porch even after he opened the screen and gestured her in.

"Say something," she pleaded, her voice now noticeably high and squeaky.

"Stunning," he said hoarsely. "Radiant. Electrifying. Stupefying."

Well, he'd got the last part right, anyway.

Stupid, stupid, stupid.

Now that he'd finally gotten his voice back he couldn't seem to shut up.

She brushed past him. "Thank you. I think."

He grinned inanely and turned as she walked by, his gaze still glued to her beautiful dress.

And smile.

And hair.

She looked him over, from the tip of his spit-shined black patent leather shoes to the top of his carefully groomed hair. Then she grabbed his arms and turned him around.

Once.

Twice.

Finally, she turned him back toward her and reached up to adjust his bow tie.

"There," she said with a satisfied grin. "Now you, also, look stupefying."

She flashed him a cheeky grin just like the one he was so fond of giving her. "And all those other things."

He roared with laughter and wrapped his arms around her small waist, lifting her up as if she were a feather and spinning her round and round until she begged for him to put her down.

When he set her back on her feet, he couldn't help but brush a kiss across her soft cheek.

She blanched and looked panicked for a moment, then pushed away from him with her palms against his chest and moved well into the room, away from him.

His throat closed until he thought he would choke.

Was his touch so repulsive to her? Had he misread the signals of all the time they'd spent together, that she would be so uncomfortable in his arms, or being kissed by him?

This wasn't at all how he wanted this evening to start, and his own panic drove him back to her side, determined not to let that one action set the course for their evening together.

He wouldn't let this night be the end for them. Somehow, some way, he had to convince her of his love, and that they were meant to be together for the rest of their lives.

Isobel had regained some of her color, but she still looked wary around him. It made him want to scream at the top of his lungs, he was so frustrated.

"So I pass muster?" he asked instead, giving her as playful a wink as he could manage.

She swallowed hard enough for him to notice. "Yes, sir, you do."

"May I suggest, then," he said in the smooth tone of a complete gentleman, "that we depart for the party immediately? I'm sure we're expected as soon as humanly possible."

"You *are* the guest of honor."

He offered his arm, but he didn't expect her to take it. "Shall we?"

"Thank you," she said with quiet dignity, and then looped her hand through his arm.

He led her to the door and opened it for her. He felt as if he was sweating like a pig, and hoped it didn't show. He did hope, however, that his first surprise of the evening would show, and quick.

"Oh, Dustin!" Isobel exclaimed as they stepped out onto the porch. "I can't believe you did this. It's so— not you."

"Yes, Isobel," he agreed wryly, "but it is very much you. Do you like it?"

"Like it?" she parroted. "Dustin, I'm absolutely

thrilled to be taking a limousine to the party. We'll make such a splash! It's brilliant. Whatever made you think of it?" Her glistening wide-eyed gaze met his.

He laughed. "You did, of course. Do you want the truth? I was thinking back to our first conversation. Do you remember?"

She hovered one white-gloved hand over her mouth and chuckled. "Oh, I do. There was something about a sports car, as I recall. You wanted to give me a zippy ride around downtown Denver."

He lifted his chin and sniffed his offense at her remark. "It *is* a sports car, thank you very much. I've worked hard on it."

"Maybe, but it's still an old piece of junk," she teased merrily, apparently having forgotten her earlier problems. "I'm surprised it works at all. I'd be *afraid* to ride in it."

"Then I'll be sure to make you take a ride sometime, just out of spite." He grinned. "Do you remember how we talked about how snooty limousines could be? And here I am splurging on one."

She met his warm gaze and held it. "Thank you for this special, once-in-a-lifetime treat. Snooty or not, you're making me feel like royalty."

"Then follow me, my dear, beautiful princess. Your coach is waiting."

"Will it turn into a pumpkin at midnight?" she queried mischievously.

"Eleven o'clock. I couldn't rent the thing all night, you know. What do you think I am, a millionaire with money hanging out his pockets?"

"I certainly hope you don't have anything hanging

out your pockets," she replied. "It's very unfashion-able—unless it's a handkerchief."

Dustin patted his chest. "I've got that, and it even matches my bow tie."

"Impressive. Very impressive," she said with a chuckle.

The driver of the limousine parked at the curb, got out and opened the door for them. He was snappy and well-dressed in his uniform, and he gave them both a friendly smile.

Dustin helped Isobel inside, sliding close onto the seat next to her, though there was a lot of extra seat space in the vehicle.

Holding his breath, he reached his arm up and around her shoulders, where he settled with nonchalant ease, almost like a teenager on his first date at a movie theater.

He thought she might object to the close quarters, but she beamed up at him, her eyes glazed over with pleasure.

It made his heart turn over.

He cleared his throat. How could one look make his head spin until he wasn't sure he could think at all, much less speak?

"I special-ordered drinks for us for the trip over to the hotel." Somehow he got the words through his tight throat and dry mouth.

She looked at him as if he'd grown horns.

"What?" she chirped.

He raised an eyebrow, perplexed.

She likewise raised an eyebrow at him, and suddenly he laughed.

"I didn't mean *drinks,* Belle, I meant *drinks.*"

He smiled and tipped the end of her nose with his

finger. "I meant *real* drinks. You know—iced tea. Orange juice. Soda."

"Water?" she asked, her gaze again gleaming.

"Ice-cold, refreshing water. Only the best for you."

She smiled. "Please."

He opened the minifridge and twisted the top on a cold bottle of mountain spring water from Colorado, then opened a bottle of orange juice for himself.

With a big smile, he held up his bottle and indicated a toast. She grinned back at him and held her bottle aloft as well.

"To my princess. May every day be a fairy tale for you," he said in a husky voice.

"To my adventurer," she replied. "May tonight be the beginning of your dreams."

They tapped bottles and then both took a sip, their gazes locked on each other. Slowly they put their bottles down, but for a long while neither of them said a word.

It was a comfortable silence, but the electricity in the air felt sizzling, at least to Dustin. He wondered if she noticed the static buzz.

Finally, Isobel broke the silence, coughing softly before she spoke.

"Are you nervous?" she asked, taking a sip of her water.

"Me?" he responded, doing his best at sounding surprised by her question, though in truth what he was really trying to do was hide the nervous tension he felt sitting so close to her.

"Nah. I don't get nervous." He waved her question away with his hand.

She stared at him a moment, looking pensive. He didn't know whether she believed him or not until she shook her head and spoke. "No, you really wouldn't be, would you?"

"You sound jealous," he teased. "Don't tell me the phenomenal image consultant Isobel Buckley is afraid her greatest work won't pan out."

"Of course not," she said, sounding at once mortally offended and yet unsure of herself. It was a charming combination.

"I won't let you down," he vowed, his voice low and serious. His gaze met hers, pleading with her to believe in his strength—in *God's* strength. "You've done too much work on me for me to fail you now."

"Dustin," she said, turning every bit as serious as he was, and making him feel immediately uneasy, "I want to tell you something. It's really important to me that you hear me out on this."

She reached out and pulled his chin toward her so their eyes would meet. "Oh, what a nice, smooth shave," she said in surprise, rubbing her hand along his cheek and jaw.

"Huh? Oh, yeah. I went out of the way for you this time. I shaved twice today. It gives a new meaning to 'clean-shaven.'" He chuckled.

"You look nice," she said softly, sweetly and almost hesitantly.

He looked her straight in the eye as he spoke. "Thank you."

"Be that as it may," she continued as if he hadn't spoken at all, "I want you to know something about tonight."

She sounded incredibly earnest and resolute, so he didn't throw a wisecrack at her this time.

"Go ahead," he urged.

"I think you look absolutely perfect. I think the things you do—known and unknown—more than account for making a contribution to society.

"In short, I think you've made progress in every area I was hired to work with you on."

"Thank you."

"Maybe you aren't taking my meaning," she prodded, though in truth Dustin thought he knew exactly what she was getting at. He supposed he didn't want her to go there, though it looked as if he had no choice in the matter, as she was pursuing it anyway.

He nodded and stared into her chocolate-brown eyes, feeling as if he could get lost in them. His arm around her shoulder tightened territorially.

"It may be," she said slowly, obviously carefully selecting her words, "that your brother will not agree with my assessment of your progress up to this point."

She took a deep breath. "I cannot fathom how that could happen, Dustin, but nevertheless, it is an eventuality we should think about and prepare for, in case the worst-case scenario becomes a reality."

"Believe me," he said gruffly, "that's almost all I ever think about anymore. That stupid trust fund. I hate it." He knew his annoyance showed in his voice, but he couldn't help it.

He didn't want to obsess over money, even if it was for a good cause. He hated that his father had done this to him, and yet here he was, on his way to *the* banquet.

"In short," she continued, interrupting his thoughts, "you might not get that money, Dustin. Addison may deny you your trust fund. You may have gone through all this agony for nothing."

"Agony?" he repeated dumbly, wondering what she was talking about.

He didn't remember any pain at all.

He remembered the way Isobel swished her long brown hair when she was irritated.

He remembered how her eyes glowed when she was happy.

He remembered the sweet, high tone of her laughter.

Was that agony?

Maybe, in a way, it was. It sure produced turmoil in the general area of his heart.

"It's okay," he said gruffly, squeezing her shoulder to show his support. "I'm fully prepared for the contingency you mentioned." He laughed, but it was an empty sound. "This is my family we're talking about, and I, better than anyone, know what they're capable of."

He paused, thrust his fingers several times through his once carefully combed curls, and said, "I love my brother, and I know he loves me. Whatever happens, happens."

"I think you do." She reached up to stroke the backs of her fingers across his cheek. The soothing movement calmed him a little.

He paused, embracing the emotion that was enveloping him completely. He struggled to gain control.

"Addison is the only family I have. No matter what the outcome of the trust fund, he is my brother—and my brother in Christ." His throat grew tighter at every word he spoke.

Isobel cuddled into his arm and laid her head upon his shoulder. His head swirled with emotion as he tightened his embrace around her.

He wanted to feel this way for his entire life. He

wanted to take care of Isobel, to hold her and protect her in his arms.

And most of all, to love her forever.

"I wish I had a brother or a sister," she said wistfully, squeezing his arm. "All I have left is my mother."

"But she's moving out here to Denver, right?" he asked, stroking her arm. "To be with you? See her grandkids?" he teased.

Isobel laughed. "Well, maybe someday. About the grandkids, I mean."

She took a deep breath. "Mom will be moving up next month, if the weather permits and she can close on her house. I've found a nice apartment for her here in one of the retirement centers.

"She likes the idea, and it will be nice to have her around. Sometimes a girl just needs her mother's advice—even if that girl happens to be approaching thirty."

She curled into him, as if seeking his warmth. It felt wonderful to him, and he pulled her in closer next to him.

Isobel sighed quietly. "You know, Dustin, I'm still working through my issues with my father. I don't think he was a good man. Not at all.

"And of course I will never be able to rid myself of the guilt, always wondering if it was me."

He groaned softly in agreement. "I know what you mean."

Oh, how he wanted to be a shield around Isobel, protecting her from the kind of pain she had experienced with her father. It made him angry that anyone could treat her with anything but respect and love.

"I'm getting through it, though," Isobel continued. "With God's help, I am."

She paused, catching and holding his gaze, though he wanted to look elsewhere.

"Forgiveness is a powerful thing, Dustin. I long for the day when that tremendous weight will be lifted from me for good. When I can finally forgive my father for all he has done—and not done—for me."

Dustin stiffened. "You've only told me a little bit about what your life was like as a child, but I can imagine the rest. What he did to you is unforgivable. It won't be easy to let go of." His voice was low and fierce.

"No. It won't be easy, Dustin. Not at all. In fact, I think it will be the hardest thing I will ever do," she said sincerely.

"And yet…" Dustin said, his voice laced with anger and frustration.

Already an idea was forming in his mind. What had really happened to Isobel's father? Something just didn't add up.

Isobel continued, breaking into his thoughts. "What my father did was unforgettable, but not unforgivable. God is not the author of 'forgive and forget,' though I think we often get confused by that."

She paused until Dustin looked her way. "God only asks us to forgive."

He frowned and creased his forehead, thinking of his own father, of the situation he was now in because of that man. "I don't know. I just don't think I'm up to that sort of thing. You have more grace than I."

"Oh, Dustin," she implored.

"I could never forgive my father," he said vehemently. "Not ever."

Chapter Sixteen

He would have said more, but the limousine came to a stop at the hotel, and the driver opened the door to allow their departure.

Dustin stepped from the car and offered a hand to Isobel, thinking that as bad as his tuxedo was, it must be that much more difficult to wear a gown.

He was glad he was a man. Especially with Isobel on his arm.

Isobel took his hand as they approached the hotel, unconsciously lacing her fingers with his. She didn't even notice until he smiled softly and squeezed her hand.

Apparently he didn't mind.

She was quite disturbed by their conversation in the car. Dustin was carrying around as huge a burden as she, and her heart yearned to help free him from it, to help his pain go away, even if she could not relieve her own.

If only he could believe her words.

What her father had done still hurt her, and it still

came to mind from time to time. That was only human nature.

Anger and distress had lessened from those memories as the years had gone on. God had relieved her of some of that pain, made her realize that no matter what had happened, it was still within the realm of God's reach, and though she hadn't known it at the time, He had taken care of her, carried her through the difficulties and on to a newer, better life in Christ.

If only Dustin could see what she saw, could know what she knew.

It would be a start.

She was shaken from her thoughts the moment they entered the hotel. Camille hailed her in a loud and boisterous voice.

"Isobel! Dustin! I've been watching for you for like—forever!"

Isobel laughed. "I imagine you have. Have the festivities started?"

Camille smiled at her friend. "Only just. And of course it won't really get off the ground until the guests of honor arrive."

"Oh, don't call us that," Dustin said with a loud groan. "I'd really rather be a wallflower than the life of the party. Or at least this once I would."

Isobel raised her eyebrow at him. The man who could and did talk to everyone without the least discomfort now wanted to be invisible?

"I do," he insisted.

Isobel squeezed his hand. "I'm afraid that's just not possible this one time, Dustin. No matter how much you wish it."

Camille's gaze dropped to their linked hands, and

she smiled widely and winked at Isobel, then made a funny face indicating that she was aware that they were entering as a couple.

Isobel flushed with embarrassment, and then realized she didn't care what Camille thought. She was proud to be with Dustin, and it wasn't something she wanted to be embarrassed about.

Dustin pulled at his collar with his free hand, yanking it around as if trying to find a comfortable place to breathe.

"So then, Camille, can you point us in the right direction?" he said in a scratchy voice.

"Certainly," she said, using all her charm on Dustin, who didn't appear to notice Camille at all. He only had eyes for Isobel, and for tonight, she was going to enjoy it.

"I think you'll find the surroundings familiar," Camille continued, "although admittedly the atmosphere has changed substantially."

"I beg your pardon?" Dustin asked, looking adorably confused.

Camille grinned at both of them, her smile like that of a cat. "Oh, surely you remember. Fifth floor? Ring any bells?"

Isobel and Dustin looked at each other and broke into laughter.

"You know," Dustin said as they entered the glass elevator, "I really dislike heights. Especially glass elevators."

Isobel laughed, shaking her head at his obvious distress. "Why didn't you tell me? We could have taken the stairs."

He pointed at her two-inch heels. "In these outfits?

We wouldn't make it up one flight of stairs, much less five. Can you imagine what Addison would say if we didn't show up because we were stuck in a stairwell?"

By then the elevator had reached the fifth floor. Isobel chuckled as Dustin stepped out and planted his feet firmly on the floor.

"It's good being on dry land again," he said, theatrically wiping his brow. "I'm so incredibly relieved. I can't even begin to tell you, Belle."

"Ha!" Isobel replied. "You think you're sweating now. Just wait until we walk in there."

She pointed to the open double doors, behind which was Dustin's one opportunity to make or break his chance at his trust fund.

Dustin scowled for a moment, sizing up the open doors, which to Isobel looked very much like a mouth—a whale's mouth, perhaps, or a tiger's.

Suddenly Dustin shrugged and grinned. "No time like the present," he said, offering his arm. "Would the lady care to accompany me to my doom?"

She curtsied playfully before taking his arm. "I'm absolutely honored to be with you under any set of circumstances."

Oh, how true her words were.

If Dustin only knew the truth.

As soon as they walked into the ballroom, they were met by Addison, along with many friends and acquaintances they both knew.

Isobel recognized many prominent faces in the room, people who would gladly give generously to a cause such as the Children's Hospital cancer ward, which Addison had picked as his charity of choice for the evening. This would be a good night for the hospital.

She was glad for that.

"Welcome, Isobel," Addison said, politely shaking her hand and giving her a friendly smile, which she returned in spades.

Then he turned to Dustin, his expression giving nothing away as he looked his brother over from head to foot.

Isobel realized suddenly that Dustin had never fixed his hair from when he'd run his fingers through it. His curls were showing.

She held her breath.

"Hello there, Addy boy," Dustin said at last, shifting from foot to foot.

Addison hesitated a minute, just staring at his brother. Then he suddenly stepped forward, smiled broadly and threw his arms around Dustin. "It's good to see you, bro."

Isobel's eyes moistened with tears, and as she met Dustin's gaze, she thought she saw a telltale gleam there, as well.

She smiled and stepped aside as Dustin animatedly returned the bear hug, giving back what his big brother had offered.

"You two look great," Addison said huskily as he moved back and dropped his arms. "Feel free to mingle around the ballroom and enjoy the food."

Addison turned to her. "Isobel, your friend Camille picked the caterer, and let me tell you, the hors d'oeuvres are spectacular, and that says nothing of the meal she has planned."

"Camille has a gift for these things," Isobel said with a laugh.

Addison waved his hand at Dustin. "From what I

can see, Isobel, you have a gift, too. I've never seen my baby brother look so spiffy."

Isobel's heart raced. Did this mean Addison approved of what had been done and saw beyond the obvious—that Dustin would get the money in his trust fund?

She could only hope.

But she was also aware that this might not be the last test of the evening. Dustin would have to continue to be on his best behavior, and he might be called upon to disclose a little more than he was comfortable with.

Dustin once again offered her his arm, and they moved deeper into the room, talking to various friends and colleagues, and making general conversation with those they did not know.

Dustin leaned down close to her ear. "This place looks so familiar," he teased. "Although I have to say it does look a lot different tonight." He laughed. "I don't see a model's runway anywhere, thank goodness. Or any racks of clothes. Whew."

"It's more like the ballroom of a prince's castle," Isobel whispered, her head swirling as she looked at the red and gold decorations that had transformed the room so completely.

"I can assure you, Addison is no Prince Charming," Dustin said with a laugh.

Isobel looked up at him, her eyes wide and her heart in her throat. She thought if her heart swelled with any more love than she felt at that moment that she might simply burst.

"I wasn't thinking of Addison," she said quietly and tenderly.

Dustin's eyebrows immediately pinched together, as did his lips.

Isobel felt an urgent sense of panic.

She had said the wrong thing.

She was making an issue out of something that simply did not exist, at least on Dustin's part. When would she get that through her thick skull?

She immediately promised herself she would be more careful about what she said and how she acted around Dustin for the rest of the night.

She could not give her feelings away.

That would not be fair to Dustin. This was his night, and she was here to support him. She would not ruin a night he was sure to remember the rest of his life by throwing herself at him.

"Camille is a wonder with decorations," she said in a rush. "Like I said before, she's really gifted as a hotel manager."

"Yeah," said Dustin, sounding dazed and confused. "Gifted."

The announcement that dinner would be served saved Isobel from further embarrassment.

Ever the gentleman, Dustin once again offered his arm as they weaved their way around the tables looking for their place cards.

Dustin pulled at his collar for the hundredth time, stretching his neck to both sides in an apparent attempt to ease his anxiety, and perhaps to gasp a quick breath of air.

Every movement he made was apparent to Isobel, who felt his anxiety so strongly and fiercely it started to become her own.

He shifted in his jacket. "Where are we supposed to be sitting?" he asked in a strained voice. "I've got

enough to think about without having to sit on the floor
to eat."

She was certain he hadn't meant the words as a joke,
as tense as he was, but though she tried to restrain it,
she couldn't help herself.

She burst into laughter.

"No matter what you think your brother thinks of
you, I doubt very seriously that he expects us to dine
picnic style."

Dustin looked at her, his eyes glazed over as if he
hadn't heard her at all.

"And if it is, hon," she said, still laughing, "I'm in a
lot more of a pickle than you are. At least you're wearing trousers."

Dustin stared at her for a moment, the same glazed
look in his eyes.

Suddenly, the clouds parted, the sun broke through
and he smiled. The happy-go-lucky man she knew and
loved appeared back in his eyes.

"Let's find Addison," he said. "Surely he knows
where he seated us."

Dustin took her hand and led her to the head table
nearest the raised platform. Addison was seated by a
famous hockey player on one side and a well-known
national politician on the other.

"It's about time you got here," Addison said, smiling at them. "I was about to feed your salad to my pet
rabbit."

Dustin raised both eyebrows in surprise, but said
nothing.

Isobel squeezed his hand.

"Well, sit already," Addison said, indicating the two
vacant chairs opposite him. "I'm sure Isobel is hungry,

even if you are not. It's really not very nice to keep your date away from the dining table, kid."

Dustin looked down at Isobel, panic in his eyes.

She knew what was bothering him. He had to sit at the lead table and act like fancy banquets were something he did every day.

"You can do this," Isobel whispered. "It's just food."

He nodded, a smile pulling slightly at the corner of his mouth. "Right. Just food. I'm hungry. How about you, Belle?"

He held the chair out for her to sit and then seated himself.

With a flair that surprised her, he selected the right fork and gently dived into his salad, taking slow, small bites.

As the courses changed, Dustin leaned toward her. "Smile," he whispered. "If you keep looking like that, everyone is going to know I'm a fraud."

"You're not a fraud," she whispered back fiercely.

Dustin spoke frequently throughout the meal. Unlike Isobel, who had to force herself to be outgoing for the sake of her business, Dustin was a people person. He got along with everyone, and made easy conversation that would have been painful for Isobel to initiate.

After the meal and before dessert was served, Addison rose and moved to the podium on the platform. He turned the microphone on and tested it, then looked down at Dustin and smiled.

"Tonight is an important evening," Addison announced to general applause.

"As you know, tonight's event was to sponsor the cancer ward at the Children's Hospital in Denver. My company, Security, Inc., has asked you all here to generously match our donation of five hundred thousand dollars."

The guests roared with approval, and it was several minutes before Addison could continue.

"I am astounded by the giving hearts in this community, and am proud to announce that not only did you match our contribution tonight, but you surpassed it. Our total tonight is one million, ten thousand dollars. I'm sure the hospital will be overwhelmingly grateful for your generosity."

Dustin whistled under his breath. "I had no idea my brother was doing such philanthropic things," he said to Isobel.

"Philanthropic or Christian?" she replied, meeting his gaze with her warm chocolate eyes blazing.

"You may have a point," he said.

"There is another reason we've gathered tonight," Addison continued, cutting off their conversation as Dustin gripped her hand.

"As many of you know, in my father's will, he left me in charge of my baby brother's trust fund, with very stringent conditions."

"Some baby brother," a man called out from a rear table.

"Point taken," Addison said with a laugh.

The crowd laughed along with him.

"Anyway, Father left strict instructions on distributing the fund to my brother, and I am happy to say that tonight I have witnessed a major change in him, exactly what I had hoped for."

Isobel became ruffled.

What did he mean Dustin had made a *major change?*

He hadn't really changed at all, except for the tuxedo he was constantly fidgeting in.

"I'm proud tonight to introduce you to my brother, Dustin, and to present him with his well-earned trust fund."

Dustin's whole body was shaking. He gritted his teeth, trying to control his emotions. This was the moment he'd been waiting for, when he would finally receive his trust fund.

All he had to do was get his legs to work, walk up to the platform and receive the coveted check.

The only problem was that he was completely frozen to the spot.

He couldn't move a muscle, except to pull at his ridiculous collar and his strangling bow tie, which felt like it was getting tighter by the moment, choking him to death.

He certainly couldn't stand, never mind walk.

He took a deep breath, trying to steady his nerves and pull himself together.

Suddenly Isobel was out of her chair, standing behind Dustin with her hands on his shoulders.

He had no idea what she was up to, but he could feel her hands shaking.

"No," she said so loudly her voice echoed in the big room.

Addison cleared his throat and tapped his fingers against the podium. "I beg your pardon?"

"I said," she repeated, emphasizing each word as if she were speaking to children, "no."

Chapter Seventeen

Panic rushed through Dustin.

What was Isobel doing? She was ruining everything they had worked for.

He could see the train wreck coming but he was helpless to stop it.

"Stand up," she whispered for Dustin's ears only, a command rather than a suggestion.

He complied, but only to turn and implore her with his gaze to stop whatever game she was playing and let things go as they were.

"Take it off," she said, once again in the loud, piercing voice that everyone could hear, even those clear across the room.

"What?" asked Dustin, in a daze.

"I said, take it off. Now."

He had no idea what she was talking about, so he stood staring at her, wondering if she'd gone completely mad from nerves or something.

"If you don't, Dustin, I'm going to," she warned in a low voice.

"Ms. Buckley, may I ask what you are doing?" Addison asked from the podium. The rest of the crowd was so silent they could have heard a pin drop.

Isobel made good her threat, and finally Dustin understood what she was doing, besides killing any chance whatsoever he might have to get his hands on his trust fund.

She started with his coat, yanking it off his shoulders and down his sleeves until she'd completely shed it from him.

Then she started on his bow tie.

She stepped back and looked at him for a moment, then reached her hand up and mussed his hair.

Dustin felt a good deal more comfortable, which he supposed was a good thing, as he was going to his own funeral.

Isobel stomped up onto the platform, her high heels clicking with every step. Addison yielded the microphone to her without a word.

She paused and took a deep breath.

Dustin was holding his breath, half terrified and half oddly interested in what she would say.

After a moment, she pointed at him.

He cringed and wondered if he ought to crawl underneath the table.

"This man, ladies and gentlemen, is Mr. Dustin Fairfax."

There was complete silence in the room as Isobel continued to point.

"I am a professional image consultant. Six weeks ago I was hired by Addison Fairfax to make over Dustin, to help him become something that would fit the terms of their father's will."

Dustin clenched his fists, unable to fathom what was going on.

"I admit I like the new haircut," she said wryly, and

the crowd chuckled along with her. "However, I cannot let this farce continue. I am here tonight to tell you emphatically that Dustin has *not* made a major change that suddenly makes him worthy of the trust fund."

Dustin groaned quietly, seeing the end in sight. He could almost hear the chop of the ax.

"Dustin is not a person who likes to dress up and attend social functions," she continued. "He is most comfortable in faded blue jeans, old tennis shoes and a plain old T-shirt.

"He is more comfortable with his jacket off—it confines his shoulders—and his tie removed. Oh, and the buttons. Dustin does not like anything too tight around his neck."

"Ms. Buckley," Addison whispered frantically, urgency in his tone.

She held up her hand to him.

"Dustin has not changed," she repeated, looking out into the crowd, "because, ladies and gentlemen, he does not need to change."

Several murmurs broke out among the crowd as Isobel's speech began to make sense.

"Dustin Fairfax is the most honest, giving, hardworking man I know. He makes all kinds of contributions to society, and we don't need to know what they are. As the Bible says, he keeps his good works a secret, so that his reward is in heaven.

"Dustin is the best man I know. He should get the trust fund simply because he completely deserves it. He has earned my respect, my confidence and my loyalty."

As she finished, she lowered her head, tears in her eyes.

The crowd was roaring with applause, many standing in ovation to her speech.

Addison quickly moved to Isobel's side and put his arm around her, whispering gently into her ear.

Dustin was on his feet in a second. Something about seeing his brother with his arm around Isobel spurred him to action like nothing else could.

He was gone in a moment.

"Do you know where we're going?" Camille asked, excitement lining her voice as she turned a corner in the clunky, boxy old car Isobel had never been able to convince her to part with.

Isobel leaned against the cool window and groaned, holding her forehead in one hand. "I thought you said it was a surprise."

Camille gave her a quick glance and smiled despite her friend's obvious agony. "It is a surprise. I just wondered—you know—if you recognized the neighborhood or something."

Isobel gritted her teeth. She didn't recognize the neighborhood because she wasn't watching where they were going.

She couldn't care less.

It had been three weeks since the banquet, three weeks since she'd seen Dustin, and she was miserable.

Addison had announced that Dustin would be receiving his trust fund, though he'd been gone by the time she'd finished her ill-fated speech.

She wondered if he knew he was getting his money.

Addison had given her a check, but she'd handed it right back, donating it to the Children's Hospital, the night's chosen charity.

It had felt like blood money.

"Oh, will you cheer up, already?" Camille chirped. "This is going to be fun."

Isobel begged to differ. Nothing was ever going to be fun again. In every man she saw Dustin's face, every voice, his voice. Every laugh, his laugh.

She wasn't sure if she would ever laugh again. The logical part of her argued that Dustin was a phone call away. She knew where he lived, for pity's sake.

But if he didn't want her, she wasn't going to go chasing him around, making a nuisance of herself.

And he obviously didn't want her.

It wasn't just that she didn't want to walk out of his life and never see him again.

It was that she wanted to be with him. She wanted to share every joy, every sorrow.

For richer and for poorer, in sickness and in health, her mind mocked her.

How had she only now figured out what must have been obvious for at least a couple of weeks, maybe since the first day, when Dustin walked into the deli with that awful haircut?

She was completely and unconditionally in love with Dustin Fairfax.

She had had relationships with other men before, but they had all been short-term and, in hindsight, rather shallow.

Stupid. Stupid. Stupid.

"We're here," Camille said, turning off the car. "Get out."

Isobel recognized where they were the moment she slammed the car door shut.

The church with the belfry and red doors.

She tried to pull on the door handle, but she had locked the door by habit when she'd exited.

"Camille, take me home. Now," she ordered, pulling on her friend's elbow.

She just laughed. "No way. Come on, girlfriend. Your future awaits you."

Then why did she feel as if she were going to a funeral?

She knew Dustin was waiting inside. She just didn't know why. And after three weeks?

She looped her arm through Camille's, and her friend patted her hand for good measure.

"Deep, slow breathing," Camille advised. "You can do this."

Camille had watched her mope about for three weeks. She knew the agony of unrequited love herself. Why was she drawing this out?

Camille was in cahoots with Dustin, that's what it was.

Then they were inside, and the real surprises were only beginning to show themselves.

The youths were there, milling about and chattering up a storm.

Dustin was at the piano. He appeared not to notice her appearance.

But then the tune changed, and suddenly the choir assembled, humming a background to an unsung melody. Addison stepped from one side of the church, her mother from the other. They were both smiling.

She was confused.

Stunned.

Elated.

In a moment she was in front of the piano, and Dustin was seated at the keyboard. His kind, flashing green eyes were on her as he stroked his fingers lightly over the ivories.

His expression was as serious as Isobel had ever seen—his brow furrowed and his lips tight.

"Hey there, Belle," he said as if they had seen each other yesterday. "How's it going?"

"I—uh," she stammered, unable to process what was going on.

She cleared her throat and looked around her. "Okay, I guess."

He nodded gravely. "Well, I—" he started and then paused, his gaze locking on hers. "I'm feeling absolutely terrific tonight."

He smiled just for her. "No, better than terrific. Fantastic. Wonderful. I can't put it into words, how I'm feeling right now."

He put his hand on his heart, still holding his earnest gaze with hers.

She tried to hold back her grin but couldn't.

"Stupefying?" she suggested, knowing her eyes were gleaming with the hilarity of the private joke.

"Mmm, yes. I was thinking more along the lines of *supercalifragilisticexpialidocious*. You know, the word you use when you can't think of a word?"

Isobel couldn't help it.

She laughed.

He smiled gently. "Well, Belle, do you remember the night of the Elway Foundation benefit?"

"Ha!" she said, letting out a puff of breath. "Do I remember it? As I recall, it was your midterm, and you flunked."

He nodded and winked at the crowd hovering around them and chuckling at the scene. "This is true," he said with a casual shrug of his shoulders. "I definitely didn't rank up to par."

"That's the understatement of the year," Isobel mumbled under her breath.

"Yes, well, anyway, I'm sure you recall that I was late that night."

"Very late."

"Very late," he agreed.

He paused for a moment, running his tongue across his bottom lip and looking deep in thought.

"I had a reason for being late that day, although I didn't tell you then what it was."

She was baffled. "Why not?"

"It wasn't finished yet."

"I'm sorry," she said, her forehead creasing as she tried to comprehend his words. "I don't think I understand. What wasn't finished?"

He looked at her then, long and hard, and yet tenderly. His expression was serious, but a soft smile quickly appeared.

"This," he said in almost a whisper.

Then his fingers ran over the ivories one more time, and he began playing the softest, sweetest song Isobel had ever heard.

She closed her eyes, reveling in the beauty of the music, and in the knowledge that Dustin had written this song.

It was so beautiful, and from the way he had phrased it, she was certain it was the first song he'd ever composed on his own.

But why hadn't he simply told her that?

Did he think she wouldn't understand?

She did understand.

She understood Dustin almost better than she knew herself. She felt inexplicably linked to him, but she knew that this was only her side of a relationship that would never be.

Suddenly, Dustin began to sing, his clear, rich baritone piercing through the sanctuary even though he had no microphone.

And he was singing about her.

When Isobel heard her name, a finger ran up her spine and gooseflesh covered her arms.

The song was about her!

She gulped down and tried to pull in air, but nothing seemed to work. She felt as if she were suffocating.

His words whirled around her, every note burrowing into her.

He was singing a love song.

A love song!

Could it be that he returned her affections, that he felt the same connection as she?

Was it true?

Dustin continued singing, but his gaze met hers, and in his eyes she could see all the love and affection and commitment that she felt for him.

He smiled and winked at her in that crazy, adorable Dustin way he had, and her heart flipped over, and then over again.

He loved her!

Oh, how she wanted to be alone with him right now, to finally express all the feelings she'd kept hidden in the depths of her heart.

Dustin finished his song, clearly spelling out his love for her—by name.

And the next minute he was beside her, holding her hand. She was unaware of the crowd gathering closer to see what would happen.

She could only see Dustin, and the love beaming from his eyes.

Part of her screamed that it was too good to be true; that there was no way her dream could be becoming a reality.

And yet there Dustin stood, softly smiling just for her.

"This took me longer than it should have, Belle," he said, dropping her hand and putting both his hands in his pants pockets.

"For what?" she asked breathlessly.

"To figure out I'm in love with you."

Her breath rushed out of her body and she stood like a statue, his words having frozen her.

"And there was one more thing."

"What?" she whispered, all choked up.

"Your father."

"My *what?*" she screeched.

Her mother put her arm around her.

"Mom?" she asked.

"This should come from me," she said.

"What?" Isobel didn't know whether to be happy or sad—but she was confused.

Dustin answered. "Before I could make things right with you, Belle, for all you did for me, I needed to find out what happened to your father. I wanted to give that knowledge to you as a gift—so we could go forward with a clean slate."

"So you went to my mother?" Isobel demanded, adding a bit of anger to the cloud of emotion she was feeling.

"Not immediately, no. First I hired a private investigator. When I found out the truth, I went to your mother for confirmation."

"What do you mean *confirmation?* Mother? You knew what happened to Dad? Why he didn't come back?"

"He did leave your mother for another woman," Dustin said gently, placing a hand on her mother's shoulder. "And he thought a clean break would be better, at first."

"But then that other woman broke it off," her mother offered, a tear sliding down her cheek. "Your father wanted to come back home again. I wouldn't let him."

Isobel was stunned into silence. Dustin put his arm around her.

"I was angry, Isobel," her mother explained. "Angry and hurt. And then—" She broke off suddenly, closing both hands over her face.

Dustin cleared his throat. "You were about five years old then, Belle. Your father, he was—he overdosed on medication. The police believe it was an accident."

Isobel burst into tears, and then, as if a light poured on her, she remembered the day her mother had gotten a certain telephone call, and what had come of that.

"Do you think...?"

But she didn't have to finish the question. Dustin nodded. "I do think. And now you can let it all go."

Still crying, her mother embraced her. "I'm so sorry for not telling you the truth. I was so ashamed of my own behavior."

Isobel hugged her tight, and they cried together. The others, besides Dustin, stayed back, letting the family renew their own vows.

After a while, Isobel turned to Dustin. She opened

her mouth to speak, to tell him she loved him, to thank him for his heartfelt consideration. But the words wouldn't form.

She couldn't breathe, much less speak.

He smiled gently and put a finger over her mouth.

There was no need for her to speak. The love between them was almost a tangible thing.

Suddenly he pulled his hand from his pocket, a white velvet box clutched in his hand.

She might have panicked, with all these people around her, watching her every move.

But the look in Dustin's eyes calmed her, and she waited to see what he would say.

He flipped open the box to reveal a lovely gold ring with interwoven aspen leaves made from genuine Black Hills gold.

Gently, carefully, he removed the ring and held it up to her.

"This is a promise ring, Isobel," he said in a soft, smooth baritone filled with the richness of his love for her.

"If you accept this ring, you are accepting my promise to you—before God—to love you, care for you, be there for you, and when the time is right, make you my wife."

She stared at him for a moment, just letting his words sink in.

How she loved this man!

Slowly and with great regard, she lifted her left hand and accepted the ring, which Dustin quickly slid onto her hand, as if she might change her mind.

This, she knew, she would never do. And she realized

she owed Dustin the same kind of vow he had given her. He needed to hear it from her.

As he started to move his hand away, she grabbed it and held it.

"Dustin," she said, her voice choking with emotion, "I love you, too. I accept this ring, not only as a token of your love, but of my love for you.

"I will—before God—love you, care for you, and when the time is right, I will become your wife.

"I look forward to getting to know everything about you, and to bond our love by our time together."

"Kiss the woman," a man in the crowd called.

Soon, everyone in the crowd was calling for the culmination of such serious vows.

Dustin grinned like a cat, amusement lighting his eyes. "What do you think, Belle?" he whispered for her ears only.

She grabbed the front of his shirt and pulled him to her, so their lips were mere inches apart.

"I think," she said with a sly smile, "that you'd better kiss me."

Dustin obliged willingly, closing the distance between them with a soft, sweet kiss.

"We're on it!" a man and a woman said. She thought it might be Addison and Camille, but she wasn't sure and she didn't really care.

A moment later, the bell was ringing, clear and loud inside the sanctuary of the church.

Around them, Isobel could hear applause.

She thought all the angels in heaven must be applauding at that moment, for the joy of a man and a woman who'd finally found each other.

Chapter Eighteen

Four and a half months later

Isobel heard the pounding on the door to her condo, but she was busy playing with her cat, Epiphany, and didn't want to move to get it.

"Camille, can you get that for me?" she called.

Camille appeared at her side, dressed, but with a towel wrapped around her hair.

"In any other circumstances, Izzy. But I think you should answer it this time."

With a groan, Isobel picked herself up off the floor and went to the door.

Not a huge surprise, Dustin was on the other side of it. What did astonish her was the man standing behind Dustin.

His brother—Addison.

She hadn't seen Addison since that time at the church when she'd received her promise ring.

It was only then she realized Dustin was holding a box with a ribbon—and it wasn't just any box, it was a clothes box.

She couldn't have been any more surprised. She felt as if he could knock her down with a feather.

"Come in," she said to the men, holding open the door. "Addison, it's great to see you."

He rubbed his hands together as if he were nervous, but then gave her the pearly-white Fairfax grin.

"You're looking as pretty as ever."

She smiled and shook her head at him.

She would have said more, but Dustin cleared his throat.

"Excuse me," he said wryly, "but isn't anyone interested in the gift I brought? The gift in the *clothes* box?"

She laughed. "You know I am."

He nodded. "Good," he said firmly. "Then you'll follow my directions to the letter."

She frowned at him, her eyebrows furrowing. Who had exchanged her sweet, carefree Dustin for a man who gave orders?

"It's important, Belle. Just do what I say, this once?" He was pleading with her now, his big green eyes like a puppy dog's. She couldn't resist.

"Okay, so what gives?" she said, giving in with what she hoped was a modicum of dignity.

Camille had wandered out to the living room, and Isobel was surprised to see her hair was not only dried, but styled.

What was going on here?

Dustin handed her the box. "There are clothes in here," he said, as if it weren't obvious. "I want you to go in and change. You have to wear what's in the box today. Promise?"

She had a feeling this was a promise she was going

to regret, but how could she say no with all these people staring at her?

"Camille can help you get dressed," Dustin suggested offhandedly.

As if she hadn't been dressing herself all her life?

But she smiled and took the box from Dustin, then allowed Camille to herd her into the bedroom.

"What did I just get myself into?" she said to Camille.

Her friend just laughed. "Why don't you just open the box and see?" she suggested merrily.

Isobel set the box on the bed, held her breath and untied the blue ribbon, gently easing the top off the box.

Blue jeans. It was blue jeans. *Faded* blue jeans, to be exact.

It figured. It just figured.

"Well, put them on," Camille suggested with a wave of her hand. "You know he said you have to wear this outfit today."

"Yeah, don't remind me," she groaned.

She picked up the jeans and found an even worse surprise.

"Oh, it's a T-shirt," she said of the carefully folded cotton material. "He knows I hate T-shirts."

"Well, look on the bright side," said Camille. "At least it's hot pink. You'll look really cute."

"I'll look really grungy," Isobel replied, but she pulled the jeans over her hips.

"Okay, okay, the shirt," Camille urged.

"All right, already. Don't rush me. I'm not in a huge hurry here."

"Well, it's not fair to leave Dustin and Addison waiting," Camille advised.

Isobel picked up the hot pink T-shirt and rolled her eyes at her friend. "So I'll get dressed, already."

She pulled the T-shirt over her head. "I'm ready. Let's go."

Camille looked at her strangely. "O-kay," she said, drawing out the word. "You first."

Isobel shrugged. "Whatever."

She stepped out of the bedroom and back into the living room to find both men smiling from ear to ear.

"Well?" asked Dustin, rubbing his hands together.

"Well, what?" she said, lifting her eyebrows.

Camille sighed loudly. "This woman cannot take a hint."

Isobel turned to her. "What are you talking about?"

Dustin laughed. "Come here," he said, leading her to a full-length mirror in the hallway. "Now, look at yourself."

She did, and then she screamed for joy, throwing her arms around Dustin and kissing him soundly.

Though the words were reversed in the mirror's image, she had still easily been able to read the words printed on her T-shirt.

Marry Me.

* * * * *

Dear Reader,

Change.

It's a six-letter word that draws fear in all of us, from the humblest to the mightiest. We can't control many of the changes that happen to us—but sometimes we become obsessed with changing ourselves.

As Dustin and Isobel learned, and what Moses himself learned straight from God, maybe life—today's life—isn't about change at all. Maybe it's about being just who God made you—right here, right now. God loves you just as you are, and has placed you just where you are—for a reason.

It's worth a thought.

I love to hear from my readers! You can write me at: Deb Kastner P.O. Box 481 Johnstown, CO 80534.

Resting in His strength,

Deb Kastner

QUESTIONS FOR DISCUSSION

1. Dustin was willing to have himself made over in order to get his hands on his trust fund. How far would you be willing to go for a large sum of money? Why or why not?

2. Dustin was elusive and went out of his way to make sure Addison didn't discover many of his activities. Why do you think he did this? (Hint: Matthew 6:3)

3. Both Dustin and Isobel had gifts and abilities they shared with others in God's name. What gifts and abilities do you have that you could use to help others in any kind of need?

4. Isobel stuck with Dustin even when things got rough. How long should you stand the antics of a person who makes you uncomfortable before you say, "That's enough"?

5. Isobel felt abandoned by her father, who left without a word when she was a young child. If we are a child of God, are we ever really abandoned?

6. At the end of the book, Dustin gives Isobel a promise ring. If he is sure, and she is sure, why do you think he didn't give her an engagement ring?

7. If God has blessed you with abundance in your life, in what ways can you think of to give back in your communities, nation and works?

8. If, like many of us, you live paycheck to paycheck, what ways can you think of to give back to God for His generosity in giving us His Son?

9. What do you think you would do if you suddenly came into a windfall of money? Be honest!

10. What is a tithe? Use a Bible concordance to look up verses to help you answer this question.

A WEDDING
IN WYOMING

But he was wounded for our transgressions,
He was bruised for our iniquities:
The chastisement for our peace was upon Him,
And by His stripes we are healed.
—*Isaiah* 53:5

To my former manager Kristie Parks at Hallmark, and all the ladies, for making my time working there so special. I told you I would!

To my editor, Emily Rodmell, for her patience and direction in bringing me back up to speed in my career with this book.

And most of all, to my family—my husband, Joe, my daughter Annie and her husband, Max, and my daughters Kimberly and Katie. You have pulled with me through the rough times and laughed with me through our joy. May God continue to bless each and every one of you with His mercy, grace and love.

Much excitement and love to the little new bobbit in the DePriest/Kastner family, my first granddaughter, Isabella! And no— I'm not old enough to be a granny!

Chapter One

The roses were perfect, and so was her plan.

This year, Jenn Washington's annual two-week family reunion would be different. She could see it already, from the way her family was fawning over the recently delivered bouquet.

"Oh, how lovely!" Jenn's mother exclaimed. "And to be delivered way out here—it's such a romantic gesture."

"A dozen red roses," Granny added, waggling her eyebrows suggestively. "The color of love."

Precisely, thought Jenn. *Thank you very much.*

She'd gone to a great deal of trouble picking out the perfect bouquet online—red roses surrounded by a scattering of baby's breath and lodged in a lovely French vase. It had cost her a pretty penny, not only to purchase, but to have them sent by special courier to the middle of nowhere in Wyoming, at her grandparent's ranch where she'd grown up.

Now, seeing her family's surprised gazes, she knew it was worth every cent.

This plan was going to work.

"Sounds fishy to me," Jenn's great-aunt, Myra, said, pursing her lips. "There's a card attached. Let's read it."

"Don't you think you ought to let Jenn read it in private? It's her gift, after all," Granddad said in his usual, pleasantly gruff manner.

All eyes were on Jenn. Her heart was pounding. This was the moment she'd waited for, her coup de grâce, so to speak. "Oh, no, that's all right. Go ahead and read it. I have no secrets."

She had more secrets than she cared to admit, but she wouldn't reveal a single one.

Not now.

Not ever.

Auntie Myra plucked up the small card and opened it with flair, clearing her throat melodramatically before reading the words.

"'Love, Me.'"

Clever, even if Jenn had to say so herself. She wanted to laugh aloud, but she kept her expression as innocently neutral as she was able.

"That's it?" Granny said, turning to face Jenn, arms akimbo. "Sounds like you've got a bit of explaining to do, missy."

Jenn did her best to look both innocent and delighted. *Delighted* wasn't so difficult. This was going to be fun. No one was going to tease her about a lack of a significant other this year. No one was going to hint at the lack of grandchildren at the reunion.

Not this year.

Exactly as she'd planned.

"They're just flowers," she said, making a dismissive motion with her hand. "I don't know why everyone is making such a big deal over it."

"What? You don't like flowers now?" teased Granny.

"Oh, I like flowers," Jenn answered with a laugh.

"So it's the *man* you don't like," guessed Jenn's mother.

Jenn laughed again and shook her head. "I didn't say that."

"Do you even know who these are from?" queried Auntie Myra, still gazing at Jenn with suspicion and disbelief. Not hard to understand, since Jenn, now twenty-six, had never brought a man home to meet the family.

"Of course I do," Jenn answered immediately.

Me, she thought with delight.

"And that would be?" Auntie Myra continued.

From the start, she'd known that her family would want to know the name, rank and serial number of any man who'd *finally* gotten close enough to Jenn to receive her attention.

"J-uh-Johnny," she stammered, and then let out a relieved breath when everyone smiled at her.

All at once, questions flew at her from every direction.

Where did she meet him?

How long had they been dating?

Why hadn't she mentioned him before?

As quick as they started, the barrage of questions were abruptly cut off by a loud pounding coming from behind them.

"What's all the noise in here?" came an unexpected voice from the kitchen doorway, where a sandy-haired man was lounging his bony shoulder against the doorway, his cowboy hat low over his eyes.

"Scotty!" Jenn was the first to see him, and launched

herself into his arms, nearly knocking him off his feet.
"I didn't think you were coming!"

"Young man," Granny said, from just over Jenn's
shoulder, "didn't your mama teach you any manners?
A gentleman removes his hat when he enters a house."

Scotty colored and swept off the dusty blue cavalry
hat, his trademark among the bull riders from back in
his teen years, tapping it mildly against his thigh. He
cleared his throat loudly. "Sorry, Granny."

Granny made an indistinct snorting sound, then
laughed, crowding Jenn to give her grandson a hug. It
wasn't a moment more before everyone was crowding
in for a big family bear hug.

Scotty was a welcome diversion from Jenn's flowers,
a fact she noticed and was happy to accommodate. She'd
rather not answer the questions her family plagued her
with about her mysterious Johnny, so it was just as well.

And she was as thrilled as the rest of her family to
see her baby brother. It had been a year, and he had
sprouted like a beanpole.

It was only then, stepping back to allow her family more access to her brother, that she noticed Scotty
was not alone. Lingering in the background behind her
brother, his hip leaned negligently against the kitchen
counter, his black Diamond Jim Stetson curled in his
hand, was another man, a stranger to Jenn.

He was tall, six-two maybe, with broad shoulders
and strong arms, but with the long, wiry frame of a
man who spent most of his time in the saddle. His deep,
curly black hair was a little long, as if he'd missed his
last haircut, and was ruffled from the removal from his
hat. He was purposefully hanging back, but his posture was relaxed and his face friendly and open. Jenn

guessed the cowboy could be called handsome, in a rugged sort of way.

If one were attracted to that sort of man, which Jenn definitely wasn't.

He'd obviously come in with her brother, though he looked to be several years older than Scotty—close to Jenn's own age, she guessed.

He didn't look uncomfortable at being overlooked. His dark eyes, a color which floated somewhere between blue and black, were brimming with amusement and understanding. His friend was home with family, who clearly adored him. The stranger appeared to be content to wait his turn.

When the man realized Jenn was staring at him, he smiled and winked at her. Flushing, she turned her gaze away and elbowed Auntie Myra, gesturing toward the unannounced guest, knowing her aunt would jump at the chance to welcome someone new to their gathering, especially a handsome young man.

"Why, Scotty," Auntie Myra exclaimed, "you haven't introduced your guest."

Scotty laughed from his belly and gestured the stranger forward, slapping him on the back affectionately. "Sorry. I was so caught up in seeing you all I almost forgot about him."

"Well, thanks," the stranger replied, punching Scotty's arm hard enough to send the boy off balance and sprawling into other family members.

"I can introduce myself," the man said, his voice deep, yet surprisingly soft-spoken, given his size. He had the slightest bit of a drawl, though not Texan nor Southern. Jenn couldn't place it.

She was pondering this when his next words blasted over her with the force of a hurricane.

"Glad to meet y'all. My name's Johnny. Johnny Barnes."

Dead silence.

Even loquacious Auntie Myra was left speechless in the wake of Johnny's declaration.

Jenn's breath left her body as if she'd been punched in the gut. And it didn't return. She wasn't even sure her heart was beating.

Johnny?

Scotty brings a wrangler from the depths of Wyoming and his name is *Johnny?*

It figured. It just figured. Now she was going to have to talk her way out of this one, too, because she knew perfectly well her dear family was never going to leave it alone.

So, what if there were a million *Johnnys* in the world? They were still going to ask if he was the *one,* Jenn just knew it. And the expressions on her family's faces only served to confirm her fears. Especially Auntie Myra, who looked as if she was preparing to pounce on the poor cowboy.

Scotty looked around, obviously confused by his family's odd behavior. Everyone else's gaze was on Jenn. No one was welcoming Scotty's new friend to the household, as her younger brother had clearly expected.

"Johnny wrangles with me. I thought it would be okay to bring him along," Scotty said, hesitantly.

Granddad was the first to recover, always the most sensible of the lot of them. "Of course he's welcome. Johnny, glad to meet you." Granddad thrust out his hand for a hearty handshake.

Auntie Myra stepped forward and hugged the man. Johnny returned the unexpected embrace awkwardly, and Jenn smiled despite herself. Obviously, Johnny was not prepared for Scotty's affectionate family, as he accepted hug after hug from the women and friendly, enthusiastic handshakes from the men.

Only Jenn remained where she was, caught in a trap of her own making. She couldn't approach the man and greet him. Stranger or friend, her family would be watching her with hawkeyes.

It took a moment, but her brain slowly started functioning again.

What did she have to worry about? This was Scotty's friend, fresh from sprawling Wyoming ranch land. Surely her family would realize he couldn't possibly be *her* Johnny.

There would only be a moment of confusion before things were set to right and she could go back to enjoying the reunion.

"So," asked Auntie Myra in a casual tone that belied her open, wide-eyed curiosity, "Are you *the* Johnny we've heard about?"

Jenn cringed inwardly, though she reminded herself again and again there was no real danger in him answering that question. The man wouldn't have the slightest notion of what Auntie Myra was really asking, and would, naturally, answer to the negative.

End of subject.

Johnny definitely looked stunned as he stared from face to face. But after a moment he quirked his lips, shrugged, and announced, "Guess I've been found out. Yes, ma'am. That would be me."

Jenn felt her legs buckle underneath her and moved

quickly to the sofa and sat before she fell down. She had no idea why the unknown cowboy had answered the way he had, but now she—and he, for that matter—had, as the old saying went, a lot of 'splaining to do.

She was suddenly furious at the gall of the cowboy. Never mind that this whole setup was her doing in the first place.

How could he say he was *the* Johnny? There was *no* Johnny! What kind of a game was he playing?

Everyone rushed at him at once, deluging him with questions.

When had he met Jenn?

How long had they been together?

And how long had it been since they'd seen each other last, what with him wrangling and all?

Johnny sent a panicked glance at Scotty, but his friend just grinned and shrugged. Obviously the boy would be no help in sorting this out.

Who was *Jenn?* What were these nutty people talking about?

Suddenly he spied the young woman seated on the sofa, the pretty woman who'd been the first to notice him when he and Scotty first arrived. She was also, he'd noted, the only one of her spirited family who'd held back in the initial greeting, not offering him a welcome, much less a hug. She must be the sister Scotty had mentioned.

She now looked a little woozy. Her eyes looked glazed over and she was gripping the arm of the sofa like a lifeline. He guessed her to be around his age—twenty-five or twenty-six at most. She had gorgeous, short golden curls, a pretty, perky little nose, intelligent blue eyes, and a face as red as a Macintosh apple.

Obviously, she was the woman they were all talking about. What he didn't know was *what* they were talking about.

He'd thought Scotty's family had recognized him from a magazine cover or a television news story, but apparently that was not the case. He didn't know whether to be relieved or alarmed.

He had to figure out what was going on, and fast. He thrust his fingers through his hair and tapped his Stetson against his thigh. If these people didn't know who he really was—and they clearly didn't—he didn't want to tip off his own hand.

He hesitated in revealing his true identity—just yet. Not to this happy, *real* family who apparently didn't keep up with national news all that well.

But he still didn't know who they thought he was. He had to figure out some way to gain the information he needed without giving himself away.

And then he realized the answer to his problem, that *other way,* was staring straight back at him, half glaring, half beckoning, as if she expected him to say something that would clear up everything. To say that he was in no way connected with her, apparently.

And he supposed he would…in time. At the moment, he just wanted to hear what was invariably going to be a highly amusing story, especially if it came from the mouth of the lovely woman on the sofa.

He grinned widely as he looked away from Jenn and tipped his head toward her aunt, his fingers tugging at the imaginary brim of his hat. *Cowboy style,* he thought, his smile growing even bigger. "I'm mighty pleased to meet you all," he said, giving a show at his most charming drawl. "But I wonder if I might have a moment alone with—uh,—Jenn?"

He couldn't remember everyone's names in the enthusiastic jumble of introductions, but Jenn's name was sealed firmly in his mind.

"Why, of course," answered a fine-looking middle-age woman who could only be Scotty and Jenn's mother. She had the same golden curls—albeit with a bit of white—and the same vibrant blue eyes as her daughter. "You two probably haven't seen each other in ages."

Which was the understatement of the century, Johnny thought, his lips twitching with amusement.

"We'll all retire to the kitchen to get sandwiches prepared for everyone," Jenn's grandmother suggested, "and give you two a little privacy."

Jenn was on her feet in an instant. "I don't think—" She stopped, looking around with wide eyes. *A deer caught in the headlights,* Johnny thought. She looked as if she were about to be run over by a blaring semitruck.

Johnny still had absolutely no idea what was going on, but it had to be one good story. He probably would have laughed out loud if the poor young woman by the sofa didn't look so pitifully miserable.

He hadn't felt like laughing—really laughing—in a very long time, and he savored the feeling. He'd let his work get the best of him, stealing away his teenage years, not to mention the first half of his twenties. Taking this summer off was the best thing that had ever happened to him.

Especially now, when he'd somehow landed in the midst of a happy, if chaotic, family, and a mystery he was eager to solve.

"Now, Jenn," said Scotty's and Jenn's grandmother, "be gracious to your guest. Fresh-ground coffee is on its way." She turned to Johnny. "Please, young man, be seated." Her forceful sideways glance at Jenn clearly indicated she should do the same.

Jenn nodded mutely at her family as all but her brother departed for the kitchen.

Scotty didn't budge. He was grinning at Johnny like he'd just roped a steer on the first try. Scotty didn't speak, but he chuckled and lifted one eyebrow.

Johnny just shrugged.

"Scotty," Jenn said, her voice just a little bit shaky and very much pleading, "please."

Scotty laughed rowdily but moved to join the others in the kitchen.

Jenn cringed inwardly. Count on her baby brother to give her trouble about this. About *Johnny.* As if she weren't in enough trouble already.

Jenn regained her seat on the sofa with a deep sigh, burying her face in her hands. Johnny sat down on an armchair opposite her, leaned his elbows on his legs, and waited.

Jenn said nothing for the longest time. This was absolutely, totally surreal. She couldn't get her mind around what was happening, never mind what to do with the situation.

She was alone in a room with a man she'd just now met—a man whom her family assumed was some sort of *significant other* in her life, a relationship obviously serious enough to warrant flowers being delivered to her out in the middle of nowhere.

Quickly, she composed her thoughts. There had to

be a simple way out of this mess, even if she couldn't see it now. She just had to think rationally. Starting with the obvious.

"Why did you call yourself *the* Johnny?" she asked, her voice more demanding than she'd intended, but she was under a lot of strain.

"We'll get to that," the man replied in his soft, rich baritone. "But first, I think you need to tell me who these people think I am."

Jenn nodded. "Yes, I suppose you're right. You must be stupefied by their reaction to your presence."

He laughed. "Yeah, well, *stupefied* isn't the exact word I'd use, but let's just say I am more than just curious."

She couldn't help but laugh with him. It *was* funny, or at least it would be in twenty years when she looked back on this moment.

Right this second though, she felt dreadfully serious. Her stomach hurt.

"It's my family. I know you've only just met them, but I'm sure you've noticed how overwhelming they can be."

"You're lucky to have a family," Johnny said, his expression suddenly serious. Then he smiled and shrugged. "I'm an orphan, myself."

"Oh, I'm sorry," she said, and meant it with all her heart. Her job as a social worker in downtown Denver brought her in contact with many orphaned and abandoned children. She knew firsthand the pain and suffering they experienced, being all alone in the world. She wondered what Johnny's story was, what he had been through. But now was not the time to ask.

"I love my family, I really do," she stated emphatically. "I look forward to these yearly gatherings. It's the only time I see most of my family, even my parents. I work in Denver, and it sometimes feels like Wyoming—where the rest of my family lives—might as well be Mars."

"You're busy with your work?" Johnny asked.

He had guessed accurately. "Yes. I'm a social worker. I work long, hard hours—sometimes seven days a week. And I'm on call many of the nights."

Johnny nodded. "I know what you mean."

She supposed he did, in a backward, cowboy sort of way. Wrangling cattle was pretty much a 24/7 job.

"There's just this one thing, you see," she explained. Oddly, she was beginning to feel comfortable in this cowboy's presence. He was a large, intimidating man, to be sure, but he had kind eyes and a playful quirk to his lips that set her at ease.

Still, she had to be careful where she trod, especially since Johnny seemed so sincere.

It was best simply to get down to business and have it done with. They needed to work out a feasible solution to the problem she'd created, not become friends. Not that she wanted that, anyway.

"You may have noticed there are no children about."

He cocked his head a little to one side, and then nodded. "I have to admit I was a little surprised—a family reunion with no kids."

"My Auntie Myra—she's my great-aunt, really—lost her husband in Vietnam. They had no children, and her heart was so broken she never remarried."

"I see," he said, though the look on his face told her he had no idea whatsoever where this conversation was leading.

"Basically, Johnny, the lot has fallen on me. Everyone wants squealing little children running rampant through this farm, and they want them now."

"Well, sure they do," he said with a soft drawl. "But you're all of what, twenty-four years old? Twenty-five, maybe? And Scotty's only just finished his high-school diploma."

"I'm twenty-six," Jenn clarified wryly. "And as far as my family is concerned, it's time for me to settle down and start popping out some sweet little babies for them to spoil rotten."

She paused thoughtfully. "It's not all that surprising, really, given everyone's circumstances. I don't blame them. It's just not where I'm at in my life right now."

Ever, she thought grimly, but she didn't say the word aloud.

Johnny pursed his lips. "So, then, let's see. The real problem is that Mr. Right hasn't come along yet to sweep you off your feet?"

Jenn chuckled. "I don't even know if there is such a man. For me, at least."

"You're pulling my leg," he replied, with a shake of his head. "You can't tell me you don't have men knocking down your door every day of the week. A beautiful, intelligent woman like you?"

He was teasing, but that didn't stop Jenn from flushing from her toes to the tips of her ears. "I really don't have time for dating."

"Well, you ought to make some." His midnight-blue eyes were alight with amusement.

Jenn waved him off with her hand. "Now you're starting to sound like my family."

He laughed and stretched like a lazy cat. He was so large he dwarfed the armchair he was seated on.

"I still don't understand where I come in," he said after a minute.

"You don't," she stated emphatically. "This is all one big misunderstanding."

"I got that much. So who is—and more to the point *where* is—this fellow Johnny your family was clearly expecting?"

She groaned and put a palm to her forehead. "That's the thing," she muttered. "There is no Johnny."

There was another long moment's pause as Johnny considered her words, and then he shook his head. "I don't get it."

She chuckled. "No, you wouldn't. I did something stupid, at least in hindsight it appears that way. My family always teases me mercilessly about getting married and starting a family, so I made up a man."

"You did *what?*" He fingered the dusty Stetson in his hand.

"It's not as complicated as it sounds—at least it *wasn't,* until you showed up and announced your name was Johnny."

"My name *is* Johnny," he said with a low chuckle.

"Unfortunately," she muttered, and then clapped a hand over her mouth. "I'm so sorry. I really didn't mean that the way it sounded."

He laughed. "I didn't think you did."

She liked his laugh. He threw back his head and chortled wholeheartedly, his blue eyes glittering.

Okay, so she was harboring a little resentment toward the man, even if she knew perfectly well it wasn't really his fault she was in this predicament. Fortunately, he couldn't tell how she was really feeling, this convulsion of emotions coursing through her heart and head.

At least Johnny appeared to be taking her revelations with courtesy and maybe a touch of humor, which, Jenn thought, said a lot about the kind of man he was. He didn't seem mad at her.

Yet.

He hadn't heard the whole story. Johnny might appear to be a nice enough man for an unpolished cowboy, but he still had no idea how big a quandary he'd innocently walked into.

There were limits to any man's patience, and Johnny's, she had to think, must already be stretched close to its limit.

Jenn was about to continue her convoluted explanation when her mother interrupted. Clearing her throat loudly to announce her presence, Jenn's mother entered with two steaming mugs of freshly ground and brewed coffee. Jenn inhaled the lovely aroma of hazelnut and crème, her favorite.

Mom didn't say a word. She set the mugs on the table and, with an encouraging smile to each of them, backtracked into the kitchen, closing the French doors that separated the rooms firmly behind her.

"I sent myself flowers," Jenn announced as soon as she and Johnny were once more alone.

"That's it?" Johnny asked, cocking an eyebrow. "That's all you did? Signed the card *Johnny* and let everyone think what they may?"

"Not exactly," she said, chuckling. "I signed the card, *Love, Me.*"

He laughed heartily, and Jenn was certain her family could hear *that* from the next room.

"Clever," he said. "Ingenious. This story gets better and better. So what happened when the flowers arrived?" He leaned forward, elbows on his knees, as if anxious to hear the rest.

In that, he would be disappointed. "There isn't much to tell. The family made a big deal of it, of course, and started nagging me for a name. I'd only just blurted out *Johnny* when you and Scotty showed up."

"Hmm," he said, stroking his strong jaw between his thumb and forefinger. His face was unshaven, as he'd been out on the range for a good week at least, Jenn thought.

She wondered why she didn't find the scruff unattractive. Stubble had never appealed to her before.

He sat back in the chair. "My showing up puts you in a bit of a pickle, doesn't it?"

"Let's just say it was a major jolt to my system, and leave it at that. I was really freaked out there for a while. But now that I've had a chance to settle down and think about it—and to talk to you—it's really not so bad. We—*I*, that is,—just need to come clean with the facts. I simply have to tell my family there's been a misunderstanding and you are not *my* Johnny."

"And yet, here we've been sitting alone all this time like we're catching up."

The man did have a point. Jenn felt herself blushing again. She hated that. "I can't think of how to explain that part—yet."

Johnny grinned. "I can."

But before he could say more, the family emerged from the kitchen, flooding back into the living room with expectant gazes on their faces. Apparently, they'd collectively decided they'd waited long enough to get the scoop on Jenn and her new beau.

Even Scotty looked curious. *How could he think for one second that...*

Her thoughts were cut off when Johnny stood, and with the athletic agility of a rugged cowboy, slid into the spot next to her on the sofa and slipped his arm around her shoulders, effectively sealing the deal.

She couldn't think. She couldn't breathe. The temperature in the room seemed to suddenly have spiked to well over two hundred degrees.

What was the crazy cowboy up to now? Didn't he realize he was making things worse by the second?

And how was she going to explain herself to her family, when Johnny was acting so cozy with her?

There was only one answer to that question.

She couldn't.

Chapter Two

"Relax," he whispered close to her ear, his soft drawl sending a shiver down her spine for any number of reasons. "I'm doing you a favor."

What? Her mind scrambled for an answer to his riddle, but she couldn't put two thoughts together rationally to save her life.

Steady, she coaxed herself mentally. *Relax. Think. Try to locate your brain.*

"Thanks, folks," Johnny said, addressing her hovering family. "It was nice to have a few minutes alone with Jenn to get—er—*reacquainted* with this lovely lady."

His arm tightened around her shoulder for just a moment. She didn't know if the gesture was meant for the family's benefit or if he was sending her some kind of unspoken message.

Maybe both.

Because she was sure, now, what he was doing.

He was playing her game.

The game *she* had initiated and no longer wanted any part of.

She tried to speak, to lay it all on the line for her family, but Johnny's statement sent the whole clan abuzz, and Jenn couldn't get a word in edgewise.

"A *cowboy*," Granny said, looking from Johnny to Jenn, and then back at Johnny again, assessing them before giving Jenn a nod of approval. "Who would have thought?"

Who would have thought, indeed? Jenn wouldn't hog-tie herself to a ranch hand in a million years. Rough-and-tumble cowboys just weren't her type, and her family, of all people, should have known that.

"The flowers are lovely," her mother offered.

Especially picked for me, by me, Jenn thought.

"And how romantic for you two to meet up this way," Auntie Myra added. "Johnny must have done some real fast talking to surprise you like this, Jenn. All in all, I think this whole reunion is going to be one surprise after another."

More than Auntie Myra could possibly know.

Granddad settled into the chocolate-colored armchair Johnny had vacated. "So, son, tell us more about you. Jenn was going to fill us in when you arrived. Where do you hail from?"

Jenn noticed Johnny's hesitation, and the way his grip on his cowboy hat tightened. He rolled the rim as he spoke. "I'm originally from Nebraska, sir, but I've lived all over the country at one time or another."

That explained the slight but unidentifiable drawl, at any rate—the accent that made her heart do that tiny, annoying flutter she was trying to ignore. Johnny spoke firmly and quietly, but the tension was definitely still present.

Jenn wondered if anyone else had noticed the way he'd suddenly stiffened. But no, of course not—they were all flying off in this wild fantasy she had created for their benefit. She wanted to crawl underneath the nearest chair and hide, but Johnny's arm was still firmly about her shoulders.

"Your family is in Nebraska?" Jenn's father asked, standing directly behind the armchair her grandfather occupied and leaning into it, resting his elbow on the cushion.

"No family," Johnny said briskly. He wanted to fold his arms across his chest in a protective move, but he didn't want to let go of Jenn to do it, so he remained where he was. He didn't want to talk about this subject—not to this nice, close, happy family. But he knew he had to say something. "I'm an orphan, sir."

Best to stay as close to the truth as possible, he decided. As a Christian, it went against every moral grain in his body to submit even the smallest white lie to anyone, but he'd suddenly discovered a chivalrous streak he hadn't even known he possessed until this moment.

At first, this charade had been about himself, about protecting his own identity and getting to spend a couple weeks finding out how a real family functioned.

Now it was about Jenn.

When the family had abruptly broken off his conversation with Jenn, he'd moved to her side without a moment's thought or hesitation, going straight on gut instinct. An instinct to protect the beautiful woman now lodged firmly, if not comfortably, in his arms.

The fact that he was protecting her from *herself* crossed his mind, but it didn't matter now. He'd made his decision and he was going to stick with it.

"Well, you've got family here, son," Jenn's grandfather said firmly. "Any friend of Jenn and Scotty's is always welcome here."

To his surprise, Johnny found himself fighting a burning sensation in the back of his eyes. He'd thought he'd put aside all his hurt and anguish at having grown up without a family, but Jenn's grandfather's words pierced his heart.

Johnny wasn't a crying man. He hadn't shed a single tear since he was five years old and his bully of a foster brother had beaten him up for being such a sissy.

He grit his teeth against the onslaught of emotion, determined to overcome it by sheer strength of will but entirely unable to speak.

"That's right, honey," Auntie Myra said, ruffling Johnny's hair as she would a young boy. "Now that you're dating our precious Jenn, you've got to consider us all your family. And I expect you to call me *Auntie Myra.* I know the rest of my family feels the same— *Granny, Granddad.*"

Johnny opened his mouth to speak but only a choking sound emerged.

Auntie Myra held up her hands, thinking he was trying to beg off. If only she knew.

"No, no, we won't hear of anything else, will we, folks?"

Her family clamored over each other to be the first to agree.

Jenn's mother placed a hand on Johnny's shoulder. "I know you must be feeling a little overwhelmed right now, Johnny. Don't let them frighten you away. I know you and Jenn are just dating. You probably haven't made any long-term plans."

That was an understatement. He and Jenn hadn't gotten so far as to what they were going to do in the next minute, much less the next two weeks. Johnny swallowed hard and nodded.

"Still and all, things being the way they are, Jenn's father and I would be honored if you would treat us like family, even if it's just for these two weeks."

Johnny looked at Jenn. Her bright blue eyes were shimmering with unshed tears, from joy or chagrin he couldn't say.

For himself, Johnny thought this might be the happiest moment of his life, and it was certainly going to be the best two weeks he'd ever spent.

He was still feeling guilty about deceiving these kind people, but it was really only a sin of omission, wasn't it?

Anyway, he was already committed. In for a penny, and all that. For the next two weeks, he decided, he was going to toss away guilt and savor every moment.

Because for the first time in his entire life, he had a *family*.

"We need to make some ground rules," Jenn said firmly, as she showed Johnny to his room. "Since *you've* decided to play this little game." Her tone was both defensive and accusatory.

"You started it," he reminded her, then clamped his jaw shut as he realized he sounded like a five-year-old bantering with a sibling.

Jenn Washington was most *definitely* not his sibling. His grip on his saddle pack increased with every step. Maybe this wasn't such a good idea after all.

"It's true. I did," she admitted quietly after a moment's pause.

At least she had the maturity to own up to her part in this charade. Johnny respected her for that.

"What I don't understand is why you decided not to call my bluff," she said, gesturing him into a small corner bedroom.

Johnny quickly scanned the room. There was a neatly made twin bed with a colorful quilt folded at the bottom, a writing table which faced one of two windows, and a clothes rack in lieu of a closet.

There wasn't space for a closet, or anything else, for that matter. Johnny had to duck his head to get through the doorway.

He set his saddle pack against the foot of the bed and then sat down, feeling less awkward sitting than standing. He looked at Jenn expectantly, wondering if she was going to keep on about the subject of why he hadn't called her bluff, or if she would move on to something else.

Thankfully, it was something else. "I apologize for the cramped quarters. This is the only spare guest room we have left."

"Not a problem," Johnny assured her.

"You're positive you won't be claustrophobic? You're used to sleeping under the stars, I'm sure."

He didn't think now was the time to mention he'd shared a dorm room smaller than this in college. "Like I said, I'll be fine. If I get the hankering, I have my bedroll. I can always go out by the barn and sleep under the stars." He winked at her.

"Yes, I suppose you can," she agreed with a smile. "And then come back inside for a hot shower in the morning. What a novel idea for a cowboy."

Actually, he *was* looking forward to sleeping inside

again, on a real bed, and most especially taking a hot shower every morning, but he didn't tell her that. He just grinned.

"Now, back to my original statement. Ground rules," she reminded him. "And I still want to know why you decided to masquerade as *my* Johnny."

"That's a simple answer," he replied, opening the frilly blue gingham curtains to let in what was left of the sunshine. Since the window above the authentic pinewood writing desk faced east, he knew he'd see a lot more of the sun come morning.

He grinned. "I've never had a family. You've just given me two weeks with one. It'll be a new experience for me."

He was surprised when she didn't smile back, but rather frowned at him. "Are you serious? You want to be a part of *my* family? You've spent more than five minutes in their combined company. Are you nuts?"

"You don't know what you have."

Jenn went silent. He *was* serious. And she felt sorry for him. She might not see them often, but she *had* family, and as curious as they were, she knew she could count on them, no matter what.

Johnny, on the other hand, had no one.

He returned to his saddle bag and flipped open the top, taking out a well-used leather-bound bible and placing it on the writing desk, his hand lingering over the cover.

"You're a Christian?" she asked, more alarmed than surprised.

He looked her straight in the eye. "Yes, ma'am. Does that bother you?"

Jenn looked away from his soul-piercing gaze. "No, not at all," she said with forced enthusiasm.

"You're in good company here. My family is all out-spoken believers."

She expected he would naturally include her in the statement, but he continued to watch her, assessing her with eyes that gleamed almost black in the twilight of the bedroom.

To her relief, he didn't press the point. Instead, he shifted back to their original quandary.

"You said something about ground rules." That low, soft-spoken voice went straight to her heart. "What did you have in mind?"

"It's not that I don't trust you," she began, and real-ized to her own surprise that she meant it. "But I think we'd both be more comfortable—and believable—if we simply devise and agree to abide by a game plan. That way there won't be as many opportunities for mistakes, faux pas, if you will."

"Okay," he said straightaway, sitting on the corner of the bed and gesturing her to the pinewood chair. "Should I shut the door, do you think, so others can't hear our conversation?"

"No!" Jenn felt a blush rising to her cheeks—again. "That's exactly what I'm talking about. My family is old-fashioned. *I'm* old-fashioned, at least in that respect. This is exactly the sort of behavior I *don't* want—"

She stopped speaking dead in the middle of her state-ment when she looked at Johnny, who'd crossed his arms and was grinning like the Cheshire Cat.

She suddenly realized he was teasing her, which only made her blush all the more.

"Seriously, now," he said. "What is it you think we

should—or should *not*—do to make our grand charade a success?"

Jenn had no idea where to start. Her mind was jumbled with thoughts, and not all were about the pretense they were initiating. He was looking at her with an intensity and amusement that sent her mind and heart completely off-kilter.

Johnny merely cocked an eyebrow, waiting.

"Well, I don't think we should spend too much time together alone," she started, and then realized that was exactly what they were doing now. "Of course, my family will expect us to hang out with each other, but let's try to do that when everyone's around."

He nodded, his lips quirking in that adorable smile of his.

"My family doesn't really believe in private time—individual or otherwise—especially during these reunions. They usually have every spare second filled with some amusement or another."

"Sounds good to me."

"It'll drive you crazy by the end of your first week here."

He laughed. "You like your private time, huh?"

"Oh, yes," she agreed instantly. "I have to have some downtime just to recover from all the noise my family makes. Trust me, you will, too."

"Naw." He shook his head. "Other than devotional time, which I usually take early in the morning before anyone else rises, I think I'm good."

"We'll see." This man was far too agreeable, which would normally set her nerves on edge, but for some reason, she liked him all the more for his positive attitude.

"What else?" he asked, leaning back on his hands.

She wondered if his curly black hair was always as ruffled as it was now, or whether it was the result of wearing his cowboy hat all day.

"I would prefer that you not try to delve into my personal business—my private life. I'll respect yours, as well. Naturally, I'll fill you in on the basics, the things you need to know to be *my* Johnny. But at the end of the day, I'm a very private person, and I'd like it to stay that way."

"Of course," he agreed immediately with a firm nod of his head. "Likewise, darlin'."

The endearment left a mark on her heart. She wanted to deny him the right to use a pet name with her, but realized it could work to her advantage, so she said nothing.

She considered what a simple cowboy like Johnny could possibly consider a *private life.* He spent all his time out on the range with *cows,* after all.

Then again, as a social worker, she'd learned the hard way that everyone had secrets. She knew she personally carried more than the usual load. But still…

"Anything else I should know?" he asked, interrupting her thoughts.

"No P.D.A.," she blurted without thinking, and then groaned inwardly. This was going to be much, *much* more complicated than she'd ever imagined.

That quirk of his lips again. She was positive that trait was going to drive her crazy within the space of a week, for better or worse.

"Public Displays of Affection," she clarified.

Johnny chuckled softly, a deep, low rumble in his throat. "I know what P.D.A. stands for. I was just wondering what your family will think if there aren't any. We're supposed to be in love, remember?"

She choked and sputtered for air.

He just grinned. He was baiting her—again, as if he enjoyed making her blush.

Maybe he did.

"You have a point," she conceded slowly. "I suppose there must be *something*. Er—uh—holding hands once in a while would be appropriate, and I g-guess you can put your arm around me from time to time." She hated how she stammered through that sentence, but she couldn't help herself.

"I feel honored," Johnny said, using his fingers to tip the rim of the hat he wasn't wearing. She couldn't tell whether or not he was teasing her again. His voice was serious, but his midnight-blue eyes were dancing with merriment.

She frowned. "I'm serious. And one more thing. Absolutely, positively *no kissing*. Not even so much as a peck on the cheek. Are we clear on that point?"

His gaze widened, and for the longest moment she thought he might object, but in the end he just nodded. "Done," he said firmly.

She let out a sigh. He had no idea of the relief flooding through her. Because, even though she didn't know this man at all, she believed he meant what he said.

She shouldn't. She knew better.

She'd keep her guard up, no matter what. At least he'd agreed to the ground rules in theory, and her gut instinct was to take him at his word. Time would tell.

At least he hadn't asked for details, or questioned her rules. Most women, she supposed, probably threw themselves at the handsome cowboy. He probably wasn't used to a woman being as reserved as she was.

She wasn't being mysterious, only cautious.

Johnny couldn't possibly understand the truth. No one could.

"Now for the backstory," Jenn said, happy to change the subject. "You know I'm a social worker in Denver, and I know you're a wrangler in Wyoming. I have absolutely no idea how we could possibly—and plausibly—have met."

"That should be an interesting concoction," he said, reaching his arms up and lacing his long, leather-callused fingers behind his neck. "I've been wrangling cows with your brother for a month."

Jenn blew out a breath. "This is impossible," she stated, as she twisted her index finger through her golden curls. "How on earth would I have ever even met a *cowboy,* much less have started dating one?"

Johnny winced inwardly. The way she said *cowboy* said it all. She wasn't the type of woman, Johnny realized, who would be remotely interested in a down-home, backward *cowboy*.

Only, he wasn't a wrangler.

Far from it.

If she knew who he really was…

No. That would ruin everything.

"Well, I'm doubting you took a trip to Wyoming to hang out with us *cowboys,*" he said in a soft drawl, stressing the word with the same emphasis Jenn had given it.

She chuckled. "Hardly."

"Which means I must have come to Denver for some

reason." Johnny was starting to enjoy this, concocting this crazy story with her. A small wave of guilt passed through him—not the larger, more convicting stabs he'd had earlier, but more like the ones he'd had as a teenager, afraid he'd be caught sneaking out of his foster parents' house late at night.

He welcomed the adrenaline rush that accompanied the thought. "I don't have any family, so…"

"You were visiting friends," she prompted. "Mutual friends, between you and me, as it turned out. I have a dozen married friends my family knows are always trying to set me up. That wouldn't be so far-fetched."

"We met, were instantly attracted to one another, and have been calling and e-mailing and seeing each other whenever possible."

The *instantly attracted* part wasn't a lie, anyway— at least on his end, Johnny thought. Jenn was beautiful, with her golden curls bobbing about her face and her blue eyes blazing with delight as the two of them solidified their story.

What man wouldn't want to spend a little more time in her company, maybe get to know her better?

She frowned, pursing her lips together in the cutest way, like a toddler who'd been told *no*. "What about Scotty?" she asked with a tilt of her head that sent those curls afloat in the most enchanting way. Johnny was having trouble concentrating on her words.

"What *about* Scotty?" he asked belatedly.

"It seems an obvious enough problem to me. You guys have been together all month. How did our *relationship* slip past my brother? Wouldn't you have said something about it—about me?"

Johnny chuckled. "For someone who studied human

behavior, you sure don't know men very well. We don't talk a lot on the range, and when we do, it's not about our *relationships*. Besides, it appears to me he's taken to the ruse as much as anyone here. If he asks about it, we'll handle it. Trust me."

"I can't believe I—*we're* doing this," Jenn said. She sounded a bit hesitant, but Johnny saw the excitement brimming in her eyes.

She had her reasons for playing this out, and he definitely had his own. It was harmless enough playacting. No one would get hurt.

Besides, he was doing her a favor.

Wasn't he?

The fair damsel in distress, rescued by her knight in shining armor—or rather, in well-worn boots and a dusty old Stetson.

He stood and reached a hand to her. "Come on. Let's go out and face the dragon."

Chapter Three

Jenn didn't know what she expected, but obviously she'd come to the wrong conclusion about this cowboy. Dinner that evening, at the big dining room table, with her grandmother's best china and crystal, was enlightening in ways Jenn couldn't possibly have imagined.

One thing was for certain—Johnny Barnes cleaned up well. When he walked in for dinner, he was clean-shaven, dressed in a crisp red Western shirt with pearl snaps, and a fresh pair of blue jeans, held up by a belt fastened with the inevitable oversize buckle that proclaimed he'd won some rodeo event at some point in his past. He'd even scraped the mud off his boots for the occasion.

Jenn found she almost had to pull her jaw off the floor, she was surprised by how good he looked. If Johnny was handsome with a week's worth of sweat and dirt covering him, he was triply so now, and she couldn't take her eyes off him, which of course he immediately noticed, if his teasing wink was any indication.

Jenn wasn't the only woman in the room to notice

him. Auntie Myra, Granny and even, to Jenn's horror, her own mother began complimenting Johnny left and right, not even allowing him to get a word in edgewise.

"My, what a lovely shirt that is," crooned Auntie Myra, hooking an arm through the young cowboy's.

"Thank you, ma'am, I—" Johnny was immediately cut off by Granny.

"And just look at that extraordinary belt buckle. What were you, son? A bronc buster? A bull rider like our Scotty here?"

"A roper, but—"

"And look at that nice square jaw you were hiding under all that scruff," said her mother.

"Amanda," Jenn's father warned, but to no avail.

Johnny just quirked his lips and shrugged. "Yes, ma'am."

"His hat is still dirty," Jenn pointed out, knowing she was grousing but not caring.

Every eye turned upon her, and everyone but Johnny was frowning their displeasure at her comment.

Johnny, of course, was grinning as if she'd just paid him the highest compliment.

She ignored Johnny's smile and shrugged at the rest of her family. Her statement was true, wasn't it?

Why would the man bring his cowboy hat to the dinner table anyway? At least he had the good sense not to be wearing it indoors, which would have set Granny on him like a pit bull on a piece of fresh meat.

Oh, who was she kidding? Jenn sighed inwardly, giving herself a mental shake. She was born and raised on a Wyoming ranch. All ranch hands had their boots and hats permanently glued to them.

"You may hang your hat on that peg over there,"

Granny said, gesturing to a large pink and blue country pig plaque, with arms made for just that purpose. Scotty's cavalry hat was already hanging from one of the pegs.

After doing as Granny suggested, Johnny returned to the table and pulled out a chair. But instead of seating himself, he offered it to Jenn, and then fussed around her until he was sure she was comfortable.

Playing his part.

And Jenn couldn't have been more uncomfortable. Especially when he leaned down next to her ear and whispered, "I tried to brush my hat to get the grime off, darlin', but I think the thing has near seen its last days."

She didn't know whether it was his warm breath on the nape of her neck, his leathery cowboy scent or the small endearment, but whatever it was, it was nearly her undoing. She shifted uncomfortably in her seat. She wasn't used to being this near a man—any man—and this handsome stranger was far too charming for his own good.

Or hers.

His sitting down next to her didn't help one bit, never mind the cheeky grin and wink he gave her. She knew it was for her family's benefit, but it still made her uncomfortable.

Not for long, though. It was only moments before Johnny was chatting comfortably with her family, making everyone laugh with his silly jokes.

She sighed inwardly, wondering once again what she'd gotten herself into. She was going to be a cowboy's girlfriend for two solid weeks. Why, oh, why did the man's name have to be *Johnny?*

The family began passing the dishes around, the

cheerful babble of voices never ceasing as they piled their plates full of food. No one picked up a fork, however, not even Jenn's cowboy.

Granddad, seated at the head of the table, cleared his throat, and everyone became silent. With the quiet reverence Jenn remembered from her childhood, her grandfather folded his hands and bowed his head.

"Let us pray," he said, the usual cheerful gruffness for once gone from his voice, replaced by the humble reverence he offered the Almighty.

Jenn followed suit with the rest of her family, though she shot a quick sideways glance at Johnny. He, too, had his head bowed over clasped hands.

Why, Jenn wondered, did Granddad always wait until *after* the food was served to say grace? Her plate was steaming with fresh beef, a pile of mashed potatoes made from scratch, and green beans.

The aroma of the feast was tantalizing and far too delectable to pass up, and Granddad's prayers were often too long and windy, at least for Jenn.

"We thank you, Lord, for all the blessings of this day," her grandfather began. "For the food you have provided, and especially for bringing a guest into our midst. We ask you to be with us this night, and to bless our good fellowship together as a family. In Jesus' name we pray. Amen."

There was a hearty echo of *amens* following the prayer, and Jenn even heard Johnny's rich, deep voice in the chorus.

Jenn hoped Johnny didn't notice that she didn't join in. None of the rest of the family had, to her knowledge, ever noticed, thankfully, not in all the years since high school. Or if they did, they never commented on her lack of enthusiasm for anything related to praising and worshipping God.

It was one of the moments Jenn hated most about these reunions—the constant stream of prayers to a Heavenly Father she had long since stopped believing in. God was a myth, like Santa Claus. She'd gotten over it a long time ago, except here, in the midst of her family, where faith in God was all too real.

And too painful.

Granddad reached for his fork and havoc set in for the next few minutes as everyone sampled the feast and delighted Granny with their praises over her excellent cooking.

Almost everyone had contributed something to the meal. Even Jenn, who never cooked anything in the city, far preferring take-out to a mess in the kitchen, had been coaxed into snapping fresh green beans.

And boy, was she glad of it now. The thing she missed most about her childhood home, other than the family members themselves, was Granny's mouthwatering home-style cooking. These were two weeks she didn't care if the gravy on the mashed potatoes was clogging her arteries. The delicious meal was just too good to pass up.

It wasn't long, though, before the family started chatting, and inevitably, the topic turned rather quickly to Jenn's relationship with Johnny.

Jenn had thought Auntie Myra would lead the way into that territory, but it was Scotty who spoke up first.

"Now I know your secret, buddy," Scotty said with an enthusiastic grin in Johnny's direction.

Johnny wiped his mouth with the edge of his napkin before replying. "Oh, and what secret would that be?"

Scotty chortled loudly. "Why you were off hugging that laptop of yours every time we hit the bunkhouse. You hinted that it might be a girlfriend, but I had no idea it was my own sister."

Johnny shrugged a shoulder, a forkful of beef hanging midair. "You caught me. I was trying to get to know this pretty young lady better. Tough to do when we're riding the range."

"My sister," Scotty said, sounding amazed. "And I never guessed it."

Johnny winked at Jenn.

"How *did* you two meet?" This time it *was* Auntie Myra doing the questioning, or rather, Jenn thought with amusement, the interrogation.

Jenn thought Johnny would field the question as he had the others, but he nudged her with his knee under the table. Apparently he thought it was her turn to do the talking.

Jenn smiled sweetly at Johnny but nudged him back. Hard.

"We met through mutual friends," she explained. "Really, it all started as a joke."

"A joke?" Johnny queried. Jenn nudged him again with her knee. *He* wasn't supposed to be asking any questions here.

"Well, yes, of course." She looked deeply into Johnny's eyes, sending him a silent warning to shut up and go along with her. "Mark and Julie were always nagging me, wanting to set me up with one of their friends or another. I don't know why young married couples always think they need to share the wealth. Mark and Julie are happily married, so they assume I need to be, as well."

"Hear, hear," called Granny, holding her glass of iced

tea in the air in a mock toast and making everyone at the table burst out in laughter.

"In any case, I finally gave in to their pressure and said I would meet one of their friends, on the condition that it be at their house, with them present."

Johnny jumped in at that point. "I didn't know anything about it," he said, lifting his right palm out as if taking an oath.

Jenn's eyes blazed intensely at Johnny before she forced a sickeningly sweet smile to her lips for his benefit more than that of her family. She wasn't going to let him fluster her—not when so much was at stake.

"I arrived early," Jenn broke in. "I think Mark and Julie planned it that way. So there I was, sitting on the sofa with Julie, when this man came in."

Everyone's eyes were riveted on hers.

Even Johnny's.

And, as unusual as it was, not a single family member was speaking. Jenn started to enjoy spinning this yarn, though she still felt a little guilty for misleading everyone.

"I took one look at him and panicked. I thought my friends had gone completely crazy."

"Because he was a cowboy?" Granny asked.

"Oh, no," she said with a cheeky grin. "It was because he was short, bald, wore little round spectacles which looked like they'd come from the last century, and spoke with the highest-pitched, squeakiest voice I've ever heard in my life."

The laughter in the room was deafening.

"Who was he?" Johnny asked curiously, then cleared his throat and continued, "I haven't heard this part of the story before."

Jenn chuckled, ostensibly about the story, but actually because of Johnny's very truthful comment. Of course he hadn't heard the story. He couldn't have, since she was making it up on the spot.

"The bald man turned out to be a neighbor, just dropping in to say hi and return something he'd borrowed, I think." She beamed at Johnny for her family's benefit. "I cannot tell you how relieved I was to hear another knock at the door and see this tall, good-looking cowboy strutting in as if he owned the world."

Johnny ruffled his fingers through his thick, dark, curly locks. "Wow," he exclaimed. "I cannot say how truly thankful I am at this moment for this full head of hair of mine."

If the story were true, Jenn thought, it might even have happened that way, Johnny being a cowboy or not. He was incredibly handsome in his nice, clean Western clothes, though she did wonder momentarily what he might look like in a business suit, his curls tamed with a palm full of hair gel.

But, no. That wouldn't be Johnny; and at the moment, Jenn wasn't sure she'd change him if she could. He was as wild and free as the Wyoming range, and he most definitely looked that way.

Oddly, Jenn found she couldn't complain.

She realized she'd abruptly dropped her story with her daydreaming when Johnny picked it up.

"I don't know for sure how it was for Jenn that night," he said, smiling softly down at her, "but for me, at least, the moment our eyes met, I knew beyond the shadow of a doubt that I was a goner."

Her gaze met Johnny's at that moment, as if their story had been true. His midnight-blue eyes were shimmering with amusement and just a touch of something else Jenn couldn't quite identify. Then his mouth did that cute little twist and Jenn thought, if the circumstances she'd concocted were true, *she* might have been a goner, as well.

Even with her past. Even with her secrets.

Johnny was getting to her somehow, and she took a mental step backward, bolstering the defenses she'd relied on all her life.

She didn't want to go there—to the past. And she wasn't about to let Johnny, with his good looks and charming ways, take her there.

Johnny wondered why Jenn's smile had turned so quickly to a frown, and he redoubled his efforts to make the light come back into her eyes.

That she had been hurt in the past, by someone or some circumstance, was a given. She was all bottled up inside. He could see it through her eyes even now, though her gaze had become distant.

The clatter of a fork against a fine china plate interrupted his thoughts. "Love at first sight," exclaimed Auntie Myra. "It's so romantic. Was it that way for you, too, Jenn?"

"Myra," Granny snapped, "don't push the young people. It's their story. Let them say what they want to say."

"Indeed," Jenn's mother agreed. "By all means, go on. We're all anxious to hear the rest of the tale."

Even Jenn's father and grandfather nodded at that statement.

Jenn went from dark to light in a split second, startling Johnny more than he realized. Did lying come so easy to her? She definitely had a knack for storytelling, and she was a phenomenal actress, for her eyes now held warmth toward him.

It almost felt like love, not that he had any experience in that area. He'd never found a woman who instigated the bevy of emotions coursing through him. Whatever he was feeling, it disconcerted him until he could hardly think.

"Just like the love songs paint it, I'm afraid," Jenn admitted with a wink. "Take a look at him," she said, smiling up at him and brushing a stray lock of hair off his forehead with the tips of her fingers. "Who could resist him?"

Johnny swallowed hard. The simple touch of her fingers running through his hair made his heart jump into his chest, thudding so rapidly he thought everyone at the table might hear it.

Jenn *was* a beautiful woman. What man wouldn't be attracted to those bouncy golden curls and bright blue eyes so full of life and intelligence?

But he was getting off-track, and fast.

He reminded himself mentally that her actions were for her family. Part of the ruse and nothing more. Her touch had seemed somehow intimate, yet he knew it was all for show.

It meant nothing. So why did he feel like it did?

"Our dinner together was a bit awkward, with us gawking at each other across the table," Jenn said, punctuating her sentence with a laugh that, at least to Johnny's ears, sounded forced. "I think Mark must have kicked Johnny underneath the table a couple of times to keep the conversation flowing."

Johnny winced visibly, then gave a rueful grin.

"He walked me to my car afterwards," Jenn said, as

Johnny slid his arm around the back of her chair. "Talk about cliché."

"He snuck a kiss!" Auntie Myra exclaimed, slamming both her palms down on the table in her excitement, making the silverware and glasses nearest to her dance. "How incredibly romantic!"

"He did no such thing," Jenn protested, with a shake of her head.

Johnny winked at her, but he couldn't help that a tiny bit of his male pride was bruised by her harsh statement. Due to the fast pace of his career and nonstop working obligations, he hadn't dated much in the past few years, but did she really believe kissing him would be so terrible?

"He remarked on how pretty the stars were that evening, and then he asked if he could call me sometime."

"Well, ya obviously gave him your number, didn't ya?" teased Scotty.

Jenn scowled at her younger brother. "I didn't have to," she stated bluntly. "He'd already gotten it from Mark and Julie on the sly."

Granny snickered behind her hand. "Quick thinking, young man."

"Of course, Johnny was busy," Jenn continued. "We spoke on the phone a few times—when *he* called, that is—the man never did give me his telephone number, no matter how many times I nagged him about it. Mostly we've gotten to know each other through e-mail."

The statement shook Johnny like an earthquake. The way she described their meeting—that's exactly how it would have happened, *if* it had happened, for he certainly couldn't have given her his telephone number for where he *really* lived.

Unless he told her the truth about his identity. Unless she knew who he really was.

Maybe if things had been different…

He shook his head mentally. This was nothing but a charade. He needed to get his head back on his shoulders, and right quickly.

Auntie Myra held her hands to her cheeks. "This is so romantic. I think I may faint."

"Oh, knock it off with the dramatics already, Myra," Granny snipped.

His supper finished, Jenn's grandfather pushed back his chair and stood. "Seems to me," he said with a slow drawl, "that given the circumstances, we ought to be giving these two youngsters some alone time."

Jenn's eyes widened. Johnny quickly slipped his arm from the back of the chair to her shoulders, where he gave her a reassuring squeeze. He was certainly aware she hadn't concocted this story in order to spend time with him—alone. She'd made that perfectly clear.

"I think that's a fine idea, don't you, darlin'?" Johnny asked softly. "Maybe Jenn and I could take a walk. It's a nice night out, now that the temperature has dropped some. She could show me around the ranch a bit, help me get my bearings."

"Sure," Jenn agreed, sounding, at least to Johnny's ears, quite reluctant. Then she chuckled, surprising him with her sudden change in spirit. "Maybe Johnny can comment on the stars again."

That got the family laughing.

"Just be sure and get *his* telephone number this time," Scotty teased. "'Course, there ain't no cell phone service out on the range."

Jenn shrugged. "So I'll get his house number. He has to go home sometime."

Johnny cringed inwardly until his gut was in knots. The last thing he wanted to think about was going home. He rose to his feet and offered Jenn his hand. "Let's go see those stars."

Jenn took his hand, but dropped it the moment she was standing. She strode to the door, not even looking back to see if Johnny was following.

Johnny barely made it out the door after Jenn before he threw back his head and laughed heartily. "Darlin', you really know how to spin a story."

Jenn scowled and turned away from him, wrapping her arms around her, both for warmth and the sense of protection it offered. "Do you know what I just did?" she ground out from between clenched teeth.

"No. What?"

Jenn turned to him, her chest squeezing so tight she thought she might suffocate. "I just lied to my family."

Johnny frowned. "Yes, *we* both did."

Jenn shook her head. "It bothers me. I know I started it with that whole sending-myself-flowers thing, but I never dreamed I would end up creating an entire back-story to go along with the flowers. I feel so awful about deceiving everyone. They asked, and the words just flew out of my mouth before I could think about them."

"I understand," Johnny said softly. "You were under a lot of pressure there."

"But I shouldn't have made up a story. I should have told them the truth."

"Yes," Johnny agreed. "The truth is always best. But even without words, we've been lying to your family since the moment I walked in the door."

Jenn clutched at her chest, which was still spasming so erratically she couldn't take a proper breath. "What did I just do to the two of us?"

Johnny shrugged and shook his head but didn't offer any kind of answer, not that Jenn really expected him to. It was right there in front of them both, whether spoken or unspoken.

"I've buried us, that's what," Jenn said with another scowl.

Johnny blew out a breath. He hadn't been prepared for the way Jenn's family had questioned them over dinner, though he realized now he should have been. Jenn's family was boisterous and openly curious. They were bound to ask questions about his and Jenn's relationship.

Johnny hadn't been ready at all, and Jenn had simply panicked and spun a quick yarn to ease them out of a tense situation. He certainly couldn't lay the blame at her feet. He didn't want to. It was at least as much his fault as it was hers.

But no matter how he cut it, what they'd done was still lying, wasn't it? What did it matter who said the actual words?

Guilt weighed heavily on Johnny, as it obviously did on Jenn. He wasn't sure *what* the right thing to do was at this point. If they went and told the truth, *he'd* have to tell the truth about who he was.

He wasn't ready to do that. Not for him, and definitely not for Jenn's sake. He knew he was being stubborn and bullheaded, but he also knew, without asking, that Jenn was purposefully shielding herself from something, and hiding it from her family.

The problem was, he couldn't straight-out ask Jenn

what was wrong. He wanted to support her, he just wasn't sure how. She'd made the rules, after all.

"I don't know what to do now," Jenn admitted in a coarse, conspiratorial whisper.

Instinctively, Johnny put his arm around her shoulder. Surprisingly, she didn't shrug him off. "I don't know, either, Jenn. Maybe we should pray together about it, seek God's wisdom on how to straighten this mess out."

She turned sharply and slipped out of his grip, moving to face him. "Can we just take a walk?" she suggested instead.

Johnny didn't miss the way she changed the subject, any more than he'd missed the way Jenn hadn't been praying at the table tonight.

Yet they'd talked about their faith in God, hadn't they? She'd asked if he was a Christian right off the bat, and he knew how much her family valued their faith.

But what had she said in response? Had she mentioned her own faith? Johnny racked his brain for the answer but couldn't seem to remember. He'd been distracted then by Jenn's presence, just as he was distracted now. The woman made his senses all topsy-turvy.

"Where are we going?" he asked, as she turned and started trekking toward a meadow.

"Just out—under the stars, like we supposedly did before," she said gruffly. "There isn't much to show you that you haven't already seen a million times. You've seen one Wyoming ranch and you've seen them all," she joked dryly.

Finally she stopped walking. They were in the middle of a meadow, with dry, waving grass in every direction. "Well, here they are, Johnny."

"What?" he asked, momentarily confused by her train of thought.

"All the stars, in country-evening Technicolor. I knew you'd want to see them. Again." She laughed at her own joke, but it sounded forced.

"It was a great story," Johnny said, catching up with her and grabbing her elbow to turn her toward him. "Maybe it could have been that way. I mean, if we'd met like you said."

Jenn looked at him for a long, silent moment before answering.

"Yes," she said at last, nodding her head ever so slightly. "Maybe it could."

Chapter Four

Morning came, and with it the dreaded announcement that this was picnic day, a yearly ritual that filled Jenn's heart with immense trepidation. Swimming was the main attraction, something Jenn dreaded in the worst way. At least she was spending quality time with her family.

And Johnny.

She couldn't get the cowboy off her mind, no matter how hard she tried. She was treading on dangerous territory and she knew it.

This morning he was wearing black jeans and a maroon snap-down Western shirt rolled up at the sleeves. With his boots and hat, of course. What cowboy would be seen without them?

Hardly picnic-by-the-lake attire, Jenn thought with an inward smile, but no doubt Johnny would change into something more appropriate as soon as he heard the family's plans for the day.

Jenn, on the other hand, would be sweltering in her clothes—jeans and a long-sleeved Western shirt she kept snapped at the wrists. And unlike Johnny, she wasn't going to change her outfit, however desperately she wanted to. It was simply out of the question.

End of subject.

His well-used hat was at his side, but it looked like he'd made an attempt, anyway, to dust off his boots.

And his smile was just for her as he pulled out her chair, then went to claim her a cup of coffee from the counter. He was so polite and incredibly dashing. She hadn't been this attracted to a man since—well, she'd never been this attracted to a man before. In fact, she'd gone out of her way to avoid feelings like these.

"One sugar, right?" he asked solicitously. "My darlin', the sweet tooth."

Her breath caught in her throat at his gentle endearment. She didn't *want* to like Johnny. She still couldn't see why she was attracted to him, yet the enticement was definitely there.

But why?

Johnny was everything she didn't want in a man. Cowboys were too attached to their horses and their freedom to give their lifestyles up for the boxed-in atmosphere of school.

And Johnny was the epitome of everything wrangler, from his hat to his spurs. He was rough-cut and rugged. He carried a day's growth of beard on his chin, not clean-cut and clean-shaven as she preferred, or at least she'd *thought* she preferred, until she'd met Johnny. He wore a cowboy's jeans, faded T-shirts under worn Western shirts and dusty boots. She'd always preferred seeing men in crisp business suits and ties.

But that wasn't the point at all, was it?

What was she thinking?

So what if he appeared to be well read and up on

current events, and able to playfully banter with her family as if he'd been there all his life. So what if her heart lit up like a candle every time he smiled at her?

The fact was, Jenn didn't want a man.

Any man.

She shuddered as the thoughts and memories she'd kept buried deep within threatened to burst out and overwhelm her once again. She felt a moment of panic, before—with all her will—she crammed those memories back where they belonged, out of sight and out of mind.

She was a woman now—a strong woman, not the foolish girl who'd once let her romantic notions lead her into the worst kind of trauma.

She wouldn't go there, not even for a moment. But it was a sharp, painful reminder to keep her distance from Johnny, both physically and emotionally.

A reminder she clearly needed. Johnny had her head and heart all out of whack. She needed to keep her distance, or she was going to be in even more trouble than she already found herself.

She placed her head in her hand and groaned. How had her life become so complicated? In Denver, she was a respected social worker. She threw herself into her work so she didn't have to think about things like this, didn't have to expose herself to the danger of really feeling anything for anyone.

Out here in the country, there was too much time to think. She rubbed her temples with the tips of her fingers.

She almost wished there *was* a God, that she could find it in her heart to believe in a Higher Power with more control over her life than she had herself—which amounted to zero. Despite her best efforts to the contrary, her life was a roller-coaster ride, and she couldn't get off even if she wanted to.

The worst part of it was, she wasn't even sure she wanted to get off. What kind of convoluted nonsense was that?

Maybe God could sort things out, if she believed. It would definitely be simpler if she were a believer, in this household where faith in God was as natural as breathing to most of its occupants.

As natural as breathing. Except to her.

Johnny slipped into the chair beside her, with his own steaming mug of coffee. He grinned at her extended family milling all around the kitchen. "So, what's on the agenda for today?" he asked.

"A picnic," Scotty said, sitting down opposite Johnny and Jenn. "We have one every year, out by the lake. It's one of the highlights of the reunion. You'll love it."

Johnny raised an eyebrow. "Speedboats and jet-skiing in Wyoming?"

Granny chuckled. "It ain't that kind of lake, son. More a grand puddle of mud most of the time, but good enough to splash in and cool off in the hot July sun. And what we lack in water, we make up for in food."

"Granny, you know the way to a man's heart, now, don't you?" Johnny asked, patting his fit stomach for emphasis. "You'd have caught me hook, line and sinker with that delicious cooking of yours…that is, if my heart wasn't already stolen by this young lady here." He tipped his head at Jenn.

Granny blushed. She actually blushed!

"You can stop with the flattery already, young man," Granny teasingly scolded. "All that is going to get you is a big bellyache from me forcing more food down your gullet."

"Oh, there won't be any force necessary," Johnny assured the elderly woman.

Jenn cringed, not so much from Johnny's words as the reminder of the picnic. As much as she loved Granny's cooking, Jenn would much rather partake of the delicious meal at the comfort of the dining room table. Jenn adjusted her shirt over her jeans and composed herself.

There were too many lies, too much deception. But she'd done it before—for years—and this time would be no different.

Except for Johnny. The cowboy presented her with a whole new set of difficulties.

A whole new set of *lies*.

She had her reasons. She'd simply do what she'd always done—sit in the shade of a tall cottonwood tree and pretend she was relaxing. That she didn't want to swim.

And hope Johnny would buy her story. For some reason, she was more worried about being found out by this relative stranger than she was by her very own family.

It wasn't long before they were on their way to the picnic grounds. All of them were on foot, as the lake was less than a mile's hike. Even to Jenn, who was in a decidedly bad mood, the day was lovely: not a cloud in the sky, and a refreshing breeze coming in from the west. Wyoming was, she had to admit, beautiful country. She wondered why she had hated it so very much when she was a teenager.

She had wanted only to leave. Now, older and more mature, she saw what she had missed when she was younger, the peace the rest of her family so loved and cherished.

Jenn sighed and wiped off a trickle of sweat that was drizzling down from the nape of her neck and down her back. Everyone was dressed to swim. Even Granny was geared up in a frilly one-piece bathing suit and matching umbrella to keep off the sun.

Jenn was out-and-out jealous. She tried to direct her thoughts to more pleasant subjects and not on how uncomfortable she was in her warm clothing.

Lost in her own thoughts, Jenn lagged behind, and Johnny, toting the largest and heaviest of the picnic baskets—at his own insistence—slowed his pace to match hers.

Something was wrong with Jenn today, but Johnny couldn't quite put his finger on the problem. The one observation he could make with any surety was that Jenn was the only one in her family not dressed for a good, fun-filled splash in the lake.

She was going to swelter in the heat, he thought; but then again, he might be accused of that, as well. He'd not changed his clothes, but rather wore his swimming trunks underneath his jeans.

Johnny at least had a good excuse for dressing as he did. Since he only had cowboy boots with him, he knew he'd look like a laugh-out-loud dork, walking around in his swimming trunks and a pair of cowboy boots.

Johnny chuckled just thinking about it, and Jenn looked up at him, questioning him with her gaze.

Johnny shrugged. "I was just thinking how hot I am," he explained.

Jenn sighed loudly. "You and me both," she agreed,

running the back of her hand against her glistening forehead. "It must be at least ninety degrees out here in the shade."

"I would have worn my swimming trunks, except that I don't have any shoes except my boots here. Can you imagine?"

Johnny smiled when his comment brought a tiny but genuine laugh from Jenn.

"You could have asked Scotty. I'm sure he has an extra pair of sneakers lying around someplace."

Johnny glanced down at his boot-clad feet. "I would have, except my feet are about three sizes larger than Scotty's. I'd never even get my toes into a pair of his shoes."

Jenn's glance fell to his boots, as if considering what he said. "Yes, you're probably right. Scotty always had small feet, even when he was little."

"Is that a nice way of not telling me I have huge feet?" he joked.

"Not at all," she said immediately. "I'd never say something like that."

"You'd think it, though," he teased.

She grinned and shrugged. "Maybe."

"You, on the other hand, had the good sense to wear a comfortable pair of flip-flops." *That was something, anyway,* Johnny thought, though he didn't voice his observation aloud.

So why the rest of her getup, he wondered? It didn't make any sense. Shorts and a T-shirt would have been way more comfortable.

Jenn didn't offer an explanation, though she already looked hot and tired, and the smile she gave him faltered on her lips.

He smiled back but didn't break the silence with questions, no matter how curious he was. She'd asked for privacy in her personal life, and he supposed that included what she decided to wear to a family picnic. He would respect her wishes. If she wanted to tell him anything, she would.

Still, she looked miserable, so he took her hand with his free one and linked her fingers with his. He knew he was taking an enormous chance with that action, with all that *public display of affection* stuff she had spouted at him the first day, but he wanted her to know he was there for her if she needed him.

Besides, it wasn't like he didn't notice her family's transparently obvious glances back at the two of them, no doubt perceiving them as a young couple in love. Surely, they expected to see some sort of friendliness between the two of them.

To Johnny's surprise, Jenn didn't pull away, and they walked quietly, their hands linked, for several enjoyable minutes, until they hiked over the top of a low incline and Johnny spied the lake. While it wasn't waterskiing material, it was larger than he had imagined it would be, and was the deep, dark blue of western water. He couldn't wait to take a cool dip. He was roasting alive in his shirt and jeans.

"Let's set our picnic blanket up there, under the cottonwood trees," Jenn suggested, pointing to the trees and glancing up at him with a forced smile.

Johnny noted that the spot she'd chosen was some distance from where her family was setting up for their picnic, but he followed silently when Jenn tugged on his hand, leading him away from the family, whose company he so enjoyed.

Still, it made sense, he supposed, that the two of them, he and Jenn, would choose a spot with a little bit of privacy, after all. If there was a real relationship between them, that's what Johnny would have wanted to do, he realized. And the thought of spending more time getting to know Jenn wasn't so bad, either.

"They're going to need this," Johnny said, lofting the large wicker basket onto his shoulder. "I think most of the food is in here. They're going to come after us and toss us in the lake if we keep all Granny's awesome cooking to ourselves."

He heard Jenn's soft laughter as he strode down the hill and placed his basket with the others. Everyone was milling about and chattering and laughing as they prepared blankets and set up Granny's umbrella, which would look more at home on a sandy California beach than on Wyoming's rough terrain.

He grabbed a couple of gigantic roast beef sandwiches, loaded with all kinds of extras, from fresh purple onions to ripe tomatoes, two apples and a couple of sodas, then tucked them in his shirt and strode back up the hill to Jenn. She was in the midst of spreading a red plaid blanket across the ground.

Aching for relief from the burning sunshine, Johnny dumped his culinary treasures onto the blanket in a heap and reached for the front of his shirt, popping all the snaps at once with one good, hard yank.

He had a black T-shirt underneath his Western shirt, but Jenn's shocked expression made him feel he'd done something completely inappropriate.

He'd never figure out a woman's mind and moods if he lived to be two hundred years old. He shook his head at her, and then shed the long-sleeved shirt entirely.

"Why did you dump our food like that?" she asked in an accusatory tone.

He raised a brow at her. "Because I'm frying in this sunshine and I want to get out of this hot shirt and jeans. Don't you think you should do the same? Half your family is already splashing at the water's edge."

"You shook up the pop cans when you threw them that way. We won't be able to open them for an hour now."

Johnny met her gaze but was unable to read her thoughts. She'd completely ignored his suggestion and continued harping on one silly action he'd made.

Maybe this was why he'd avoided having a girlfriend. A woman could make a guy go crazy.

Hoping to distract her from the shaken soda and whatever else was bothering her, Johnny hopped around on one foot, trying to remove one of his cowboy boots, thinking his antics might amuse Jenn.

Her look hadn't changed. She was still scowling, her arms wrapped about herself as if she were trying to fend off the cold. *In this heat?*

Suddenly, in one fluid movement, she stood from where she had seated herself on the blanket. Wide-eyed, Jenn backed away from him. She looked disoriented, like she wasn't quite seeing what was really before her, but some kind of nightmare behind the shadow of her eyes.

Johnny opened his arms in a gesture of friendship but she didn't seem to notice. When he stepped forward, she backed up. One step, then another, until Jenn was backed against the firm, thick trunk of the cottonwood tree shading them from the heat.

"What are you doing?" she asked, her voice cracking with strain. Johnny knew it was obvious, and he'd already said as much. He was just following the lead of the rest of her family, and getting ready to splash in the cool comfort of the lake.

But for some reason, he realized suddenly, his actions had been taken wrong. And it wasn't him dumping their lunch into an unglorified heap on the picnic blanket, either.

Jenn looked like a little filly ready to bolt, and he knew if he didn't somehow save this situation now, it was going to get out of control in a hurry. He might never win back the peaceful coexistence he and Jenn had formed on the walk over to the picnic site, and that bothered him more than he cared to admit.

He had to act now.

Johnny stepped forward slowly, closing the gap between them. "I was just getting comfortable," he explained gently, though he'd already voiced the words once. Somehow, he knew he needed to say them again in order for her to really hear them. "Jenn, I don't understand. Why aren't you doing the same?"

Jenn shook her head vehemently. "I don't, uh— swim," she said with a quiver in her voice.

Everything inside Johnny made him want to reach for her to give her a reassuring hug, but he sensed she'd balk. It was in her eyes. Instead, meeting her gaze squarely, and moving with infinite care, he placed his hand on the tree, just over her head, ignoring the roughness of the bark cutting into his palm.

He'd just backed her into a corner, figuratively speaking, and they both knew it; but he'd also given her a chance to retreat if she wanted to, to duck under his arm and run away from him and whatever it was that was bothering her so.

Johnny was surprised and relieved when she didn't budge, though her fingers clutched at the tree behind her, as if for support. She was looking everywhere except at him. The sky, the ground, his boots.

Just not his eyes.

With his free hand, he tipped her chin so she had no choice but to meet his gaze. "Don't be frightened," he said, the words tumbling out of his mouth before he could stop them.

Her blue eyes blazed with indignation. "I am *not* frightened," she ground out, brushing away his hand from her cheek.

There was a long, silent pause as they just looked at one another, sizing each other up. Johnny was just trying to figure out what she was thinking, how she was feeling.

Something had set her off, and he still had no idea what it was.

"I would never hurt you," he continued, knowing the words needed to be said, even if she didn't want to hear them.

There was another long pause as Jenn stared into his eyes, measuring the strength of his words. Johnny didn't move a muscle, didn't even breathe. Surely, she could see the truth in his eyes.

Then, as quick as it came, the moment passed. Jenn reached up and tipped his cowboy hat over his eyes. "You going to go swimming in that thing?" she asked a little too brightly. "One boot off and one boot on, Deedle Deedle Dumpling..." she teased, and then swiftly ducked out from beneath his arm.

Jenn sat down on the far edge of the blanket and picked up an apple, gnawing in small bites, as if to give her something to do with her hands.

Her chest was rising and falling with rapid breaths. Johnny had promised not to pry into her personal affairs, and he hadn't. Not really. But he could tell he'd shaken her up with his gentle words—words that hit far too close to home, even for him.

Chapter Five

Johnny would never hurt her.

How she knew that, how she could possibly hope to believe it, was beyond her comprehension. Hadn't she learned anything from her past experiences?

Hadn't she heard those words before?

Yet her gut instinct told her this was different. Johnny was a different sort of man than those she'd encountered in the past.

But could she really trust him? Did she dare?

Johnny flipped his hat off his head and tapped it against his thigh with a laugh. "Guess I look pretty ridiculous at the moment, don't I?" he drawled. "One boot on, one off, like you said?"

Not ridiculous, Jenn thought. *Not even limping around in one boot and one sock. Outrageously handsome, perhaps.* Incredibly charming with that easy smile of his, for sure. But she wasn't about to say *those* thoughts out loud, not in this lifetime, so she merely chuckled.

Johnny stretched himself full-length on the blanket, murmuring something between a groan and a sigh. He picked up one of the sandwiches and unwrapped it, then took a large bite.

"Incredible," he said, still chewing. "I never knew a roast-beef sandwich could taste so good."

Jenn nodded, her face solemn, but smiling inside in a way she'd never felt before. "It's the ambience."

Johnny threw back his head and let out a peal of genuine laughter, a trait that did strange things to her insides. "Did anyone ever tell you that you have a way with words, Jenn?"

"Mmph," she answered. "More than once. Maybe a few times too many."

He laughed again—hearty, free and sincere. It showed in his eyes as much as on his lips.

Jenn glanced down at the lake. Apparently, either her family was finished eating or they'd opted to forego food in favor of the cool water. Everyone, even her grandparents, were splashing around in the shallow lake and laughing raucously, enough for it to be heard all the way up the hill to where she and Johnny sat.

She slid a glance at Johnny, who was also watching her family's antics, the little quirk of amusement on his lips twitching more than once. He appeared to be genuinely enjoying himself as he munched on his sandwich and watched the lake below.

"Don't feel obligated on my account," Jenn said immediately, gesturing to the lake. Johnny hadn't even bothered to finish stripping down to his swimming trunks. He still had one boot on and one off, his legs stretched out on the blanket, one ankle crossed over the other. "Go get yourself cooled off in the lake," Jenn urged. "The water will do you good, and I can see you want to go."

He looked at her for a long moment, then stretched and stood. But instead of divesting himself of his remaining clothing and racing down the hill to the water's edge, Johnny reached for his maroon-colored shirt, slipping it around his shoulders but not buttoning it.

"What are you doing now?" she asked, puzzled, as he hopped around, replacing his other boot on his foot with an exaggerated lack of grace.

He winked at her and slung his hat back on his head, tipping it at her for emphasis. "Swimming is not really my style, anyway," he stated with a negligent brush of his hand. "I'd rather be on a horse."

Jenn's eyes widened in surprise. She could see right through him. There was no doubt in her mind that he was making his decision based on her needs, to make her feel more comfortable at his own expense—and it wasn't any small sacrifice he was making for her. It was way too hot for jeans and long sleeves, as well she knew.

"Johnny, you really don't have to do this," she insisted.

He just shook his head and resumed his stretched-out position on the blanket, hat and all. "Aw, don't worry about it," he drawled softly. "I don't feel fully dressed without my boots and hat, anyhow."

She couldn't tell him how much she appreciated his kind gesture. Full of emotion, her heart welled into her throat and she was certain she couldn't speak, to thank him for his kindness.

Anyway, what would she say? She had no reasonable explanation for her own behavior—at least no explanation she cared to share.

Ever.

So she said nothing, and he appeared to be okay with that.

Johnny and Jenn spent a pleasant few minutes in silence, simply watching her family playing in the water, shouting and laughing. It was odd how comfortable she felt with Johnny, Jenn thought. She could just sit here in silence without feeling the need to speak, and without feeling awkward and needing to fill the void with words.

It was…*peaceful*. Jenn wasn't sure she'd ever felt that way before. She smiled at him and he smiled back, giving her a friendly wink Jenn interpreted as his way of telling her he felt the same way.

Johnny didn't mind sitting quietly with Jenn. Ostensibly, he was caught up in the action below at the lake, but every so often he glanced at the beautiful woman at his side. He couldn't help himself.

What made her tick? Why was she vacillating between hot and cold, like a faucet?

Eventually he broke the silence. While Johnny enjoyed the serenity between them, he wanted to get to know Jenn better, and that required speaking. She was supposed to be his girlfriend, after all. The more he knew about her, the better—for the sake of the charade, of course.

"Tell me about your work," he said, intentionally breaking one of her rules, but hoping she trusted him enough to let it go.

She glanced at him, obviously weighing her options in her mind before she spoke.

At length, she sighed. "I work in the foster care system," she said softly. "There are so many needy children out there. I guess you already know that, with your past and all. I don't mean to remind you of anything you'd rather forget. It's just that it frustrates me sometimes that I am able help so few kids when there are so many out there."

"Every child matters, Jenn," Johnny said. "You make a real difference in the world. That's more than I can say for the work I do."

Jenn laughed, her tone bitter. "Most days, I only see the bad. It's agonizing and frustrating, but every so often something wonderful happens and makes all the terrible stuff worth it."

"Do you have anyone back in Denver to share your triumphs and disappointments with?"

Jenn shook her head. "So much of what I do as a social worker is private. Most of the time, I can't talk about my work at all, and even when I can, it's hard for me to put into words what I'm doing, and how I'm feeling. I think that's probably a lot of the reason I don't have many close friends, though I do have a few colleagues I spend time with. Not that I have much time. My work schedule doesn't make for much of a social life."

She paused thoughtfully. "It's tough on relationships—with other women or with men. I can't seem to create an emotional bond."

"Other social workers find meaningful, fulfilling relationships outside their jobs," Johnny pointed out gently.

Jenn nodded. "True."

"But not you."

"But not me, what?"

She was avoiding the question and they both knew

it, so Johnny didn't push her or try to explain himself. He just waited.

After a while, Jenn blew out a breath. "Yes. You're right. Other people are successful with relationships and I'm not. I just can't seem to connect. It doesn't happen for me. Maybe I've got faulty wiring. I really don't know."

"Give yourself some credit, Jenn," Johnny said softly. "You're special. Anyone who has been around you for more than five minutes knows that. But you're lonely." It was a statement, not a question.

"Oh, no," she protested immediately, with a firm shake of her head. "Not lonely. *Alone.* And it was my choice to make, Johnny. Now, can we drop the subject and move on? I'd ask you what you do for a living, and for fun, I imagine, but I already know you play with cows all day."

Johnny internally winced at her weak attempt at a joke. It hit way too close to home. Wrangling cattle *was* fun for him, but it sure as shootin' wasn't his real job. He didn't want to be thinking about that right now.

Besides, his heart went out to her, feeling her pain as if it were his own. He felt an inexplicable need to help her, to rescue her, though he didn't have any notion as to why he felt that way, or what it was she was trying so desperately to avoid.

When she said the word *alone,* he knew she meant it. He'd watched her at dinner last night as they all politely bowed their heads for grace. Jenn had been the only one who hadn't joined in prayer.

Her whole family appeared to be fervent believers. They thanked God for every good blessing. There was a beautiful wooden cross in the living room over the stone fireplace, and prayer plaques spread on walls throughout the house, even in his own bedroom.

But Johnny deeply sensed there was something different with Jenn, something missing, and he thought he might know what—Who—it was.

He was fishing around for a way to ask her about her walk with the Lord, without it coming off as condescending, when there came sudden shouting from the bottom of the hill. Everyone was crowded around the lake, and Scotty was squarely in the middle. He was waving his hand in the air and then submerging under the water.

The calls from shore sounded to Johnny like those of distress.

He didn't give it a moment's thought. He sprinted down the hill as fast as his legs would pump, taking only a moment to toss his hat on the shoreline before diving into the water.

Jenn stood, mouth agape. What was the crazy cowboy doing? He'd plunged into the water, boots and all, yet was swimming with strong, even strokes toward Scotty.

Didn't Johnny know Scotty was just fooling around? Obviously not.

Jenn skittered down the hill, reaching the bank just as Johnny reached Scotty's side.

"It's okay, you're safe" she heard Johnny call out. Johnny was trying to flip Scotty into a supportive position, to swim them both to shore, but Scotty was fighting tooth and nail to get away from him.

"Just relax and go easy," Johnny coaxed. "I can't help you if you fight me."

Jenn looked around, wondering what she should do. Should she call out to Johnny, let him know Scotty wasn't in any real danger? Or should she just let the scene play out? Either way, in her mind, Johnny was a bona fide hero, always thinking of others before himself.

Her relatives were hooting and hollering for all they were worth, egging Johnny on with their chatter.

And they were laughing.

Jenn couldn't stand by and let her family make fun of a man who would risk his own well-being for someone he'd only known for a short while.

"Johnny," Jenn called loudly. "Stand up."

"What?" he yelled back, submerging momentarily under the water as Scotty continued to struggle in his arms.

"Stand up," Jenn repeated, louder this time. She shaded her eyes from the sun, trying to see what was happening through the brilliant glare of the sun on the water.

Johnny must have understood her words the second time, for he did as she asked. With the man being six-two and the water at six feet in the deepest part of the lake, the waves barely met his hair line.

Everyone was laughing in earnest now, even Scotty, who was playfully splashing water at his wrangler friend.

Everyone, that is, except Jenn.

Johnny hadn't wasted an instant when he thought Scotty was in trouble. He had been there, without a thought for his own safety, and had dashed to the rescue, not guessing for one second he had been hoodwinked.

Now his heroic act was being—albeit playfully—mocked by her family.

Jenn didn't want to laugh at Johnny. She wanted to hug him until he couldn't breathe.

Johnny trudged to shore with his arm draped around Scotty, bellowing out a full-bodied laugh of his own, throwing his head back in a way that made Jenn's insides feel like mush. He swept up his cowboy hat, used his free hand to slick his hair back, and then planted his hat on his head, low over his eyes.

He looked around at her family, his features unreadable. Everyone stopped laughing and stared back at him. Jenn wondered if they were as troubled by their teasing as he must be. Jenn was appalled and ashamed of her family's behavior.

Johnny had every right to be angry, or embarrassed, or maybe a little of both. Surely, his male pride had been wounded, if nothing else.

Suddenly, Johnny gave a toothy grin and tipped the edge of his hat with his fingers. "Thank you. Thank you very much," he said in an absurdly exaggerated Elvis impersonation.

Even Jenn laughed. How could she not, when Johnny managed to take even the most uncomfortable circumstance in stride—and with a contagious grin on his face to show for it.

She and Johnny were as opposite as day and night, Jenn realized. Jenn fretted over every little issue and was far too conscious of her own pride. She would have been fiercely wounded by the kind of cavalier behavior her family had shown Johnny.

She couldn't just let it go, not like Johnny so very easily did. What was the cliché? Like water off a duck's back? That was how Johnny took everything; while Jenn herself would let that same water drown her.

How were the two of them going to continue with this act? They were too different in personality to have been genuinely attracted to one another, much less to have tried to make a relationship. Surely, someone would see right through the ruse.

How could they not?

Jenn took a mental step backward, trying to see her family through Johnny's eyes. Clearly, he didn't perceive the incident the same way she did. He was all smiles and laughter.

She looked around at her family, who were still joking and laughing with Johnny.

With Johnny. Not at him. What Johnny was experiencing was genuine and familiar—the loving family life Jenn took for granted. Those things about her loved ones that drove her crazy were the same things making Johnny grin so widely now.

It was an epiphany long in coming. There was much in her life she needed to reevaluate.

But not now, not when Johnny, still sopping wet, moved to her side and dropped a wet arm over her shoulder, giving her a friendly nudge.

He was getting her soaked, and obviously intentionally, at that.

Funny, though, it didn't seem to matter to Jenn as she thought it might. Not when Johnny smiled down at her with his dancing blue eyes and that irritating, adorable quirk of his lips.

Johnny winked at her, then gave the family another broad grin. "Well," he drawled slowly, "at least my hat's dry."

Chapter Six

The following day found Jenn so angry she thought steam must be rushing from her ears. And for once, it had nothing to do with her family boxing her into a corner about faith or relationships. Surprisingly, it didn't even have anything to do with the gigantic mess—and it was a mess—she had created with Johnny Barnes, or even the man himself.

It was her stupid, useless, piece of junk laptop computer she was about to chuck out the window and have done with altogether. She'd been fiddling with the uncooperative piece of electrical equipment for over two hours now, to no avail.

Vacation or no vacation, she had work to do, and she was never going to be able to access her files if she couldn't get her worthless computer to work. And with no computer tech within miles around who could help her, Jenn had little hope she'd actually be able to toil through the problem on her own.

She didn't spend any more time with her computer than she had to, preferring her work in the field, with real people. Perhaps she hadn't paid enough attention to the modifications made on her computer so she could access her work on her holiday.

Accessing her files from the wide expanse of Wyoming ranch land had sounded like a piece of cake when the computer tech back in Denver had showed her how it was done. She wasn't a complete illiterate, or idiot, for that matter, where computers were concerned, but at the moment, she felt like one.

Her stupid one-click-of-the-button software wasn't *clicking*.

Now how was she supposed to change that?

Anger was rapidly turning to sheer panic. She had a couple cases she'd left with coworkers, and they weighed heavily on her mind. No matter how long she worked at her profession, she'd never forgotten a single face of those dear, sweet orphaned or abandoned children she worked with. She just *had* to know what was happening on her latest cases, on the off chance she could offer some assistance or advice.

Just to know, really.

A knock at her door startled her so much she nearly jumped out of her seat.

"It's Johnny," came a soft drawl from behind the closed door. "I started to worry about you when you didn't come down for breakfast. Are you feeling okay? Is there something I can do for you?"

Glad to have something to do other than pound her computer into the ground and jump on it until it was smashed in dozens of tiny pieces, she slammed the lid on the laptop, hopped up out of her chair and swung the door open wide.

Apparently, Johnny had been leaning against the other side of the door, for he came crashing into the room off-balance, and swerved right into her desk, slamming his palms down with both hands and nearly sending her computer careening to the floor.

He could have saved his pride, but instead, he saved her computer, snatching it up and hugging it tightly to his chest with both arms before falling ungracefully to the rug on his backside.

Frankly, Jenn thought he should have saved himself and let the computer fall where it may; but she knew voicing her thoughts aloud would do more harm than good at this point, so she remained silent. She couldn't help but smile at the adorable, rumpled picture Johnny made, sprawled out on the floor, hugging her computer, but she hid her grin behind her fist so Johnny wouldn't see.

"Sorry. Sorry," he apologized, righting himself and returning the computer to the desk. "Mercy, woman, you ought to warn a man before you swing open the door like that."

She crossed her arms over her chest and glared at him, though she suspected her eyes were still twinkling with mirth. "You were the one who knocked. If you didn't have the good sense to stand away from the door before I opened it, how is that my fault?"

He didn't have his cowboy hat with him, for once, but he nonetheless tipped the nonexistent brim at her with a conciliatory grin. "Touché, darlin'. You spending some time on your computer? Not doing work on your vacation, I hope."

Not doing work was exactly right, and this time Jenn scowled for real, remembering her recent tussle with the contrary piece of electronic equipment, a fight in which she'd lost by a landslide. Johnny's presence could only make her humiliation all the more viable, so the sooner she got rid of him, the better.

"Okay, first, don't call me darling. Second, if I'm hungry, I'll come to breakfast. If not, I won't. Third— and I think we agreed on this point earlier—you are not my keeper."

Inside her heart, she knew she wasn't being fair to him, ranting like this, but she couldn't seem to help herself. Johnny had simply picked a very, very bad time to come knocking on her door.

"Look, darl—uh—Jenn, your granny sent me lookin' for you. She said you're an early riser and it's not like you not to come down and join the family for breakfast. Everyone was worried about you. That's all."

Jenn ran her fingers against her scalp, attempting to ease the tension headache building there, and not caring if she looked a mess.

"I apologize," she said, because that's what she knew she was supposed to say, and not so much because she was feeling it at the moment. "I'm not angry with you, Johnny, or with my family." She blew out a breath.

This time, when his smile showed amusement, Jenn didn't think it was cute. She wanted to punch his lights out.

She sighed again. No, she didn't. Not really. She wasn't being fair to Johnny, and she knew it. He was just being his same old, likeable, distractingly charming self, even if it was grating on her nerves like crazy at the moment.

"Grrrr," she growled out in barely suppressed frustration. "It's not you, Johnny. It's this dumb, stupid, idiotic computer!"

He lifted a brow. "Seems like a lot of adjectives for that little piece of equipment there."

"Yeah? You try it sometime. That *little piece of equipment* is supposed to interface with my work computer, and I can't even get it on the Internet."

"In the middle of Wyoming? Does that really surprise you, darlin'? I'm half surprised they have a working telephone up here. This pretty much has to be no-man's-land, or something, where the Electronic Age is concerned, don't you think?"

"For my cell phone, yes," Jenn answered, still glaring at her computer. "I never expect to get service way out here. But the computer tech at my office assured me he had me wired up for this dumb, stupid, idiotic piece-of-junk computer."

Johnny chuckled loudly. "There go those adjectives again."

Now she glared at him in earnest. He wasn't helping her mood any with his glib comments. "Okay, so my vocabulary turns to mush when I'm angry. Thank you so much for pointing that out to me."

He threw back his head and laughed—at least, until Jenn advanced on him like a cougar on a rabbit, her hands planted on her waist so she wouldn't be tempted to flat-out strangle the man.

"Whoa, there, darlin'," Johnny said, holding his hands up as if she'd held a gun to his head. "I was only teasing."

With another frustrated growl, she backed off and slumped into the desk chair. Couldn't he see she didn't need to be teased right now?

Fighting a losing battle with her computer was one

thing. Fighting that same battle with the gentle cowboy smiling down at her was another.

He stepped before her and kneeled so he was eye to eye with her. His smile disappeared. "I can be a big dumb ox sometimes," he stated bluntly, his eyes changing to a color that was almost black in its intensity. "Here I am, trampling all over your tender feelings, when I ought to be lending you a hand."

His gaze took the fight right out of her, and his words confounded her. She was afraid to ask, but she did, anyway. "Lending me a hand, how, exactly?"

He chuckled. "I think your exact words were, 'You try it sometime.'"

Her eyes widened. The man couldn't be serious. Okay, sure, Scotty had said he'd seen Johnny with a laptop in the bunkhouse where they wrangled, so he obviously was at least familiar with computers. But almost everyone e-mailed in this age. Fiddling around with a high-tech computer program was another thing entirely.

If she couldn't click the link and make it work, it was highly improbable it would suddenly work for Johnny. Cowboy charm only went so far after all, and she doubted it extended to inanimate objects, she thought, with a grim smile.

"Look, I've already tried everything and then some on that dumb—uh—computer that the tech support guy in Denver said to do. Nothing works. There's nothing you can do about it."

There went those lips again, curling in amusement, as if she'd said something funny. Which she hadn't. "Don't be so sure about that."

He reached for her computer, but Jenn blocked him. "Look, Johnny, I appreciate what you're trying to do here, but I think it would be better if I just put the thing away and admit defeat."

"Defeat? I didn't think that word was in your vocabulary."

It wasn't. But if it was between that and having some cowboy try his hand at fixing her computer, she'd choose defeat—at least for now. She'd no doubt have the annoying laptop out within the hour, trying once again, and probably unsuccessfully, to make the interface work.

"Why do you need it to interface with your work machine?" Johnny asked softly.

"What?" she asked in confusion, having been abruptly pulled from her own thoughts.

"The interface. Why do you need it? I thought you were on vacation here."

"I am," she said immediately. "It's just that there are a couple cases I'm working on—a couple kids caught in the bureaucracy of the system. I'm kind of worried about them, is all, and wanted to check up on how things were progressing with them."

He reached out a hand to brush the backs of his fingers against her cheek, but she instinctively pulled away from his touch. He dropped his hand immediately, but his eyes were so warm and gentle, it made her insides hurt.

"You really care about these kids, don't you?" he asked in that soft-spoken voice of his.

"Every last one of them," she whispered, her heart tightening with all kinds of emotion.

"Then," he said simply, "let me have a pass at your computer."

"Johnny…"

He reached out his hand again, this time using just his index finger to tilt her chin up just slightly, so there was no way she could turn away from him. As if she could have, anyway. His gaze had locked her eyes to his.

And this time, much to her own surprise, she didn't flinch from his tender touch.

"Trust me," he said softly.

"I do, but…"

"Trust me," he said again.

With effort, she broke her gaze from Johnny's. Elbows on her knees, she buried her face in her hands. She couldn't think straight when she was looking into his eyes like that.

It made absolutely no sense to hand her computer over to this cowboy. He was still a stranger, even if she felt an inexplicable closeness to the man. Her computer tech back home would have her hide.

But then again, what could it hurt? What harm would there be in allowing Johnny to see what she'd already discovered? It wasn't as if he could somehow harm the computer. Johnny would just try the same links, get nowhere and shrug it off.

Shaking her head at the wisdom of her action, she stood and moved out of the desk chair, making a sweeping gesture toward the laptop. "Be my guest. Quite frankly, I'm on the verge of throwing the stupid computer out the window anyway. And I don't think you can break the thing by punching a few keys."

"Yeah, probably not," he agreed, sliding into the seat she'd vacated. He opened the laptop and stared for a moment at the screen she'd left on—the interface which wasn't working.

"The tech in Denver told me all I had to do was push

on this little link here," she said, pointing to the blue line on the screen, "And then my work station desktop was supposed to appear out of nowhere. As you can see, nothing's happening."

Johnny scrubbed his hand through his hair, making his curls go every which direction, then winked at her. "You're right. Nothing's happening…"

She nodded vigorously, just short of saying *I told you so.*

Then he grinned at her. "Yet."

Brushing his hands over the keyboard as if he were a virtuoso pianist about to begin a piano concerto, he began typing at lightning speed. This in itself was an enormous surprise to Jenn—a cowboy who typed eighty words a minute?

Johnny continued to surprise her at every turn, and she wondered what else she didn't know about him. It was worth looking into, she thought—and then she glanced at the computer screen, horror gripping her insides.

Little boxes began appearing and disappearing, and then the screen went black, with only a tiny white cursor blinking in the far upper-left corner.

Jenn wanted to scream. What had the crazy cowboy done to her computer?

"Johnny," she squeaked, her voice barely sounding from her throat. "Please. Just stop."

"Stop?" he asked with a chuckle. "Darlin', I'm just getting started."

With that, he began punching in what Jenn now recognized as computer code—*complex* computer code. Line upon line upon line of it, without stopping for a moment to consider what he was doing.

Jenn didn't know whether to laugh or cry, but one thing she knew for sure—she knew absolutely nothing about the cowboy who called himself Johnny Barnes.

In mere minutes, Johnny had her machine back up and running—and this time, when he pressed the interface link, her Denver work station appeared instantly.

"I made a few modifications," he said with a grin. "That tech you have in Denver isn't as good as he thinks he is."

"M-modifications?" Jenn stammered, staring blindly first at the computer, and then at the handsome cowboy-slash-computer genius.

"Mmm-hmm," he murmured with a low, soft chuckle. "You can now access every file in your system, rather than merely your current caseload. Facts, figures, pictures. It's all there. Your communication system on this computer was a bit outdated. I fixed that, as well. And of course I pumped the speed up for you."

"Of course," she echoed vaguely.

She shook her head to clear her mind, feeling as if she'd just stepped off another planet.

Or else *he* had.

She was in limbo, somewhere between reason and insanity, and wasn't exactly sure which side she was hovering the closest to.

"Johnny, you're a genius," she said at last, laying a hand on his shoulder.

He tipped his imaginary hat again. "Why, thank you, ma'am."

"No, I mean it," she continued. "You have to take me seriously here."

"Darlin', I always take you seriously," he bantered. Johnny had been there for her, ever since he'd stepped in the door that first day. He'd been doing all the giving in their pseudo relationship, and she'd been doing all the taking. He'd even put up with her bad mood this morning, letting her take verbal swings at him without even trying to hit back.

This was her chance to do something for him—if she could get him to listen to her. She wasn't sure he was paying attention, not with the lazy, catlike grin lining his face and his eyes half-closed.

"You have an extraordinary gift. I have to say, I'm astounded." Jenn shook her head. "Why didn't you tell me you were able to do such spectacular work programming computers?"

He shrugged. "You didn't ask."

"Yes, but don't you see? You're out there herding cattle when you could be making money—*loads* of money—in the computer business. Based on what I've witnessed today, with your talent, you could probably open up your own company if you wanted to, or at least troubleshoot for the big guys."

Johnny frowned and looked away from her. "Money isn't everything, Jenn."

He was missing her point entirely, and her frustration once again began to build. "That's not what I'm saying, or at least that's not all I'm saying. Sure, money is part of it. You can't possibly make a decent living wrangling cattle. But it's so much more than that. Johnny, can't you see you're wasting your God-given talent out there on the range?"

"Am I?" His gaze met hers, this time with an intensity so fierce his eyes were once again almost black in color.

"Just think, Johnny, how much you could benefit. Why—"

"Jenn," Johnny barked, cutting her off. It was the harshest tone she'd ever heard him use, and her gaze widened even as her mouth closed.

"Sometimes," he said slowly—not hesitant, but obviously taking time in selecting the right words, "men choose to be cowboys because they don't want to be involved in any part of the corporate rat race. Not every man wants to spend all his time in a claustrophobic office environment, in some small cubicle with telephone gear practically growing out of his ear.

"Out on the range, a man is a free spirit. No buildings, no commitments, just a man, his horse and the cattle he's herding."

Johnny paused. His gaze had never left Jenn's, and she was blinking back at him with her enormous, glittering blue eyes, looking for all the world as if he'd just said the moon was made of green cheese.

Clearly, she didn't comprehend a word he was saying, and for some indefinable reason, he desperately wanted her to understand his point of view.

But of course she wouldn't get where he was coming from; Jenn thrived on the very life Johnny was trying so desperately to avoid.

And why was he trying to explain himself, anyway? Why should he care what she thought about him or his genius skills?

But he did care. He cared very deeply. And he wanted her to care, too—not just with a token understanding, but with real appreciation.

That wasn't likely to happen, especially not now,

when he'd revealed far more of himself than he ever meant to. Feeling more than a little trepidation, he suddenly realized he'd nearly given himself away this morning, all in an effort to help her.

Who was he kidding? He'd been showing off with his skills in order to impress her in the field he knew best. He been strutting his stuff like the vainest rooster in the barnyard.

Unfortunately for him, it had worked—all too well for his own good.

Jenn had been impressed, all right. Enough to want to send him straight to the corporate prison many people called their lives.

The very life he was trying to escape.

Chapter Seven

Johnny managed to avoid Jenn for most of the day, more because she had locked herself in her room with her computer than because of anything he did. Although, he thought wryly, if he had any sense he'd be out of this house and out of Jenn's life at the first opportunity, before he betrayed himself, or more accurately, exposed his betrayal to a family Johnny had come to hold dear to his heart. Especially Jenn.

But he couldn't bring himself to even consider leaving before his two weeks were up, so he stayed and prayed he wouldn't be found out. With every passing second during the afternoon, Johnny missed Jenn's radiant presence; but even so, he managed to enjoy the cheerful company of her extended family. Granny and Auntie Myra were a riot, bantering back and forth like a couple of old hens.

Even funnier was the way Jenn's grandfather withstood it all with the patience of a saint and the gruff good nature borne of decades of love.

Love Johnny had never known, and certainly had never seen in action. This family continued to surprise him with their love of God and their affection and support for each other. He was really going to miss them all when he left at the end of next week, to return to the Double Y ranch to finish out his summer as a wrangler.

This was what a family was supposed to be, everything he'd dreamed of in his childhood.

And Jenn?

Well, beautiful, fiery-tempered Jenn was definitely the icing on the cake.

More than likely, he'd never see any of them again in his life, except, of course, Scotty, since they still had another month's work on the Double Y.

Johnny had an ache in his gut so fierce he couldn't even eat a decent supper. He must have looked as green as he felt, for no one commented when he excused himself from the table early.

Marching straight to his room, he grabbed his bedroll and headed for the peace and openness of the starry night sky. He never got tired of lying on his back, stargazing in the depths of Wyoming ranch land. Where he could actually *see* the stars.

Where he was from, the only stars he could make out were the Big Dipper and sometimes Orion's Belt, on especially clear nights. Out here, it was all he could do to *find* those constellations amidst the millions of stars twinkling down on him.

He didn't know when he finally drifted off to sleep, but it was much later in the night. Not even the stars had helped him turn off his racing mind, or ease the throbbing pain in his chest.

When he awoke, it was to Scotty's laughter.

"I'm with you, buddy," the youngster said, sliding

down to the ground beside Johnny. "Sleeping inside drives me clear out of my mind."

Groggily, Johnny sat up, shoved his curly mop of hair back with his fingers, and planted his hat on his head, pulling the brim low over his brow on the off chance Scotty might see any of his feelings in his eyes. He cleared his throat before speaking. "Yeah, sport."

"I wish you would've come got me. We could've camped out together."

Johnny chuckled. "Boys' night out?"

Scotty grinned. "Something like that. Why are you out here, anyway? No—I know. They all drive you nuts, don't they?"

"Your family? No. No—they're all great."

"Liar. My sister is especially bad on that count. She jams herself right under your skin like a bad splinter, and just keeps on rubbing so you can't ever forget she's around."

Johnny bit his lip to keep from laughing. *That* much was true, anyway. Scotty's sister was a hard woman to forget about, even for a minute.

"You wanna get away from everything?" Scotty asked enthusiastically. "Just you and me?"

"What did you have in mind?" Johnny asked, curious, but reluctant to part with the family, much less Jenn, for *any* of what little time he had left.

"A good, long horseback ride. I can show you the ranch."

"That sounds nice, Scotty, but, uh—I was really hoping to spend some time with Jenn today. You and I have the rest of the summer to ride together. I only have a few days with your sister."

"Yeah," the young man said, obviously disappointed by Johnny's answer.

Johnny put a hand on the boy's shoulder. "I have an idea that might work for all of us, if you don't mind having your sister around."

Scotty grunted. "I always mind having my sister around."

Johnny laughed. "Spoken like a true brother." Then he paused, frowning slightly. "I envy you."

This time it was Scotty who reached out to Johnny, giving him a friendly slap on the back. "Hey, buddy, I forgot about that. I'm really sorry. And I'm just joking around about Jenn. She and I get along pretty well, all things considered. And I haven't seen her in a year. So not horses, then, I guess. What'd ya have in mind for us?"

"Not horses?" Johnny queried lightly.

"Naw. Not with my sister."

Johnny smiled at Scotty's continued use of drawled, slang speech. He knew the only thing the boy had ever wanted to be was a cowboy, and though Johnny knew perfectly well Scotty was educated enough to speak correct English, he found it amusing that the boy stuck to his guns—pun intended.

And Johnny could relate. He rather wished he could keep on with the humble, carefree life of a cowboy forever, but he knew it couldn't last.

Not forever. Not even close.

Hopefully, for at least these two weeks, and if God was merciful to him, the rest of the summer.

"I don't see why we still couldn't take that horseback ride you mentioned. I wondered if I could just invite Jenn to go along with us?"

Scotty belted out a laugh, looking utterly relieved. "You can ask, old man, but she ain't about to go with you…us."

"And why is that?" Johnny cocked a questioning brow at his friend.

"Because, big guy, your Jenn is deathly afraid of horses. I thought she would have told you that in one of your '*conversations*.'"

Johnny ignored the boy's teasing, preferring to go straight to the point. "She grew up on a ranch. How could she be afraid of horses?"

Scotty rolled to his stomach and cupped his chin in his palms. "I dunno if I should be telling you this or not. Maybe you should ask Jenn. But I always wondered if that was what sent her flying into the big city as fast as her wings would flap."

"What did?" Johnny asked, his patience wearing thin. He knew exactly what kind of response he'd get if he tried to ask Jenn anything remotely personal, yet he was determined to find out more about her, even if he had to wring it from her younger brother's neck.

"She never liked living on a ranch," Scotty said, now rolling onto his back and lacing his hands behind his head and staring straight up at the sky.

"I got that much," Johnny said dryly. "Now tell me what I don't know."

Scotty chuckled. "Testy. You must really like my sister a lot."

Johnny didn't want to think about that statement, so he continued to press the boy for details. "Just tell me what happened to her, Scotty, and spare me the lectures on the state of my heart."

Scotty laughed again. "Did I say anything about your heart?"

"Scotty," Johnny warned.

"All right, already." Scotty chuckled and pulled in a deep breath. "Jenn was about, I don't know, five or six when she got her first horse. 'Course, I wasn't born yet, so I've only heard the story secondhand, but it's one of those stories the family passes around."

He winked at Johnny. "Anyway, she'd been on horses before plenty of times, bein' that we lived on a ranch and all, but this horse was all hers, a birthday present from our folks."

Johnny didn't say a word to interrupt, now that Scotty was speaking freely.

"I think she must've been too excited or something. My folks knew how to pick good horseflesh, and they chose a real gentle gelding for her, a horse that had been around the block a few times, you know?"

"Mmm-hmm," Johnny answered.

"But Jenn was just a kid—an excited little girl with her very own horse. She'd been riding around the corral for several minutes when the gelding suddenly spooked and started rearing like a buckin' bronc. No one really knows why, even to this day. He dumped her but good, right into the corral fence. If I recall the story right, she broke a wrist and sprained both her ankles, but it wasn't really serious."

"Then what?" Johnny asked. "You aren't a real horseman until you've taken your first digger. Surely your parents knew to get her up and back on that horse riding as soon as possible."

"Oh, they tried, believe me. Still do, sometimes. But Jenn would scream like a banshee every time they tried to get her near a horse. After a while, my parents stopped trying to force the issue, though, like I said, they still offer to take her out on a horse every year when we're up here for the reunion."

"And every year she refuses."

"Exactly. Now, you might be able to charm Jenn into a few moonlight kisses, but don't expect to be able to get her to ride with you."

The part about the moonlight kisses had Johnny's mind going in all kinds of directions for a few seconds, but he reeled his thoughts in—reluctantly.

"Be that as it may, I'm still gonna try," he said, standing to his full height and stretching to take the kinks out of his muscles.

"Brave man," Scotty said with a wink.

Stupid man, probably, Johnny thought, though he didn't say it aloud. Still, he couldn't shake the feeling that he needed to ask.

This was something he could help her with. The woman was still a complete enigma to him, but he'd seen the fear in her eyes. Maybe this whole horse thing had her rattled, being on the ranch and all.

He could help with that. He knew he could.

If she'd let him.

"So what's keeping you?" Scotty teased.

Johnny gave him his best frown, and then grinned widely. "You're lying on my bedroll."

Johnny couldn't find Jenn anywhere. The ranch house was sprawling, but it wasn't that big. He'd walked around it twice, crossing paths with nearly every member of the family along the way, some more than once. He thought about asking someone if they would be able to point him to where Jenn might be, but he knew enough about her now to know that, if she wanted her privacy, she wasn't going to announce her whereabouts to everyone.

He'd just about decided she must be out on the grounds somewhere, when he saw the slightest brush of the curtain next to the windowed alcove in the sitting room. On a hunch, he crept up to it, trying to keep his cowboy boots from clunking on the hardwood floor.

"Jenn?" he said softly, before brushing back the curtain with the back of his hand, not wanting to startle her by his sudden appearance.

He'd expected to find her reading, or just taking a few minutes of quiet time away from the hustle and bustle of her family, to bask in the sunshine like a lazy cat.

What he actually encountered when he pulled aside the curtain shocked him to the core, causing his breath to freeze in his lungs.

Jenn's blue eyes were huge as she met his gaze, and an expression of guilt and panic crossed her face as she instinctively skittered away from him into the far corner of the alcove. In the same moment, she quickly tried to pull the sleeve of her shirt down over her arm and hide a tube of antiscar liniment behind her back so Johnny couldn't see.

But he did.

Jenn knew she was too late, that her movements hadn't been quick enough for Johnny's keen gaze. Johnny's eyes turned to a deep, forbidding shade of black as he slid in beside her and placed his hat on the seat next to him.

"Jenn," was all he said, as he took her wrist in one

hand and carefully rolled up her sleeve with the other, baring her forearm. His touch was gentle and his gaze tender and understanding. His Adam's apple bobbed as if he were trying to speak, or swallow, but appeared to be able to do neither.

Which was why, if she could have, Jenn would have run as far and as fast as she could away from the man. Blockaded herself in her room and never come out.

But Johnny was holding her wrist like a vise. She couldn't move, but neither could she sit there and envelope the warmth of the sympathy in his gaze.

Not Johnny. Please, not him.

She'd thought she was alone, that no one would bother her. All she'd been doing was rubbing some scar-reducing cream onto her forearm, something she did several times a day when no one was looking.

Or at least when she *thought* no one was looking. This time she'd been caught.

And of all people, by Johnny Barnes.

She couldn't imagine anything worse. Except maybe the tears that sprang to her eyes. She would have dashed them away, except that she felt completely paralyzed by Johnny's presence.

"Jenn?" he asked softly, brushing his fingers along the scars on her arms.

She wished he would stop repeating her name and just come out and say what he was thinking. Actually, she wished he wasn't here at all.

"Just go away, Johnny, and leave me alone."

"No."

That one word stopped her cold. It wasn't harsh or condemning, which made it all the worse. Uttered

gently and with that soft-spoken voice she couldn't resist, she looked everywhere but at him, or at her arm.

"Did you get these injuries from falling off the
horse?" he asked, in the same mild tone. "No wonder
you won't go near the animals."

"What?" She hadn't planned to talk to him at all,
and she waited until he eased up on her wrist and she
could pull away and make a dignified exit, or at least
as much as she was able in her current state of mind.
But his words confused her.

"When you fell into the fence," he explained gently.
"Scotty said it was a corral. I just assumed it was a
wooden fence. Was it barbed wire? Did your arm get
tangled up when the horse threw you?"

Jenn still had no idea what he was talking about, and
neither did Johnny, apparently. She scrambled to fill in
the missing blanks, so she could answer him without
giving anything away.

Horses?

Barbed wire?

Her mind flashed through a number of scenarios,
but she still came up blank.

"I looked all over for you this morning. I wanted to
ask you to take a ride with me tomorrow—on horseback. Scotty warned me you wouldn't want to go. Now
I think I know why."

Jenn breathed an internal sigh of relief. Finally, she
understood what he was talking about—when she'd
been thrown from her horse as a youngster. Falling off
horses she could deal with.

Not so much the truth.

And he'd brought it up, after all. She didn't have to
say a thing, didn't have to invent a single falsehood. She

could let him think whatever he wanted to, and have him be none the wiser as to the real source of her scars.

But it still felt like a lie, and Jenn had it up to her ears with lies. On one hand, adding this to her already enormous heap of fabrications seemed like such a small thing, especially considering the circumstances. If there was ever a reason to hide the truth, this was it.

Johnny dropped his free arm behind her, not quite touching her, but close enough to make her feel warm and cherished, as if he were hugging her close. She closed her eyes, savoring the feeling, if just for now.

She was an idiot, she realized. She knew she wasn't going to get out of this situation without some damage to her heart, but at the moment, she didn't care. The only thing that mattered was that Johnny *did* care.

And he wasn't anything like other men.

She felt the brush of his fingers against her cheek, and she leaned into them, savoring the rough calluses of this cowboy's work-worn hand.

"You've really been hurt, haven't you?"

His words made her freeze both inside and outside. Was he still talking about horses?

Part of her hoped so, and she wanted to let it go at that, or at least, she knew she should.

Yet there was a part of her, in the deepest recesses of her soul, which cried out to be released. She'd carried her secrets around so long, the ache had become a part of who she was, an integral part of her being. Her scars went far deeper than the flesh wounds she'd been tending, and she'd never told a single soul about either type of injury—inside or outside.

Until now.

She opened her eyes and met Johnny's gaze. His full,

bow-shaped lips were pressed together as if he were experiencing pain of his own, merely by empathizing with hers. She saw it in his eyes, as well, so full of warmth and compassion.

He cared.

And he'd be gone in a week.

Suddenly, it didn't seem so far-fetched to share the real story with this man. It was a burden she'd carried around far too long. From what she knew of Johnny Barnes, he wouldn't judge, and he most certainly wouldn't tell anyone.

He couldn't.

Hot tears sprang once more to her eyes, as the pain and agony she'd kept bottled up for years rushed to the surface. She didn't even try to wipe away the moisture, knowing many more tears would be shed before she could say what she wanted to—*had* to say.

"These scars aren't from getting thrown from a horse, Johnny," she said, her voice twisted and scratchy. "I—I fell through a bay window."

"You did *what?*" Johnny asked, disbelief and fury warring on his face. "How?"

Her silence must have been answer enough, for he continued. "Who did this to you, Jenn? I'm going to take that man and—"

Jenn cut him off. "That wouldn't change my past, Johnny. Or my future."

His gaze, so focused on her own, was piercing her straight to the heart. His lips worked, but no sound came out for several seconds. Finally he whispered a coarse, "What?"

"This is going to be really hard to explain. I'm not sure I really understand all the implications myself.

Some social worker I am, huh? I can't even handle my own problems."

"Who did this to you?" Johnny repeated, sounding as angry as Jenn had ever heard him. She wondered if he was angry at her. For hiding the truth. For being stupid enough to have put herself in the position of being thrown out of a window in the first place.

Jenn was angry enough at herself. She didn't need Johnny's censure. But she could hardly blame him. It was a shocking story.

"The scars are a constant reminder of what was. Is," she said, correcting herself. "The pain—the emotional pain—never really goes away."

"What happened?" Johnny asked again.

Jenn shook her head. "I think it's best if I start at the beginning."

Johnny nodded and gave her shoulders a comforting squeeze.

She took a deep breath and plunged in before she lost her nerve. "I never liked living on a ranch," she explained. "Not even as a small child. Maybe it was the whole getting-thrown-from-a-horse thing, I don't know. I just know I wanted out, and the older I got, the closer I was to graduating high school, the more I hated it."

She brushed at her tears with the palms of her hands. "The long and short of it is, by the time I was sixteen, I rebelled against everything good I'd been taught by my family."

"All teenagers rebel." Johnny sounded almost as if he were making excuses for her, but Jenn knew the truth: there was no excuse for her actions back then.

Or now, for that matter.

"Yeah? Well, not like I did. I was raised by a loving

Christian family, and I knew better. I'd been taught well, but I didn't care to be anything like them. I couldn't see past the nose on my face, if you'll pardon the expression.

"Like most teenagers, I thought I knew everything. So I did anything I could to prove what a smart grown-up I was. Everything I'd been taught better than to do. I drank, I smoked and I ran with a bad crowd."

"I still don't understand," he said gently. "Lots of kids do that. But most people don't get thrown through a window." His fingers were soft as he traced the scars on her arm. "Don't tell me you got into a bar fight, like in the movies."

Johnny's light, teasing tone made it easier for her to face the truth. Jenn closed her eyes to shut out the painful memories, but they were coming fast and furious, and she opened her eyes again, finding more comfort in the strength of Johnny's gaze than in the darkness, the self-imposed, agonizing isolation she'd lived with all these years.

"There was this guy I really liked. He was quite a bit older than me—ten years. He was twenty-six years old, and I was sixteen. I was so flattered that he paid attention to me, that I didn't see the warning signs. I'm not even sure I knew what they were back then. Or else I was ignoring them."

"Warning signs?" Johnny asked gently.

Jenn shrugged. "I was always attracted to the bad boy image, and this guy had it in spades. It didn't occur to me that it was more than just an image, that the clothes he wore were an indication of what he was like inside his heart. He—I—"

She paused, regrouping. "At first he doted on me. He drove a Mustang and would give me rides home from school. He brought me presents. I'd been with him for weeks before he started slapping me around." She looked away from Johnny, her face reddening. "I was young enough and stupid enough to think he really cared for me, even when he hit me. He always apologized afterward, always told me how much he loved me."

Johnny's eyes turned a dark black and were filled with a look Jenn had never seen before. She rushed on, afraid to stop.

"You can probably guess the rest. Duke—his name was actually Darryl Duke, but everyone just called him Duke—took me back to his house one night. He was angry and drunk, but I didn't see it then. Here I was, thinking how mature I was, how special it was that Duke noticed me at all.

"He offered me a drink. When he came on to me, I didn't know what to do. I might have been rebellious, but I was a good girl at heart, and he scared me."

"He didn't take no for an answer."

"He was so nice at first, flattering me with romantic words. But when I started balking, he changed. He called me all sorts of names. Said I had led him on."

"Oh, Jenn."

"When he grabbed me, I struggled. I tried to get away from him. That's when he backhanded me hard across the face. The force of the blow set me off balance. I twisted in the air and realized too late I was going to…" Her sentence drifted off into the thick air.

"You don't have to say it, Jenn," Johnny said softly. "He knocked you through that window."

"I was so young, so stupid. I've asked myself over and over again why I got in that car. And I was so scared someone would find out, my family especially, that I didn't say a word to anyone."

"But you must have been badly hurt, to have scars like that," Johnny pointed out, gently tracing the lines on her arm. "You didn't go to the hospital?"

"No. That's why the scars are so bad. I think I must have instinctively held my arms over my face when I fell, because they got the brunt of the glass. But I didn't dare seek medical help. A doctor would have been obligated to call my parents."

"So, what did you do?"

"Went to a friend's house. She pulled out all the shards of glass left in my arms and bandaged me up. I've kept my arms hidden ever since."

"Which is why you wore long sleeves to the beach… why you didn't swim with the rest of your family."

"Yes."

Johnny snorted and shook his head. "And I thought you just didn't like to swim. I'm so sorry, Jenn. I'm as thickheaded as they come."

"Don't apologize," Jenn said, astounded that he would even suggest he was to blame for anything. "This is a secret I've kept for a long time. I wouldn't have expected you—or anyone—to guess the real reasons behind my actions. Please don't take that on yourself. It's my fault and my fault alone."

"It wasn't your fault." Johnny's voice was no longer soft-spoken, but as deep and hard as she'd ever heard it.

Jenn brushed at the tears on her cheeks. "I know," she said, and a wave of relief engulfed her so fiercely she began shaking. She *had* known she wasn't to blame, yet, until she'd said the words aloud, she had never—

she realized with a flaming burst of insight—really forgiven herself.

She chuckled dryly. "I'm a trained social worker, remember? But knowing the truth and believing it are two different things."

"I wish there was something I could say, but there isn't," Johnny said, his soft voice back.

"I know. I don't expect anything from you, Johnny, except for you to keep your mouth shut."

Johnny nodded immediately. "Done."

Johnny wondered at the wisdom of the promise he made her, but he knew in his heart that, no matter how much he wanted to let her family know, to have them help and support her through the trauma she'd carried for so long, it was Jenn's decision to make.

And it was a decision she'd made long ago. That she'd confided in him filled him with a guilt-ridden sense of pride. He wanted to be there for her and was glad he was, but so many questions lingered.

Why him?

Why now?

And what could he do to help? He still didn't understand, and had the deepest feeling that he didn't know half of the story.

"I understand why you didn't say anything at the time," he said gently, again tracing the uneven, ragged edges that marked her forearm. "But why have you never told your family? I'm sure they would understand. And then you wouldn't have to hide anymore."

"It has been years, but it may as well have been yesterday. The wounds are so fresh. I have so much rage, guilt, fear. Deep, gut-wrenching emotions I can't even put a name to. At one point I even wanted to take my own life, though my folks put enough of the fear of God in me that I was too chicken to take the permanent way out, no matter how bad things were."

Johnny frowned. "Okay," he said, blowing out a breath. "You asked me to keep your secret, and I will. You can trust me, Jenn."

Jenn squeezed her eyes closed. "I know," she whispered raggedly.

"You are still in so much pain." Johnny didn't mean it as a question, and he didn't state it that way.

"Sometimes. Most of the time I just shove it down so far inside me I can hardly feel it. I've lived with it so long, it's only a dull ache now. Most of the time I hardly notice. It seems worse when I'm here at home, for some reason."

"I can only imagine," he said softly.

He would have said more, but suddenly he heard footsteps approaching the alcove.

Johnny didn't have time to think. All he knew was that Jenn's arms—her scars—were exposed. The secret she'd kept from her family for years.

He did the first thing that came to mind, something he knew would distract Jenn's family long enough for her to cover up.

He threw himself in front of her, framed her face with his hands, and kissed her.

Jenn's heart had leapt clear out of her chest when she'd heard footsteps. And then, before she had the chance to so much as even take a breath, Johnny was kissing her.

Her head swam, her senses overwhelmed by the tender way he framed her face with his large, callused hands. By the soft, gentle warmth of his lips on hers.

One week ago she would have slapped any man who would have come anywhere close to kissing her. Now, she leaned into the kiss, wanting to forget everything but the comfort Johnny offered.

Dimly, she heard the curtain open, and Granny and Auntie Myra call out, "Gotcha!" She didn't even care if her family was watching.

Then she felt Johnny nudge her arm with his elbow and immediately realized his true intent. He was blocking Granny's and Auntie Myra's view, so she could cover up her arm before they saw the scars.

So she could keep her secret.

Bless the man. Even if it was next to impossible to think rationally enough to roll down her sleeve with Johnny kissing her that way.

And he just kept on kissing her.

She didn't fight him.

Just the opposite, in fact. She leaned into his kiss, wrapping one arm around his neck and threading her fingers into the soft, curly hair at the nape of his neck.

It wasn't that she'd never been kissed before. She'd kissed more than her share of young, inexperienced boys—part of the reason, maybe, why she'd been drawn to Duke, who, at twenty-six years old, had appeared so different to her—better: a man. Not a boy.

At least, until she'd met up with Duke's cruelty. Since the brutal encounter which had made her distrust, even hate, men in general, she'd been a card-carrying member of the Never Been Kissed Club.

Didn't want it.

Didn't need it.

Just leave me alone, thank you very much, Jenn had thought.

Now she realized what she'd been missing. Johnny was a man, not a gangly teenage boy. And he was as kind and tender as Duke had been cruel.

There was no denying it anymore, no matter how she told herself differently. She was experiencing undeniable, flag-waving feelings for Johnny.

"Hello-o-o," Granny hooted with an earsplitting chuckle. "Take a breath, for mercy's sake, before you both pass out!"

Johnny broke off the kiss with a laugh. "If you insist," he said, casually turning toward Jenn's relatives, his arm still firm around her shoulders. "Though I've got to say, kissing your granddaughter is a good site more interesting than bantering with you two."

Auntie Myra clutched a hand to her chest, over her heart, staggering dramatically. "You wound us, Johnny," she teased. "And look at Jenn's face. She's as red as a ripe tomato."

Jenn knew that much was true. She'd felt the blood rush to her face the moment Johnny had drawn away. His arm was still around her, but she felt as if she'd lost something very valuable, and she desperately wanted it back. She wondered vaguely if kissing Johnny would be like that every time, or if it had only been the circumstances.

So much for no public displays of affection. What would her family be expecting of them, now that they had seen what looked like stolen kisses?

What did *she* expect?

She couldn't answer that question, especially not with Johnny so near. She stood quickly and turned to

Johnny, brushing her thumb across his scratchy cheek. "Thank you," she said for his ears only. "I owe you one."

He reached an arm around her neck and pulled her closer, brushing a soft kiss against her cheek before whispering, "You don't owe me a thing, darlin'."

Chapter Eight

Johnny slept under the stars once again. He could hardly sit through supper, with all the smothered grins and speculative glances Jenn's family was laying on the two of them. He had a good notion to slam his palms against the table and tell them to just knock it off, that Jenn had already been through more in one day than any woman should have to bear, not to mention the constant agony of the past she'd confided in him.

But in the end, Johnny remained silent. For one thing, her family was just being…well, her family. Laughing, teasing and joking all the time. They loved one another and meant no harm.

Even so, Johnny had reached for Jenn's hand underneath the table when it was time to say grace.

She'd pulled her hand away.

And why wouldn't she? The true source of her embarrassment and pain today was *him*.

After all she'd revealed to him in confidence, all the fear and loathing he'd seen in her eyes when she mentioned her past, he'd gone right ahead and done the stupidest, most hurtful thing he could possibly have done under the circumstances.

He had kissed her.

He could justify his reasons until the end of his days, but the truth was, he was no better than Duke, the man Jenn so abhorred.

Johnny had taken advantage of Jenn in a weak moment, and he knew it.

Never mind that it was the only solution he could think of in such a short and supercharged moment. No matter that his action had been to save Jenn, to keep her scars from her family's notice. What had started out as another one of his unprecedented gallant moves had turned into something else entirely.

He could have—*should* have—let her go the moment she'd tugged her shirtsleeve back down to hide her scars. Instead, he'd allowed the moment to linger. Truth be told, he'd wanted that kiss to go on forever.

But throwing himself so wholeheartedly at a woman so clearly—and rightly—gun-shy of men, well, that was just plain stupid.

Stupid.

The act was done, and he couldn't take it back. But there was something he could do.

He'd make sure it didn't happen again.

Even if his own heart was shattered in the process.

Jenn was up early the next morning. The sun shined brightly through the windows and there wasn't a cloud in the sky.

It was a good day to learn to ride a horse.

She didn't know exactly when in the night she'd made that decision, but by morning her mind was made up. Johnny had reached out to her with an offer to help conquer her fear of horses.

He was already well on his way to helping her conquer her fear of men.

She'd been living in fear too long, she realized as she laced up her running shoes, not having a pair of riding boots to don. Fear of the past had chained her future. As a social worker, she recognized this in others, but she'd never seen it in herself.

It had, she realized with a secret smile, taken a humble cowboy to do that for her.

She was beginning to think—*hope,* really—that this charade she and Johnny had started might actually have turned into something real. Something valuable, that would last far beyond these two precious weeks.

Never in a million years would she have imagined herself falling for a cowboy, but there it was, in black and white.

At least she thought so, until she entered the dining room for breakfast. Johnny and Scotty were speaking in low tones when she arrived. Johnny took one quick glance at her and then looked away, a frown creasing his brow as he stared down at his breakfast plate.

Jenn had dressed with special care this morning in her skinny jeans and a soft pink cotton shirt. She'd spent extra time arranging her silky curls, though she knew they'd soon be hopelessly windblown on the Wyoming range.

The least the man could do was appreciate her efforts, but he wouldn't even look at her. She stared at him, trying to force his gaze upon her, but he stubbornly refused to glance her way.

It was Scotty who finally said something to break

the awkward silence. "We're goin' riding, sis, not to a fashion show," he teased.

Jenn supposed that was her brother's gangly way of a backhanded compliment, but she glared at him anyway, just for good measure.

Johnny looked up then, but not directly at her, shoving his fingers through his thick black curls.

"You're going *riding,* Jenn?" he queried, sounding astonished, though not at all the kind of surprise Jenn was hoping for.

He almost sounded as if he wasn't the one who'd asked her to come in the first place. She didn't know whether to be angry or hurt.

Jenn sat down at the side of the table opposite Johnny, clattering her dishes on the hard oak. Why did he not want her to go? What had happened to change his mind?

"I—I can see I'd just be in the way," she stammered. "I'll just—" She stood, unable to finish her sentence. She didn't want to be where she wasn't wanted, especially where Johnny was concerned.

Johnny reached across the table and gently but firmly grasped her hand to keep her from leaving. "No. I promised to teach you to ride, and I will."

"This I gotta see," Scotty quipped with glee. "Better than a circus."

Finally, Johnny met Jenn's gaze, but it was as if the sparkle, the light in his eyes Jenn had so grown to appreciate, had been smothered out. His gaze was hooded with shadow, his midnight-blue eyes appearing almost black. The adorable, amused quirk of his lips was gone, as well, and his jaw was clenched so tightly Jenn could see a muscle working there.

She was once again batting a thousand, Jenn thought.

She had completely misread the situation from yesterday and now Johnny was acting like a cougar trapped on a bluff.

Jenn felt foolish. She had spent so many years running away from relationships, that the first time a man kissed her, she'd fallen right into his arms.

And why not? Johnny was handsome, charming, witty—and definitely *not* interested.

Jenn had known perfectly well why Johnny had thrown himself in front of her the way he had in the window nook yesterday, and why he'd kissed her. It was to help her keep her secret from her family, and nothing more.

She'd obviously misread any other emotion or intent on Johnny's part. Considering her self-imposed limited experience with the opposite gender, that insight shouldn't have surprised her.

But it did.

And it hurt.

Johnny stood and moved to the wall, where he took his hat off the peg and planted it on his head. "I'll go out and saddle you a horse, Jenn."

Jenn sat staring after him, her elbows on the table and her fingers clasped together, but did not immediately get up to leave.

Scotty looked from Jenn to the door Johnny had so abruptly exited, and then back again. "Did I miss something here?" he asked. For once, there wasn't a trace of brotherly teasing in his voice.

Jenn shook her head, thinking her brother's quiet concern was harder to deal with than if he'd simply made fun of her as he usually did. It wasn't that she didn't want to confide in Scotty about her feelings for Johnny as much as that she didn't know what she would say.

She didn't know *how* she felt.

"It's nothing," she said at last, feeling she had to say something, even if it sounded flat to her own sensitive ears.

"You guys have a lovers' spat?"

Jenn chuckled, but the sound was empty. "Believe me, Scotty, we most definitely did *not* have a 'lovers' spat,' as you put it."

How could they? She and Johnny didn't have a *lovers'* anything.

"He really likes you, you know." Scotty's usually loud, boisterous voice was barely more than a whisper, and even more surprisingly, her brother refused to look her in the eye.

Jenn perked up for just a moment, hope sparking to life at her brother's simple, direct words. "Did he tell you that?"

Scotty shook his head, then stood and reached for his own hat. "No. He didn't have to."

With that, her brother also exited. Jenn sat motionless, though she was shaking inside. Her mind felt like it was being pulled a billion ways at once, not to mention her heart and emotions.

She wished she'd never created this tangled web. She wished even more that Johnny hadn't played along. Most of all, she wished it wasn't a farce at all.

That the kiss had meant something—something real. As it had to her. But if Johnny's peculiar behavior this morning was anything to go by, all her wishes amounted to nothing.

With a sigh, Jenn stood and stretched. This was

going to be a long enough day just trying to learn to ride a stupid horse, without having to think about her relationship, or rather lack of a relationship, with Johnny.

With effort, she shifted her thoughts to the ride to come. Her fear of horses was real enough to distract her, at least for the time being.

By the time she'd gathered sufficient courage to approach the corral, Johnny already had a dapple gray quarter horse gelding saddled, bridled and tied to the corral fence by a rope halter. Reluctantly, Jenn moved to Johnny's side, though she stayed on the opposite side of the fence from both the horse and the man.

"You can do this, Jenn," Johnny said, his voice so low she could barely make out the words.

"I think so," she replied, not completely truthfully. She wasn't sure she could find the courage to actually mount the horse, much less make any reasonable attempt to ride him.

But then again, she never thought she'd trust a man, either, and Johnny had worked through that barrier in the space of a week, merely by his patience and charm.

She only hoped that *charm* extended to horses, in particular the gray in front of her.

"This here's Silver," Johnny said, running his hand down the horse's neck and affectionately rubbing the tuft of mane between his ears.

"Oh, now that's an original name," Jenn quipped, glad to be thinking about something other than actually mounting up.

Johnny threw back his head and laughed. Jenn was glad to see the calm, steadfast gelding didn't shy away from the boisterous sound, or even appear particularly

interested. Johnny truly had taken care to select a calm
mount for her, for which she was especially thankful.

Johnny raised an eyebrow, and then winked slyly.
"Come on over the fence, darlin'. You aren't going anywhere from there."

"Wasn't the Lone Ranger's horse white?" she asked,
trying to continue that wayward train of thought even
as she slipped through the space in the wooden fence—
still a good two feet away from both horse and man.

Johnny had winked at her. And he'd called her darlin'. Maybe she'd overreacted to his behavior at breakfast. Now Johnny appeared nearly as calm and unruffled
as the nickering horse he was urging her toward.

Johnny reached out a hand to her. "Come on over
here, Jenn. You don't have to mount up until you're
completely comfortable with Silver."

She didn't move, and he wiggled his fingers to indicate he was waiting for her.

"You have nothing to worry about," he said in a low,
composed tone she was certain worked at least as well
on her mount as it did on Jenn. "I'll be right here with
you," he promised earnestly. "And as for this old gray,
he's the calmest, gentlest horse you'll ever have the
pleasure of riding."

Yeah, Jenn thought. *That's what they said last time,
and look where it got me.*

Even so, she stepped forward slowly, tentatively
reaching out to take Johnny's hand. The feel of his
rough, callused palm in hers was oddly reassuring, despite her unrelenting reluctance to continue toward her
waiting mount.

When she reached Johnny's side, he didn't speak.
Neither did he try to force her to touch the gigantic

beast. They just stood quietly, Johnny looking down at Jenn and Jenn eyeing the horse.

Johnny was every bit a man of his word, Jenn realized with relief. He wasn't going to push her in this. The cowboy could be so incredibly thoughtful sometimes, despite how gruff he'd been with her at breakfast.

Knowing Johnny was by her side gave her the courage she might otherwise have lacked. So, with a deep breath, she reached her hand out and brushed it along the gelding's neck as she'd seen Johnny do earlier.

The horse didn't flinch. Jenn wasn't sure if it was because of Silver's gentle nature or because of the way Johnny held the halter tightly in his grip, but whatever it was, it was working.

"Hello, Silver," she said in the voice she instinctively used with animals and small children. She had to smile when the horse nickered and leaned into her hand.

Johnny's reassuring smile helped, too. He spoke to the horse quietly while Jenn continued getting to know Silver, brushing her hand along his mane, his side, and eventually even down the blaze of his muzzle.

After a few moments getting to know the horse, Jenn dropped Johnny's hand and turned to him, looking him straight in the eye. "I'm ready," she said firmly, but refusing to look back at Silver.

"You sure?" Johnny asked gently. "You don't have to hurry this along, darlin'. Take all the time you want. I'm not in a hurry, and you shouldn't be, either."

"Look, Johnny. If you are going to get me on that beast's back, you'd better do it now, while I've still got the guts to try. Just tell me what I have to do."

She eyed the saddle horn and the stirrup on the side of the horse that was closest to her. The saddle horn she could reach if she stretched, but there was no way she could see herself getting a foot in the stirrup.

"I think I'm going to need a little help with this mounting business," she muttered, more to herself than to Johnny.

He chuckled softly. "Not a problem."

She expected Johnny to give her a foothold, but instead he simply grasped her by the waist and lifted her onto the saddle, with no strain on his part. The act left Jenn dizzy and a little out of breath, and not because she was six feet off the ground, on top of a shifting animal.

Once Johnny was sure she had her balance in the saddle, he moved back to once again firmly grasp the halter. He was positive Silver was a good match for her, but he didn't want to take any chances that the horse would start moving around.

"Feet in the stirrups," he instructed calmly. "Heels down. You want to balance with your knees, not with that death grip you have on the saddle horn."

Johnny winked at her to let her know he was teasing, and Jenn gave a nervous laugh. Even so, she straightened in the saddle and balanced herself with her legs.

"I'm going to slip the bridle reins over the saddle horn for right now, then lead Silver with the halter," he explained as he did just that. "Nice and slow. If you feel like you have to hold on to the saddle, do, but I want you to feel the rhythm of the horse. Try to move with him, not against him. We won't go any further until you can balance without holding on."

"Johnny, are you sure—" she started, as Johnny untied the halter from the fence.

He looked up at her, locking her gaze with his. "Do you trust me?" he asked softly.

"Yes," she immediately answered. "It's the horse I don't trust."

"I've got Silver well in hand. He's not going anywhere I don't tell him to. Now, I'm going to start leading him around the ring at a nice, slow walk. You just relax and enjoy the ride."

She made a soft, strangled sound in her throat, but Johnny kept his chuckle under his breath.

He started off in a slow circle, walking next to Silver's head and keeping his gaze on Jenn. Surprisingly, it wasn't long before her grip on the saddle horn loosened, and then fell entirely as she placed her palms on her thighs.

"I'm getting this!" she exclaimed, then clamped a hand over her mouth. "I can't help being excited, Johnny, and I think that's what got me into trouble last time. I'm afraid I'll freak Silver out and he'll balk like the last horse did."

"Any cowboy worth his salt gets excited when he's in the saddle. You think those rodeo guys aren't pumped with adrenaline? Horses can sense agitation, but it doesn't necessarily follow that your horse will freak out and you'll get thrown or anything."

"Those rodeo guys know how to stay on a horse at a dead run. I'm still not positive I can keep my balance at a walk."

"We can call it a day," Johnny suggested mildly. "If you want to, I mean." He was consciously baiting her, appealing to her stubborn streak.

Jenn frowned at him. "Look, cowboy, I came out

here today to learn to ride, and that's exactly what I'm going to do."

Johnny tipped his hat at her. "An admirable quality, stubbornness."

Her frown turned to a smile. "Whatever works. What do I do next?"

"Slide the reins up off the saddle horn, but keep them loose." Jenn did as he said, but kept the reins extended so far down they were nearly slipping right off the horse's neck.

"Not that loose," Johnny said with a laugh. He reached up and adjusted the reins, threading them through her fingers in the old western style. "Now you can lead the horse on your own. It's like driving a car. Want Silver to go left, move your hand left. Right is right, stop is backward—gently."

"And go?"

She had loosened up while he'd been leading her around the corral, but now she looked as stiff as an ice sculpture. The poor woman really was terrified, but her determination was greater than her fear.

Johnny felt his own sense of determination rising. He wasn't going to let anything happen to Jenn. Not on his watch.

"Loosen up, darlin'. Your posture, not the reins. I'm not going to let old Silver bolt on you."

"You'd better not."

Johnny loosened the halter to where it had a couple of feet of lead on it, but he did not entirely release his hold on the rope. "I'm not letting go, see? Just nudge your heels lightly into Silver's side and he'll go."

Jenn's first few attempts at nudging were barely visible to Johnny's eye. He grinned. "A little harder than that, hon. The horse has to feel it."

Jenn squeezed her eyes shut and gave Silver a good prod with her heels. The horse moved off at the same slow walk he'd had when Johnny was leading him around. Jenn's eyes popped open and widened in surprise.

"Well, how about that?" she asked, sounding amazed. And pleased.

"Try a couple of turns," he suggested when she'd walked Silver around the corral a few times in a clockwise motion. "Now, halt."

Jenn was magnificent, Johnny thought. Not too many people would be able to face their fears with as much courage as this woman did. More to the point, if she kept this up, she would end up an excellent horsewoman. Too bad he wouldn't be around to see her triumph.

"I'm ready," Jenn announced, joy evident in her voice. "Let's do it, Johnny."

"Do what?" he asked. Her big blue eyes were sparkling with a new light that made Johnny's chest feel like it was going to explode.

"Go for a ride. That's what you asked me out here for, isn't it?"

"Yeah, but—"

"But nothing. Saddle up, cowboy, and let's ride the range."

His gaze locked with hers, intense and questioning. "You're sure about this?"

Jenn chuckled softly. She wasn't sure about anything. "No. But I'm going to do it anyhow."

Scotty sauntered from the house, walking to the corral fence and leaning his arms on it. "I've been watching from the window," he said, amazement in his voice. "I gotta hand it to ya, Johnny. I thought only God worked miracles."

Johnny frowned at him. "It wasn't a miracle. And it wasn't me. It was your sister. She's fantastic, isn't she?"

Scotty snorted loudly and made a face at the both of them.

"Johnny and I are going riding," Jenn announced, holding her chin high against the disbelief in her brother's expression. "Are you coming along, or not?"

Scotty looked from Jenn to Johnny and back, scratching the peach fuzz under his chin. Jenn held her breath, secretly hoping he would decline. While she loved her brother, she wanted this time alone with Johnny.

When Scotty raised an eyebrow at her, she knew her thoughts had been transparent on her face. "Uh, I don't think so," he said, snickering at Johnny's back as Johnny made his way to the stable to saddle his own mount. "Three's a crowd, and all that."

Jenn felt guilty about not including her brother. They'd never been close, with their age difference and all, but she loved him. "Come along. It's probably safer for me to ride with two seasoned cowboys than just one."

Scotty beamed at Jenn's compliment. "Naw. Really. I promised to play chess with Granddad anyhow. You two go and have your fun."

Her brother turned and walked back to the house just as Johnny entered the corral, leading his own sturdy quarter horse, a large black mare which he'd brought with him in Scotty's horse trailer.

"He's not coming with us?" Johnny asked as he opened the corral gate.

"No," replied Jenn. "I believe he thought he might be infringing upon—well, a romantic rendezvous between you and me." She felt the blush rise on her cheeks and she looked away from Johnny.

He chuckled. "Scotty's loss. I guess I'll be the only one lucky enough to share your company."

Jenn thought back to their first meeting, when she'd so sternly demanded "no alone time" with this handsome cowboy. Now she couldn't wait to be alone with Johnny for an entire afternoon.

"We'll keep it at a slow walk, all right?" Johnny said, as he mounted up and led his horse outside the corral. "If you ever feel uncomfortable, just let me know. Remember, I'll be right by your side."

Funny, but she wasn't afraid. At least not of the horse. Her feelings for Johnny, maybe. And she wasn't the least sure she could rein those in with a simple backward tug.

Johnny held his horse until they were evenly paced. They rode for a while without talking, but Jenn didn't feel uncomfortable, either with the horse or with the man. There were no awkward gaps that made her need to fill the space with words. It was enough just to be out here with Johnny, riding side by side, enjoying the magnificent view of the ranch.

"Thank you," Jenn said softly a few minutes later.

"For what?" Johnny asked, his voice low and a little scratchy.

"You know perfectly well for what. For getting me up on this horse. I never realized how spectacular the landscape really is up here."

"Like what?"

"Well, for one thing, I thought it was all dead grass. I had no idea so many types of wildflowers grew on my grandparents' property."

"No?" he asked with a sideways glance at her. "Pull your mount to a halt for a moment, darlin'. Just hold steady there, okay?"

Jenn did as she was asked, wondering what was wrong. Had her cinch loosened, and she was sliding off her mount without even knowing about it?

Johnny slid off his horse and pulled the reins over the animal's neck, dropping them to the ground and leaving the horse free.

"Should you be doing that?" Jenn asked, wondering how they were going to get back to the ranch if Johnny's horse decided to take off on his own.

"Lucy here comes when I whistle," Johnny said with a laugh.

"Lucy? You named your horse Lucy?" It just didn't seem like the name a cowboy would give his horse. She shook her head and laughed.

"Yeah. Just fit her personality, I guess."

"I guess," Jenn repeated, still laughing.

Johnny started walking, looking around at the ground, as if he'd lost something.

"What are you looking for?" she asked, not so impatient as curious.

"Shh," he said, holding his index finger to his lips. "Just give me a second."

Jenn raised her eyebrows but said nothing.

"Here it is. I knew I'd find it if I looked close enough." His back was to her so she didn't see what he reached down and grabbed until he'd turned back toward her, a long-stemmed wildflower with dangling blue petals in his hand. "Bluebells," he said. "Or at least, that's what I call them. They remind me of your eyes."

Jenn choked up as he handed his heartfelt gift to her. No one had ever given her anything so thoughtful. The single wildflower held far more significance than the fancy roses she'd sent herself.

She tucked the precious flower into her hair, thinking she'd press it into a book when she arrived back at the ranch house. It was certainly a moment she didn't want to forget.

Ever.

"Thank you," she choked out belatedly, as Johnny remounted.

Johnny just shook his head and looked away from her. "Let's go that way," he said, pointing to the west. "Looks like some nice terrain."

Jenn turned her mount that direction, wanting to say more, but not knowing what to say or how to express what she was feeling.

She wasn't even sure *what* she was feeling, only that her emotions were in such a jumble, she was surprised they didn't cause her to fall right off her horse.

She was about to say thank you again, she realized, but Johnny had already blown off her gratitude twice. She was relatively certain, she thought with a soft smile, that he wouldn't want to hear it a third time.

She was still pondering what she *should* say when she suddenly heard a sound she'd been taught to recognize from childhood and which she had been afraid of all her life.

The chilling rattle of a snake.

Chapter Nine

Jenn didn't have a second's time to consider what that might mean to her or her mount, before Silver bucked sideways and bolted at a dead run. The horse's sudden jerk back should have thrown her, but she'd been concentrating carefully on riding just the way Johnny had taught her, and somehow, some way, she'd remained in the saddle despite the horse's lurch.

But she had only ridden at a slow walk. Now the horse was galloping at a speed so fast the countryside was flying by her in a blur. Instinctively, she leaned forward, desperately gripping the saddle horn and the horse's mane for dear life with her hands, while trying to remember what Johnny had taught her about using her legs and heels to keep the horse under her. She still held the reins in her left hand, along with the saddle horn, but only because they'd been laced through her fingers by Johnny.

Now she knew why.

At first, her concentration was solely on staying in the saddle and keeping her stomach from lurching, both from the fear of losing her seat and the feeling that the earth was coming up to meet her with each stride of the horse.

She could hear Johnny calling to her in the distance. "Pull up, Jenn. Pull up on the reins!"

Except, she couldn't pull up on the reins, or otherwise steer the careening beast, because she knew if she let go of the saddle horn, even for a brief moment, her ride would be over.

Her *life* might be over. No telling what a fall from a horse going this speed might do to her—and that was if she didn't hit her head on a rock when she fell.

No, she was going to have to continue holding on for dear life, and hope that eventually the horse would tire and stop on its own.

It was then she realized just where Silver was headed. She didn't know the ranch as well as the rest of her family, but if she wasn't mistaken, there was a steep ravine ahead, with a drop of at least twelve feet or more. There was no way she'd survive if the horse went over the edge, and she was helpless to stop him.

She closed her eyes, gritting her teeth against the inevitable. Either she would have to jump from the horse or she would hit the ravine.

Neither option looked good.

It was as if time slowed down, though the clatter of hoofbeats never ceased.

She was going to die. And she hadn't even made peace with herself, let alone God, not that she believed in God. But her life was suddenly over, and what did she have to show for it?

And what did it mean—*really* mean—to die?

A giant nothingness?

Would she simply cease to exist?

Her soul cried out against that thought. How could she *be,* and then suddenly *not be?*

And still the horse continued on at a gallop, headed straight for the ravine. Jenn was barely aware she was screaming, no longer caring if Silver might be affected by her own terror. The situation had gone far beyond that now, and the ravine was closing in on her.

She could still hear Johnny yelling but could no longer make out his words. She was beginning to feel dizzy, with the world whirling around her. Maybe she would pass out entirely.

Maybe it was better that way.

And then Johnny was in front of her, just at the edge of the ravine, his horse rearing up and Johnny, hat in hand, waving his arms and yelling for all he was worth.

It took Jenn a moment to realize what he was doing, and even longer still to recognize that his plan had worked. He'd risked his own life for hers, putting himself and his own horse directly in the path of the ravine, forcing Silver to divert to the side, to safety.

It worked, and Silver, frothy and snorting from the run, quickly slowed and began sidestepping in his agitation. Jenn didn't let go of the horse or the saddle, but she turned her head to see Johnny still on the edge of the cliff.

He appeared to be having trouble controlling his own mount, though Jenn struggled to understand how that could be, consummate horseman that Johnny was. He held a good seat despite Lucy slip-sliding on the loose gravel near the edge of the ravine. Johnny appeared to be helping her, guiding her away from the danger.

Then his horse lost her footing and half reared to avoid the deep, deathly fall into the ravine.

Lucy recovered and quickly skittered away to safety. Johnny was not so lucky.

Jenn slid off her now still mount, screaming in terror as Johnny was heaved off the saddle, his hands grasping desperately at the air as he plunged down the side of the ravine.

Jenn hit the dirt at a dead run, not caring when she slid on the gravel and had to right herself with her palms, not even noticing they were bleeding from the small, sharp rocks.

She slowed only as she reached the edge of the ravine, dropping to her stomach to look over its edge. Johnny's body lay unmoving at the bottom, his neck cocked at an odd angle.

Had he hit his head on a rock? There were certainly enough ominous-looking stones down there, many around Johnny's still body.

"Johnny!" she called, over and over, but he didn't respond.

He obviously couldn't, Jenn thought.

He was dead. And she'd killed him.

She scrambled down the ravine, ignoring the sound of tearing cloth, as thorny branches reached out to scratch her skin raw. "Johnny. Oh, God, please don't let Johnny be dead."

She didn't even realize she was praying.

It was only when she knelt before Johnny's body that she realized his chest was rising and falling. Relief flooded through her, followed quickly by terror. Johnny was alive, but he was unconscious, which meant he'd suffered a good knock to the head. She could now see his head had, in fact, landed on a sizeable stone.

What should she do now?

For all she knew, every bone in his body could be broken. And she was out in the middle of nowhere, with nothing and nobody but the horses, presumably still on the ridge above her. She reached for the cell phone she always carried with her. It was a lost cause. There was no service this far out in the middle of nowhere. With an audible growl of frustration, she jammed the phone back into her pocket.

Think, she commanded herself.

Okay. First aid. She could administer some sort of help to Johnny. She'd taken courses in first aid from the community shelters where she worked. Mostly what she remembered, though, was CPR, and that wasn't going to help her now.

Johnny's heart was beating, and he was breathing, albeit shallowly. What was the correct course of action for a bump on the noggin?

Concentrate.

Johnny's face was becoming paler by the moment. Beads of sweat had formed on his forehead.

Was he going into shock?

Quickly, Jenn unbuttoned her long-sleeved shirt, glad she'd worn a T-shirt underneath for the ride today. She rolled her shirt into a makeshift pillow and slid it as gently as possible under Johnny's head, trying not to move his neck any more than she had to.

She found a medium-size rock which had a flat edge, and put it underneath his feet to raise them slightly.

A blanket. She needed a blanket. The sun was roasting down on them, but a shock victim might not feel the heat, and even so, she knew she needed to cover him.

And water. He needed water.

Jenn knew both items were tied to her saddle, so

she quickly scrambled back up the ravine's steep incline, hoping she'd find her horse, or Johnny's, when she made it to the top.

Both horses were grazing just east of the ravine, looking for all the world as if nothing had happened. Her horse didn't even spook as she approached. Silver let her get what she needed from the saddle without bothering so much as to stop nibbling at the grass.

She only wished Johnny could recover as quickly from the trauma of the past few minutes. If he didn't... Well, she wasn't going to let herself go there now.

She needed to stay alert. Focused.

Positive.

With the needed supplies tucked under one arm, Jenn slid back down the ravine to Johnny's side. Murmuring light, comforting words under her breath, she quickly covered him up with the scratchy wool blanket and then splashed her handkerchief with some of the cool water from her canteen.

"Come on, Johnny, don't do this to me," she whispered as she gently dabbed the fabric against his brow. "You can't leave me now. I just found you."

She was putting a second splash of water on the handkerchief when Johnny groaned.

"Oh, my head." He lifted an arm toward his forehead, but Jenn stopped him.

"Shh. Don't try to move, Johnny. You fell down the ravine. You've been hurt."

To her surprise, Johnny chuckled, if weakly. "Yeah, that much I got."

Lying on death's door and still cracking jokes. Or maybe she was being overdramatic. Maybe his injuries looked worse than they were.

There was only one way to know for sure.

"I don't want you to move. Not a muscle, do you hear me, cowboy?"

"Uh," he answered, his eyes flitting open for just a moment before he closed them again. "Don't think I could if I wanted to."

"I've got to ride back to the ranch and get help," she stated as calmly as possible, though her heart was racing on the inside. There was no use making Johnny panic by her going into hysterics, so she pushed her apprehension to the back of her mind.

"Uh-huh," he answered in a quiet, scratchy tone. "I'm not going anywhere." He sounded as if he weren't quite all together, and Jenn's heart clenched. Maybe the head injury was worse than she thought.

"I'll be back as quick as I can. In the meantime, you just lie still. I *will* be back," she promised him fervently, laying a gentle hand on his forearm for emphasis. "It won't take nearly as long to return for you in a four-wheel drive."

Johnny lay unmoving, and Jenn thought he'd passed out again. She laid her hand on his chest, over his heart. "I'm praying for you, Johnny."

She didn't know where the words had come from. Maybe from being around her family too long. Maybe from the lack of having anything else to say.

He couldn't hear her anyway.

She was about to rise when Johnny's hand snaked out and grabbed her wrist. Startled, she tried to pull away, but even in his weakened state, Johnny was stronger than she was.

She felt one moment of panic, the sheer terror her experience with Duke had branded into her.

But this was different. This was Johnny. And he wasn't hurting her, on the off chance he was truly capable of doing so in his present condition.

He just wasn't letting go.

"Are you really? Are you really, Jenn?" he rasped through a dry throat.

Jenn took a moment to dribble some water from the canteen down his throat before she answered.

"Really what?"

"Really praying."

"I guess so. I don't know." She paused and shook her head. "Why are you asking me this?"

She should be racing for help, but Johnny wouldn't let her go. His eyes had reopened and his midnight-blue gaze was clear, holding her every bit as firmly as his grip on her wrist.

"I pray with my eyes open, Jenn," he said in a coarse whisper.

Jenn had no idea what that statement meant. Maybe the man was delirious, though his eyes were clear and piercing straight through to her soul.

"Look, cowboy, you're going to be in a world of hurt if I don't get back to the ranch and get you some help."

"Yeah," he agreed, dropping her wrist and covering his ribs protectively. "It hurts, all right."

"Don't move," she warned him again, pressing the canteen into his hand. "Not a muscle, Johnny. I'll be back as soon as I can."

She didn't wait to see his response, but rather hiked up the ravine wall as fast as she could, ignoring the sharp pain in her ankles when her feet slid on the treacherous gravel.

One thing at a time now. Ravine. Horse. Ranch.

Horse.

Great. She'd made a lot of progress today, but she wasn't even remotely over her fear of horses, and now she was alone with a great, big giant of a horse, and without Johnny to help guide her.

Or to assist her in mounting.

She approached Silver and took up his reins, glad when the horse didn't balk at her presence. Surely, he must sense her fear of horses, not to mention the apprehension she was feeling at Johnny's precarious condition, but he remained calm.

Why had Johnny given her such a gigantic animal to ride? How was she supposed to get into the saddle? Johnny had lifted her onto it before.

But she had to get in that saddle. One way or another. *Now.*

She knotted the reins and slid them over the saddle horn, which was right about level with her forehead. This was not going to be easy.

You've seen this done a thousand times, she coached herself. Everyone in her family rode horses all the time—and they didn't need handsome cowboys hoisting them into the saddle. Just like on television, the members of her family made it look easy to swing up on top of their horses. Jenn had the sinking feeling it wasn't as easy as it looked in the movies.

Standing to the left of the horse and as close as possible, she raised her leg, trying to get a foothold in the stirrup. If she could just get one foot in, maybe she could boost herself up by the saddle horn.

This was one time when being short was definitely not an advantage. Her foot didn't even come close to the stirrup, no matter how she twisted, turned or hopped.

There had to be another way. She looked around for something big enough to stand on—a boulder maybe, or a tree stump. But there was nothing in sight.

Her heart continued at its frantic pace, and Jenn felt as if it might burst right out of her chest if she didn't find a solution.

Then she saw the tree, a lone cottonwood waving in the soft breeze as if beckoning to her. Jenn eyed the sturdy tree for a moment, an idea forming in her head. A *bad* idea, probably, but what other choices did she have?

Sliding the reins back over Silver's head, Jenn led him to the base of the tree and tied the reins to one of the lower branches.

Trees she could climb. Horses not so much. But if she could climb onto a branch high enough to be over the horse, but not so far as to make some sort of crazy leap…

She didn't give herself time to think up all the disadvantages of her plan. She scampered up onto the middle branches with the same ease she'd done in childhood.

But that was the easy part. Still holding tight to the tree trunk, she used one foot to test the strength of the branch nearest the horse. It gave a little, but held.

"Okay, then," she muttered to herself. "Time to see if I still remember how to play on the monkey bars."

She eyed the horse one more time, attempting to judge the distance from the branch to the saddle. Then, holding her breath, she swung out onto the branch, dangling directly over the horse.

Her plan had worked! Or at least she thought it had, before she heard the dry, crackling snap of the branch above her breaking. She had no more time to steady herself or position herself over the saddle before she came tumbling down—right onto the saddle.

"Whoa," she said aloud, both to steady the dancing horse and as an exclamation of the pain she felt. But she was in the saddle, and a sense of elation rushed over her, making her already adrenaline-soaked nerves stand on end.

She nudged the horse forward with her knees, until she could reach the reins still tied to a lower branch of the tree. It didn't take much to loosen them, though getting them back over the horse's neck was a bit problematic.

It was only a moment before she'd turned the horse toward the ranch, giving one backward glance at the ravine where Johnny still lay, in God only knew what condition.

Literally, God only knew.

Chapter Ten

Johnny groaned. He didn't know how much time had passed, or how many times he'd drifted in and out of consciousness. Once Jenn was gone, he'd tried to sit up, but the pain that cut through the back of his head was like a sharp blade, so he lay back down again to wait.

It was hot, and he was thirsty. He knew enough to take only small sips of water at a time, but since he was lying down, he had to pour the water into his mouth from the canteen, and he was certain he dropped more water down his shirtfront than into his mouth.

But what was really worrying him most wasn't his condition, or his safety.

It was Jenn.

She'd only learned to ride today. How would she fare getting back to the ranch on her own? Silver was a reliable horse, but he was also a big one. Johnny wasn't even sure she could mount him on her own.

Presumably she knew her way back to the ranch, having been here so often, but he didn't know for sure. The mere idea of Jenn getting lost was more terrifying to him than the thought of no one coming to his aid.

What if Jenn *did* get lost and no one came to *her* aid?

It would be a couple of hours before anyone would miss them, and by then dusk would be approaching. It would be hard for the family to look for them in the dark, though Johnny knew they'd try.

He had to get up, to get back to his horse and find Jenn. He sat up, and then winced at the blinding pain stabbing through his head. The earth spun around him. Lights turned to shades of gray as blackness engulfed him.

He wasn't going anywhere.

Jenn managed a slow canter, surprised at how easy it was to remain balanced on Silver once she'd gotten used to the easy, somehow comforting rocking motion. It wouldn't take her much time at all to reach the ranch house at this speed.

Johnny would be safe.

Johnny.

What had he meant by his statement—that he prayed with his eyes open? She half thought he was delirious, but deep in her gut she knew his words had been co-herent. And serious.

He was trying to tell her something.

And then it hit her.

He prayed with his *eyes open.* Literally.

Which meant he'd observed that she wasn't praying at all. She'd once asked him if he was a Christian, way back on the first day they'd met, but Johnny had never pursued the same subject with her, a point for which she'd been thankful.

So why did Johnny pick now of all times to bring it up? She'd only been saying something random in order to comfort him, not to start a theological debate on the merits of Christian belief.

She thought it didn't matter, but she'd been wrong about so much, why should this be any different?

Johnny obviously *did* care about her relationship— or lack of one—with God. It mattered to him enough to confront her when he might even be dying.

The thought of Johnny dying was almost more than she could bear. Of course, Christians believed they were going to a better place, not simply having their life snuffed out like a candle.

But Jenn didn't want Johnny in heaven. She wanted him with *her*.

"It's not fair," she said aloud, realizing only after the words were spoken that she was yelling into the wind. "You let this happen, God. You let *all* this happen. Maybe I deserved what Duke did to me. I wasn't being faithful to You, and we both know it.

"But Johnny? He's a good man—honest and decent and…and a Christian!" she stammered. "And now Johnny's hurt, maybe dying. What kind of God are You?"

Tears streamed down her cheeks but were brushed away by the wind. Fury had risen to such intensity in her, she thought she might spontaneously combust. Never had she felt such agony ripping up her insides, not even with Duke.

And then it struck her, as hard and as deep as a bolt of lightening.

She was talking to God.

The God she didn't believe existed.

Or did she?

She was certainly furious with Him now, so angry she wanted to lash out at something.

Someone.

She urged the horse forward into a gallop, appalled at what she'd discovered about herself. She believed in God, all right. And she blamed Him for everything.

It was all God's fault. All of it. Every bad thing that had happened to her. To those in her family. To the kids she worked with.

To Johnny.

And yet, so many of those nearest and dearest to her were believers and loved the Lord with all their heart, strength and mind. She couldn't reconcile it. How could that be?

Her tears had abated, along with her fury, her anger spent and her voice hoarse from yelling. She slowed Silver to a trot, knowing the ranch house was over the next knoll and she could soon send help for Johnny.

She didn't know much scripture, but part of a verse kept repeating itself in her head, despite her constant denial.

I am with you always.

What about when Duke had backhanded her through the bay window?

I am with you always.

What about Johnny, lying in a ditch, terribly hurt or maybe even dying?

And suddenly she knew. She knew it with the same certainty as if she'd been slapped in the face or punched in the gut, yet the realization in her heart had come softly. Silently.

She'd been taught all the right principles and, perhaps more importantly, had seen those principles lived out in faith by her family's love in action. Yes, it was true she had been a victim of Duke's cruelty, but instead of turning to God for solace, she'd run away.

From her family. Her home. Her God.

Her God.

She wasn't sure what that meant, but the peace that swept over her at that moment was as indefinable as it was sure and certain.

She had no more time to ponder her thoughts or relish the peace in her soul, for she had reached the ranch house and pulled up in front of it. Most of her family was already outside and running toward her. They must have sensed something was wrong.

She slid off Silver, tossing the reins to her brother. "Dad, Mom, get the four-wheeler. Johnny's been hurt."

Scotty had fetched the country doctor from the nearest town. The doctor carefully examined Johnny's head and taped up a couple bruised ribs. A mild concussion was the worst of it, the doctor pronounced. Nothing to worry about. A couple days in bed and he'd be right as rain.

It was when the doctor shook Jenn's hand that she realized her arms were exposed and her family was all around. There was no hiding the truth now.

She wanted to run away from the situation, curl up in a blanket and never come out, but she knew it was too late. By the looks on their faces, a sympathetic mixture of shock and compassion, it was all too obvious what they were thinking.

There was nowhere to hide.

At first, no one said a thing. Scotty excused himself with a tip of his hat, explaining that he needed to rub the horses down.

With a sigh, Jenn sat down on the couch. Her mother and father seated themselves on each side of her, Mom's arm around her waist and Dad's around her shoulders. Granny and Auntie Myra pulled chairs in close, each of them also reaching out to touch her in some way—Auntie Myra with a shaky palm on Jenn's knee, and Granny gently but firmly taking one of her hands. Granddad remained standing, pacing back and forth, his hands clasped behind his back and his face grim.

With courage she didn't think she possessed, Jenn looked every one of them straight in the eye, one by one. She felt like a suspect in a police investigation, with all eyes on her, as if waiting for a confession.

She wasn't a criminal. She was a victim. Yet that was exactly what she needed to do.

Confess.

Tell the truth for once.

She held her arms up so everyone could see the ragged scars clearly in the muted light of the late afternoon sunshine, barely glowing through the living room windows. Slowly, she turned her arms over so her family, so dear to her now more than ever, could see the full extent of the damage.

Would they hate her when they knew the full story?

Jenn knew better. Her family was the most forgiving of any people she'd ever known. But that deep, persistent fear that belonged to the latent child who'd been afraid to go home, was resurfacing with a vengeance.

Swallowing with difficulty, she struggled to form an explanation. "These are from—well…" She paused and gasped for breath. "The truth is, a long time ago, I was pushed from a bay window."

Granny's eyes narrowed. "By whom?" she asked,

sounding for all the world like she was going to take a sawed-off shotgun and blast the culprit's head off.

Her mother's grasp tightened around her waist, and for a moment Jenn wished she'd used the word *fallen* instead of *pushed*. But she was done lying, even though she knew the truth would bring more hurt to her beloved family members than in her worst nightmares.

In a way, this *was* her worst nightmare.

"Who did this?" Granny asked again.

Granddad hovered over Granny's shoulder now, his face looking equally sober and angry. It was as much of an emotional expression as she'd ever seen on the old man's face, and Jenn cringed that she'd been the one to put it there.

But then again, she had it coming to her, didn't she? Granddad—the whole family—had every right to be angry with her.

"It was a long time ago," Jenn repeated, her voice cracking. Her heart pumped rapidly, echoing into her head.

"That is why you left home so suddenly," her mother said softly. Jenn could hear the agony of the statement, and it pierced her heart. At the time, she hadn't even considered what pain and anguish she might be causing her family by her sudden flight to Denver. Her only thoughts had been for herself.

"It is," Jenn acknowledged with a slight nod.

"But you were just a teenager," Auntie Myra said, tears running down her face. "Oh, you poor, poor girl. Why didn't you come to us, sweetheart?"

"It doesn't even look like you went to a doctor for those," Granddad said, and for once, his voice didn't carry its usual gruffness.

Jenn looked up at him in surprise. Granddad's eyes were so full of compassion and understanding, Jenn felt even worse than she did before.

Her family loved her unconditionally. She could see that now. If only she'd been able to see that when she was a stupid, naive teenager.

"I'm sure it's no secret to you all that I ran with a bad crowd when I was a teenager. What you didn't know of was my relationship with a certain man," Jenn continued her explanation, revealing every awful detail to her family.

"Why didn't you come to us?" Mom asked, her voice low and rough with emotion when Jenn finished her story.

"I was too ashamed to face any of you. And I knew you'd tell me to rely on my faith. Only, I didn't have any faith. I couldn't find it in my heart to believe there was a God who would just sit back and let such horrible things happen in the world."

She dropped her gaze to her lap, waiting for the judgment she deserved. She'd made one bad mistake after another, and she'd just confessed to her own lack of faith in God. That had to be the worst of it for her family.

No one spoke for the longest time. Jenn squeezed her eyes closed against the tears burning there.

"Jenn," Granny said softly, taking her other hand and squeezing both. "Jenn, look at me."

Jenn raised her head. Granny's eyes were full of compassion and kindness.

No condemnation, no censure.

Only love.

Jenn looked around. Everyone met her gaze square-on, and there wasn't a hint of judgment in any of their eyes.

"You must think I'm a real hypocrite," she said, her voice full of self-loathing.

"We think," stated Granddad clearly, "that you have been through enough."

"We love you, Jenn," her father said. "All of us do. When you go back to Denver, go back with that knowledge in your heart."

Jenn smiled softly through her tears. She hadn't given her family enough credit. Not when she was a teenager, and not now. "There is one more thing I'll be taking back to Denver with me."

"Johnny?" asked Auntie Myra, some of the old glow returning to her eyes, though the tears had not yet dried on her rosy cheeks.

Jenn shook her head emphatically. "God."

Chapter Eleven

Johnny was a bit uncomfortable with Jenn's family hovering over him as if he were facing a terminal illness and not just a bruised ego. He did, though, enjoy Jenn's company. She rarely left his side, and then usually only to get him something to eat or an extra pillow to make him more comfortable.

He slept way past sunup, and when he awoke, he found Jenn dozing in a chair next to his bed, an open bible in her lap.

A bible.

Thank You, Lord, for the good that has come from this accident. Thank You for reaching Jenn with Your love and compassion. Her soul is so desperately in need, and only You can fill the void. Help her to see Your truth and feel Your love.

"Jesus can help you, Jenn," he whispered through a dry throat and cracked lips.

Jenn jumped, her bible falling to the floor at her feet as she used the palm of her hand to wipe the sleep from her beautiful blue eyes. Johnny remembered the first time he'd seen her, all made up and fancy. She looked as good to him now—better, even—with a fresh face and sleep-tousled hair.

Or lack of sleep. Johnny doubted she'd had much rest that night, as uncomfortable as that pinewood desk chair was.

"I really think you should go into Cheyenne and get a CAT scan done," Jenn said, as Johnny yawned widely. He wondered if she was deliberately changing the subject.

Maybe she was. But he'd let it drop for now, knowing he'd bring it up again when he was feeling better.

"No need." His voice sounded gravelly even to his own ears. He cleared his throat.

With a soft smile, she leaned over and smoothed the hair back over his brow. He closed his eyes again, savoring the sensation of her soft fingertips against his skin, and the sweet, soft floral scent that always accompanied Jenn's presence.

"If it's a money issue, I'll take care of it. It's my fault you hurt yourself in the first place," she said gently.

Johnny lurched up in bed, spilling the mug of coffee on the nightstand. The jolt of pain in his head was nothing compared to the shock he'd just experienced in his heart.

"*Your* fault? How do you figure?"

She refused to meet his gaze. "You were trying to save my neck when you fell. I would have gone right off that ravine, otherwise."

Johnny quirked a grin. "And I suppose you were galloping toward that ravine for the fun of it?"

"Of course not. A rattlesnake spooked Silver and off he went. I had absolutely no control over the beast. It was all I could do to hang on."

Johnny nodded briskly, and then winced as pain shot through his temple. "So how do you figure it's your fault, darlin'?"

"You and your chivalrous streak," she said with a shake of her head that made her hair bounce delightfully. "First you gallantly agree to play the role of my significant other for the sake of my ego, and then you race your horse in front of mine to keep me from plunging to my death."

"First off, Jenn," Johnny said patiently, reaching for her hand, "I had as much to benefit from our—uh, mutual friendship as you. And second, I think you're being overdramatic."

She glared at him. "Am I?"

Johnny shrugged, but the movement hurt his ribs and he winced from the pain. "Silver probably would've turned anyway. Horses don't have death wishes any more than humans do."

"So there was no reason for you to ride in front of me, is that what you're saying?" she asked caustically, casting out his logic.

"Just call it an extra precaution," he said with a grin.

"Which left you at the bottom of a ravine with a hard knock to the head."

"Maybe God thought I needed to have a good conk on the head," he joked, then sobered when Jenn's expression became serious.

"About that, Johnny. I—"

He stopped her from completing her sentence. "You don't owe me an explanation."

"No," she agreed. "But I'm going to give you one anyway." She picked up the bible from where it had fallen and carefully placed it on the desk. "You were right about my faith. Rather, my lack of faith."

"When did I say that?"

"You didn't. Not exactly, anyway. But I was aware you knew I was faking it for my family's sake. I think they knew, as well, but were waiting for me to have the courage to face up to it."

"And now?"

"Well, let's just say it was a long ride back to the ranch. I *am* a coward. I was afraid to face myself. Even worse, I was afraid to face God."

Despite the ache in his head, Johnny pushed himself up until he was sitting at the edge of the bed, glad he was still clothed in the jeans he'd been wearing the day before, though now he wore only a loose T-shirt over his bandaged ribs.

"Come here," he said tenderly, reaching his arms to her.

Jenn hesitated only a moment, before shifting to a spot beside him where she could rest her head on his broad shoulder and hear the comforting beat of his heart.

It hurt a little to have Jenn leaning against his ribs, but Johnny didn't care. He wanted her in his arms.

They stayed that way, silently, for a few moments until Jenn shifted so she could look into Johnny's eyes. He grimaced when she bumped his ribs. "I'm sorry," she said quickly, shifting away from him so she wouldn't accidentally bump him again.

"Woman, will you stop apologizing for every little thing?" Johnny asked through gritted teeth. His gaze was full of amusement, and he chuckled.

Jenn laughed with him. "I'm embarrassed to say I yelled in anger at the Almighty God."

"He understands," Johnny said, stroking her hair off her face.

She looked away. "I know that now."

Johnny reached for her hands and kissed her knuckles. "I'm so happy, I think I might just jump up and dance."

"I don't suggest that in your current condition," Jenn said with a laugh.

Suddenly Johnny's eyes became serious as he looked down at her hands, which he still held gently in his.

"What is it?" she asked, her heart nearly stopping at the seriousness in his expression.

"Your arms. They aren't covered." He brushed his fingertips along the scars of one of Jenn's arms.

She pulled away. She didn't want Johnny looking at her like that, full of pity and concern.

"My long-sleeved shirt was your pillow in the ravine," she stated bluntly. "My secret is out."

"One of them, at least," he reminded her soberly. "How did your family take it?"

"Like I should have expected them to. As they would have years ago, when the accident first happened, if I'd just had the nerve to come forward."

"With love, care and concern," Johnny said softly. "You've got a real special family, Jenn."

Tears blurred her vision, but she didn't brush them away. "I do. This time with you has shown me how much they mean to me."

"And how much you mean to them."

"That, too." Jenn nodded. "Which brings up another point."

Johnny said nothing, though his gaze was questioning hers.

"My family needs to know the truth, Johnny. The whole truth. About us, I mean. I'm ready to come clean about it. Don't worry—I'll let them know the entire blame falls on my shoulders."

"Oh, no, it doesn't," he said determinedly.

"It does," she argued. "It was my dumb idea in the first place, sending myself flowers. I don't know what I was thinking. It's not like I could have kept up the ruse for two whole weeks, with or without a real man at my side. But then you showed up. My Johnny."

"You would have confessed the truth at the beginning if it weren't for me," Johnny reminded her, reaching once again for her hand. This time she didn't pull away, and Johnny stroked her palm with the pad of his thumb. Her skin was so soft and smooth, Johnny never wanted to let her go.

Ever.

"If I hadn't put my arm around you when I did," he continued, "you would have told the truth right then. It was my own foolishness that got us into this mess. I was so eager to see how a real family functioned that I compromised my integrity. And yours. I'm deeply sorry for that, more than you know."

Jenn's blue eyes were glistening with tears. "I've never met a man like you."

"I've been waiting my whole life to meet a woman like you," he countered, then realized belatedly what he had said.

Every word of it was true, but he sure shouldn't have spoken his thoughts aloud.

He was even more certain of his thoughtless blunder

when Jenn's face went suddenly pale. She looked like she might fall over. Johnny steadied her by the elbow.

"What did you say?" she whispered, her voice ragged with emotion.

Johnny pinched his lips together, wishing he'd managed that particular action a moment sooner. But Jenn deserved to hear the truth, and since he'd already made his spontaneous declaration, he had to say something to back it up, to let Jenn know once and for all how he really felt about her.

No more lies.

"Do you remember the day of the picnic?" he asked in a voice so gentle he would have used it on an unbroken filly.

She nodded.

"I told you I would never hurt you."

"I remember."

She wouldn't meet his gaze, so he reached out his hand, brushing two fingers down her cheek before tipping her chin up so she would have no choice but to look at him and see the truth in his eyes.

"I meant it then, and I mean it now."

Jenn stood suddenly and walked away from him, jamming her hands into the pockets of her blue jeans as she stared unseeingly out the east window. "I know you do."

What this man could do to her with a look was almost more than Jenn could bear. And when he put words to those unspoken expressions, it became too much for her.

She didn't know what to think, how to feel. Johnny had stirred emotions she didn't even know existed. He'd won her trust. Despite her past, she believed him when he said he'd never hurt her.

That was probably the worst part of it, she thought miserably. He *was* going to hurt her—when he walked out the door of her family's ranch house for the last time and she would never see him again.

"Jenn. Look at me," he softly urged.

She was afraid to turn, to see the sincerity in his gaze, but found herself helpless to do otherwise.

"Stop me if this is too much for you," he said, wincing as he stood.

"Sit down, Johnny. You're going to hurt yourself." She was glad to have something to say that didn't have to do with what she was feeling right now.

He groaned but did as she asked. "All right. If you promise to hear me out."

She wrapped her arms around herself as if for protection, but nodded briskly before she could think better of it. She owed him that courtesy.

"I had good motives for sticking around here and masking as your boyfriend," he said, then shook his head. "But it was not well played. I never should have forced your hand."

"You said that already," she reminded him.

"I did, didn't I?" He chuckled, and then grasped at his rib cage. "My point is, somewhere all this became… more than that for me."

He paused and jammed his fingers through his tousled locks. "I truly care for you, Jenn. I admire so much about you, and I want to know more. The bottom line is that I don't want this to end when the reunion is over."

Neither do I, Jenn thought, turning back to the window so Johnny couldn't read her expression.

"Now, I know you've been through a lot, and I don't want to chase you off with my words, but I have to speak what I feel. I want to see you again after this week is over. Do you think that's possible?"

If there was one thing Jenn had learned in her time with Johnny, it was that anything was possible.

And this request was something she wanted, too. *Needed.* To move on with her life, maybe have the first real relationship she'd ever had with a man, even if it had started out as a lie.

Who knew what the future held for them?

She couldn't answer with words, but she turned to face him, allowing him to see the tears now coursing down her cheeks as she smiled and nodded.

His answering smile lit up the whole room, assuring her beyond words she was doing the right thing to trust this man.

Jenn was enjoying a steaming cup of coffee in the window nook when the doorbell rang. Granny, Auntie Myra and Jenn's mother, she knew, were all quilting on the back porch, so she set her mug on the nearest end table and went to answer the door.

She couldn't have been more surprised by the man on the other side of the door if he had been purple and sporting a pair of antennae.

The first thing she noticed was his suit, a silk tie, and even a well-placed silk handkerchief in his jacket pocket.

In Wyoming.

Slowly, her gaze rose to the man's face. Close-cropped blond hair, blue eyes, clean-shaven, a nice smile. And an expression that bore witness to his feeling out of place. Jenn almost wanted to laugh, if the man standing in her doorway didn't look so serious.

He shifted from one foot to the other, rubbing his hands in front of him. "Good afternoon," he said, his voice a pleasant tenor.

"Hi," Jenn replied, raising her eyebrows and smiling at him. "Can I help you?"

"I'm sorry to bother you," the man began hesitantly, "but I am looking for a colleague of mine. A Mr. Jonathan Whitcomb."

"I'm sorry for your trouble, but there's no one by that name here." She started to close the door when the man barred it with his hand. Surprised, Jenn opened the door back up, gazing expectantly at the well-dressed man.

"I understand," the man started, then paused. "That is, I think he may be going under the alias Johnny Barnes."

Jenn's heart stopped cold.

Her Johnny Barnes? What could this man possibly want with him?

"I think you'd better come inside," Jenn said, opening the door wider and ushering the blond man into the ranch house.

"Thank you," he said. "My name is Blake Edwards III, but most people just call me Trey."

"Glad to meet you, Trey. I'm Jenn Washington. Now why don't you sit down and tell me exactly why you're looking for Johnny Barnes."

Trey ruffled his fingers through his hair, but somehow managed not to displace a single strand. He looked every inch the high-classed businessman, as different as night and day from her sweet, unassuming Johnny.

Jenn seated herself on the sofa and gestured to the

chocolate-colored armchair across from her. It occurred to her that this was where she'd had her first conversation with Johnny, when she thought him nothing more than an ignorant cowboy.

How much had changed in such a short time.

"Perhaps I should start at the beginning," he said, seating himself and leaning forward on his elbows, clasping his hands in front of him. "My business partner and I own the Zandor Corporation. Specifically, the Zandor computer software system. Perhaps you've heard of it?"

Of course Jenn had. It was only the top of the line business software company in the world.

Come to think of it, she'd heard of Jonathan Whitcomb, as well. She'd read about him in the papers. Teenage prodigy of some sort, she remembered. He'd started his company at the age of sixteen and it had exploded on the market.

"What does this have to do with Johnny?" she asked again.

"He's here, then," Trey said, sounding relieved. "It's taken me a great deal of time and expense to track him down."

"I'm afraid you'll be disappointed, then," Jenn said. "I don't mean to discourage you, but I'm afraid there's been a mistake. The man I know as Johnny Barnes couldn't possibly be your business partner, Jonathan Whitcomb."

Trey frowned. "And why is that?"

Jenn chuckled. "Trust me. The man I'm talking about wouldn't be caught dead in a business suit. He's been wrangling on the Wyoming range all summer."

"So that's where he went." The glimmer of hope returned to Trey's eyes. "He just up and left, saying he had to get away from it all for a while. Didn't tell me where he was going or anything. I've been going crazy, trying to run the company without him."

"I still don't think—" Jenn began, but was interrupted from the door to the kitchen.

"I thought I heard the doorbell ring." It was Johnny, looking a bit peaked and clutching at his rib cage, but up on his feet. "What, did you get another delivery of flowers while I…"

His sentence drifted off to nothing as his eyes made contact with Trey's. If Johnny had looked a bit weak in the knees before, he now looked as if he'd fall down flat on his face.

Without thinking, Jenn moved to his side, slipping her arm around his waist to support him. She was about to tell him he shouldn't be out of bed when his next word stopped her cold.

"Trey."

"Jonathan."

"What are you doing here?" Johnny's voice was as hard and cold as she'd ever heard it. He stiffened noticeably in her arms.

Jonathan?

Jenn couldn't wrap her mind around it. Her cowboy, the man she'd given her trust to, a man she might even be starting to fall in love with, wasn't really a cowboy at all?

No way.

It couldn't be.

Her arms still around his waist, she stared up at Johnny, but though he rested his arm around her shoulders, he refused to look her in the eye, choosing rather to glare at the newcomer.

So it was true, then. Johnny's actions were speaking far louder than any words he could have said, and guilt, not denial, was written plainly on his face.

Johnny Barnes, wrangler, was actually Jonathan Whitcomb, millionaire computer prodigy.

Which meant he'd been lying to her from the moment they'd met.

Now she was the one to stiffen. How could he have done this to her?

Her mind raced through all the special moments she and Johnny had shared—the picnic, the horse ride. She'd shared her deepest, most intimate secrets with him.

She'd trusted him.

Anger and betrayal rushed hotly through her veins, an angry haze shadowing her sight. She opened her mouth, trying to breathe, trying to speak, but then clamped her jaw closed again. She had a million and one things she wanted to say to Johnny—Jonathan—right now. She wanted to push him away, scream at him, do something to show the agony she was feeling at her heart being shattered into a million pieces.

She'd *trusted* him.

What a fool she'd been.

There was so much she wanted to say, but she ground her teeth with the effort to remain silent, unwilling to lose what little poise she still possessed.

She would not voice those thoughts. Not now, anyway, with company in the house. She had that much dignity left.

She unwrapped herself from Johnny and turned toward him, knowing he could hear the anger in her voice, even if he refused to look at her face. "I'll leave you to your friend, *Jonathan*," she whispered harshly. "I'm sure you two have a lot of catching up to do."

She twirled around on her toes and, breathing deeply, tried to make a slow, steady exit from the room, her chin held high. She would not dignify the moment by giving him a chance to respond—but she would not run away from him, either.

It was only when she reached the safety of her room and had closed the door behind her that she broke down, sliding to the floor in a crumpled heap, with the cold, wooden door for support, crying for a man she now realized she never really knew at all.

Chapter Twelve

Johnny strode to the couch and sat down opposite his friend. "What are you doing here?" he asked through gritted teeth. "You may just have ruined everything."

Trey chuckled. "What everything?"

"My life," answered Johnny, deadly serious.

"Don't you think that's being a little overdramatic?" Trey asked. "After all, you were the one who left me high and dry without a word. I had no idea where to find you, even in an emergency."

"Was there?"

"Was there what?"

"An emergency."

The blond-haired man frowned, his cheeks staining with color. "Well, no. But I don't see how you could just walk out of your job like that. We've been best friends since childhood. Doesn't that mean anything to you?"

"Of course it does," Johnny said with a shake of his head. "But I couldn't handle it anymore. I've—*we've*—been working nonstop since we were sixteen. We missed being kids. Doesn't that ever bother you?"

Trey's eyebrows shot up. "Yeah, but look at the money we've made."

Johnny slammed his palms down on his knees in frustration. "I don't care about the money. I was going crazy in New York. I needed a break, and I knew if I told you what I was going to do, you'd either talk me out of it or tail me until I relented. And I wasn't so far off, now was I?"

Trey just stared at him, stunned.

Johnny jammed his fingers into his hair. Whatever mess he was in now was his own making. It wasn't Trey's fault Johnny had dropped off the planet without leaving word of his whereabouts. It had seemed a good idea at the time—but then again, so did a lot of the actions he'd made recently, actions he now regretted with all his heart.

Especially where Jenn was concerned.

But first he owed Trey an apology. His friend was looking at him as if he'd grown a third nose, and rightly so. They had been close, as Trey had pointed out, since they were kids, and they'd built their company from the ground up.

"I'm sorry," Johnny said contritely. "I'm taking my frustration out on you and that's not right."

"I can see you're upset, buddy. I'm sorry if I've made things difficult for you. I've obviously come at a bad time, if that pretty woman who just stalked from the room is any indication. Maybe I should just leave."

"Not until I explain things to you," Johnny said, punching his fist into his palm. "I owe you that much, at least. I'm in a world of trouble, especially with Jenn, but it's all my own doing."

"So, then, what's up?" Trey said, leaning back in the

armchair. "I don't understand any of this. Why did you disappear the way you did?"

"Like I said, I short-circuited. Don't you ever feel like we missed out on something, starting our company as early as we did?"

Trey shrugged. "Yeah, I guess we did. I mean, rooming with you in college was fun and all, but we didn't do much, other than work and study, did we?"

"That's an understatement. So you understand why I needed a break, then?"

Trey shook his head. "Not entirely. We're living our dreams, Jonathan, doing all the things we talked about as kids. We travel the world, attend fancy parties, and run a multibillion-dollar corporation."

Johnny shook his head vehemently. "I hate those parties. And while I admit I enjoy traveling, it's not exactly like a vacation when you're on business, is it?"

"Guess not," Trey conceded.

"I'm finding that, lately, the things I thought were important don't hold the same sparkle they used to. My priorities," Johnny said softly, gazing at his hands, "have changed."

Trey glanced at the French doors where Jenn had exited. "You have a new girlfriend?"

Johnny scowled in earnest. "Can we just leave her out of this?"

Trey shrugged. "I guess."

"I didn't leave because of her. I didn't even know her at the time," Johnny said, with a weary sigh. He wrapped an arm around his rib cage, which was aching mercilessly. Or maybe the ache was deeper inside.

He tried not to think about it. Not now. "I hired on for the summer as a wrangler at a Wyoming ranch. I thought it'd be good for me to sleep out under the stars for a change."

Trey made a face. "Ugh. Not my idea of a good time, but whatever. I've got to say, buddy, you aren't looking so good right now. Are you feeling all right?"

Johnny nodded, knowing he was unable to hide the misery of his expression. "I'm okay."

Trey apparently chose to take Johnny's word at face value. "Glad to hear it. Now, what I want to know is, when are you coming back to New York?"

Johnny glanced at the door where Jenn had left moments earlier and winced inwardly. If he had any sense in him at all, he'd run back to New York this instant, with his tail tucked between his legs. He'd made a huge mess of things all around. It would be the easiest thing in the world to just up and leave—maybe even easiest for Jenn, too, in the long run. She couldn't be very happy with him right now, that was for sure.

Then again, he'd never been a man to run away from his problems, especially those he'd brought upon himself. He would stay this one out, though he had little hope of regaining what trust he'd built with Jenn.

Johnny scrubbed a hand down his face, vaguely realizing he was unshaven. Between that and the way he still favored his rib cage, it was no wonder Trey thought he wasn't at the top of his game.

Johnny caught and held Trey's gaze. "I can't leave right now. I have some unfinished business to take care of here."

"Meaning the woman."

"Meaning a lot of things," Johnny snapped back, angry that his friend should bear such a cavalier attitude toward Jenn. "Up to and including the fact that I have another month left of wrangling. I signed a contract."

"Which our lawyers can easily handle."

"I gave my word, Trey. Right now, that doesn't count for very much. I'm not going to make it any worse than it already is by breaking my contract with the Double Y."

"So you're not coming back."

"I didn't say that. Just not yet."

"I just don't like being left with all the responsibility."

"Tell you what," Johnny offered. "When I get back to New York in a month, I'll let *you* take some time off for a change."

"I don't need—" Trey began, but Johnny cut him off, raising his palms to halt Trey's words.

"Nonnegotiable," Johnny insisted. "You've worked every bit as hard as I have. You deserve a vacation and you're going to get one."

Trey shrugged. "I don't get you, Jonathan. I finally find you, and here you are, way out in the middle of Wyoming, looking like a cowboy, working like one. What's up with that?"

"I obviously can't explain it, at least to you. It was just something I had to do. Can we leave it at that?"

"Yes, if that's what you want."

"It's what I need. We can talk about it more later, when I get back to work. In the meantime, I appreciate you covering for me. I shouldn't have left without telling you where I was going, and I apologize again for that."

Johnny took a piece of paper from one of the side tables and jotted down a telephone number. "You can reach me here if I'm not out on the range, or leave a message if I am. You can also e-mail me. I've been avoiding work mail, but I promise I'll check my messages often and get back to you as soon as possible."

Trey shook his head skeptically, then stood and offered his hand to Johnny. "I wish you the best, pal, with whatever it is you have going."

"Thanks, Trey," Johnny said, and meant it. "I promise I'll make it up to you."

"I'm sure you will," Trey answered dryly. "In the meantime, tell that pretty blonde it was nice to meet her for me, will you?"

This time Johnny cringed outwardly. That "pretty blonde" was probably never going to speak to him again, and if she did, he doubted he'd get the opportunity to pass along Trey's message to her.

He had the distinct feeling Jenn was never going to listen to a word he had to say about anything.

Ever.

As soon as he saw Trey off, Johnny went straight to Jenn's room, figuring, as likely as not, she'd holed herself up in there. Maybe permanently.

As he expected, Jenn's door was closed. He gently tried the handle just to see if it gave, but not surprisingly, it was locked. He listened quietly, his ear to the door, and thought he heard soft sobbing from the other side.

It tore up his insides to know *he* was the reason Jenn was crying. He took a deep breath and knocked. He couldn't make things right if he didn't face her head-on.

"Jenn, it's Johnny," he said, his voice just over a whisper. "Let me come in. I need to answer all your questions, darlin'."

At first there was no answer. When he knocked

again, he heard movement on the other side of the door, but still no answer.

"Just go away," Jenn answered through the closed door the third time he knocked. "I don't want to talk to you. You don't have to answer to me."

"Oh, yes, I do," he replied, resting his forehead and both palms against the cool oak of the door. "Please. Just open up the door, will you? I need to explain what is going on here."

"You don't *need* to do anything, mister," she replied bitterly. "Just leave me alone."

Johnny sighed miserably but turned away from the door. Who could blame Jenn if she didn't want to talk to him? He could hardly stand his *own* presence right now. He couldn't imagine how she felt.

Defeated, he trudged back to his own room, closing the door behind him and dropping painfully to his knees beside the bed.

It was a long, excruciating few minutes before he could pray. Images of Jenn rushed through his mind. The first moment he'd seen her. Her gorgeous blue eyes gleaming with unshed tears as she told him about her past. Her joy when she shared her new love of the Lord with him.

And he'd ruined everything.

He'd meant to tell her the truth a dozen times, yet he had stalled, convincing himself the moment wasn't right, that she wasn't quite ready to hear what he had to say.

He didn't know what really held him up. Jenn worked in the city, loved everything about its fast pace.

She only came to the country for her family, and she clearly didn't like cowboys at all. No doubt, she would have been thrilled to hear he wasn't a wrangler, but rather a successful businessman.

So, why hadn't he told her the truth while there was still the opportunity to do so?

Because, he finally admitted to himself, he'd liked things the way they were. He liked being a humble cowboy and not a jet-setter. He was, he realized, a simple cowboy at heart, no matter what kind of business he ran in New York.

And more than anything in the world, he wanted to hang on to the sweet simplicity of the relationship he'd developed with Jenn.

Except that it had all been based upon a lie.

He groaned. He didn't want to face himself, much less his Heavenly Father. But he couldn't ask forgiveness from Jenn until he'd asked forgiveness from God.

"Dear Lord," he prayed earnestly. *"I've made a royal mess of things. I've deeply hurt a woman I've come to love, and I don't know how to make it right. Be with her, Father, and care for her wounded spirit. I only pray she'll find strength in her new faith in You. I pray that what I've done won't shake her tenuous newfound faith. I know she trusts You now, Lord, and You will never betray her. Let her rest in that confidence now, more than ever. Amen."*

Jenn barricaded herself in her room all day, not even coming out for dinner. She didn't expect Johnny to be at the dinner table, but she didn't want to take that chance. Not until she was ready to face him.

At the moment, she wasn't ready for much of anything. Her thoughts were muddled, her emotions clustered so tight in her chest she thought she might burst from the pain.

Maybe she should just go talk to Johnny, lay it out on the line.

Make him go away.

Yet, the thought of the ranch house without Johnny in it was almost more than she could bear. He had brightened up her whole world with his smile. What would it be like when he was gone?

She'd have to face that inevitability sooner or later, she realized. Just this afternoon, it had sounded like Johnny wanted to pursue a relationship with her, something beyond the farce they'd created.

Something built on truth, not lies.

But Johnny had lied. About himself. About everything. Who knew whether anything he'd ever said to her was true.

There was one way to find out.

Bolstering her confidence, she quietly slipped through the hallway and across the vacant living room to the opposite hallway, where Johnny's bedroom was. She stopped before the door, her hand raised to knock, but paused momentarily, trying to gather her thoughts.

This might be her one and only opportunity to speak her mind. She had the feeling Johnny might be leaving a little earlier than planned. She would have already packed and shipped off if she were him.

She bit her bottom lip until it hurt, concentrating on the physical pain instead of the emotional throbbing of her heart. With a deep breath, she rapped sharply on the door.

She heard Johnny stirring a moment before he said softly, "Come in, Jenn."

He was certainly sure of himself, believing it was her on the other side of the door. That made her anger surge. How dare he presume *anything?*

She slipped through the door, closing it behind her and leaning back on its cool strength. She needed all the support she could get.

Johnny—Jonathan—whatever his real name was, was seated in the chair, an arm sheltering his rib cage. He wasn't looking straight at her, and Jenn could see a muscle working in his jaw.

"Thank you for coming," he said at last, sounding as if he had invited her to a party or something. He hadn't invited her anywhere. *She* had come to *him.*

"Hmmph," she answered, crossing her arms.

"I want to explain."

"I'll just bet you do," she snapped, wondering whether she'd made the right decision confronting Johnny right now, while she was in such a vulnerable emotional state.

"Jenn, please," he pleaded quietly, his midnight-blue gaze finally meeting hers. Gone was the amused quirk of his mouth, replaced by a thin, straight, grim line. "Just listen."

"No, *you* listen, cowboy," Jenn bit back. She had a few things to get off her chest before he launched into whatever pathetic explanation he cared to share.

"Jenn," he groaned.

"I can't believe you lied to me," she said accusingly. "Johnny Barnes? Jonathan Whitcomb? You didn't even tell me your real name."

"Actually, I did," he admitted gravely.

"Oh, yeah. Right. So now I am supposed to believe your friend Trey, who traveled out here, clear from New

York, in order to find you, I might add, was mistaken when he called you Jonathan Whitcomb?"

Johnny jammed his fingers into his black curls. Unlike with his friend Trey, whose similar movement hadn't disturbed a hair on his head, Johnny's action ruffled his dark, curly locks, reminding Jenn of a little boy.

She'd always appreciated the unpredictable, windblown look his hair often had. But she didn't want to think about that now. She didn't want to think about the many things which had so completely attracted her to Johnny. Most of it, except perhaps his outward appearance, was a lie. And even that—the cowboy hat and boots—appeared to be a ruse.

"My full name is Jonathan Barnes-Whitcomb. I just dropped the last part when I was with you."

"And you couldn't tell me the truth because...?" she prodded, and then continued before he could say a word. "Because you didn't trust me enough to tell me the truth, that's why. You told me I could trust you, but where was your trust in me?"

She knew her own hurt and pain was flowing through the high-pitched strum of her voice, but she didn't care.

"Was it all a lie, Johnny? Everything you said, everything you did?"

"Jenn, no. I—"

She cut him off again. "I don't want to hear it."

"But—"

"But nothing. You let me—" She paused and sucked in a pained breath. "I told you things I've never told another living soul. And all the while you were hiding your true identity from me."

"That's true, but—"

Jenn held up her hands for silence. "I said I didn't

want to hear it. Not from you. Not now. How can I believe a word that comes out of your mouth? I came clean to my family and told them everything. But you…"

Johnny clenched and unclenched his fist around the arm of the chair but remained silent, no longer attempting to jump to his own defense.

Good, Jenn thought. There was no defense for such abominable actions. He might as well save his breath, for all she was concerned.

"I know God wants me to forgive you," she continued testily, "and…and I will. Someday. I don't feel it in my heart right now. I don't feel anything."

She stared at him pointedly. "I don't feel a thing."

Now she was the one who was lying, and she knew it. Did it count that she desperately wanted her words to be true? Oh, what she wouldn't give *not* to care, *not* to feel anything for this man.

Johnny sucked in a deep breath and winced, probably from the pain in his ribs, Jenn thought. Or perhaps from her verbal jabs. Either way was just fine with her right now.

She wanted to hurt him, make him feel some of the pain she was feeling from his betrayal. She knew it wasn't right, that it wasn't what God wanted her to do, but she couldn't seem to help herself.

"Anyway, it doesn't matter, does it?" she hissed. "You'll be gone tomorrow."

"What makes you think I am going anywhere?" he ground out through clenched teeth, his voice coarse.

"Aren't you?"

"No. Not until the end of the week, at least. Face it, Jenn. You're going to have to deal with me sometime in the next three days."

Jenn leveled him with a stare. "No. I don't. I won't. This is my house, cowboy. You're my guest. If I tell you to go, you go."

"I'm Scotty's guest," he reminded her. "And he drove me and Lucy out here in his truck. I couldn't leave even if I wanted to." He paused thoughtfully. "Which I don't."

Jenn felt as if he were backing her up against that cottonwood tree again, as he had at the picnic. But this time she didn't want to stand her ground with him. She wanted to duck and run.

Except, she wasn't the one who should be running. And she would not back down. "Fine. Just stay out of my way. No more lies, Johnny."

"Don't forget, Jenn," Johnny replied bitterly, "The lies started with you."

Johnny clamped his mouth shut the moment he'd said the words, but the damage had already been done. Jenn's face, once red with fury, now drained of color, and she swayed on her feet.

He stood and strode to her side, wrapping his arms around her to keep her from falling, but she made a small squeal of protest and immediately squirmed out of his grasp, bumping into his bad ribs in the process.

He groaned and backed up, clutching at the spot her elbow had hit, wondering if her action had been intentional or simply panic.

Not that it made any difference. He'd promised himself he would not lash back, no matter what she said to him, and then he'd gone and opened his big mouth again. He deserved whatever was coming to him.

The words had just slipped out. Jenn *had* started it. But that didn't make Johnny any less culpable, as well he knew. "Jenn, I'm sorry. I didn't mean it."

She was backing up toward the door, her doe-eyed gaze never leaving his. "Yes, you did."

"No. I—"

"And you're right. This is all my fault. I did this to myself."

"No, Jenn. We both—"

"Just stay out of my way, Johnny. Please?" This time she was pleading, not demanding. Johnny found it almost impossible to bear. His heart was being ripped to shreds, and he felt each and every tug, every tear, more painfully than the bruises on his ribs.

It was better—easier—when she was accusing him. He couldn't bear to see her take the blame upon herself, to see the self-loathing in her eyes and know that he'd put it there.

She wasn't completely without blame, or his words wouldn't have found their mark. But he shouldn't have said anything to begin with.

Jenn had backed all the way to the door. She reached behind her, grasping for the handle without taking her gaze off him. "I'm sorry I got you into this mess," she said softly, unshed tears glistening in her eyes.

He heard the handle click open before he moved, but when he did, it was fast. Two quick strides and his palm was on the door over her head, slamming it closed behind her. He couldn't allow her to leave this way, taking all the blame on herself.

"No way are you walking out that door without hearing my side of the story," he said, his voice a soft rasp. "I'm not going to try to defend my actions, but you need to know the truth. The *whole* truth."

She tipped her chin up defiantly and her eyes locked with his. For the slightest moment, just before she shielded her gaze from his, he saw a plethora of emotions washing through the brilliant blue depths of her eyes.

Pain. Anger. Betrayal.

And what else? Fear?

Johnny stepped back, clenching his fists until his arms were shaking from the effort. What was he doing? He was scaring her with his oafish actions. That was the last thing he wanted to do, now or ever.

What he wanted was to make things right with her, to make her understand that, no matter what he had said, or more to the point, *hadn't* said, he truly cared for her. He wanted to pursue the tenuous relationship they'd built together, not remind her of Duke and the past that had haunted her for so long.

But that was exactly what he was doing, however unintentionally.

Hurting her.

Again.

He stepped back and jammed his fingers through his hair with one hand while gesturing her out the door with the other. "Go," he whispered hoarsely.

Jenn reached for the knob, but her gaze never left his. "I—I'm sorry, Johnny," she stammered weakly, then turned and slipped quietly out the door.

Chapter Thirteen

Jenn was sorrier than she could ever say. She'd marched
into Johnny's room and struck him with her words more
harshly than a physical blow might have been. Regret
mixed with remorse in the pit of her stomach.

Johnny had been wrong for not telling her the truth,
or at least the whole truth. But, as he'd so aptly pointed
out, she was equally at fault.

More so, even.

She'd started all this. Johnny's reasons for masquer-
ading as a cowboy couldn't be any more complicated
than the charade she'd played out with her family. She'd
thought she had good reasons, just as Johnny must have,
and look where that had gotten her.

No more lies!

God's spirit settled within her the moment her mind
was made up. If the snarled web of her life had been
woven with deceit, could it possibly be untangled by
telling the truth?

Jenn didn't know, but she was about to find out.

She strode into the living room, determined to find
her family and tell them everything. Scotty was the

only one present, his legs dangling across the arm of the plush chocolate-colored easy chair, his cowboy hat on his lap, as he watched cartoons on television.

"Still watching baby stuff, I see," Jenn said teasingly, as she entered.

"Funnier than anything else on," Scotty replied, making a face at her. "Better than your soap operas."

"Probably," Jenn admitted, sitting down on the couch across from her brother.

"Huh?" Scotty queried, obviously surprised that his sister was, for once in her life, agreeing with him.

"I just said you are probably right," Jenn repeated.

"Okay. What's going on? Who kidnapped my sister and replaced her with you?"

Jenn sighed. "It's complicated." She stared at her brother for a moment, realizing how much he'd grown up since she'd seen him last. Time moved so fast. Things changed in a heartbeat. She needed to make more of an effort to see her family.

If they ever wanted to see her again after tonight.

"Do me a favor?" she asked.

"Sure, sis."

"Can you round up Mom and Dad for me? Granny and Granddad, too."

"And Auntie Myra?"

Jenn cringed inwardly, knowing Auntie Myra would be the most outspoken of the bunch, and would no doubt have a good deal to say about what Jenn was about to reveal.

"And Auntie Myra," she conceded, with a reluctant shrug of her shoulders.

"What for?"

"I'll tell you when everyone is here."

Scotty planted his hat on his head, tipped the brim at her, and left the room to find the family. It only took him a minute before everyone was gathered, curiosity lining every face in the room.

"What's up, Jenn?" Granny asked, as soon as everyone was sitting. Count on Granny to be the one to cut straight to the chase.

"I just—I have something I need to say," Jenn said, stopping and starting again. "It's about Johnny."

For once, it seemed nobody in her family had anything to say. Jenn wished the floor would open and swallow her. It figured, the one time they were quiet was the one time she desperately wanted to hear voices.

"What about Johnny?" her mother asked, when Jenn didn't immediately continue.

"Well, for starters," Jenn said at last, "His real name isn't Johnny Barnes. It's Jonathan Barnes-Whitcomb."

"As in Jonathan Whitcomb the computer guru?" her dad asked with a low whistle.

"One and the same," Jenn admitted miserably. "He was apparently taking some time off to wrangle over the summer, which is where he met Scotty."

"Hmm," murmured Granddad, cocking an eyebrow. "Shouldn't Johnny be telling us this?"

Jenn nodded. "You're probably right on that account. But I have some things I need to tell you all, and it would be better, or at least clearer, if you understood up front who Johnny really is."

Again, there was a deafening silence in the room, as everyone waited for Jenn to continue.

"The thing is, I need to ask your forgiveness. I will-fully mislead you all into thinking Johnny and I have—

had—a relationship. The bouquet of roses I received that first day, well, they weren't from Johnny."

"What do you mean, sweetheart?" Mom asked gently.

Jenn stammered out the entire story. When she finished she looked from face to face. "I'm sorry. I didn't think—"

"No. You didn't think," Granny answered, cutting her off.

"But we're glad you've come clean," Mom added, reaching for Jenn's hand. "It can't be easy for you to make this kind of admission in front of us all."

"Can you forgive me? For everything I've done, all the lies I've told?"

"Jenn, honey, of course we can," Mom said softly. "We've always known that you had some bad things happen to you in your past, things you never talked about, until this year."

Of course they knew. She'd left home the day after high school, not even waiting for September and the start of college to get away from home.

From her memories of Duke.

From her shame.

Even after she discovered in her college classes that what had happened to her wasn't her fault, that there was no shame in being the victim of abuse. Wasn't that what she told so many battered women on the street, who were running from their own pasts?

Yet, she'd never quite forgiven herself. Instead, she'd chosen to blame God and stuff her painful feelings deep inside her heart, rather than face them and move forward with her life.

And look where that got her.

Here.

With a family that loved her unconditionally, who were now rallying around her with support and consideration, even when she admitted lying to them.

"Can I ask you a question?" Dad queried, moving to Jenn's other side and dropping a gentle arm over her shoulder.

"You can ask me anything," Jenn answered sincerely.

"Why now? Why did you decide to set things straight tonight?"

"Because," said Jenn, "I discovered I could no longer run from God. I don't want to. I've been so angry for so long. I just don't want to do that anymore. No more running. No more lies. I need to face my life— my whole life—head-on."

Mom kissed her cheek. "Do you know how proud we all are of you? You're a strong, compassionate, caring woman, Jenn."

Her mother's words cut like a knife. Jenn wasn't any of those things. She wasn't strong. And she sure hadn't been acting caring and compassionate, especially to Johnny. She had a feeling she was going to be eating a lot more crow before the week was through.

"And Johnny?" Granny queried, an amused gleam in her eyes.

"Yes," Auntie Myra seconded. "What about our Johnny?"

Jenn shook her head. "I don't know. I'm really confused right now."

Mom laughed and squeezed her hand. "Confused? Or in love?"

"What?" she squawked, standing suddenly to her feet and turning to meet the gazes of each of her family members. They all looked at her expectantly, as if waiting for another confession.

Were her feelings that obvious? Here she'd thought she'd been keeping everything boxed in, when really, they had known about her all along. Maybe better than she knew herself.

"I thank God for having a family like you," she said, hugging her mother and father, who were nearest to her, and then moving on to Granny and Auntie Myra.

"That," quipped Auntie Myra with a short laugh, "most definitely sounded like an abrupt change of subject."

Jenn laughed with her. "It's true. I'm not making any more confessions tonight. But I really meant what I said about you guys. You're the best."

"We think *you're* the best," said Granny, giving Jenn another tight hug.

"Okay, I'm out of here," Scotty said, giving Jenn a peck on the cheek. "This is getting way too mushy for me."

"Hmmph," Granddad added.

"Okay, okay," Jenn conceded. "You're right." She moved to the door and then turned, throwing her family members a kiss with her palm. Suddenly impish, she knew she just had to have the last word, for once.

"I love you, though," she said mischievously, then turned and ran down the hall to her room.

Johnny had been pacing his room all night. He couldn't sleep. He couldn't eat. He couldn't think straight, not since Jenn had come in and railed on him like that.

He'd already packed his saddlebags.

It was time for him to leave.

He was no longer running from anything. Jenn wanted him gone. She'd made that fact perfectly clear. And it wasn't as if he couldn't afford a taxi, even to as remote a spot as this ranch. Scotty would probably be willing to drive Lucy back.

Before he left, though, Johnny had one more thing he needed to do. Picking up his bible, his index finger marking the passage he'd selected, he strode from his room and down the hallway.

He knocked on Jenn's door, but there was no answer. He tried the knob, and it turned. "Jenn?" he called softly. He didn't want to intrude on her privacy. "Jenn? You here?"

When there was no answer, he peeked in the door. The room was empty.

He breathed a sigh of relief. No need to have another scene like the one yesterday. Johnny didn't want to cause her a moment's more grief. Just this one thing and he'd be out of here.

It only took him a moment to do what needed doing. He set his open bible on her bed, took one deep, poignant breath of the floral scent of the woman who occupied the room, and made his exit.

It was time for him to go home.

Never an early riser, Jenn surprised herself by waking with the dawn. Spontaneously, she'd taken a long walk on the ranch in order to clear her head, along a trail which had, to her own surprise, ended in the stable.

"Hey there, Silver," she said, approaching the gray gelding. She grabbed an apple from her pocket, which she'd brought along for her own breakfast, and fed it to the friendly horse, who nickered playfully as he chomped down the fruit.

Jenn laughed as the horse nudged her shoulder, obviously looking for more goodies. "Sorry, boy. That's all I have."

She wasn't afraid of the horse anymore. Not even a little. Her fear had dissipated like dew in the morning sunshine. She might not ever *like* horses that much, but it was nice to know she no longer feared them.

Thanks to Johnny.

She inhaled deeply, enjoying the pungent scent of fresh hay and horse. She used to associate the smell of horses with all that was bad in her life, but now she found a smile lingering on her lips.

Johnny truly had changed everything.

Silver nickered again. Impatiently.

"You're right, boy," she said, more to herself than to the horse. "What am I doing out here? No sense putting off the inevitable. I need to go find Johnny, don't I?"

Silver shifted and bumped her shoulder with his muzzle again. "Yeah, yeah, I get your drift," Jenn said with a laugh. She patted the gray on the neck. "Next time I'll bring more fruit, I promise."

Giving the horse one last pat on the muzzle, she left the stable, determined to find Johnny. First, though, she wanted to go back to her bedroom and spend some time in bible-reading and prayer.

This time, nothing was going to daunt her, nothing would get in the way of telling Johnny all that was in her heart. She needed all of God's good grace to make sure her mouth didn't once again get the best of her.

She paused before the door to her room, her heartbeat increasing markedly. She was certain she'd closed her door when she'd left earlier this morning, but now it was cracked open. She had the oddest feeling she wasn't alone, and half expected Johnny to be waiting inside her room.

She pushed the door back and peered inside.

Empty.

Sighing with relief, she entered her room and closed the door behind her. As much as she wanted to see Johnny, she needed her time with the Lord first.

And then she saw it—a well-worn bible lying open on her pillow. One thing she knew for certain—it wasn't *her* bible. Hers had only recently been opened, and the pages were still neat and crisp. This bible had been used. A lot. Its pages were dog-eared and the leather worn.

Johnny's bible.

She remembered it from the first day he'd come, when he'd so reverently taken his bible from his saddle-bag. She remembered the tender way he'd handled the book, running his long, calloused fingers over the cover.

Curiously, she sat on the edge of the bed and picked up the holy book, careful not to lose the page to which it was opened. She inhaled the scent of the soft leather, which reminded her of Johnny.

Johnny the cowboy, anyway.

Glancing down at the bible, she scanned the page. It was opened to the Book of Isaiah. Jenn didn't remember much from the Old Testament, except perhaps a few of the better-known stories she'd learned in Sunday school—Abraham, Isaac, Jacob, Joseph, Moses.

But not Isaiah.

She'd been reading through the gospels, trying to get to know her Savior better through His own words while

He was here on earth. She supposed she'd eventually get to the Old Testament. After her change of heart the day Johnny was injured, she was achingly, unquenchably thirsty for God's word, and spent hours every day reading the bible.

Curiosity turned into fervency and she glanced over the open pages. There was something here Johnny wanted her to read. But what was it?

That Johnny had gone to the trouble to leave the passage for her affected her heart in the funniest way, making it flitter around like a swarm of butterflies. She'd thought he might never speak to her again, and with good reason, the way she'd ranted off on him.

Yet, despite their differences, Johnny was still thinking of her, perhaps praying for her. Again, she was struck by his kindness, a trait that had gone so far to restore Jenn's faith in humanity and in men in particular.

And among men, Johnny was the cream of the crop. She knew that now.

Curling up at the head of the bed, a pillow under her elbow, she started reading Isaiah, chapter 52. It was a beautiful, poetic passage, but Jenn found nothing that jumped off the page at her.

Then she moved on to Isaiah 53 and suddenly Jenn knew exactly why Johnny had left this particular page open for her. Though written by an Old Testament prophet, the passage was talking, to Jenn's amazement, about Jesus, as surely as the gospels, which had been written after His birth.

A man of sorrows, acquainted with grief. Her Savior had already trodden the path she walked, and had risen victorious from it. And through Him, she realized with a light heart and joyous spirit, she could do the same.

She kept reading, anxious to learn more.

And then she read words that pierced her more sharply than the double-edged sword her parents had always sworn the word of God to be.

By His stripes we are healed.

His wounds were in many ways similar to the scars Jenn bore on her arms. Jesus, too, had been the victim of a violent, senseless crime.

Well, not senseless, perhaps. Jesus had suffered for her so she wouldn't have to suffer, so she could live her life for Him. That was what Johnny wanted her to see, wanted her to understand.

And she did. She did believe.

She closed the bible and brushed the cover with a reverent hand, then bowed her head to pray. If God could heal her, He could heal the rift she had created between her and Johnny.

All she needed were the right words, and the spirit of God could help her with that. She was sure of it.

Johnny stood on the front porch, his saddlebag, packed and ready, over his left shoulder. With a long sigh, he inhaled the crisp, cool morning air. How he loved the country. He'd miss it when he returned to the stuffy, polluted air of New York.

Not as much as he'd miss being here with the Washingtons, though. And especially not as much as he'd miss Jenn. Time, it was said, healed all wounds, but Johnny wasn't convinced.

It would be a long, long time before he had Jenn Washington out of his system. The way he felt right now, maybe never. She was one special woman—the woman he'd been waiting for all his life.

And because of his lies, he'd never see her again.

Spying the porch swing, he swung his saddlebag to the ground and took a seat. No telling how long it would be before the town car he'd ordered would arrive. This ranch wasn't exactly easy to find. Most of the roads surrounding it weren't even on the map.

Johnny stretched his legs out in front of him and tipped his cowboy hat over his eyes. He didn't think he could rest, but it was worth a try. Every time he closed his eyes he pictured Jenn, laughing, riding a horse, scowling adorably at him with her arms perched on her hips.

He'd memorized her face—every look, every expression. He'd remember her blazing blue eyes as long as he lived.

He wondered if the ache in his heart would ever ease, or whether he was looking at a lifetime of regret.

Regret. He was sure of it.

It only took Jenn a couple of minutes to find Johnny sitting out on the front porch swing, his cowboy hat tipped over his eyes. He was breathing deeply and evenly, and she wondered if he was sleeping.

She tiptoed to his side and stood looking down at him, her heart fluttering wildly. He was so handsome he took her breath away, but that wasn't all that made her heart go wild in her chest.

Not even mostly.

Johnny was the best man Jenn had ever met. He was kind, gentle and loved the Lord with a quiet passion Jenn only hoped she could emulate. He had helped her in so many ways.

She was no longer afraid. Not of horses. Not of God. Not of men.

Most definitely not of Johnny.

She had been kidding herself by thinking she could just walk away from this man. So he had secrets. She wasn't exactly a role model in that area. Heavens, she could be crowned the patron saint of liars.

"Johnny?" she whispered.

He leapt to his feet, one hand grabbing at his hat to keep it from falling off his head and the other gripping his rib cage.

He winced and groaned.

"Sit down, Johnny." Jenn took his elbow and guided him back to his seat. "I'm sorry," she said. "I didn't mean to startle you."

"You didn't startle me."

"No?" she asked, grinning at him.

He looked stunned for a moment before giving her a cautious smile in return. "Well, maybe just a little bit. I guess I must have dozed off."

"Long night?" she guessed.

"Mmm," he answered pensively.

"For me, too," she admitted.

"Yeah?"

"Yeah," she replied, still smiling at the adorably rumpled cowboy. "Don't you want to know why?"

"I'm not sure I want to hear this," Johnny said, punctuated by another groan. He leaned back on the chair and tipped his hat forward over his eyes, just as he'd been when she first walked up.

"Well, you may not want to hear it, but I have some things to say to you that will not wait."

He sighed heavily. "What did I do now? Whatever it is, I'm really sorry, Jenn."

"Will you stop that already?" she snapped, sounding more irritated than she was feeling. Couldn't the man just be quiet for one minute so she could speak?

"Stop *what* already?"

"Interrupting me!"

"Oh. Sorry."

"And stop saying you're sorry." Now she *was* irritated.

"Okay. Sorry."

She leveled her gaze at him, though his eyes were hidden under the brim of his hat. His lips, however, gave his true feelings away, as they quirked in that endearing way of his.

So he was amused. Teasing her again.

She blushed despite her best efforts. Johnny could get under her skin like no man she'd ever known. He could make her laugh or cry, send her spirit into the heavens or crashing down to earth. It could be frightening, that he had so much power over her, but it wasn't.

Because, she realized without the shadow of a doubt, Johnny would never hurt her, at least not intentionally. What he'd said to her that day at the picnic was true, and she believed it, now that she knew his heart even more than on that day when he'd been a relative stranger to her.

"Given the circumstances," Johnny said, his voice so low and soft, she would hardly have known he was speaking if his lips weren't moving, "I think I should go first."

"You're interrupting again," she reminded him.

"Maybe."

"There is no *maybe* about it."

"But I have some things that need to be said." He tilted his hat up and met her gaze head-on, his midnight-blue eyes serious.

"Be that as it may, you are going to hear me out first," she demanded stubbornly.

"Jenn," he pleaded.

"No. No. Not this time, Johnny."

"What do you mean, *this time?* Seems to me you always get to talk first."

She glared at him, but it was halfhearted. He was right. More often than not, she didn't let him speak first, if at all. Even so, this was one time Jenn *needed* to go first. If she didn't, she might never have the nerve to say what needed to be said.

"I'm going first, and that's all there is to it. You can say anything you please when I'm finished."

"All right."

"All right?" she echoed, having expected at least a token argument from him.

"All right. If there's one thing I've learned about you these past two weeks, Jenn, it's that you're a stubborn woman. No sense fighting with you when I know I'm gonna lose. May as well save my strength."

"Fighting? Johnny, I haven't come to—"

Johnny raised his hands, palms outward, cutting off the flow of her words. "Kidding, Jenn. I'm just pulling your leg."

"You like to get a rise out of me, don't you?" she asked, just a bit surly.

"Yep," he answered, with a cheeky grin. "That I do. Now why don't you sit down here beside me and tell me whatever it is you think I need to hear."

She slid onto the seat next to him, close but not actually touching him. She wanted to reach out to him, but didn't know quite how.

"I just wanted to say I forgive you," she started, deciding the best part of valor was simply to dive in head-first. "I know you've been keeping secrets from me, but I also know God would not want me holding a grudge against you for your actions, which I'm sure are justified. Even if I don't understand why you hid your true identity from me, I should have realized it didn't matter."

"But it does matter," he argued.

"Johnny, you're interrupting again."

He looked like he was about to say something else, then abruptly clamped his jaw closed.

"The reason it doesn't matter," she continued, "is because I know you. The real you. No matter what your name is. I should have trusted that what I knew in my heart was true about you, rather than go off on a rant the way I did."

"You had every right."

"I had no right. And no excuses. You once told me that you can judge a man by his hat. I've learned a lot in these two weeks, Johnny. I'm not judging you by your hat. I'm judging you by your *heart,* when my own heart has come up wanting."

"Jenn," he whispered in the soft voice that turned her knees to mush. She was glad she was sitting down, or else she might have simply melted into the wooden beams at her feet.

"You are the sweetest, most honorable man I've ever known, Johnny. I was wrong to blame any of this on you. Everything that's happened here is my doing, and

I just want you to know I am now taking full responsibility for my actions."

"Jenn," he said again.

"And one more thing."

He reached an arm around her and pulled her close to his side. "And what is that?"

"I wanted to say thank you."

"For?" he drawled lazily, tipping his hat back so his gaze met hers.

"For leaving me that passage in Isaiah. It really spoke to me."

"I'm glad."

"It also reminded me why you're so special."

He groaned and tried to tip his hat back over his eyes, but Jenn wouldn't let him.

"I'm serious. You may not want to hear this, especially now, but I—I care for you very deeply, Johnny. I can be really thickheaded at times, and it's taken me longer than it should have, but I finally realized how happy I am that God brought you into my life."

"Uh—Jenn," Johnny protested, sitting up straight and pulling away from her.

"I'm sorry," she apologized immediately. "I said the wrong thing. Count on me to be candid."

Johnny shook his head, but she waved him off and didn't let him continue.

"I know it's probably too little too late, but I wanted you to know the truth—the whole truth—before you left here forever."

Johnny pulled at the collar of his forest-green Western shirt and shifted again. This time Jenn saw what she'd missed before—Johnny's saddlebags, which had been half-hidden by his boots.

"You're leaving now," she croaked, her voice suddenly giving out.

Johnny pulled his hat off and jammed his fingers through his hair. "That's what I was trying to tell you. After everything that's happened, I thought it would be best if I took off earlier than planned."

"But you can't," Jenn pleaded.

Johnny hadn't expected Jenn's admissions, the way she forgave him even before she knew why he'd deceived her.

He should have seen this coming, he realized belatedly. From the first day they'd met, Jenn had always owned up to her own responsibilities, admitting her own part in whatever she perceived as a problem.

"I've already called for a town car," he explained softly. "It should be here anytime now."

Jenn clasped her hands in her lap and looked away.

"What is it?" he asked. She looked so sad, so distant, that he wanted to reach out to her and wrap her in his arms. But if he did that, he knew he'd never be able to let her go, so he remained still.

It was a long time before Jenn spoke. When she did, she slipped her hand into Johnny's and met his gaze squarely. "I don't want you to go," she said in a voice barely above a whisper.

Whatever Johnny had expected, it wasn't that. Sure, she'd just openly admitted to having feelings for him, something that made his heart soar. But he still thought he should leave.

Even if Jenn didn't realize it right now, his leaving would be best for everyone involved. He'd already caused Jenn more pain than he ever would have wished. All he wanted to do was protect her and care for her.

Love her.

All the more reason he ought to walk away right now, before things got even more complicated. Before he managed to hurt the woman he loved even more.

"I think it would be best," he said at last.

She stood and glared down at him, her hands planted firmly on her hips. "Best for whom?" she bit out.

He stood and faced her, ignoring the pain in his rib cage. "For you, I think," he replied, trying to keep the emotion he was feeling from showing in his voice, a task at which he was not entirely successful.

"Why don't you let me be the judge of that?" she said, leaning over to pick up his saddlebags, which she promptly shoved at his chest.

He winced. "Look, Jenn, I thought a lot about this last night, which is why I didn't get any sleep, as you so adroitly pointed out. I really think it would be best for me to leave today. Now."

"Well, I don't," she snapped back. "And neither does my family. Did you think about them when you made this rash decision?"

"Of course I thought about your family," he replied, testily. "Jenn, these have been the happiest two weeks of my life. I've never spent time with a real family before, and I can't tell you what a blessing it's been to me. What a blessing *you've* been to me."

"Then stay."

"I can't. I just can't." How could he try to explain to her the anguish in his heart? How could he make her understand that he just had to walk away now—before he couldn't walk away at all?

"Yes, you can. And you will. For me, Johnny. If you care for me at all, like you told me you did, then you will be man enough to stick around and see it through to the end."

"I just don't want to hurt you anymore," he said softly, looking away from her piercing gaze.

"Johnny Barnes, you could never hurt me. You told me that yourself, the day of the picnic."

"But I have, don't you see?"

"What I see is a dumb, obstinate cowboy who doesn't know when to say give. You aren't going to wrestle this calf to the ground, Johnny, so you may as well give up and accept it."

He chuckled lowly. She was quite a woman, his Jenn. Bullheaded as the day was long.

And he loved her for it.

Gazing straight into her wide blue eyes, he dangled the saddlebags in front of her and then dropped them at her feet.

"That's better," she said with the brightest smile he'd ever seen from her lips. Her entire face lit up when she smiled that way. If she was pretty before, she was knock-down, drag-out beautiful right this second.

It was all he could do not to pull her into his arms and kiss the daylights out of her. He clenched his fists against the urge, groaning with the effort.

She was by his side in a second, supporting him with her arms around his waist. "What is it, your ribs? Sit down, Johnny."

He closed his eyes. Her scent, all flowers and beautiful woman, wafted around him until he was dizzy. His resistance was weakening by the second, and he knew it. "If you stay where you're at," he warned her with a low growl, "I'm going to kiss you."

She threw back her head and laughed. "Is that supposed to be a threat—or a warning?"

"It's a warning," he rumbled low in his throat. "I suggest you take it to heart."

"Make no mistake," she said, shifting her arms so she was face-to-face with him. "I intend to."

It was as if time slowed. Johnny forgot to breathe when Jenn reached up and stroked his jaw with her long, soft fingers. She reached around to the back of his neck, drawing his head down toward hers.

He couldn't fight her. He didn't even want to. His eyes drifted closed as their lips met. Her kiss was soft and innocent, like the woman herself.

He was lost and he knew it. Without a care for his rib cage, which he couldn't feel anyway, beneath the pounding of his heart, he wrapped his arms around her and drew her closer, putting all the emotions of the past few days into a long and thorough kiss.

At long last he pulled away, tucking Jenn's head into his chest, where they stood for the longest time, unmoving. She clung to him as much as he was clinging to her, and he was glad for that, thinking they might both fall over if they were to be separated.

The sound of a car driving up the dirt road to the ranch house pulled Johnny out of his reverie. The town car he'd called for was here to pick him up.

"Jenn," he said hoarsely.

"Mmm?"

"My town car is here."

"Oh." She sounded confused. Flustered. "I forgot about the car."

"So did I," he said with a chuckle. He'd forgotten about everything but Jenn and the myriad of feelings still coursing through him.

"What are you going to do?" Her voice was as rough as his, an observation which made him smile all the wider. The poor woman looked genuinely distressed, and for some reason, that made his chest well up with so much emotion he thought he might burst.

He chucked her under the chin. "No worries, darlin'. Just give me a second."

Jenn's breath caught in her throat as she watched Johnny approach the car and speak with the driver. He'd left his saddlebags at her feet.

She hoped it meant what she thought it meant. After the special moment they'd just shared, she couldn't see how he could possibly leave.

They had a lot to talk about.

After a minute, Johnny stood to his full height and tapped his hand a couple times on the hood of the car. The car pulled away and Johnny turned and grinned at her.

"I paid him for his time," he explained, as he approached her, "and sent him on his merry way—without me tagging along."

Jenn smiled back. She still couldn't breathe, never mind speak, around the lump of emotion in her throat.

"So then, I'm all yours for the next couple of days. If I have my way, we'll be spending every second together. There's so much I don't know about you. So much more I want to learn."

"I want that, too," Jenn said, finally regaining the

use of her voice. "Johnny, that must have cost you a fortune, sending the car away."

Johnny laughed and winked at her. "Darlin', don't worry about it. I *have* a fortune. And I'd gladly spend a hundred times the amount I gave that driver, if it meant I got to spend the rest of the week with you."

"Will you go back to the range with Scotty?" she asked, not liking the feeling she got at thinking of Johnny going anywhere away from her.

"Yep," he answered without hesitation. "I signed on for the summer, and I'm giving them the summer, no matter how hard it might be for me to fulfill my obligations to the ranch."

Jenn nodded slowly. "I understand, even if I don't like it very much. And I respect your decision to honor your contract."

"Thank you," he said in that soft, low voice of his. "It looks like we'll be doing just what you said we were doing at that family dinner of yours—e-mailing each other and making phone calls whenever my cell phone has service."

"This is going to be hard, isn't it?"

"Maybe the hardest trial I've ever had to endure," Johnny said, sincerely. He stroked a hand down her cheek. "But we can do this, you and I. And I have the feeling I may be spending an awful lot of time in Denver, once I get back to my regular job."

"You live in New York. That's an awful long way from Denver."

"Not for a jet-setter like me," he teased. "I spend half my time on an airplane, as it is. I'll just make sure the airplane in question is headed for Denver."

Warmth filled Jenn at Johnny's words. He was willing to go to any lengths to be with her. He genuinely cherished her, something that she'd never before felt from a man.

And this wasn't just any man. This was Johnny Barnes. Or more precisely, Jonathan Barnes-Whitcomb. No matter what his name was, he was hers.

Impulsively, she threw her arms around Johnny and hugged him tight, making him wince and laugh simultaneously.

He would always be Johnny Barnes, the cowboy, to her. She couldn't even picture him in a business suit, with his wild curls tamed and slicked back.

It would be interesting, getting to know that side of him, the teenage prodigy who'd contributed so much to society with his genius.

But for now, she was simply going to enjoy the sweet, humble cowboy in her arms. She tilted her head up to look into his face. His midnight-blue eyes were twinkling, and his lips turned up in amusement.

"Darlin', if you keep looking at me like that, I'm going to have to kiss you again."

"I was hoping you'd say that."

Johnny obliged her readily, tilting his head down to kiss her once again. She loved the paradoxical combination of strength and tenderness in his touch.

"Well, well, if that don't beat all," Auntie Myra said loudly, from behind Jenn's left shoulder.

Jenn and Johnny broke apart instantly, both of them looking as guilty as kids with their hands stuck in the cookie jar.

"Oh, don't stop on my account," Auntie Myra said, with a cackling laugh. "Don't mind me at all."

"Ahem." Jenn cleared her throat so she could speak, or at least attempt to speak. "Did you want something?"

Johnny slipped an arm around Jenn's waist and laughed wholeheartedly. "Looks like you caught us again, Auntie Myra."

"I'm sure I did," Auntie Myra replied, with a wink at Jenn that made the younger woman blush in mortification.

"Actually, I was sent to find you both for luncheon. Granny has outdone herself, as usual. There's enough food on the dining table to feed a whole next generation of Washingtons—or whatever their last name might happen to be."

Auntie Myra laughed at her own joke, and Jenn found, if it were possible, that she was blushing even more than before.

A whole new generation...

Epilogue

December

Jenn had a backlog of paperwork to be done and was preparing for yet another late night, when the office secretary buzzed her desk.

"Ms. Washington, Mr. Whitcomb is here to see you."

Johnny.

This was a surprise. It had been two weeks since she'd seen him, and hadn't expected him again until next week, when they planned to spend Christmas Eve together, going to the midnight church service and exchanging presents afterward.

She'd even bought a tree, albeit a predecorated, artificial pine, for her apartment for the occasion. Never before had she had a Christmas tree in her home. Never before had she felt like celebrating the way she did this year, with her dear Johnny.

She would never get used to seeing him in Armani, his gorgeous curly hair gelled and slicked back. He cut a fine picture, to be sure; but somehow, Jenn felt something was always missing from the picture.

Probably a cowboy hat and boots, she thought with a smile.

To think, she was in love with a cowboy.

"Hey there, darlin'," Johnny drawled from the doorway.

Jenn looked up from her paperwork to find Johnny casually leaning his broad shoulder against the door frame, that amused quirk on his lips and a bouquet of roses thrust forward in one hand.

"Love, Me," he said with a chuckle.

"Johnny," she exclaimed, rising from her chair and launching herself full-force into his arms. "I didn't expect you until Christmas Eve."

"Maybe Santa's coming early this year," he said, throwing his head back for a hearty laugh. "Watch it, love, you're squishing the roses."

Jenn didn't care about the flowers. All she wanted was to be in Johnny's arms, and to stay there.

It was only then, in his arms, that she realized her cheek was nuzzling flannel, not fine silk. Glancing at the man she held so dear, she was pleased to find him in jeans and cowboy boots, his black Diamond Jim hat in one hand.

"I like you better this way," she whispered, hugging him tightly.

"I like me better this way, too," he said, framing her face with one hand for a most welcome kiss. "Now, then, I've come to rescue you from that huge pile of paperwork I see on your desk. You were planning to work late again, weren't you?"

He made the idea sound so awful, Jenn tried to shrug it off. "It has to be done," she said, just a tad defensively. "I always feel like I'm behind."

"Darlin', it's Friday night. This is *definitely not* how you should be spending your Friday nights."

"No?" she teased lightly. "You have a better idea in mind?"

"Actually, I do."

"And that would be...?"

"Reservations. At the finest, most exclusive dining facility in the whole Denver metropolitan area."

"Which restaurant?" she asked.

"It's a surprise. Come on, get your coat. We're going to swing by your house so you can change into something more comfortable—say jeans and a Western shirt?"

"I'm quite comfortable in my work clothes," she informed him, brushing down her wool skirt. "Besides, how is it that we can be going to an exclusive restaurant dressed in jeans?"

"Now *that* is for me to know and you to find out. Trust me on this one, please, Jenn?"

How could she resist, when he was asking so nicely?

In half an hour, Johnny had her back to her apartment, her lovely red roses carefully arranged in the vase she had purchased for the family reunion.

It was fitting, as if her life had come full circle. Her world was beginning to make sense to her. Things were falling into place at last.

She hoped.

Jenn quickly changed into blue jeans and an emerald-colored Western shirt with pearl snaps. She even had cowboy boots now, the real kind, meant for riding horses, for when she next made a trip to the ranch.

"You look fantastic," Johnny said, as she slipped into the back of the limousine he'd rented.

"Thanks, I think," she replied, making a face at him. "How did I get hooked up with a cowboy, anyway?"

He chuckled. "That, darlin', is a long story, and you'd never believe a word of it. Anyway, we'd better hurry now, or we'll lose our reservation."

"Are you going to tell me where we're going?" she asked again.

He smiled. "Chez Barnes," he said. "I finally broke down and bought a condo here."

"That's wonderful!" she exclaimed, and then stopped short and shot him a pointed look. "Don't tell me you cooked a meal."

"Me? I don't think so—not unless you want baked beans out of a can, cooked over an open fire."

Jenn scrunched up her nose. "So we're having take-out, then?" It still sounded romantic, and Johnny had obviously gone to a lot of trouble for her.

"Something like that," he said wryly.

When they got to his condo, he stopped in front of the door, his key in his hand. "This is it," he said with a grand sweep of his arm. "Chez Barnes. And you are a most welcome guest here."

He swept open the door and Jenn peered into the dark room, unable to see any more than the shadows of the sparse furniture there.

Jenn had expected something bigger, more elegant, somehow. Johnny had the money, after all. But his condo was small and practical.

Humble, like her cowboy.

Johnny ushered her in the door and to the middle of the room, not pausing to turn on any lights.

"Very romantic, Johnny, but don't you think we need

at least a few candles, or a fire in the fireplace, or something? I can't see a thing."

Suddenly the whole room lit up.

"Surprise!" yelled a cacophony of voices from around the room.

Jenn screamed—literally screamed—in surprise.

Surprise didn't even begin to cover it. All her family members were merging on her—every single one of them, even Scotty.

"A little birdie told me it was your birthday," Johnny whispered into her ear from behind her, his breath soft on the nape of her neck. "Surely you haven't forgotten your own birthday."

She turned and rested her palms against the wide expanse of his chest. "That little birdie should have kept her mouth shut," she grumbled good-naturedly. Actually, she was thrilled to see her family again. She'd been missing them.

"*His* mouth, actually," Johnny replied with a chuckle.

Jenn sent a friendly glare in her brother's direction, but Scotty just tipped his cavalry hat at her and grinned from ear to ear.

"Is this a conspiracy?" she asked the room at large, planting her fists on her hips for emphasis.

"Count on it, darlin'," Johnny replied, wrapping his arm around her shoulder. "We can't have you working late on your birthday, now can we? Ask yourself, what would your family think of me if I didn't make a big celebration for you?"

Tears welled in Jenn's eyes. No one had ever made a birthday celebration for her, not since she'd left home. She'd always been alone on her birthday, and had planned to be alone yet again this year.

Johnny had changed all that. And now her family, too. Her heart welled with gratitude and love, until she thought she might burst from feeling.

"Aw, don't cry, darlin'," Johnny crooned. "I hate it when women cry. It breaks me all up inside."

"Me, too," Jenn said with a half-chuckle, half-hiccup as she dabbed at the tears in her eyes. "I never cry. I don't know what's wrong with me."

"I do," crowed Auntie Myra. "Love. That's what it is, sweetheart. Love."

"Cut it out, Myra," Granny demanded. "You're embarrassing the poor girl."

Granddad grunted his concurrence with the statement Granny had made.

"You know your Auntie Myra is just poking fun at you," Jenn's father said, as Johnny drew her farther into the room, which she now saw had been decorated with purple and gold balloons and streamers.

Her favorite colors.

How had Johnny known? He'd obviously been in touch with her family.

"Do you like your cake?" Johnny asked, every bit as expectant as a small boy, his expression clearly eager for her answer.

Jenn gazed at the homemade masterpiece, two layers smothered in chocolate buttercream frosting. A ballerina music box had been carefully placed in the middle, in between the words *Happy Birthday, Jenn*.

Johnny leaned around her and wound up the music box. The soft, tinny melody of "Lorelei" drifted across the room, but in Jenn's mind, it was the Elvis Presley lyrics she was hearing, a love song.

"Do you like it?" Johnny asked in that rich, soft-spoken voice Jenn so loved.

"I love it."

I love you.

She didn't say the words aloud, but she was certain they were in her eyes for all the world to see.

"I made it," Johnny said excitedly.

"You did *what?* I don't believe you," Jenn exclaimed, jabbing Johnny's arm. "You don't cook any more than I do."

"Well, I made this cake," he said with a mock-defensive posture.

Granny chuckled. "With a little help from his family, that is."

"Oh," Jenn said, drawing out the word. "Now I get it. You got to lick the frosting out of the bowl, right, Johnny?"

"He baked the cake," Scotty said with a laugh. "I watched him. If you look real close, you can see it's kind of lopsided."

"Hey," said Johnny, "thanks for pointing that out to her, sport. I was hoping she wouldn't notice."

"You really made a cake for me," Jenn said, wonder lining her voice as she believed him at last.

"I did. And it *is* a little lopsided. But it's the thought that counts, right?"

"Most definitely," she assured him. "And I'm sure it will taste just wonderful."

"Let's get this party started, then," Granny announced without preamble. "Someone light the candles."

Jenn's mother lit the two candles—the number Two

on one side of the cake and the number Seven on the other.

"Time to cowboy-up and make a wish, darlin'," Johnny said softly, guiding her to the front of the cake, with his hands on her waist. "Make it a good one."

Jenn closed her eyes for a moment, enjoying the peace and joy of the moment. Then she made her wish, a simple prayer, really, that she might find many more of these special times with her family.

And with Johnny.

She opened her eyes and blew out the candles. Everyone hooted and applauded.

"Let's rodeo!" Scotty exclaimed with a hearty laugh.

"Speaking of rodeo," Johnny said to Jenn, but loud enough for everyone in the room to hear, "I think it's about time I cowboy-up, as well."

With that, he dropped to one knee in front of Jenn and held out a small velvet jewelry case. "How 'bout it, darlin'? Will you marry me?"

Jenn stared down at him for a moment, not believing her own eyes. At length, she shook the feeling and smiled as she reached for Johnny's hand to pull him to his feet.

"The cowboy or the businessman?" she quipped.

Johnny chuckled and shrugged. "I'm afraid you'll have to take the whole lot."

"I see." She paused thoughtfully. "That's quite a challenge. However," she said, staring deeply into his brilliant midnight-blue eyes, "I do believe I'm up to it. I will marry you, Johnny Barnes and Jonathan Whitcomb."

Her family, which Jenn had temporarily forgotten were even in the room, broke into applause, hoots and cheers.

"Well, whatever my last name will be," she said, with a soft, happy smile, "I think there might be a few more little Whatever-Their-Last-Name-Is feet pattering around in future family reunions. Hopefully, at least one with his father's gorgeous black curls."

Johnny wrapped his arms around her shoulders and squeezed her close. "I can't vouch for hair color," he said, close to her ear, "but as for little ones? Nothing would make me happier."

"Or me," Auntie Myra chimed in.

"Or me!" added Granny. "And it's about time, too, if you ask me."

For once, Jenn agreed with her family.

* * * * *

Dear Reader,

This book is a direct result of one of my favorite hobbies. I was researching and watching the complete filmography of my favorite television actor, Dale Midkiff, whom you might know from his role as Clark Davis in the *Love Comes Softly* movies.

I ran across a television series from the late nineties called *The Magnificent Seven*. This wonderful series was a take-off on the old movie. These seven delightful gunslingers renewed my interest in writing a dashing cowboy hero, and from that came *A Wedding in Wyoming*.

I hope you have as good a time reading about my charming cowboy as I enjoyed writing about him.

I love to hear from my readers. You can contact me by email at DEBWRTR@aol.com, or my Facebook page. I look forward to hearing from you!

In Christ's Love,

Deb Kastner

Questions For Discussion

1. Jenn struggles with circumstances beyond her control. What circumstances in your life feel beyond your control? Discuss how you handle these situations. How can you trust God when things go wrong?

2. Jenn had been physically abused in her youth. Have you suffered from physical abuse, or do you know someone in this situation? How can you minister to those who have suffered physical abuse? Can you ever move on, or do you just learn to live with it?

3. In the book, Jenn wants to control everything. It is only when she realizes she is *not* in control that she can trust God and move on with her life. In what practical ways can you "hand over the reins" to God when it seems life is moving beyond your control?

4. To which character in *A Wedding in Wyoming* do you most relate? Why?

5. What do you consider the themes of *A Wedding in Wyoming?* How do they relate to your life?

6. Jenn has issues with lying. Is it ever right to lie? What about little white lies? How can you resolve to tell the truth in your own life?

7. During the course of the book, Johnny wears a couple of different "coats," or identities. All of us

wear a number of "coats," such as wife, mother, daughter, career woman, etc. What "coats" do you wear? How do you balance them?

8. Jenn's extended family was a very important part of her life, and Johnny didn't have a family. What kind of role does your extended family play in your life? Who are the spiritual patriarchs/matriarchs in your family?

9. Some people don't come from a Christian background when they come to faith in Christ. Specifically, in what ways can they start, where they are at, to develop their own Christian legacy?

10. Jenn struggles with her own fear—fear of the past repeating itself and fear in trusting God with her life and her future. Share a fear you have in your own life, and how you can give that fear to God and find peace.

11. In the book, Johnny takes a sabbatical from his "real" life and in the process grows closer to God. Do you need to distance yourself from anything or anyone in order to renew your strength and your focus on God?

12. Jenn forgives Johnny unconditionally, without waiting to hear his explanation for his actions. Why do you think she does this? Read Matthew 6:12, which is part of The Lord's Prayer, and discuss the implications in your own life.

13. Because of her past, Jenn was angry with God. Have you ever been angry with God? How did God work in your life to resolve that situation?

14. Johnny uses bible verses to minister to Jenn, when his own words are not enough. We can't use the scriptures to speak to others unless we know them ourselves. In what ways do you place the word of God in your heart? How can you do better?

15. Has there ever been a situation where you used the bible to minister to another person? What was the result?

We hope you enjoyed these classic **Love Inspired** stories.

Love Inspired stories show that faith, forgiveness and hope have the power to lift spirits and change lives—always.

Love Inspired

Uplifting romances of faith, forgiveness and hope.

Enjoy *new* stories every month from Love Inspired, Love Inspired Suspense and Love Inspired Historical!

Available wherever books and ebooks are sold.

SPECIAL EXCERPT FROM

Love Inspired

Don't miss a single book in the
BIG SKY CENTENNIAL miniseries!
Will rancher Jack McGuire and former love
Olivia Franklin find happily ever after in
HIS MONTANA SWEETHEART by Ruth Logan Herne?
Here's a sneak peek:

"We used to count the stars at night, Jack. Remember that?"

Oh, he remembered, all right. They'd look skyward and watch each star appear, summer, winter, spring and fall, each season offering its own array, a blend of favorites. Until they'd become distracted by other things. Sweet things.

A sigh welled from somewhere deep within him, a quiet blooming of what could have been. "I remember."

They stared upward, side by side, watching the sunset fade to streaks of lilac and gray. Town lights began to appear north of the bridge, winking on earlier now that it was August. "How long are you here?"

Olivia faltered. "I'm not sure."

He turned to face her, puzzled.

"I'm between lives right now."

He raised an eyebrow, waiting for her to continue. She did, after drawn-out seconds, but didn't look at him. She kept her gaze up and out, watching the tree shadows darken and dim.

"I was married."

He'd heard she'd gotten married several years ago, but the "was" surprised him. He dropped his gaze to her left hand. No ring. No tan line that said a ring had been there this summer. A flicker that might be hope stirred in his chest, but entertaining those notions would get him nothing but trouble, so he blamed the strange feeling on the half-finished sandwich he'd wolfed down on the drive in.

You've eaten fast plenty of times before this and been fine. Just fine.

The reminder made him take a half step forward, just close enough to inhale the scent of sweet vanilla on her hair, her skin.

He shouldn't. He knew that. He knew it even as his hand reached for her hand, the left one bearing no man's ring, and that touch, the press of his fingers on hers, made the tiny flicker inside brighten just a little.

The surroundings, the trees, the thin-lit night and the sound of rushing water made him feel as if anything was possible, and he hadn't felt that way in a very long time. But here, with her?

He did. And it felt good.

Find out what else is going on in Jasper Gulch in
HIS MONTANA SWEETHEART by Ruth Logan Herne,
available August 2014 from Love Inspired®.

A reclusive Amish logger, Ethan Gingerich is more comfortable around his draft horses than the orphaned niece and nephews he's taken in. Yet he's determined to provide the children with a good, loving home. The little ones, including a defiant eight-year-old, need a proper nanny. But when Ethan hires shy Amishwoman Clara Barkman, he never expects her temporary position to have such a lasting hold on all of them. Now this man of few words must convince Clara she's found her forever home and family.

BRIDES OF
Amish Country

Finding true love in the land of the Plain People.

The Amish Nanny

by

Patricia Davids

Available August 2014 wherever
Love Inspired books and ebooks are sold.

LI87902

Love Inspired HISTORICAL

The Wrangler's Inconvenient Wife
by
LACY WILLIAMS

With no family to watch over them, it's up to Fran Morris to take care of her younger sister, even if it means marrying a total stranger. Gruff, strong and silent, her new husband is a cowboy down to the bone. He wed Fran to protect her, not to love her, but her heart has never felt so vulnerable.

Trail boss Edgar White already has all the responsibility he needs at his family's ranch in Bear Creek, Wyoming. He had intended to remain a bachelor forever, but he can't leave Fran and her sister in danger. And as they work on the trail together, Edgar starts to soften toward his unwanted wife. He already gave Fran his name…can he trust her with his heart?

WYOMING *Legacy*

United by family, destined for love

Available August 2014
wherever Love Inspired books and ebooks are sold.

Find us on Facebook at
www.Facebook.com/LoveInspiredBooks

LIH28274